Price of Passage

A Tale of Immigration and Liberation

Larry F. Sommers

Elizabeth —
May the journey
be worth the cost!

Larry F.
Sommers

This book is for Joelle, who made it possible,
and for Katie, Elsie, and Tristan,
who made it necessary.

NORWEGIAN NAMES

Most Norwegians in the nineteenth century based their last names on their fathers' first names—for example, Gunstensen "the son of Gunsten" or Haraldsdatter "the daughter of Harald." What they had was a patronymic, which varied from one generation to the next, rather than a family surname that carried on through generations. This naming practice can confuse today's American reader.

Thus, schoolmaster Gunsten Gundersen's second son was named Anders Gunstensen (not Anders *Gundersen*). Anders' own male children ought to have been Andersens. Instead, Anders' sons George and John turned out to be Gunstensens, taking their father's patronymic as if it were a true surname—just because Anders Gunstensen decided to go to America.

I have tried to keep the names of Norwegian characters as simple as possible without sacrificing either authenticity or atmosphere.

One other note about Norwegian: The language forms the plural of its nouns with *–er* instead of *–s*. Thus, a word like *skurk*, which means a scoundrel, becomes *skurker* when there are more scoundrels than one ... as there sometimes are.

1. Anders

Norway
February 1853

Anders Gunstensen jumped up from his straw pallet, struck a match, and re-lit the oil lamp. What was the time now? How soon could he start for North America?

He teased open the gold case of the watch Grandfather had given him.

At that moment Uncle Torgus burst into the barn with a great bang of the door. "Anders, you oaf—wasting my lamp oil in the middle of the night!" The old man swayed left and right. He smelled of hard spirits.

The cattle, accustomed to Torgus' rages, neither lowed nor bellowed.

Anders took a deep breath and stood tall. "Uncle, what can I do for you this evening?"

Torgus lashed out with a fist. The blow stung Anders' cheek. Having been born under the caul might ward off injury by fire or steel, but it was no charm against simple battery.

Anders raised his hands, palms out. "Uncle, calm down. Why do you strike me?"

"None of your lip, now! I can beat you whenever I want. I own you."

"I am not your slave," Anders said. "Our agreement—"

"Seven years' labor." Uncle Torgus leaned forward, his sour breath in Anders' face.

"Skilled service, Uncle! You sent me to college to help improve your farm. I am a trained agriculturist. Instead, you have me cleaning stables, prying up stones while the stock goes untended—"

"Honest work. The schoolmaster's second son sneers at picking stones! The labor's beneath you, is that it?"

Anders bit back a sharp reply. He took a deep breath. "Even honest labor should have some point to it, Uncle. This time of year, the cold earth fights you for every chunk of granite you try to pull up. The land will have just as many stones to offer in the springtime."

"Your father loathes hard work, too. That's why the farm came to me and not him."

The farm came to you simply because you were the eldest, Anders thought but did not say. It was only a bit of education that saved Father from abject dependence on his bullying elder brother.

Uncle Torgus' voice rose as he extended his lecture. "Your fancy ideas are not needed here. We need farm labor, pure and simple. A great bargain I made, binding you to a seven-year indenture—or it will be, once I teach you to work." He leered, proud of having bested his nephew in trade.

"I'll not take seven years of this," said Anders. Surprised to hear that he had spoken his thought aloud, he was even more surprised to note that it was true.

Uncle Torgus took a step back. "It's not your place to talk to me that way." His brow darkened. "You think because you wore the caul at birth, nothing can wound you. Well, let's see about that." He picked up a pitchfork and ran at Anders, the tines glinting.

Anders stepped aside. Seized by a fit of anger, he grabbed the wooden handle and wrenched the fork from the old man's grasp.

Torgus reeled into a barn pillar headfirst. He fell to the floor.

Anders fingered the sharp steel tines, which had just missed him, and trembled.

Uncle Torgus lay silent.

Anders dropped the pitchfork. He carried the oil lamp to where the old man lay, his head at a queer angle to his body, his chest neither rising nor falling. Anders knelt and placed a finger near the slack nostrils. Felt for a pulse in the man's neck, to no avail. He gasped, rocked back on his heels, and made the sign of the cross.

Anders had often wished his uncle dead. Now it had come true. He felt dizzy and wretched. This was not what he had intended.

What did it mean? With Uncle Torgus lying so still, who would be there to scream at his sons and daughters and farmhands on the morrow? Who would be there to kick and curse them about their duties?

Uncle Torgus lies dead by my hand. The thought caused Anders to shudder. *Does that make me a murderer?*

He had not tried to kill Uncle Torgus. To fling him away, yes, deliberate, anger-fueled. But Uncle's careening into a post and breaking his neck—that was an accident.

Please, Lord, let it be so.

Lord Jesus would believe Anders, surely. Father and Mother would believe him, surely, and his brothers also. Others might not.

The sheriff. What about the sheriff?

What a mess.

Anders sighed. "You should not have tried to use a steel weapon against me, Uncle." A chill came over him.

None of the family or servants would find Uncle Torgus till dawn, for no one ever sought out the nasty old man on purpose. Eventually, of course, the word would spread to Anders' parents in Øiestad. What would Father say? Too late to think about that.

Anders went back to the vacant stall where his straw pallet lay. He donned trousers, shirt, coat, and hat. Already grieving the cattle he must leave behind, he slipped on his boots. With shaking hands, he stuffed his spare clothes and his few possessions into the carpetbag he had brought with him last year when he arrived, filled with bright ideas learned in agriculture school.

Where should he go now?

Menard County, Illinois. Where Gunder Jørgen Nybro had gone.

If he were meant to reach America, this would be his chance.

Father's voice came back to him: "I had to find my own way in the world, and you had better make up your mind to do so as well," he had often said.

But, the cost of an ocean voyage ... As he pondered, Grandfather's gold watch ticked its way into his brain. The watch, of course! All by itself it must be worth the price of passage.

On his way out of the barn, Anders paused. With guilty tread, he approached the stall where Nidaros, a yearling calf, slept under the watchful eye of Dagros, his mother. Anders rubbed the little bull's unkempt head.

4

"Good night, Sweet Prince. May you find a home this side of the knacker's block."

Who would care for the cattle tomorrow?

It will have to be somebody else, he thought wretchedly. He marched out into the dark.

#

Anders approached Arendal ten hours later. Sleepless and alone, having walked all night, he felt wrung out, unready for the tasks ahead of him. He was a rumpled countryman, dazed by pangs of loss and guilt, on the threshold of a waking city he had never set foot in. Could he match the wits of the sharp townsmen?

He strode with false confidence into a warren of houses and shops huddled close under a leaden sky. As he neared the shore, the smell of fish and brackish water, and the feel of his foot-strikes on the cobbles, awakened his spirits.

Over the tiled roofs loomed the masts and spars of a ship. The sharp cries of gulls urged Anders forward until he stood on a wooden wharf, facing the brig *Victoria*, a handsome square-rigged vessel. She stood calm at wharf side, a lioness of the seas, content for now to loll in the sheltered waters of the harbor.

A skinny sailor lounged at the top of *Victoria's* gangplank, back splicing a hemp rope.

"It's a nice ship," said Anders.

"Aye, she is," said the sailor. "A sweet ship—though what would a farm boy like you know about such things?"

"Well, I won't always be a farm boy." Anders brushed a straw stem off his coarse wool coat. "Where are you bound next?"

"New Orleans, America," said the sailor. "We sail tomorrow."

Anders grinned. "What a great convenience, for I aim to be an American. Do you have room for another passenger?"

"You'd have to talk to the captain about that." The sailor peered slantwise at Anders. "But, well . . . yes."

He disclosed that the fare to New Orleans was twenty-five speciedaler, that each passenger must provide his own food stocks for an eight-week voyage, that a store near the wharf specialized in assembling eight-week food bundles for passengers, and that each passenger must have a passport from the police office in the town.

The gray fog that filled Anders' head lifted amid the whirlwind of his preparations. He sold Grandfather's watch to a jeweler in the main street, purchased his ticket at the wharf and an eight-week food supply at the nearby store to be delivered on board in his name, bought an English-language primer in a small bookshop, and got a passport signed by the police chief.

The police had not yet heard of Uncle Torgus' death, for they made no objection to the departure by ship of Anders Gunstensen, agriculturist of Evje.

However, back on the farm, Uncle's body would have been discovered at first light and Anders' absence noted at the same time. The sheriff would have been summoned. He would have arrived to investigate by now. Anders quivered to think that the law might be on his trail already. Would the sheriff seek advice from his boss, the bailiff in Kristiansand, a day's journey away, before acting? Or would he send out deputies posthaste to search for Anders? He did not know the sheriff well enough to guess.

If deputies began now, they might be combing the countryside near Arendal by tomorrow morning.

What Anders needed right now was a place to sleep until tomorrow. A place of warmth and safety. And most of all, a place out of sight.

2. Maria

Norway

February 1853

Maria Nybro grabbed the black iron hearth tongs—the closest tool at hand, weapon enough to bash a skurk.

This skurk—this scoundrel—had entered Pappa's boathouse and lit a fire. In her seventeen years, she could not remember when she had been so mad.

Wrapped in Pappa's old jacket, which was twice her size, Maria ran down the icy path, burst in the boathouse door, and swung the heavy tongs through a red haze of rage. The tongs stopped in the large hands of the skurk, who had jumped up from his seat by the stove.

"Careful, jenta mi," Anders said, teeth clenched on the stem of his pipe. "You could do harm with these things." His handsome face was more serious than she had ever seen it.

"Anders!" She shook with fury, frustrated that the skurk turned out to be the schoolmaster's second son, a man she had known all her life. A grown man, yet also the most wayward of children. "You dim lout, I might have brained you. Ought to have, in fact."

"Tch-tch, jenta mi, next time try a wooden club. Iron and steel don't seem to harm me." He raised his eyebrows after saying it.

"Don't peddle old wives' tales to me. A stray flap of skin the midwife removed from your head means nothing to me. And stop calling me *my girl.*"

"Only a mode of speech, jenta mi."

"Quit it! Your precious caul is no license to break into a man's workplace and steal his firewood, and speak ... familiarly ... to his daughter."

Anders eased the tongs from her hands. He set the tongs down, dashed out the ashes from his pipe, and refilled its bowl. "I won't be any trouble. Just need a place out of sight for one night."

"Out of sight? Why?"

Anders looked down his nose at her. "Lest anyone seek me out whom I don't wish to encounter." He struck a match. Its flare etched his bushy, honey-colored eyebrows as he re-lit the pipe. "Let me show you something."

Maria frowned. She had seen smoke from the boathouse while Pappa slept in the bedroom, dozing off his mid-day akevitt. She had acted on her own to drive out the squatter. Now that the squatter turned out to be Anders, things were different. Her anger, however, once kindled, would not be quenched. It soured her stomach.

"Look here." Anders pulled two slips of paper from the carpetbag at his feet. He showed them one by one. "My passport, which permits me to leave Norway. And my ticket on the brig *Victoria*, which sails tomorrow for America."

"America!" She put a hand on her cheek. "But, why?"

"It's the land of freedom, jenta mi—at least, so says your cousin Gunder Jørgen. It's a new world where men

8

hold their heads up. They meet one another's eyes. People go about with an air of confidence and mutual respect— not like us poor crofters and serfs here, scraping and bowing to the bishop on one hand and the sheriff on the other. My Uncle Torgus made a slave of me for two meals a day. I won't put up with it."

"Uncle Torgus. And how is your Uncle Torgus?"

Anders' face clouded over. "Not well, jenta mi."

"That's too bad."

"Yes." He chewed his lip for a few moments, then brightened. "In any case, I'm done with his bullying. Once I reach America and learn the language, I'll become a schoolmaster, like Father. I'll have a place of honor among the men of Illinois."

Illinois. The very word seemed exotic. It sounded like a place where the daughter of a besotted boat builder might get a new start in life too.

She crossed her arms. "So you plan to run off to America while I am stuck here."

Anders chuckled. "What do you mean, stuck? Rumor goes round that Lars Jensen spends his nights carving a mangle board for some lucky girl." He waggled his eyebrows.

The mention of Lars Jensen, all by itself, made her ill; never mind the suggestion that Lars might offer her the momentous courtship gift of a hand-wrought garment presser.

"No," Anders said. "Maybe not Lars, I can see that on your face. Somebody else, then."

He stood there, sucking on his pipe. He looked pleased with himself.

She added and subtracted him in her head. Anders: one of a kind, not always practical. You might say happy-go-lucky. If you threatened his freedom he would balk, for he had a high regard of himself. Yet, not a bad man

9

altogether. Six years her senior, not too great a difference. He had flirted with her, more than once, after church. And of late, he had gotten in the habit of calling her *jenta mi*.

"Take me with you, Anders."

The pipe fell from his mouth. He caught it in his hands and juggled it amid fresh sparks that fell to the floor.

He stared at her, wide-eyed. Struck another match and lit a lantern, for the daylight waned. Held the lantern near her face and gazed into her eyes. Slowly, he shook his head.

"Please," she whispered.

"Ninety pounds of extra baggage, you would be," he said gruffly.

Bile rose in Maria's gorge. The red haze of rage returned. She seized Anders' head with both hands, as an eagle grips a big fish. "Hear me, Anders. Pappa, the great boat-builder, drinks and snoozes the winter away. As for Mamma, living with the ghosts of her dead children, she's got a foot in the grave already."

Anders' face puckered with sympathy.

"Help me, Anders." Maria released his head. "You promised you would take me."

"Promised! Just when did I say that, jenta mi?"

"When Cousin Gunder Jørgen wrote back from America. His brother read the letter out to everyone after church. All the men stood around, stamping their feet, waiting to hitch up their horses. When you heard the letter, you said: By Odin's eyepatch, I too shall go to America!"

"Perhaps I did. And so?"

"Just then I happened to walk by. You took me and swung me by both hands, and you said: I shall take this fair jenta with me for my wife."

She stared him in the face.

"That must be five years ago. We were both younger then."

She could not confess that she loved him. "If only I could leave this sad place behind! Won't you take me with you?"

He enclosed her hands in his, turned his fathomless blue eyes upon her, and smiled.

"No," he said.

3. Anders

Norway to America

February – March 1853

Anders left the boathouse at dawn.

He feared he had affronted Maria. She had turned around and stomped out of the boathouse when he turned down her plea. Not that a life with a slender, high-spirited girl like Maria would be so displeasing a prospect, or so far-fetched in concept. But, under the circumstances, how could he take her? How could it be practical? In a day or two she would get over her pique, he felt sure.

He hiked three miles from the Nybro boathouse in Øiestad, where he had spent the night, to Arendal. With the sheriff's men on his mind, he felt eyes on him the whole way.

As he neared the city, more people moved about. Unlike his relaxed feeling of yesterday, Anders now feared that any face could be a deputy on the lookout for him.

A crowd had gathered before *Victoria's* berth in the excitement of her imminent departure. The sheriff might have watchers in this crowd. Anders hunched over low, shoved his way forward, sprinted up the gangway, showed his ticket and passport to the officer at the top, and went straight below.

He huddled in the darkness of the ship's hold until the floor tilted under his feet, the motion of a ship under sail. Then he came out to the open deck.

The ship sailed down the channel that led to the sea. When it cleared the land and set its keel among ocean waves, Anders felt his heart lifted free of former cares—the stone-bound farm, the seven-year indenture, Uncle Torgus' bullying. His memory of the old man's corpse laid out on the barn floor under the flicker of the oil lamp—as somber as it was—now receded with the shoreline of Norway.

On the other side of the ledger, he was sailing away from the only home he had ever known, from Father and Mother and all his friends and neighbors—never to set eyes upon them again in this life, most likely. A depressing prospect. But he had made his choice. His face was set towards the New World.

Anders resolved from this point forward to think as an American on his way home after a sojourn abroad. He would look everybody in the eye and speak his mind frankly. With a bit of practice, he could do it.

#

Victoria sailed out the Skagerrak strait, across the North Sea, and through the English Channel on her way to the Atlantic.

Anders satisfied himself on the first day that the law had been left at wharf side. None of his new shipmates knew him or had ever heard of Uncle Torgus.

Since this one-hundred-twenty-foot vessel would be his home for up to two months, he had best get acquainted

14

with it. For an overall view, Anders mounted the rail to start toward the crow's nest at the top of the mainmast. His foot jerked backwards before it found the first rung on the Jacob's ladder that ascended the mast. Anders fell. He landed on the scrawny sailor he had met yesterday, who had just now yanked his foot.

The wiry man hauled Anders to his feet. He held his arm in a vise-like grip. "No landsmen aloft, Sonny. Our able seamen muddle the rigging well enough, but they can't fuck it up properly with farm boys in their way. Now be off with you."

The sailor released Anders' arm, then swung a belaying pin. Its club-like shape whirled into view but stopped—just short of Anders' head.

"That will not do," said a fresh-faced fellow built like an ox. He squeezed the sailor's hand until the belaying pin fell from it and clanked on the deck. "We passengers will not be treated as sport."

"Passengers best stay off the bloody rigging, then." The sailor flexed his hand to test whether the fingers still worked, then curled them into a menacing fist.

The youth with the iron grip returned the glare of the sailor, who swaggered off.

"Thank you," said Anders. "You saved my noggin."

The dark-browed young man smiled. "I am Thor Osmundsen, at your service."

#

Thor, three years younger than Anders, traveled with his mother, Kirsten Haraldsdatter; his older brother, Reier; and two teenage sisters, Karen and Britta. The family hailed from Tvedestrand, a few miles up the coast from Øiestad. What most interested Anders was their ultimate destination in America: Menard County, Illinois.

15

"Ja," said Kirsten Haraldsdatter. "We chose this sailing because it goes direct to New Orleans. From there a great river leads to Illinois. If we went by way of New York, we would have to go bumpety-bump over wagon roads, or else ride those newfangled steam wagons—a recipe for disaster. You must know all this, since you chose the New Orleans route also."

"Indeed, Kirsten Haraldsdatter." Anders did not wish to admit that his whole idea had been to get the first ship out of Arendal. "At any rate, it seems we will travel together all the way to Menard County. So we might as well get acquainted."

Thor explained to Anders that his mother led the family expedition because his father was already in Menard County, working the farm he had purchased.

"Here," said Kirsten. She fumbled in her flowered reticule and brought out a silver half-disc. "This is half of a one-speciedaler coin that my Osmund gave me before he took ship for America. He left this half with me and took the other half with him. He said: I shall plant one half in the prairie. By the time you arrive with the other half, it will already have multiplied many-fold."

"That is quite a promise."

"Well, just a bit of foolishness, if you ask me." Kirsten frowned. "I could not believe that Osmund cut right through the image of good King Oskar. Sometimes my husband does crazy, irresponsible things. He calls it humor. I don't pretend to understand, but he is my man and will provide well for all of us."

#

From that time on, Anders spent most of his time in the company of Kirsten and her family. He learned of their life in Tvedestrand and of their decision to emigrate.

16

Osmund, a traveling shoemaker by trade, believed he could make a better and more honorable livelihood as a farmer on his own land. He had gone to America in 1851, had spent a year exploring the country, and had purchased eighty acres of land in Menard County. Then he had written Kirsten to pack up and come over at the first opportunity. So here they were.

Anders also told them his own story, except the part about Uncle's accident. Sad as it was, Uncle's death had been accidental. It need not cast gloom over Anders' new friendship. So he dwelt instead on the novelty of seeing Arendal and boarding an ocean-going ship.

The two girls, robust blond Karen and the petite redhead Britta, were smitten with Anders' whimsical approach to foreign travel. Kirsten warned them not to be the silly kind of girls who would throw themselves at the first handsome man they met.

Reier, Thor's rail-thin older brother, seldom spoke. He preferred to bring out his fiddle and entertain fellow passengers with rousing country dances.

Anders spent much of his time studying English and practicing its pronunciation, as best he could, from the book he had bought in Arendal. He encouraged Kirsten's family to practice with him. None of them, however, approached his own level of dedication.

That's because, unlike my new friends, I am an American already, coming home after an extended stay in Europe. I need only the language to make it so.

#

After seven weeks, *Victoria* came into subtropical waters. She passed the Bahamas and Cuba. Then, three more days' sailing across the Gulf of Mexico, and the ship stood outside the mouth of the Mississippi River, a hundred

17

miles south of New Orleans. After a three-day wait for the ship to be towed by steamboats up the river, they stood at last on the vast wooden wharf of the Crescent City.

They purchased tickets on the steam packet *Belle Vista*, scheduled to leave at four-thirty in the afternoon. With several hours to wait before boarding, Kirsten chose to spend that time on the wharf near the steamboat, her children close about her. Thor, however, broke free of Kirsten's apron strings and accompanied Anders on a ramble about town by foot. "After all, Mother," he said, "we will be in New Orleans just once."

"Just make sure you come back here by three o'clock to board the boat," said Kirsten. "Otherwise, we shall have to leave you behind."

The two young men roamed through city streets, stunned by America's second-greatest seaport. The buildings were finer and fancier than either of them had seen before—elegant slender columns, walls painted in soft pastels, balconies and catwalks guarded by wrought-iron balustrades. The streets teemed with rich, poor, old, young, male, female; people of every color; people in bright finery and drab slave clothes; people who spoke English, French, Spanish, and every other language except Norsk. What a riotous carnival of sights, sounds, and smells! He wondered what Father would say. Would the ever-curious scholar revel in the experience of a new culture, or would the prim Lutheran reject such gaudy excess? He wished Father could see this scene as he saw it and be exhilarated.

After several blocks they encountered a grand building, the City Exchange Hotel at the corner of St. Louis and Chartres Streets.

Thor tried to puzzle out the sign. "What does it mean, Exchange?"

18

"It's a word about business, commerce. This must be a hotel for merchants."

Men swarmed in the hotel entrance, wearing beaver top hats, silk cravats, and long coats. Seeing them, Anders longed to be one of them, to have a place of honor in their society. Despite his coarse provincial garb from the Old World, he aimed to match their independence of gait and manner. He nudged Thor and demonstrated how to hold one's head high. Thor pulled back his shoulders and lifted his chin.

"Let's go in," Anders said.

They moved with the crowd into a grand, high-ceilinged room opposite the lobby. Men stood on platforms, hawking art works and real estate. The crowd showed little interest in such items, pressing instead toward the back of the room. There, Greek pillars flanked a small stage. Anders and Thor found a spot where, between the heads of others, they could see the wares displayed on stage.

A family of Negroes. A tall black man wearing suit, tie, and top hat stood beside a downcast woman in a calico dress and white kerchief. The woman held a baby. Two barefoot toddlers clung to her dress—a little boy with close-cropped hair and a little girl with large, wide-awake eyes, her curls adorned with bits of red ribbon. The boy and girl leaned against their mother, their faces alive with a great adventure, unaware of their own plight.

"These people are up for sale," Anders said, amazed at the words he spoke.

"They are slaves? That can't be."

"What do you mean?"

"See how they dress," said Thor. "They've been well fed, too."

Anders snorted. "You would fatten a cow or sheep, too, and groom it well, if you wanted to sell it." This was a side of America he had not anticipated.

The salesman banged his gavel. "Gentlemen, this lot is from a large plantation upriver a ways. Adapted as well to housework as to fieldwork. What will you bid for this fine family? Who'll start at fifteen hunnert?" He raised his voice to speak a few whoops and hiccups with the number "fifteen" interspersed between them.

Anders recalled hearing similar babble back home— an auctioneer's chant when a crofter's widow had been evicted from her cottage, thus losing her slippery foothold in Norwegian society.

The auctioneer fell silent, with a look of chagrin. "Twe've, then. Who'll give me twe've? Hup! Twe've, twe've, hup! Who'll . . . All right, then, one thousand. For this whole family. Gentlemen, you can't get that kind of value—"

"I'll give you four hundred for the buck." It was a deep voice, near the stage.

"A handsome offer, sir. However, we're taking bids on the whole family. They're a set."

"Four hundred, him alone."

The auctioneer glanced around the crowd. "Ain't there no one who'll bid the whole lot?"

"Four hundred and *one*, for the whole lot!" called a voice from the back. The room exploded in laughter. The auctioneer glared at the jokester.

"Gentlemen, we're an honorable house. We won't sell children away from their mama, 'tain't right."

A man near Anders yawned.

"Now if we must sell the *father* off, so be it. I have four hunderd, who'll give me five?"

"Four-fifty!"

The auctioneer played the bidders against each other until it seemed certain the first bidder, a pudgy man in a frock coat, would prevail.

A sob broke forth from the woman. The seller's man shot forth a meaty hand and pinched the woman's neck, right below the ear. She winced in pain. The two children at her feet cowered in fear.

The pudgy man frowned. He aimed a stream of brown juice at a brass spittoon on the floor. "I can't afford *all* y'all. Couldn't afford to clothe and feed you if I bought you."

"Sold!" cried the auctioneer, with a bang of his gavel.

The pudgy man turned and walked away. Two hulking men who had stood behind him now walked forward. They laid rough hands on the man who had been purchased as the man's wife sobbed and the tots wailed.

"They have sold him away from his children!" Anders blurted. Gentlemen in frock coats turned to stare. He glared back at them. "Shame on them, that they do such a thing."

"We have nothing like this in Norway," whispered Thor.

"Let's go," said Anders, sick with powerlessness. He led the way out, plowing back through the crowd.

#

Belle Vista left the dock at four-thirty in the afternoon, March 29, 1853.

Anders would sleep in a cabin shared with Thor and Reier. Until then he kept watch from a spot on the top deck, just ahead of the starboard paddle wheel. From there, he could take in the whole scene: red brick warehouses fronted by acres of wooden barrels wafting forth aromas of ham and sugar-cured bacon, long

21

stretches of small wooden houses, and vast green lawns dotted with blossom-filled trees and white-columned mansions.

The city mansions gave way to plantations where black workers knelt in the dirt, the men wearing white shirts and broad-brimmed hats, the women in long dresses, heads covered by shawls or turbans. Some laid wooden sticks in long trenches. In other fields, a stubble of sticks poked upright through the ground as workers pulled weeds from between the rows.

An old man in a white suit shuffled by on deck, sporting a Malacca walking stick. Seeing Anders' keen interest in the shore, he stopped. "Sugar cane," he said.

"Ah," said Anders. "And are those workers slaves?"

"Of course."

"And how many of them, do you think, have been torn away from their children?"

The man fingered his moustache, shrugged, and walked on.

As the cane fields on the shore sank into darkness, Anders wondered what Maria Nybro would think if she saw him now, riding high over the Mississippi River—he who had never set foot outside a twenty-mile circle that embraced Uncle's farm, the agricultural college, and the village of Øiestad, where Father kept school and where Maria's father built boats.

Now, he had seen more of the world than Maria or Father or poor dead Uncle Torgus could imagine. He had seen Arendal! He had seen the coast of Denmark, the English Channel bounded by its white cliffs, and the stormy North Atlantic. He had seen dolphins and flying fish. He had seen New Orleans, with its gasworks and concert halls and slave markets.

And he would sleep tonight on such a vessel as had never been seen in Norway, a ship as long as a farm field back home, five stories high with its own dining room and saloon, its steam engine pulsing through the night, pushing this water-borne palace into the wild heart of North America.

To be more precise: The United States. The paradise where every man could own land, make his own future, and think his own thoughts. Or rather, every white man. If you were of darker hue, you could be imprisoned, held to unpaid servitude all your life, and bereft of your family on a white man's whim. He recalled the brightness of the little girl's red ribbons and the shimmer of her tears as she began to learn her family's fate.

America: Land of the free, and land of slaves.

How could these two exist side by side?

4. Daniel

Mississippi, Tennessee
April 1853

Daniel felt like a motherless child. His heart thumping, he crouched in the weeds between two of Mister Davis' warehouses, not far from Mister Davis' wharf. Barefoot, he wore the white shirt and trousers that Mister Joseph Davis of Hurricane Plantation issued to all his male slaves in January of their sixteenth year, with a new set to come every January after that. This was Daniel's first set of white clothes, which he reckoned made him an adult. All he lacked now—besides his dead mammy, for whom he wept by night—was freedom.

The steamboat idled a few yards away.

Torchlight from the wharf made his task more difficult, yet not impossible. Having Mister Davis himself on the wharf, however, might make the trick easier, if Daniel timed it right. The frail old man stood under the big signboard and chatted with his departing guest—a Yankee, by the odd sound of his speech.

The boat's gangplank touched the wooden wharf. Mister Davis in his top hat, tailcoat, and gloves, the long-jawed Yankee dressed in a plain suit and carrying a carpetbag—the two white men spoke courtesies of departure. Mister Davis valued courtesy at all times.

Now. While they jawin'. Go.

Daniel darted across the open ground. He slipped into the water. His toes sank in warm mud. He waded chest-deep in brown water to the boat. With strong shoulders, he pulled his slim body over the low rail. The Yankee's footsteps sounded on the gangplank behind him.

As the boat clerk stepped forward to collect the Yankee's fare, Daniel crept between two crates in the mid-deck cargo pen. The deck gang shouted as they drew in the gangplank. The side wheels churned, and the boat backed away from Hurricane Landing.

Nobody had noticed Daniel, as if he had become invisible. His fear mask melted into a smile of satisfaction.

Light from the landing faded away when the boat turned upriver.

Daniel had been born on Hurricane Plantation, had never left its boundaries. Now he would see the rest of the world. As the wooded shore slid by, lit by stars and a sliver of April's waning moon, he reckoned he had never traveled so fast. *Oh, Mammy, look at me now.*

He slipped his head out. A speck of orange marked the cigar of the leadsman who squatted in the bow, ready for a call from the pilothouse above. White folk on the upper decks would be promenading, drinking, flirting, and playing cards. The main deck hosted only the paddle wheels' cascade and the welcome darkness.

Yellow light splashed into Daniel's crawlspace.

"Why, there you is," said a deep, soft voice.

A lantern swung above Daniel's head. A thick man with an African face held it.

Daniel gulped. "You wouldn't bark on a fellow slave gettin' free, would ya?"

"Hush up." The man chuckled, a throaty rumble. "What you take us fer? Stokers be slaves. Us deckies is free men. We aim to stay that way. Ain't that right, Willis?"

"Mm-hmm," said another voice, a slender man who hovered by the big man's shoulder.

The big man glared at Daniel. "What that means to you, honey? Just this. Won't none of us take a fall fer the likes of you, see? So keep your head down and say your prayers."

#

Chained men clanked across the deck in the dead of night. Daniel eased out to sneak a look. A man with a shotgun herded four men in leg irons toward the boiler room in the center of the boat. The shotgun man opened the boiler room door. Orange light and a blast of heat carried all the way to Daniel. The five men entered and closed the door.

A minute later, five men, four in chains, came out. They shuffled off toward the stern. Daniel reckoned he had just seen a shift change. The two brief openings of the door had shown sweat-slick bodies, naked from the waist up, stuffing logs into the boiler furnace.

Daniel reckoned he would lose his invisibility when daylight came. After relieving himself over the side of the boat, he found a place in a cabinet outside the boiler room door. A canvas drape over its front concealed its contents. Letters were stenciled on the canvas, but Daniel knew the place for a broom closet when he lifted the drape. He re-stacked buckets to make space for himself.

He closed his eyes.

When he opened them, daylight filtered under the edge of the canvas. The air smelled of frying bacon. His stomach gurgled. He had not thought to pack any food.

Voices conversed just outside the canvas. "Don't reckon we scrub this deck today, Willis. What you think?" It sounded like the big lantern man from last night.

"Fine by me. Unless Cap'n come down and says we gotta do it."

Fingers scrabbled at the bottom of the canvas. They lifted its edge a few inches. Daniel held his breath, transfixed by the fingers.

A whole hand came under the canvas. It placed a slice of bread and a hunk of salt pork on the deck inside. The hand reappeared a moment later with a wire-capped brown bottle. The fingers vanished, the canvas dropped to the deck. Footsteps walked away.

Daniel ate the bread and pork, then washed it down with half the water from the bottle, saving the rest for later. Throughout the day, footsteps and voices sounded from the deck outside. None intruded into his broom closet. Sometimes there were shadows of legs in front of the canvas as Willis or the big man chatted with passersby.

At dusk, another meal came. The silent hand took back the empty water bottle.

They watchin' out for me anyway, he thought. Mammy would be pleased.

He stole across the deck after dark to relieve himself, then hustled back to his hidey-hole. Later, the clank of chains again marked the stokers' shift change. This time, Daniel did not stick his head out to rubberneck. If he kept doing that, he reckoned, he would run out of luck.

Abruptly, the canvas drape lifted away.

The big man stood there. "Get up out of there, Sonny, and foller me."

Daniel's legs seized up with the rush of blood as he jumped to his feet. He stumbled out and followed the big man as Willis fell in behind him.

"Where we goin'?" Daniel whispered.

The big man turned around at the stairs that led to the upper decks. "We comin' to Memphis in the mornin'. That's where they'll be waitin' for you, if anywhere."

"How could they catch up? This boat's faster than any horse."

The big man shared a smug glance with Willis.

"White folks got a thing now called the tellygraph," Willis said. "Ain't you heard of it? Your massa can send a wire to have you picked up."

"A wire?" Daniel stood there with his mouth open.

"A tellygraph message," said the big man. "If the law meets the boat at Memphis, you better pray they keep the search to the main deck. Come on." He led Daniel up the stairs.

The big man stopped at the first landing. "Looka here. That there's the saloon, where the fancy peoples chat and drink and hobnob. They's a bar at one end. That's where we're goin'."

He led the way into the dark saloon and down its length to the bar. Willis opened the lower doors of a cabinet behind the bar. The two men pulled out wooden cases to make space.

"In there," said the big man.

Daniel crawled in. He tried to stretch out full length. "Listen," he said, "you're free men. Why you-all doin' this for me?"

Willis laughed. "We ain't doin' it. You dreamin' it."

The big man grabbed Daniel by the collar. "You better understand. If they come after you all the way up here, ain't nothin' we can do. You're cooked. We never did nothin'. Or the barkeeps, neither. Remember that." Then he shut the cabinet door.

Daniel heard clinks and clanks for a few minutes as the big man and Willis re-arranged the liquor cases his body had displaced. Then silence.

He lay in the dark, fear playing on his mind. He just had to stay on this boat till it reached free soil. Could that be so hard? How would he know free soil? Not Memphis, for sure. What about St. Louis? Would St. Louis be free soil? He didn't know. How could he not recognize free soil when he came to it? Would not the very air breathe different?

Meanwhile, how long could his stomach hold out? Would the big man and Willis keep on feeding him? What if somebody discovered him by accident? What if he went crazy in this cramped space, lost control of his limbs, started to jerk around? What if somebody heard him thrashing inside the cabinet?

Oh, Mammy, protect me.

#

Daniel woke as the cabinet door flew open. Daylight flooded in.

"There he is!"

Big hands reached into the cabinet and pulled him out. A lawman, a bear with cold blue eyes. "You Daniel?"

"Y-Yes, sir."

A big paw smashed the side of Daniel's face.

Something cluttered his mouth. Teeth. Or pieces of teeth.

"That's for runnin' away," the man said. "Take him, Jack."

Another lawman yanked Daniel's arms behind his back and clamped iron cuffs on them.

30

Two Negro bartenders in purple livery stood against the wall, silent.

The big man approached them. "You boys hidin' your friend here, was you?"

The bartenders regarded their shoes. The gray-haired one said, "Never saw him before, Mister Deputy. We din't know he's in there." He gazed at the star on the lawman's shirt. The younger barkeep just trembled.

The big deputy spat on the floor. He grabbed Daniel's arm. The two of them marched him out the saloon door and downstairs to the main deck, where a crowd had gathered.

White men leered at Daniel. Passengers with luggage frowned, their debarkation delayed by Daniel's arrest. Black deck hands also watched, their faces bland or sad.

One white face showed sympathy—the Yankee guest who had boarded at Hurricane.

Daniel's clothes were brown with river mud, his bare feet bruised, his chin bloodied. The deputies shoved him haphazard through the crowd.

A tall, straw-haired man seized a loaded baggage cart and pushed it across to block the gangplank. He stood defiant. "Look you here! Halt now. How behandle you a young lad, so? You have damaged him."

The deputies hauled Daniel up short. They stood frozen in the moment.

The big bear, the one in charge, drew his pistol. "Shut your foreign yap, Mister." He cocked the gun and aimed at the man's chest. "Move it or lose it."

"You ought to put back your gun. It is a useless item in this case."

"Anders," croaked a dark young white man. He stood near his yellow-haired friend.

The big deputy lowered his gun. With a casual blow of his left hand, he sent the blond man sprawling into the arms of his friend.

Blood spurted from the nose of the man called Anders. "Now you have damaged me, too," he said.

The deputy pulled him from his friend's arms and cuffed his hands behind his back.

The long-boned Yankee—the one from Mister Davis' landing—stepped forward. "Sheriff, this fellow here comes from overseas. He don't know our ways."

"Maybe we can teach him down at the jail."

They dragged Daniel and the blond foreigner off the boat.

5. Anders

Tennessee

April 1853

Anders stumbled from the wharf into the street, his hands manacled, his nose a large red ache in the middle of his face. Townspeople hooted to see a white man and a black youth, both bloodied, herded in tandem by lawmen.

Now I've done it. I shall be imprisoned in America, just off the boat.

Anders wondered how he could get free. And something else puzzled him: The lantern-jawed American, the one who tried to intervene moments ago.

Where have I seen him?

The traveling carnival arrived at the jailhouse. The sheriff, a gray-haired man with a droopy mustache, rose from his desk. "Well, who have we here? . . . You'd be Mister Davis' Daniel." He made a wry face at the black slave, then turned to Anders. "Then who you?"

"This here's a troublemaker," said the big deputy. "Tried to interfere—"

"Shush." The sheriff stared at Anders.

"My name is Anders Gunstensen."

A sharp glance. "Not from Memphis, are you?"

"*Nei*—no."

"Hm." The sheriff peered at Anders' nose and clucked. "Got yourself all messed up for some nigger. On top of that, you've committed a federal offense."

Anders glared at the sheriff, though the matter-of-fact accusation unnerved him.

The street door opened. Kirsten Haraldsdatter marched in. She launched herself at the sheriff. "How can you abduct an honest woman's eldest son? I need him back, at once!"

Her sharp words were in Norsk.

The sheriff, stumped, stepped back and threw up his hands.

Not thwarted by language, Kirsten addressed Anders. "Tell him. Tell him you're my son and I need you on our farm."

"But I am not your son, Kirsten Haraldsdatter. I—"

"*Tell him.* Go on." Kirsten's head did not reach Anders' top button, yet he felt like a small boy scolded by Mamma.

Thor had entered with his mother. He stood behind her.

The lantern-jawed American had come along, too. He now stepped forward. "Sheriff, these people have just arrived from Norway. They don't know our laws and customs. The woman needs her son for the family farm."

What? Had the American taken Kirsten's lie to tell as his own?

"Who are you, sir," inquired the sheriff, "and what is your interest in this? You sound like a Yankee."

"My name is Benjamin Lake. I have a farm in Menard County, Illinois."

34

Menard County, thought Anders. *He will be my neighbor.*

"I knew it!" cried the sheriff. "A Yankee."

Benjamin Lake scowled. "Is it a crime here to hail from a sister state?"

The sheriff squinted. "Listen here. Miss'sippi's a sister state. Loosiana, Arkansas the same. Illinois ... that's a different matter."

"Free soil. Is that the problem, Sheriff? A man must own slaves, or he's an enemy?"

"Abolitionist blather."

Lake tipped his long chin toward Daniel, who stood spellbound. "You got your Negro, Sheriff. He's all yours. This young white man"—he raised his hand toward Anders—"is innocent. He don't know our laws. If we can get these people to Illinois, where they're bound for, you won't have to fear that they'll free any of your precious slaves."

The sheriff frowned. "Interfering with the Fugitive Slave Act is one thousand dollars and six months in jail."

Anders' heart sank.

Thor, with scant English, read the sheriff's face. "What did that man say, Anders?"

Anders, nose throbbing, merely groaned in reply.

"We can't stay here talking," wailed Kirsten. She turned back to the sheriff and badgered him, again in Norsk. "I need my son, whom you have hurt!"

Her squeal made the sheriff wince.

The American laughed. "If you throw the book at him, Sheriff, you'll have a wounded mother on your hands till October."

The sheriff raised his eyes toward the ceiling. "I could reduce the charge to disturbin' the peace."

"What's that worth?"

35

The lawman's eyes measured Lake from his brushed felt hat to his polished calf's-leather boots. "Fifteen dollars?"

"Fifteen dollars!" cried Anders. "I do not have that much. I sold my grandfather's watch to buy the ticket. There are but a few dollars left."

The sheriff ignored this outburst, his eyes fixed on Lake.

"Highway robbery," Lake said. "And would there be jail time?"

"Not if his foreign ass gets on the first boat north."

Lake reached into his pocket, drew out two gold coins, and laid them on the sheriff's desk. "I'll need a receipt."

The sheriff snorted. "Of course you'll need a receipt. Yankee busybodies always need receipts." He rummaged through a desk drawer, found a receipt book, sat down, and dipped a nib in an inkwell on the corner of his desk.

"Make it out to Benjamin Lake, Sweetwater, Menard County, Illinois."

The sheriff began to write.

Lake, who now faced the slave at a distance of two feet, said his name and address again. "Benjamin Lake . . . Sweetwater . . . Menard County . . . Illinois."

The slave's eyes opened wider.

Anders was glad to have the loose-jointed, long-jawed American paying the fine for him, but—why? *Who is he?*

The big deputy gave Daniel a shove. "Come on, darky. We got a cell in back for you." He dragged the slave toward a door in the rear wall. The boy's face held terror. He glanced back at Anders, like an orphan losing his guardian, then vanished through the door.

Anders moved to follow. He found his arm locked in Lake's iron grip.

36

The sheriff raised his head and glared at Anders. He tore off the receipt and handed it to the American. "There you are, Mister Lake. Come again when you can't stay so long."

#

A hansom cab loitered near the jailhouse. Lake hailed it. He bundled Anders, Thor, and Kirsten inside. "To the wharf, please."

The cab had barely space for the four of them. They all started to talk at once, then all went quiet in embarrassment.

Anders wondered whether the steamboat would still be at the landing. Instead, he asked Lake, "What will happen to Daniel?"

"They will return him to his owner, in accordance with the law." Lake clasped his hands as if in prayer.

"He will be punished for running away, ja?"

"Fortunately, not every planter in the South is harsh and vindictive."

"Still, I wish—"

"There was nothing we could have done for him at present." Lake turned to Kirsten. "At least, Madam, we have got your son back."

"Mister Lake," Anders said, "this woman is Kirsten Haraldsdatter. I am not her son. I am a friend of her real children."

"I misunderstood, then. It all worked out, though, didn't it?"

Anders could not deny it.

"So, you're old family friends?"

Anders smiled. "Ja—I think after eight weeks on a small ship together, we have become old friends."

37

The cab dropped them at the landing. Kirsten's other children stood waiting. They waved with relief as they spotted the returnees. Anders introduced them to Lake. "That thin one is Thor's older brother, Reier. The two girls are his sisters, Karen and Britta."

Kirsten tugged at Anders' sleeve. "Tell him, please, that I would not travel on my own, except that my dear husband, Osmund, went to Illinois without us, to prepare our farm. So I must be father and mother to my children."

Anders translated that for Lake and added, "She thinks it is improper to cross an ocean without her husband, so she wants you to know there is a good reason."

#

As the pilot backed the boat away from the wharf and turned upriver, a crewman led Anders and Lake up to the captain's cabin on level called the Texas, just under the pilothouse.

"What wants the captain with us?" Anders asked.

"Let me do the talking," Lake said.

They entered the captain's lair, a trim space with white walls, windows on three sides, and a large logbook in the middle of a table.

The white-haired captain assailed them. "I held *Belle Vista* in Memphis an extra half-hour so you all could get back. At your request, Mister Lake."

"We appreciate it, Captain."

"You can express that appreciation to each of the hundred fellow passengers you delayed by your rash actions this morning."

"I am sorry," said Anders. "I was a slave myself in Norway. When I saw the way they treated that boy, I had to do something."

The old man's frown lines deepened. "You want to hear about bad treatment, chappie—it's us that's been ill-used. Them deputies impounded my boat, under authority of the Shelby County Commissioner for Fugitive Slaves, and I'm standin' there fuming. Just 'cause one little nigger boy took it in his head to run away."

"Distressing, I'm sure," Lake said.

"I was fit to be tied," the captain said to Lake. "Then, just when there's a happy ending in sight, your boy here disrupts the course of justice and gets himself took. Which causes a further delay."

"I am sorry," Anders said.

The captain curled his lip. "How long are you on this boat?"

"We both get off at St. Louis," said Lake.

"Stay out of my sight. And don't rescue no more slaves or do anything that causes trouble, or I'll set you both down on the nearest sandbar."

#

Lake led Anders to a dainty table in the saloon. White-painted columns supported the high ceiling of the long, sunlit room, and warm scents of sugar and cinnamon wafted from the bakery at its far end. A white-coated black waiter brought coffee. Anders paid from the few coins he had left.

"I am in your debt for fifteen dollars," he said to Lake, "and I do not know when I can pay back to you."

"Not everybody would bother themselves about repayment," Lake said.

Anders boggled. "How can people not pay debts?"

"Oh, something about money spent for the Cause."

"Cause? What cause?"

39

"Antislavery. Some people expect support when they work against the Slave Power."

"What do you mean? If they oppose slavery, then must you get them out of jail, no matter what?"

Lake took a sip of coffee. "Sometimes it seems that way. And you—what you did, which the captain called rash action, was opposing slavery, in your own way."

"Well. I never thought to find slavery here."

"No?"

"I heard that America is the land of freedom."

"Not for black people in the South."

Anders sighed. "I did not know North from South. I got on the first ship for America. It was winter, so we took a southern route. Kirsten Haraldsdatter told me the destination would be New Orleans. I thought—New York, New Orleans, what is the difference? Both are new."

Lake guffawed.

"In New Orleans," Anders said, "while we waited for the steamboat, Thor and I visited a hotel where they sold black people. They broke up a family. They sold the father to one farm, the mother and children to another. It was worse than anything my uncle did to me in Norway."

Lake frowned.

"So you see, when I see them capture that boy to drag him off, I had to act."

"Yes," Lake said. "I do see."

"But why should you pay the cost for me to be a fool?"

Lake examined his fingernails. "It seemed you could use a hand."

"I think it is more to it than that. I know you from somewhere, Mister Lake, and now I remember. You got on this boat from Hurricane Plantation."

Lake raised his eyebrows. "Indeed I did. I was a guest of Mister Davis, the planter. Sold him a pair of fine Illinois horses. The man knows horse flesh and demands the best."

40

"Hurricane is where Daniel also crept aboard the boat, at the same time you boarded."

"Is that so?"

"It is so, Mister Lake. I see everything. I spend many hours on the top deck, just forward of the paddle wheel." He flung his arm in the direction of the starboard paddle box. "I am so excited to ride the steamboat through the center of America, I cannot stop watching."

"It interests me that you saw a slave in the act of escape yet did not report it to anyone."

"You know how I feel about it. I wanted him to succeed. You also did not report it."

"You think I saw him?"

Anders did not feel the need to dignify this with a reply.

A black waiter hovered nearby. "No more coffee, thank you," said Lake. The waiter bowed and departed.

Lake leaned across the small table. "You have noble impulses, my friend. Such impulses can get you in trouble here—bigger trouble than you know. Slavery is lawful in the southern states. We also must deal with a new law that requires every white citizen, South or North, to help catch slaves who escape. Not only can you be punished for helping a slave escape—you can be punished if you witness an escape and do nothing."

Anders shook his head in dismay.

"For that reason," Lake said, "the fate of most slaves is sealed."

"That is terrible."

Lake gnawed his lower lip. "On the other hand, if a man wants to help slaves get free by illegal means, he had better know what he's about."

What?

Anders sipped his coffee and scrutinized the man across from him. "Mister Lake, I cannot read your heart.

41

You seem to know what freedom means to a slave. Yet you also do business with slave owners."

"Mister Joseph Davis, who owns Daniel, breaks no law by owning slaves," Lake said. "He also needs horses and pays top dollar. Did I mention I am a horse dealer?"

"You approve slavery?"

"No, Anders—may I call you Anders? Life is complicated. For example, since you insist on repaying my fifteen dollars, how will you do it?

"In Menard County, I will find a yob—job, excuse me."

"Do you have a job already arranged?"

"No, but my friend Gunder Jørgen Nybro will help me get one."

"You know anything about farming?"

"I am a certified agriculturist," Anders said.

"Well ... I need a regular farmhand. I'll pay an honest wage, and you'll be able to work off that fifteen dollars in no time. What do you say?"

Anders pressed his lips together. Could Lake be trusted? Would this offer lead to honor and respect among Americans? Or would Anders just trade one servitude for another?

Despite his qualms, Anders shook Lake's hand.

6. Anders

Illinois

April 1853

"Anders, you can't be serious."

"I am serious, Kirsten Haraldsdatter." How could she think otherwise?

"This railroad is a newfangled thing," Kirsten said. She stopped on the pier at Alton, Illinois, on the first day of April, just off the packet boat from St. Louis, where the steamboat *Belle Vista* had landed them. "There shall be no steam wagons for us, thank you."

"But the boat goes no farther. I want to get to Menard County, don't you?"

"What if the steam engine blows up, Anders?"

Boat passengers in a hurry to get off the pier cast annoyed glances at the little knot of Norwegians who blocked their way.

"Mamma," said Reier, "our boat was powered by steam. It did not blow up."

Kirsten stood adamant.

"There is a stagecoach," Anders admitted. "The train, however, goes much faster."

"My Osmund would never forgive me if we all died so near the end of our journey."

Anders was eager to reach their destination. On the other hand, Kirsten and Thor had stood by him in his hour of need. So in the end, Kirsten prevailed.

Anders buttonholed Benjamin Lake. "Kirsten Haraldsdatter insists on taking the stagecoach. I am sorry. I must stay with the family until they reach their farm."

Lake frowned. "Can't they make it on their own?"

"Maybe," Anders said. "But they could use my help."

Lake sighed. "I suppose you're right."

"I shall come to your farm as soon as I have them settled."

So while Lake went on by train, Anders stayed with Kirsten and her family. They jolted over dusty roads in a four-horse coach and sampled the overnight hospitality of a rat-infested log tavern in Carlinville.

The railway ran close to the stage road. Twice each day the steam train passed them on its way to or from Springfield. Karen and Britta waved at the locomotive as it chugged by and overtook their stagecoach.

"Sooner or later, that thing will cause a great calamity," Kirsten Haraldsdatter said.

It took them two days to reach Springfield, the capital city, by stage. From there they set out to walk the twenty miles to Petersburg, pulling a two-wheeled cart loaded with the family's baggage. They walked through a green land, a flatter land than they were used to.

"There are slight hills, yes," said Thor. "Nothing like those at home."

"Look at their fences," said Reier. "Rickety contraptions made of wooden rails. Why do they not they build them in stone?"

Anders grinned. "I've heard the black soil is three feet deep. Not a stone to be found in it. Must we long for every inconvenience of home?"

Now, on the afternoon of Wednesday, April 6, dust-caked from the dirt road, burned by sun and wind, sore from hauling by turns on the shafts of the unstable cart piled high with luggage, they approached Petersburg, the chief city of Menard County.

Not to be compared with New Orleans or St. Louis, Petersburg was yet a true city, as large as Arendal though less ancient. Houses and shops gleamed, some with fresh white paint, others with new, unpainted timber. Commercial establishments rose two or three stories above the board sidewalks, their flat fronts towering over the squat premises behind them.

Anders and Kirsten marched ahead, down the center of the main street while Thor and Reier pulled the cart. The two girls walked behind. Local passers-by stood on the boardwalks watching the small parade of Norwegians who had arrived in their midst.

They are curious, Anders thought, *not hostile.*

Dark clouds overhead pelted them with large raindrops. The rain became a soaking downpour. It turned the dust of the street to a soupy mud. In a minute, the squall passed over, leaving a rainbow behind.

The bystanders, who had ducked into doorways on both sides of the street, emerged to stare. *We must be a sight*, Anders thought—*soggy Norwegians, five days of swallowing the dust of the road, then a pleasant shower, and here we are, latest additions to the Land of the Free.* He couldn't help smiling, for he had arrived.

Down the street loomed a tall block of whitewashed wood—a true three-story building, forty feet on a side, with no need for a higher façade.

Anders pointed. "Look, it's a hotel. Let us step inside."

"We must not pay for rooms now that we are so close," said Kirsten. "Our farm cannot be far, and my Osmund will be eager to see us."

"We'll just go in to ask for directions."

Kirsten curled her lip, then nodded.

Anders helped Kirsten step from the muddy street onto the boardwalk and two steps up, through the hotel's mullion-lit front door, into the lobby. The room smelled of waxed wood, worn leather, and cigar smoke. Chairs upholstered in leather or chintz, studded with rows of big brass tacks, lined the walls. Here and there stood a shrub grown in a pot.

A counter of dark wood dominated the wall opposite the front door. Behind it stood a tall man with sparse brown hair and a harried countenance. A sign on the counter read W. A. Schallert, Manager.

The man stared through Anders. He seemed at first not to hear his request. "I'm sorry, sir. Who did you say?"

"Osmund Reiersen. He has a farm nearby."

Schallert knit his brows. "Oh, dear." He settled a pair of pince-nez on his nose and peered at Anders. "Please have a seat, sir. Let me do what I can for you."

Anders and Kirsten sat down on a settee covered in green-and-purple-striped chintz.

A boy in a purple uniform, who had slouched near the front desk, now dashed out the door to the street. The manager slipped through a door behind the hotel desk.

"Did he tell you where to find our farm?" Kirsten asked.

"No. He is making inquiries."

Kirsten raised her eyebrows. "Is not this a peculiar welcome to North America?"

46

"That is one word for it." *Evasive would be more accurate*, Anders thought.

The front door flew open. Thor came in. "Have you found any directions?"

Kirsten snorted. "They make inquiries."

She turned to Anders. "When Osmund left Norway, he said to all of us: Fear not. I go to prepare the way for you. The same words Our Savior told his disciples, except that He was not talking about America, of course."

The front door opened again. This time a bearded man in a black suit entered. He approached the settee where they sat. "Excuse me, Madame, are you Missus Reiersen?"

Hearing her husband's name, Kirsten sat forward.

"I am Brother Andrew Claymore, pastor of the Petersburg Methodist Church. I regret to tell you that your husband, Osmund, has gone home to the Lord."

Anders gasped. The good Osmund, who already seemed a family friend, gone so soon?

Kirsten's face clouded with uncertainty.

"Excuse my English," Anders said. "We must be sure what you have said."

"Mister Reiersen is dead. We buried him one week ago."

Kirsten gasped. Her face held horror. "Dead means *død*, ja?"

"I'm sorry," said Brother Claymore. "It was heat stroke. Neighbors found him in the field. Weather's been hot this spring."

#

Anders brushed aside Kirsten's caution and rented two upstairs rooms, one for her and the girls, the other for himself and the two brothers. It had been four days since

47

he told Benjamin Lake that he would soon report for work. Now his friends' grief meant that Lake must wait a bit longer. Anders would not abandon them at this moment of vulnerability.

Brother Claymore sent for ladies from his church. They came to the hotel, sat in the lobby with the family, prayed, and spoke sympathy in English to Kirsten, Karen, and Britta.

Claymore read scriptures in his deep voice. After each phrase of the preacher's resonant English, Anders echoed the verse in Norsk dialect from his own Danish Bible, so his friends would understand the words of comfort.

> *For none of us liveth to himself, and no man dieth to himself ... whether we live therefore, or die, we are the Lord's ...*

"That is good for us to remember," Kirsten said. Blond, doe-eyed Karen and elfin, red-haired Britta wept. Kirsten squeezed their hands.

> *For this corruptible must put on incorruption, and this mortal must put on immortality ... Then shall be brought to pass the saying that is written, death is swallowed up in victory.*
>
> *O death, where is thy sting? O grave, where is thy victory?*

Anders, however, considered that the grave had scored a victory. Kirsten's sons would not yield to public grief, but surely they felt the sting of their father's death. He thought of his own father, Schoolmaster Gunsten Gunderson, back in Øiestad. Already he missed him bitterly. The difference was, Thor and Reier would never see their father again. Was it really a difference? Although Father was alive, he was an ocean away. It was very unlikely Anders would ever see him again. He wept for Thor and Reier, and he wept for himself.

Anders did not know what Methodists were. Brother Claymore said there was no Lutheran church for miles around. It seemed one must be content with Methodists.

At midnight, the family thanked these strangers who had cared for the departed father at the end of his time on earth. Kirsten Haraldsdatter had Anders ask Brother Claymore how to find her husband's farm. Then they retired to the two rooms Anders had rented.

#

They set out the next day, pulling the baggage cart on the rutted road that led west.

They found Osmund's forty-acre farm two miles west of Petersburg. The impressionable Thor, seeing the gaslights of New Orleans, had predicted his heroic father, Osmund, would find a way to furnish his farm with like conveniences. They found instead a cabin of logs with a plank door, a stone fireplace, and two small glass windows.

The grass grew high as their heads. A few acres of prairie had been planted with corn and potatoes. Weeds already towered over young shoots of corn, threatening to choke them.

A mound of fresh earth rose a hundred feet east of the cabin. At one end stood a wooden cross; at the other, a flat bit of sandstone in which the name Osborn Ryson had been scratched.

"They misspelled Father's name," said Reier, frowning.

49

"At least they gave him a marker," Kirsten said. "And they buried him here at his home, not in some city cemetery or a Methodist churchyard. This land is still his—now ours. His grave proves it." She wrinkled her brow. "I wonder, what happened to the livestock? He wrote that there was livestock."

"Hello, the farm!" called a male voice.

A stocky man wearing soiled clothes and a broad-brimmed hat stood in the road. He had with him a black mule, a yellow cow, and a gangly lad who looked like him.

Anders and Thor walked out to the road to greet the man and boy.

"We've brought Osborn's animals for ya," the man said.

"Thank you," said Anders.

"You-all his kin?" The man shuffled his feet. "My name is Hiram Johnson. I'm the nearest neighbor. This is my boy."

He thrust out his hand. Anders and Thor shook hands with him and with his son.

"Mister Johnson"—Anders did not know how to ask politely—"are there no more animals? Just the one cow and the mule?"

"Not bad for a newcomer," Johnson said. He cast his eyes down. "I'm sure he woulda got himself some piglets soon. Right now, yah, the cow and the mule is all there is. We been keepin' them at our place, so they wouldn't wander off and get lost."

Reier stepped forward. "Thank you. Er . . . how much are costing, their food?"

"Cost? For a week? Shucks, we just put them out on picket lines to graze, gave 'em a little cornmeal and water. Didn't cost us nothin'. Well, good day to ya." Johnson touched the brim of his hat. He and his son walked away.

"Thank you, very much!" Thor called after them.

Kirsten shouted to Anders, "Ask them the name of the farm!"

Anders shouted after the Johnsons, "How is it called? The name of this farm?"

Hiram Johnson stopped in the road, lifted his hat, and scratched his head. "Well, this would be Township Eighteen, Range Five, Section Five, west half of the southeast quarter." He put his hat back on his head and took his leave.

Anders translated Johnson's reply for Kirsten.

"Township Eighteen, Range Five? Southeast quarter? What kind of a name is that?"

"It's very American, Mamma," said Britta. "Modern, efficient, like gaslights and steam wagons."

"We Nordmenn have proper names for our farms. From now on, this place shall be called Osmundsgarden." She gazed at the flat stone with its inscription. "My Osmund purchased this garden, this farm, with his life."

Anders thought about the departed Osmund, whom he had not known. For some reason, Uncle Torgus flashed across his mind—not as he had last seen him, dead on the barn floor; rather, as he had known him in life, pugnacious and profane, stunted in his outlook. Had Uncle always been that way, from the cradle? Or did he get that way after years of wringing his bread from Norway's soil? Like Osmund, perhaps it was his farm that had cost him his life.

Father made his way as a teacher. Not a great man, perhaps, but one respected for his role in the community. Paid an adequate, if small, wage. Anders would begin life in America as a mere helper for a prosperous farmer. He vowed he would not be trapped in that role. He would become a respected member of the community, whatever it took.

51

Reier brought out his fiddle. For once, he did not play a country dance. Instead, the bereaved son stood by his father's grave and played a lament that sang the sorrow of his loss. It left Anders with a hollow feeling inside.

#

Anders set out the next morning, a Monday, to find Benjamin Lake's farm. He strode eastward, carpetbag in hand, through a sweet land. The warm April air smelled of manure and fresh-turned earth.

Birds swooped over the prairie—black birds with red stripes on their wings, lemon-breasted birds that teetered on tall grass stems burbling out notes of joy.

Houses and barns dotted the land, some made of logs and some of framed lumber. Men and boys followed plows drawn by oxen, mules, or horses. Anders shouted "Hei!" as they trod their furrows. He waved, and most waved back, ogling him with undisguised interest.

Sweetwater lay east of Osmundsgarden by twelve miles. The sun had climbed high overhead by the time Anders reached the tiny hamlet. No sign marked the town limits, so Anders could not tell for sure it was Sweetwater. But it was a town of some sort, neat frame houses crowding both sides of the road.

In front of the houses on each side of the main street ran a boardwalk, which Anders recognized as a sign of civilization in Illinois. Rather than continue to walk in the street, he mounted the boardwalk on its north side.

A woman hurried along the uneven walk, carrying a baby. She stared at Anders as she passed. He touched his nose to confirm what he already knew, that it was healing. It had been almost a week; the bruises must have faded by now. Maybe she stared because he had a foreign appearance. He carried a carpetbag and wore coat and trousers of coarse wool. His trim hat could not be compared to the broad, flamboyant hats worn by men of the prairie. He even walked differently. He had not mastered the free-loping swagger common to American males. Perhaps his Norwegian gait looked tentative or mincing.

Near the center of town, in front of a structure with a sign that read Sugar Grove Tavern, a man lay face-down on a bench. The man's shabby dress and rank odor showed that he had lain there drunk since the night before. With a crashing snore he rolled halfway over, his face full of seams and creases, whiskered with gray stubble, edged with ringlets of greasy hair. He opened his eyes, saw Anders, and shuddered.

Perhaps he takes me for a hallucination.

Fifty yards ahead stood a large frame building with the sign:

SWEETWATER GENERAL MERCANTILE C^o
RANSOM ELIOT, PROP.

A store, this would be. Anders thought he should talk with the storekeeper. He, if anyone, would know the whereabouts of Lake's farm.

Half a dozen rigs stood outside the store, farm wagons with two-horse teams. A sturdy black man loaded kegs of nails on one of the wagons.

Two white men on the store's shady porch leaned against barrels labeled molasses and shouted at each other.

"It's in First Timothy!" said the side-whiskered older man. "It says the laborer is worthy of his reward."

"Shore 'nuff does, you old Whig," said the beefy younger man. "But right in the same place it says thou shall not muzzle the ox that treadeth out the corn!"

The old Whig scoffed. "What's yer point, York?"

"Well, it don't say to cut the ox's traces and turn him loose. See, the niggers are like that ox. You got to feed them so they'll work, but you can't deny they was naturally meant to be slaves. That's in scripture, too."

The Negro who loaded the buckboard stood in easy hearing distance. Did the white men's conversation offend him? Was he a slave or a free man? Illinois was called free soil—yet Anders kept having his views of America upended.

The loud voices had stopped. Both white men scrutinized Anders. Did they suspect him of eavesdropping?

He showed a broad smile. "Good day, gentlemen. I am pleased to meet you. My name is Anders Gunstensen. Is one of you Mister Eliot?"

The old man with the wiry beard smiled back. "Charlie Simmons, I am. My unlearned opponent is York Blodgett. Welcome to the Sweetwater Debating Club." He extended his hand. Anders shook it.

Blodgett shook Anders' hand hastily, as if shamed into it by Simmons. "Storekeeper's inside." He shouted toward the open door, "Rance! Some durned fool wants to see you."

Anders tipped his hat. "Thank you." He entered the store.

The large room smelled of coffee beans, cooking spices, and new leather tack. Shelves, counters, and free-standing merchandise lined each long wall. Strings, ropes, and harnesses hung from the ceiling. Two assistants waited on customers.

Eliot had to be the slender man who stood watching. About thirty-five years of age, he wore a ruffled shirt, silk cravat with stickpin, and swallow-tailed coat. His black hair flowed down to both shoulders.

"I declare," he said, "we have a newcomer. I'm sure I've not had the pleasure."

Anders shook hands and said his name. "I am seeking for the farm of Benjamin Lake."

Eliot smiled and nodded. "Yes, sir. Follow Main Street south. When you have gone three-quarters of a mile, you will see the Lake farm beyond a coppice of woods on the left."

"Thank you." Anders felt a shiver of anticipation. The puzzle of Benjamin Lake would soon start to untangle itself.

"Wait a moment," Eliot said. "You can ride with Josh."

The black man Anders had seen outside stepped up to the counter.

"Mister Gunstensen," Eliot said, "may I present Josh Quimby."

The muscular Negro shook Anders' hand with a gentle smile.

"Thank you for the offer," Anders said. "That would be good, but you need not take extra trouble for me."

"No trouble, sah," said Quimby. "I'd be goin' back that way anyhow."

Eliot's eyes gleamed. "Mister Quimby is Benjamin Lake's foreman."

He seemed to enjoy Anders' surprise.

7. Daniel

Louisiana

June 1853

"Thirty-nine lashes, well laid on."

Daniel, trussed at the post, trembled. He had never in his life been whupped. It was all he could do to hold still and keep his insides from running out at both ends.

"Shame on ye, Son of Ham, for makin' me do this wearisome thing." The white overseer, McCutcheon, picked up the whip.

The gathered slaves stood mute.

The planter, Mas' Petitbon, sipped an iced drink on the veranda nearby, in the company of his wife and three children.

WHSSHK! *Christ!*

Thirty-eight to go.

WHSSHK! *Jesus, help me!*

Thirty-seven.

The master's cold stare from the veranda confirmed what Daniel already knew. His so-called shiftlessness had been an excuse. His real crime was smiling at the new girl, Betsey.

WHSSHK!

Thirty-six.

It had been a quick smile, meant to cheer the slender wench brought home from New Orleans last week by Mas' Petitbon, for she appeared jittery as a fawn.

WHSSHK!

WHSSHK!

WHSSHK!

After he laid on the tenth stroke, McCutcheon paused.

What's keepin' him? Why don't he go on? Daniel feared to turn his head around to look. On the veranda, in his direct line of sight, Petitbon's wife moved to the master's side. She whispered something in his ear. He frowned, gazed at McCutcheon, and made a swift, dismissive gesture.

McCutcheon's voice spoke very near Daniel's ear. "Ye've been given a reprieve, you black devil. See that you don't abuse your master's mercy."

#

Quintus and Micah, Daniel's two friends, dragged him to the cabin.

They laid him on the floor, face down. Spare old Quintus, the soul of caution, and his bold, blocky companion Micah. When Daniel had come to this Godforsaken place, they—his cabin mates—were the first two men he met.

Lame Hattie, cook's helper, brought a jar of something. "Balm from the maroons in the bayou," she murmured. She poured it on a cloth and laid the cloth across his back.

58

Daniel moaned when the cloth touched his wounds. Its sting gave way a warm, tingly sensation. His moan subsided to a low rumble of relief.

"Thass all right, Son," said Hattie. "You rest."

#

Daniel woke with the usual sounds of Quintus and Micah snoring on either side of him. He raised himself to peek out the cabin window. By the moon's height, it must be past midnight. His work in the cane fields would start again in six hours, whupping or no whupping. The stripes on his back howled anew.

Shutting the pain out of his mind, he rose to his feet and shuffled to the cabin door.

Quintus woke. "Where you goin'?" He raised up on his pallet.

"I got to get away from here," said Daniel.

"Put that out your mind, Son. When Mas' Petitbon get you back—"

"He ain't gone get me back, Quintus."

Micah, wakened by their voices, rose to his feet. "You fixin' to 'scape?"

"Not fixin' to, Micah—I'm doin' it. Right now."

"I'll go with you. Let me put on my trousers."

"All right. Make it quick."

Quintus stood up and blocked the door. "Hold on a minute, you two. You don't know what you's doin'."

"Gettin' free, thass what I'm doin'."

"Where you gonna go? The swamp? How you gonna live in the swamp?"

It was not a question Daniel wanted to hear, yet it was important.

"How 'bout them maroons in the bayou? Hattie said they's maroons in the bayou."

59

"You won't find them, 'less they wants to be found, which they don't."

In the moonlight from the cabin window, Micah frowned.

"Listen," Quintus said, "don't you think we wants to get free, too?"

"Well, yes. Of course."

"But it's just too hard, Son."

"No it ain't," Daniel said. The screaming wounds on his back outshouted Quintus' mature wisdom. He had to move before he, too, got bogged down in doubt. "It ain't too hard, and I'll prove it. And when I do, then I'll come back and show both of you the way out."

#

Scurrying from one moon-shadow to the next, Daniel made his way in the dark to the special shed where old Patrice, the hunter, stored his traps, weapons, and supplies. Patrice went down the bayou most days to hunt meat for the slave quarters. Mas' Petitbon trusted Patrice because Patrice always came back, and when he came back he brought with him wild game. This spared Mas' Petitbon some of the expense of slaughtering beeves or hogs just to feed Negroes.

Mas' Petitbon's slaves had long been so docile—what was wrong with them?—that he locked up nothing, not even the weapons shed. Daniel crept inside. He came out a few minutes later with Patrice's long musket plus two horns of powder, two pouches of lead balls and percussion caps, a Bowie knife, and a fine pair of hunter's boots— much better than the slave brogans he left in their place.

Daniel did not know how to make the gun shoot. He would figure it out later.

60

At the bayou, he stashed the weapons in Patrice's pirogue. He untied the master's bateau, somewhat larger, and tied its painter to the back of the pirogue. He would cast the bateau loose once well gone into the swamp.

"Here now, what you doin'?" Patrice half-whispered as he trotted down to the landing barefoot, in his nightshirt. "Who that? I heared you from my cabin. Oh, it's Daniel. What you think you doin', boy?"

"Runnin' off," Daniel said.

"Oh, now. It's a shame what they done, but you can't go runnin' off."

"Why not?"

Patrice glanced around. "Mas' Petitbon punish us all." He shivered in the warm night.

Daniel beckoned Patrice closer. "Do you want to know something?"

The old man leaned forward.

"Here's the thing," Daniel said. He clubbed Patrice with the musket. The old man fell.

He lay on the ground, unconscious.

Daniel listened above him until he heard regular breathing. "Hope I din't hurt you too bad." *Mammy, I had to do it.* He stepped into the pirogue and poled away, pulling the bateau behind him.

#

Daniel had no idea where to go. There had been no time for plans. His back, scored with raw welts, proved the urgency of escape. Somewhere, far across the swamp, rolled the Mississippi River, the one sure highway North. Somewhere inside the swamp were those maroons that Hattie mentioned. They would be friends if he met them, not enemies.

61

Right now, he could only pole the pirogue away from the plantation. He hoped he was headed right. The bayou twisted and branched. Scant moonlight sifted through the trees.

Unknown animals grunted in the swamp. Some of them must be 'gators.

There could be others that would make no noise, like snakes. A moccasin might slither out along any tree branch and drop on him from above. He had to keep his wits sharp. He was on his own. He should have brought Quintus and Micah along.

Above all, he had to avoid circling around, coming back to the plantation.

This did not much resemble his first escape, up in Mississippi. Slaves up there said a man would be a fool to flee from Hurricane Plantation. Mister Davis treated his slaves better than any other master. If you had to be a slave, Hurricane was the place to be one. But Daniel did not want to be a slave.

When they captured him in Memphis, he had been brought back to Mister Davis at Hurricane. The old man sat in his library, on the hill above the river, flanked by walls of books. He frowned. "Come, Daniel. Sit down. Let's have a talk."

Daniel, one of more than three hundred slaves at Hurricane, had never in his life spoken with the master. Now, because he had run away, he had been invited to sit.

Ben Montgomery, Davis' black shipping and purchasing manager, sat in a chair at the end of the table. He wore a suit with a tie. Flecks of gray salted his dark beard. He tipped his head toward the empty chair, as if to instruct Daniel in its use.

Daniel sat.

Mister Davis gazed at him. "What is the cause of your dissatisfaction?"

62

Daniel thought about the question. Could it be a joke? "No dissatisfaction, sah. I want to be free, is all."

Mister Davis peered across the table and stroked his wispy beard. "Observe the portrait above my head, Daniel. Who do you see?"

A painting hung on the wall. Daniel peered intently. "Is it your father, sah?"

Mister Davis' eyes squinched up. He shared a chuckle with Ben Montgomery.

"Oh, mercy me. No, boy. That is a likeness of Robert Owen. The most advanced thinker of our age. He said: There is but one mode by which man can possess all the happiness his nature is capable of enjoying—that is by the union and co-operation of all for the benefit of each." The old man stared at Daniel with burning eyes.

Daniel made no reply.

"The union and co-operation of all for the benefit of each. Don't you see, boy—that's what I want to create here at Hurricane. So we may all be as happy as ever may be." He smiled as one who has spoken a self-evident truth.

"I be happy if I am free," Daniel said.

Mister Davis frowned. "Under the present constitution of society, Daniel, it is necessary that you, like most of your race, be placed under the supervision of men such as me. Men of property, of good standing in society. You see that, do you not?"

Daniel sat mute.

"You may wonder why I asked Mister Montgomery to join us here." Mister Davis tilted his head toward Ben Montgomery. "It is because he is the last person, before yourself, who ran away from Hurricane Plantation."

Montgomery sat still and stared forward.

Mister Davis smiled. "He was not much older than you are now when he attempted his escape. He was about eighteen, as I recall. After he was brought back to me, I

63

inquired closely into the cause of his dissatisfaction—just as I am doing now with you—until we reached a mutual understanding about his situation. Isn't that right, Ben?"

"Yes, suh," Montgomery said. He cast his eyes to the ceiling.

"As a result, Mister Montgomery has been given an education and entrusted with large responsibilities. So you see, he is a valued member of our society here—a union and co-operation of all for the benefit of each."

Daniel did not know what Mister Davis wanted him to say.

"I think we may assume you also will benefit greatly and become an important member of our little society. Now, you must promise not to run away again."

Ben Montgomery stared at the ceiling.

"What do you say, Daniel?" asked Mister Davis. "Give up this phantasm of freedom, in exchange for education, income, a place in society?"

Montgomery, after all, had taken Mister Davis' offer and had prospered.

But now, with Mammy gone, what could Hurricane Plantation offer to Daniel?

"No, sah," Daniel said. "I reckon I'll just keep tryin' to get free."

And so, Mister Davis had sold Daniel downriver, where he wound up as a field hand on the sugar plantation of Mister Lot Petitbon in Bellefontaine Parish, Louisiana. Mas' Petitbon, unlike Mister Davis, had no vision of the union and co-operation of all for the benefit of each. His system was brutality.

Now Daniel, on the run again, this time with no ally but his own courage and wits, feared mainly that he would double back and return unknowingly to that brutality.

Dawn would soon appear. Cypress and tupelo trees, trumpet vines and greenbriar became visible, etched in pearly gray light. A shrill *kent* sounded behind him. A big black bird with a long ivory bill swooped low over him and flew into the trees ahead. In a moment came a *thud . . . thud-thud.* Some kind of woodpecker, he reckoned. Huge.

Daniel steered the pirogue to a bank, grounded it, and stepped onto the mud. He had cast loose the master's bateau long ago. That would delay pursuit, if not for long. He stilled his breath. He listened for sounds of dogs or men, tried to hear them through the awakening sounds of the swamp.

"Thought you got away clean, din't you?" said a deep male voice.

Daniel turned around.

A burly black man in earth-colored clothes stood before him.

"Who you?" Daniel asked.

"My name Luc," the big man said. "Who you?"

"I'm Daniel."

"You make enough noise to wake the dead. We been follerin' you the last two-three mile. Not hard to do."

"We?"

Something dropped over Daniel's head from behind, something like a gunnysack. Someone pinned his arms at his side.

"Daniel," said Luc, "meet Sammy. No point strugglin'. You won't break his holt."

Sammy's arms clamped around him so tight that Daniel gave up struggling.

Luc's voice came from the direction of Daniel's beached pirogue. "Oh, Lordy. Looks like I got me a gun at last."

8. Daniel

Louisiana

June – August 1853

Daniel lay bound and hooded in the bottom of the pirogue. The flat-bottomed canoe pushed off from shore and glided, with a pulse every time Luc or Sammy poled.

Since arriving in Louisiana, he had been whupped by Mas' Petitbon, had laid poor old Patrice on the ground with a vicious blow—*I'm sorry, Mammy*—and had now become the prisoner of wild men. Such a violent place made him shiver when he thought about it.

He couldn't just lie there mute. "Where we goin'?" he asked.

A pole cracked his head.

"Hush up," said Luc. "You make noise, we drop you in for the 'gators."

Daniel reckoned he ought to wait. He would get answers later, if allowed to live. Would they kill him? Why would they kill him? *For the gun.*

He imagined bargaining with Luc, in a make-believe world with free speech allowed. *You can have the gun,*

Mister Luc. Please spare my life. Naw, too much like begging. Besides, it made no sense. Luc already had the gun.

The pirogue bumped into land. Sammy jumped out the front end and pulled the canoe up on shore. Luc hauled Daniel to his feet. He dragged him out of the boat. "There. You on dry land now. Stand up."

They marched him forward, still hooded, over squdgy ground. A hundred steps on, the earth rose under his feet and got more solid. A hand on his chest halted him. The hood whipped off his head.

Luc stood before him in dawn's pink light. He clutched the musket to his chest.

A crowd of black people, dressed no better than Luc, stood nearby. Stone silent, they stared at Daniel. What would he say for himself? Was he a man or just something wiggly from the swamp?

"I want my gun back."

Luc flashed a gap-toothed smile, as if Daniel had passed a test. He handed the musket to a man behind him, turned back to Daniel, and smashed him in the mouth. "Speak when you spoken to, boy. That gun mine. Not yours no more. Ever."

Daniel scowled as blood dripped from his mouth.

Luc drew a knife from a scabbard. He held it to Daniel's throat.

"Welcome to Camp Réponds Pas."

They stood in a clearing, at the edge of which rose half a dozen peak-roofed huts. The huts, built of sticks, vines, and leaves, mimicked the forest. Anyone viewing from a distance might not see them.

"What is this? Who you all?"

Luc touched the knife to the skin of Daniel's throat. "Who you gonna tell?" His eyes were slits, his mouth grim.

"Uh, nobody, I reckon."

"You reckon?"

"Nobody." The blade vexed Daniel's skin. "Nobody a-tall. Never," he whispered.

Luc relaxed but kept the knife near Daniel's throat. "Why you come here?"

"You brung me."

"Before that. What you doin' on the bayou?"

"Runnin' away from Mas' Petitbon."

Luc chuckled: a low, menacing sound. "You 'spect us to believe that?"

"It's truth."

"Or maybe you is a Judas goat. Know what a Judas goat is?"

Daniel shrugged. "We din't keep no goats where I come from."

Luc kept the blade at Daniel's throat. "Soon's we let you go, you run back and lead your massa straight to us."

"No," Daniel said. "Mas' Petitbon and me don't do each other no favors. You don't believe me, talk to my back."

Sammy lifted Daniel's shirttail from behind.

Luc sheathed his knife. He examined Daniel's back. "Mm-mm. ... How come they stopped befo' thirty-nine?"

"I don't know. Miz Petitbon say something to the master."

Luc spoke near Daniel's ear. "She's your savior then, Brother Daniel. If they do the whole thirty-nine, you wouldn't be walkin'. Bijou, honey, bring some of that balm over here."

A large-boned woman slipped into one of the huts and came back with a pot. "This gone hurt some." She slapped lotion on Daniel's back. It did hurt, yet in seconds he felt relief.

"This be that famous balm," said Luc. "We gets it from the maroons."

Some of the bystanders laughed.

"Oh, thass right," said Luc, his eyes dancing. "We is the maroons."

"Thass what I reckoned," said Daniel. "Say, what is in this maroon balm?"

"Maybe I tell you next year." Luc squinted. "Then again, maybe not. We'll let you stay here for a while. You like that?"

Daniel merely nodded. A wrong word might cost his life.

"Listen here. You earn your keep, and you foller the rules."

"Rules?"

"I make the rules," said Luc. "Anybody don't like my rules gets to go out in the swamp and feed the 'gators."

#

Daniel slept in Luc's hut. "Always be where I can see you," said Luc. The other occupants of Luc's hut were his woman, Bijou, and his son, Sammy, a wiry woodsman about Daniel's age.

Sammy was Luc's shadow. Sammy had dropped the gunnysack over Daniel's head and bound his arms and had raised Daniel's shirt so Luc could see his back. Sammy also appeared to be second in command of the whole maroon colony, which numbered forty-eight souls.

In the first days with this leadership family, Daniel rode herd on his mouth and walked softly. He never forgot the big knife that Luc always wore at his waist.

After a few weeks as the lowest member of the community, Daniel began to feel accepted—or at least, taken for granted. Better than living under threat, he supposed—but it did not feel like freedom.

70

Luc remained stern and forbidding, so Daniel worked on Sammy. "Luc wants me to earn my keep. If I had my gun back, I could go huntin' in the swamp, bring back game for all of us."

Sammy put his hand over Daniel's mouth. "Just hush up. When you gonna start believin' that gun ain't yours no more?"

Daniel swept Sammy's hand away. "It's my gun. 'Tain't right."

"Course it's right. If Papa give you the gun back, what you say you do?"

"Go huntin' in the swamp."

Sammy snorted. "Just shows you don't know the first thing about huntin'."

"Get my gun back, I show you."

"Yeh, you go shootin' at some possum or wild hog. Just what I mean."

Daniel couldn't believe his ears. "What else a gun for?"

"Don't you see, Brother Daniel—we can't make noise like that. You hear a gun in the swamp, it's a hunter from one of the plantations round here. They's no way we would make a loud bang. That would show everybody where we at. We do all our huntin' the quiet way."

"What quiet way?"

"I'm goin' in the morning. I'll show you."

#

Sammy led him along a dim trail through the woods, all on solid ground though in the middle of the swamp. He showed Daniel how to move quietly by putting his toe down first, then his heel.

"Thank you for learning me that," Daniel said. "Now, when we gone do some huntin'?"

71

"Shh." Sammy stopped. He held Daniel back with his hand. He whispered. "You see that cabbage leaf? Over by the log?"

"Yeh. What about it?"

"What it's doin' there? This supposed to be the woods. That cabbage leaf musta come from a garden. You pick it up."

Daniel reached out to grab the cabbage leaf. Just before his fingers closed on it, his wrist was seized and jerked upwards.

"Hee-hee," said Sammy, with glee. "Lookit you, Brother Daniel."

A strong cord of braided plant fibers held his wrist.

"What is this?"

"You see? Thass how we goes huntin' without a gun. It's a snare. Old Brother Rabbit go for the cabbage, pretty soon he swingin' by his neck. We catches lots of meat that way."

In the following days, Daniel learned silent ways to bag almost every animal in the bayous, swamps, and wooded uplands. Sammy showed him how to set snares for rabbits, squirrels, muskrats, and possum; how to shoot turkeys, quail, and deer with bow and arrow; how two hunters together could even kill a black bear or 'gator, using knives and vine ropes.

Daniel collected hunting and trapping tools of his own. Bit by bit he extended his range into areas that Sammy and other maroons did not already patrol. He also enjoyed going out with Sammy. He made it a point to hunt with him at least once or twice in seven days.

Daniel began to see that the maroons, under Luc's control, yet had a kind of freedom. He had wanted freedom, but he was not yet satisfied. Most of the maroons were paired up in couples and families. He thought about Betsey, the girl he had encouraged with a smile that cost

72

him ten lashes. He considered the smoothness of her limbs, the softness in her eyes. He thought she would prefer Camp Réponds Pas to the Petitbon plantation.

The maroons ate a communal meal late every afternoon. It included all the fish and game the men had brought in, plus vegetables and herbs from hidden garden patches the women worked. Most items were wrapped in cabbage leaves with red peppers and onions and then cooked in the ashes of the central campfire. They also made a delicious corn bread, cooked the same way, called ash cake.

Daniel wondered where the women got the cornmeal to make the ash cake, for they grew no corn in their garden patches. Certain other items—vinegar, molasses, white sugar, salt, butter, and corn whiskey—also appeared, though the maroons had no means to make them.

The mystery lifted when Sammy returned from a solitary overnight hunt. In addition to a couple of rabbits and a few fish from the bayou, he brought a couple of jugs of liquid and something soft, wrapped in cloth. Bijou's eyes glittered at these offerings when Sammy handed them to her.

"How you get these things?" Daniel asked Sammy.

"What things?"

"You know. Things in jugs and bottles."

"Ain't you caught on yet, Brother Daniel?"

Daniel fidgeted. "Well, no. I mean, I never thought about it, 'fore now."

"Did you think we made all our own whiskey and molasses and such? No sir, it's your Mas' Petitbon, and some other planters. They's generous enough to provide us with those kinds of things."

"What, they just give you things?"

"No. We just take 'em."

"You steal from the plantations."

73

"Papa says we ap-prop-riate. They's a difference."

"Yeh?"

Sammy smiled. "Everything the masters have, come from our work. They never give us half what they owe us. So, we appropriate what we need. Thass just fair. 'Tain't stealin'."

"So, you the one that goes and appropriates?"

"Late at night. Risky work."

"Take me with you."

Sammy frowned. "I don't know, Brother Daniel. It's right dangerous."

9. Daniel

Louisiana
September 1853

Daniel jumped out onto the moonlit stream bank. He pulled the pirogue up on shore. Sammy got out.

"What we doin' here?" Daniel asked in a whisper. "This ain't the Petitbon landing."

"Course it ain't. We don't come the reg'lar way 'cause we don't want to be seen. I knowed if I brung you along, it'd be nothin' but stupid questions. Just stay here and guard the boat. I be back 'fore you know it."

Sammy, carrying a jug of maroons' balm and several bunches of swamp-grown herbs, disappeared into the brush that lined the shore.

Daniel watched him go. He tried to reckon where they had landed. In a few moments it came to him. They had stopped about half a mile short of the plantation's landing. Where Sammy had plunged into the bushes there must be a path leading to the trail that ran behind the slave cabins, a trail Daniel knew.

Leaving the pirogue to defend itself, Daniel went where Sammy had gone. He could scarcely make out the trail. Sammy had chosen a moonless night for this venture, so Daniel's eyes were useless. He got down on all fours and found a trace of hard-packed earth which ran between bushes. Soon it widened and became easier to follow. Just after that it joined the main trail. He knew where he was now, less than a quarter mile from the slave shanties.

He found Betsey easily. She had a cabin to herself, separated from the other cabins and served by a trail that ran through the woods to Petitbon's big house.

He rapped on the door. "Hsst! Betsey, you in there?"

The door flew open. There, backed by firelight, stood a stout man. Mas' Petitbon.

"Who you?" the master asked.

Wide-eyed with fright, Daniel punched him, first in the gut, then, as he doubled up, a fist under the jaw. The master crumpled to the floor.

Betsey stood by her bed, a spirit in her cotton shift, mouth open in amazement.

Petitbon groaned, began to rise. Daniel grabbed a log from the firewood bin and smacked Petitbon on the back of the head. The master fell and lay still.

"Come on," Daniel said. "We leavin' right now."

Betsey slipped her small feet into clunky slave brogans. She scooped up a daytime dress and tow-linen jacket from her one chair and followed Daniel from the cabin. They ran into the woods and down the path to where he had left the pirogue.

"I never run away before," Betsey said, breathing hard.

"I have. It's easy. I know a free place. Run fast."

When they reached the edge of the bayou, the pirogue was gone. Daniel, by starlight, made out movement on the stream. "Sammy! Stop! Come back here!" He ran along the bank to get nearer the pirogue.

Sammy stuck his pole in the bottom to halt the boat's movement. "What kind of tricks you playin', man?"

"Nothin', Sammy, I just brung a friend, is all. Come on back."

"You fixin' to betray me, I can't take the chance."

"You got to save us. We left the master knocked out on the floor. When he come to, our goose be cooked. This Betsey. I bringin' her back whether you like it or not."

#

"You what!" Luc fumed. He paced back and forth like a caged cougar, his rage illuminated by light from the candle Bijou had lit. "You bash Petitbon and kidnap his pretty girl. Now you bring your problem here to my hut."

"She need a place to live."

"Thass the least of it, you fool. Mas' Petitbon gone take us apart. We goin' back into slavery." He reached under his bed, where he kept the musket, and pulled it out. "Bijou, honey, you know where I keep them balls and powder."

Without a word, Bijou left the hut.

"Now, hold on," said Daniel. "Mas' Petitbon can't hurt us. He don't even know where this place is."

Luc gave him a glance of disgust. "You tell him, Sammy."

"We only a couple mile from the plantation, as the crow fly. Petitbon din't find us 'cause he never really search. Couple no-count slaves run off now and again, ain't worth his trouble. Now this different. You took his treasure." He glanced at Betsey, who sat in quiet solitude.

"Not only that," Luc said. "You beat him up. He will make it out a great slave revolt. He will go to th' other

77

planters. They will make up a posse to come hunt us down like dogs, once and for all. They will scour the swamp till they find us."

Daniel hung his head. All he had meant to do was help Betsey.

Bijou re-entered the hut, carrying two pouches of balls and caps plus two horns of powder, all on leather straps. She gave them to Luc, who draped them over his shoulders.

"What we gone do, Papa?" asked Sammy.

Luc cast his eyes around him. The corners of his mouth drooped. "We gone move."

#

The maroons gathered their goods—a few pots and utensils, some crude tools, scraps of clothing, dried vegetables—and set out at daybreak for their new home. Sammy and Daniel poled the two pirogues, laden with two old women, a young mother with two small children, plus old Marcellus the basket-maker. Everyone else hiked through the swamp on foot.

"You know this place we goin' to?" Daniel asked.

"Reckon I do."

"What kind of place is it?"

"Like the last place, only deeper in the swamp. Be harder to get back to the plantation for vinegar and such. It's a special place Papa scouted out years ago."

"Why for?"

"Case some young buck draws down the whole parish on our heads. Papa ain't like us. He thinks ahead."

When they arrived after hours of poling their canoes along the sinuous bayou, the chosen place turned out to be a raised clearing, screened by trees and vines—very much like the camp they had just left.

"The others won't be here till tomorrow. Come on, we got to build the camp."

They worked by a plan that Luc had devised. Sammy had long since memorized it. They used machetes to cut saplings and laid them out where the huts would stand. The two old women and the young mother helped drag branches to the campsite. By the end of the day, Sammy and Daniel had planted the uprights around which the huts would be woven. They stopped to rest. The old women built a fire in the middle of the clearing, where they cooked food they had brought from the old site.

Late the next morning, Luc and Bijou arrived with the rest of the maroons, all of them laden with utensils, tools, clothes, and foodstuffs. After a midday meal, Luc rose, picked up his musket, and beckoned to Sammy and two other men, Jerry and Amos.

"What you doin'?" Daniel asked.

Luc frowned. "Ain't we the curious one? Well, you see, Brother Daniel, on accounta your heroic slave rescue, some of us got to go back and draw the posse off—away from this direction." He gazed up to where the sun, already high in the sky, filtered through the trees. "Reckon by this time tomorrow they'll be formed up and startin' through the swamp."

"I'll go with you."

"No. You shall not." Luc's face flared with anger. "You stay here, help build the new camp. You caused enough trouble already."

#

Daniel labored with the others for the next three days, building the new camp. The men cut branches from throughout the woods. The women tied branches across the saplings already sunk. They wove gossamer walls and

79

hung them on the hut frames, stowed possessions away, built and tended the central campfire.

Three times as the maroons worked, they heard far-away gunshots. Each fusillade brought grimaces, for they knew that Luc's decoy party had only one single-shot musket.

A smell of smoke wafted through from the direction of the old campground on the day after Luc's departure. "Somebody done fired our old home," said Horatio, a gaunt, toothless graybeard. "Either the planters' posse or our boys."

Daniel scoffed. "Why would our boys torch the old place?"

"Some kind o' trickery, make the white boys think they's hot on our heels maybe."

"Truth is," Bijou said, "we don't know nothin'."

Daniel and a few other men went out hunting. They searched for game trails and water holes, set out snares and traplines, and brought home a few rabbits.

Two nights and two days passed. Where could the decoy party be?

Near sundown on the third day, Luc stepped out of the woods with Jerry and Amos.

Bijou shrieked. "Sammy! Where Sammy? My Sammy!"

Luc stomped up to the central fire, one arm cradling the musket. He wrapped his other arm around Bijou. "Sammy dead," he said.

Over Bijou's head, Luc glared at Daniel, shriveling something inside him. Would he be blamed for Sammy's death? What could he have done? Left Betsey to Petitbon's mercies?

The women left the supper cooking. Everybody gathered around Luc.

"We set a half mile from the old camp till we see the posse comin' on," he said. "Then we run back to the camp, set every hut afire, took off runnin' through the swamp. They reckoned our whole comp'ny was close by. We broke plenty branches, left lots of sign to make them think so."

"Thass just right, Luc," said old Horatio. "Jus' the thing to do."

"We stayed just ahead of them for the next day and a half. Sometime we was close enough to hear 'em talkin', so we know they thunk they was chasin' more of us than just four.

"Sammy doubled back to shoot a coupla arrows, just to tease them, like. Then some of the planters got ahead of him. They caught him and started in on him. I's hunkered in the bushes, close enough to hear their questions. Where was we? How many? Which way did we go? Wasn't we plannin' to raid the plantations and kill all the white folk in they beds?

"It was terrible to hear, and to watch. They tortured Sammy, beatin' him to get him to say what they wanted. Started to flay the skin off his arm, he was screamin'.

"So I line up my gun and shoot one of them dead."

The maroons gasped. "Served 'em right," someone said.

"All the white men, they lookin' every which way, where the shot come from? Sammy broke loose. They chased him. I din't have time to reload. He dove headfirst in the bayou. They fired at him in the water, hollerin', laughin', and havin' a grand time till they was sure he dead."

Bijou let out a wail and collapsed on the ground.

"Somebody hush her up, thass too loud." Tears flowed down Luc's face.

81

The maroons closed around Luc and Bijou, embraced them, spoke in hushed voices. A few cast harsh glances at Daniel, who stood off to the side.

What did they want me to do? Leave Betsey? He knew he had been right to rescue her from the brutal master. Any one of them, if they had stood in that cabin door instead of Daniel, would have done the same. *Wait*, he wanted to say. *What about Luc? How could he let Sammy take such a terrible risk, teasing the planters that way?*

A hand touched his shoulder. A small, soft hand.

Betsey stood beside him, her mouth puckered up. "This all on account of me."

"No." Daniel felt dizzy. How could it be her fault? She was the victim.

"Yes. Mas' Petitbon din't get up no posse when you run off. But he did when I run off, because his lust."

"Well, but—"

"The other night, when you come to my cabin and laid the master out, I made up my mind to go with you, just like that. Din't have no time to think, it was yes or no."

"Course you come. Who wouldn't?"

"Lotsa folk wouldn't. Only I got a special reason. I don't want my child born and raised under Mas' Petitbon's thumb, be just another slave like me."

"Your child?"

She hugged her round belly. "I'm with child. It's Mas' Petitbon's doin'."

10. Maria

Illinois

June 1854

Maria Nybro smiled up at the Petersburg Hotel waiter. "And plenty of butter for bread, if it please you."

"Yes, Madam. Will that be all?"

She handed back the menu. "Ja, I think that are all. Ja?"

Cousins Anne and Tarald, and old Aunt Osa, were silenced by the language.

Maria gave the waiter a decisive nod. He departed.

Relieved of the burden of English, Maria turned to her male cousin, fifteen years her senior, and spoke Norsk. "Cousin Tarald, how goes the search for a suitable farm? Anne and Tante Osa have been wondering, too— have you not, ladies?"

"Best to have the butter on the bacon, where you can see it," said Tante.

Cousin Anne, Tarald's sister, stared at their square-headed old aunt, whose face was all odd angles and jutting bones.

Tarald's eyes widened behind his round spectacles, as if he had been struck by a detail forgotten amid weightier concerns.

"It is not that we are impatient," Maria said. "We have so little to keep us busy here in the hotel. And after two weeks in Illinois, our lodging costs must be adding up, ja?"

She hoped her question did not smack of desperation. But in truth none of the four of them would be here in Menard County, or even this side of the Atlantic, had not she plotted tirelessly within her family—planting and watering the seeds of emigration in her cousins' minds, then promoting the logic that Tante Osa should accompany them and that she, Maria, must make the trip as guardian to the dotty, goggle-eyed old woman.

Anders Gunstensen, the skurk, had inspired Maria when he squatted in Pappa's boathouse the winter before last. Considering the scandal of his flight from Norway, good riddance to him! She had to admit, however, that it was Anders who had got her thinking of America and of Cousin Gunder Jørgen, the first of their family to emigrate, who now toiled as a farmhand somewhere hereabouts to save up money for his own farm.

Gunder Jørgen had welcomed them warmly to Menard County. He, however, could not give them a place to stay, for he himself lived in his employer's bunkhouse. So, they had rented two rooms in the hotel—one for Tarald and one for the three women. After conferring with Gunder Jørgen about local conditions, Cousin Tarald seemed to have gotten bogged down in his research on farms, soils, and land prices.

Tarald now cleared his throat for an important announcement. "As a matter of fact, Maria—and Anne, and Tante—I have reached a conclusion." He looked like a weasel that had swallowed a finch. Why did it seem that he had just this moment chosen what finch to swallow? That if not for Maria's query, he might still be considering other finches?

"That is wonderful, Brother," said Anne. "And what did you conclude?"

Tarald beamed. "We're going to Kansas."

"Kansas?" Anne set down her teacup. "What is a Kansas?"

"I'm sorry, let me explain." Tarald smiled like an indulgent father. "Kansas is a new territory, somewhat west of Illinois, with wonderful farmland."

"There is good land right here," Maria said. *Land good enough for Anders, at any rate.* "Did not Cousin Gunder Jørgen say so?"

Tarald peered over the top of his spectacles. "Yes, my dear, he did. And he was right."

Anne knit her brows. "Then why go elsewhere?"

"Because at five to ten dollars per acre, we can buy only a small farm here in Illinois. The land in Kansas, at approximately one-quarter the price per acre, is just as good. We can get four times the acreage for the same money."

Anne frowned. "If the land there is so good, why is it so cheap?"

"Because it's farther west." He spread his hands wide. "We shall be pioneers."

The waiter brought their meal. As roast beef and boiled potatoes went round the table, Maria thought about pioneering in Kansas. The very concept of pioneering seemed dangerous. Cousin Gunder Jørgen had chosen Illinois, and Anders had ratified his choice by settling here. Kansas seemed a bad idea.

Tarald said grace and they began their supper.

Anne, spearing a potato, asked, "What about Red Indians?"

85

"I have been assured they are no problem in that part of the country."

"There are frogs in the moss," said Tante as she buttered her pudding.

Just then Maria's heart skipped a beat. Behind Tarald's head, who should walk by the archway door of the dining room but Anders Gunstensen? Though he now wore a ridiculous high-crowned felt hat and squired a rotund old woman, she would know Anders anywhere.

In the blink of an eye, they disappeared.

Maria jumped up and raced out to the lobby. She could not let him get away. "Anders! You skurk!"

Anders froze in his tracks. He turned around. "Maria!" He beamed at her, just as anyone might on meeting an old friend in a foreign place. Better than that, the warmth of his smile anchored itself in the depths of his ocean-blue eyes. Leaving aside his act of desertion in Pappa's boathouse, Anders' face now showed real and spontaneous joy. That softened her heart toward him. A bit.

"What a pleasant surprise this is," he said in English.

The old woman beside Anders glanced from him to Maria and back.

Anders doffed his preposterous hat. "I dared not hope we would meet again," he said in Norsk. "I'm like butter melting in the porridge."

What a nice, home-cooked compliment. "You talk like a Nordmann," Maria said, "but you look and act like an American."

"Well, jenta mi, we are Americans now, are we not?"

"Of course you'd rather be an American, having abandoned your farm, your family, your country—" *And me, you skurk.*

The smile on Anders' face faded, replaced by a frown.

Tarald, Anne, and Tante came in, napkins at their chins, from the dining room.

"Come see!" she called to them. "It's Anders, the deserter."

"So it is," said Tarald. "See here, young man—"

"I am no deserter," said Anders. He spread his hands wide before Tarald. "Is it a crime to seek a better future?"

The old American woman beside Anders seemed baffled and astonished. "These are old friends from Norway," he explained in English. "Naturally, they are excited to see me."

The woman smiled, creating two extra chins below her original God-given one.

In Norsk, Anders said, "May I introduce you all to Mistress Lake, my employer's wife."

Anne and Maria curtsied. Tarald bowed. Tante stared and smacked her lips.

"I am escorting Mistress Lake to a meeting of the Anti-Slavery Society. I shall see her to her place in the meeting room and then join you all for a chat." He nodded to them and led the old woman away.

What a cool customer this skurk has become, thought Maria.

#

"A cheeky fellow," Tarald commented as he took a slice roast beef.

Maria bit her lip. "Well, Cousin, he has always been that way." *However*, she thought, *there is something more now, is there not? He stands straighter, that's it.*

"Those born in the caul," said Tante, "always think they are something special."

"Hsst!" Anne tipped her head toward the doorway, where Anders had just appeared.

87

He came to the table. Standing behind Tante, he spoke to Tarald. "So? Am I a deserter?"

Tarald sighed. "Take a seat, Anders."

No empty chairs remained. Anders pulled one from the next table, wedged it between Maria and Tante.

"Can you do that?" asked Tarald.

"Do what?"

"Should you not ask the headwaiter's permission before you move the furniture?"

"Here we do not stand so much on ceremony."

"Nor did you respect propriety when you broke faith with your uncle Torgus and lit out for America." Tarald sat upright as any judge.

Anders sat up straight, a waspish look on his face. "When I left his farm, Uncle was knocking on the door of Valhalla, demanding to be let in."

"Anders!" Maria slapped him on the shoulder. "What a way to talk of your poor uncle. People said you not only broke your indenture. You caused his death as well."

"I am sorry if people have thought ill of me." Something like a drawn curtain darkened his countenance. "It was Uncle, however, who tried to skewer me with a pitchfork."

"So you killed him."

Anders shook his head. "No, jenta mi. He ran into a post. And I did feel bad about his death. However, he was dead. So, I left."

"What about your poor mother and father? People think they raised a murderer."

"Father and Mother know me, jenta mi. They cannot think I would do such a thing."

"What your parents think about you does not matter. It's what people in town think of *them*. Don't you see that?"

88

Anders frowned. "I never thought of it that way. I wrote them a letter soon after I arrived, in which I explained why I emigrated. I shall write again, this very night, with all the details about Uncle's death. They can show my letter to all the neighbors."

"That's the least you can do."

"I agree," Anders said, with obvious feeling. The headstrong lummox had taken her words to heart. "Now you must tell me, how do you come to be here, in Menard County?"

Tarald cleared his throat. "We are on our way to Kansas."

"Kansas?"

"Yes. We just stopped here to get advice from our brother, Gunder Jørgen. Did you know he lives here, in Menard County?"

"Of course," said Anders. "In fact, we see each other often. I introduced him to Kirsten Haraldsdatter and her family. He sometimes joins us at Osmundsgarden for Sunday dinner."

"Osmundsgarden?" Maria asked.

"It is just the name of their farm, jenta mi." He turned back to Tarald with a keen look on his face. "Tell me, did Gunder Jørgen Nybro recommend Kansas to you?"

"Well . . . not in so many words."

Anders pulled out his pipe and stuffed it with tobacco. "You would be well-advised to reconsider," he said.

Maria leaned forward. "Why do you say that, Anders?"

"Yes, why?" Anne leaned forward as well.

Anders tipped his head toward Tarald, his eyebrows raised.

"Go on," Tarald said. "Give us your . . . opinion."

Anders exhaled a cloud of smoke. "First, a few facts. A law has been made by which Kansas is to decide for itself whether to have slavery." He held up one finger. "Second"—raising his next finger also—"pro- and anti-slavery mobs rush into Kansas so they can vote for or against slavery. Third, a preacher in the East sends rifles to the anti-slavery men—because pro-slavery men already range the land with rifles." He closed the three fingers he had raised. "So, this next bit is my . . . opinion . . . as you say." He pointed the stem of his pipe straight at Tarald. "There is sure to be a lot of trouble in Kansas. Your lives may be in danger."

Sixteen months ago, in Pappa's boathouse, when Anders mentioned Illinois, the prospect of sailing to America had filled her with excitement. Now, to hear the facts about America's dangers, straight from Anders' mouth, sent chills through her.

Skurk he might be, but she trusted Anders' knowledge to be as deep as her cousin's would be shallow.

Tarald glared at Anders. "Come now," he said. "The situation is not as dark as you make out. First, as you yourself say, they do things by vote here in America. There is no need to take up arms over political questions. Secondly, if people like us go to Kansas, the outcome will be favorable. I don't know any Nordmann who would vote for slavery—do you? I thought not."

"Of course there will be an election," Anders said, "and I pray that free labor wins. Do not delude yourself, however, that the pro-slavers will accept the results." He leaned forward, the bowl of his pipe cradled in his hands. "They are not only armed, they are mad on the subject of slavery. And it is a fact about Southrons—they take umbrage at trifles. Violence is apt to be their first resort." He frowned and took a puff on his pipe.

Tarald had no rejoinder.

90

Anders turned to Maria. "Jenta mi, I beg you to consider your safety. It is one thing for a warrior like your cousin Tarald to sally forth in battle. It is another thing for women and children to face the conditions that may develop in Kansas."

"Be that as it may," said Tarald, "we are going to Kansas."

Maria seized Anders' free hand with both of hers. "Tell me. That night in Pappa's boathouse, why did you spurn my offer to come with you?"

Tarald and Anne gasped.

"I was traveling light, jenta mi." Anders hesitated, then plunged on. "Also, I did not know whether I would be seized by the sheriff or allowed to board the ship for America. It would have been unfair to involve you in my risk."

"At any rate," said Tarald, "we leave for Kansas next week."

Maria pushed her plate aside, placed her elbows on the table, and leaned forward. "No," she said. "Tante and I will stay right here in Menard County."

11. Maria

Illinois

June – September 1854

Maria closed the door of the hotel room when Anne and Tante left.

"You two go down to supper," she had said to them. "I'll join you in a moment." If they thought Maria feared to face Tarald, who had sulked in his room since he stormed away from the table last night, then let them think it.

But privacy, not fear, kept her in the room this evening.

She laid her money on the bed and counted it. Just right: One hundred speciedaler in Norwegian banknotes, another twenty-five in silver coins. Her funds remained intact, because Cousin Tarald paid the joint expenses for the four of them.

She also had a few gold coins that Pappa's cousin Christen Nybro had sent along for Tante Osa's needs.

Plus a special asset, hidden away, that only she and Pappa knew about. That, however, would be held back for a dire emergency—which Tarald's bad mood was not.

Maria figured that one hundred twenty-five Norsk speciedaler would buy about one hundred fifty U.S. dollars. She swept the money back into its small bag, returned it to her locked trunk, left the room, and went downstairs to the lobby.

The coast was clear. Tarald, Anne, and Tante had already gone into the dining room.

Maria marched up to the desk.

The nearsighted manager, Schallert, looked up from a book he jotted notes in. "Yes, Miss . . . Nybro, is it not?"

"It is," she said. "I need to know, how much is our room costing?"

"Well, let's see. You have two rooms, one for Mister Nybro and one for you three ladies. Both rooms cost the same. That is"—he stopped himself with a hand to his mouth—"Oh, dear me. He takes care of all those charges, doesn't he?"

"And how much are they?"

Grinning an insipid grin, Schallert removed his pince-nez. He waved them in the air as a schoolmaster might wave his pointer. "No need to bother yourself about it, is there? Mister Nybro will be happy to reassure you. I can tell you that your rooms have been paid through the end of the week."

Maria took a deep breath. She slowed her breathing and counted to ten.

She squinted at Schallert, leaned in, and spoke softly, making him bend forward to hear. "We Norwegians do things our own way. My young cousin Tarald has no money but what I give him. And he will soon run out."

"What? Your young cousin? Surely you are younger."

"I am near forty." Maria put steel in her eyes.

Schallert fumbled with his pince-nez, raised them to his face, and stared.

Maria squinted even harder. "I need to change some notes at the bank soon, so young Tarald will not be embarrassed. How much gold must I give the boy, so he can rent the rooms for two more weeks?"

"Um ... in that case—a double eagle. Twenty dollars."

Ten American dollars per week. Each room costs five dollars. If Maria rented one room for herself and Tante, her money would last thirty weeks. Not that long, for they must eat, too.

"Thank you, Herr Schallert."

"Happy to be of service, Madam."

"Oh, by the way, I cannot help noticing you are short of staff. Could you use another cook in your kitchen?"

Schallert chuckled. "We always need cooks."

Maria smiled. Her plan was taking shape. She went to the dining room to soothe her cousin Tarald.

#

"Not like that, you moron!" Bessie, the chef who ran the hotel kitchen, snatched the knife from Maria's hand. "Do it like this." With swift strokes, the huge woman, clad in a white tunic and toque, reduced the loaf to neat slices of uniform thinness. "There. You cuttin' yours three times too thick. Our customers don't pay enough for thick slices like yourn."

Maria grabbed the knife from Bessie. "I can do it!" she shouted. Fuming, she sliced thin as thin could be, to match Bessie's slices. The massive cook stood over her, sweating, and watched. When a dozen thin slices lay on the board, Bessie said, "Keep it up like that, Ioway." She stalked away.

95

Why Bessie called her Ioway, Maria could not guess, unless it was from her accent. Perhaps Norwegians talked as people from Ioway talked.

After luncheon, when the kitchen riot died down a bit, Maria was sent to help the chief housekeeper, Mistress Stephenson. The prim, cheerless woman showed Maria how the Americans liked their beds made, where to place washing linens and small cakes of soap by the washstands, and where to dump debris swept from the floors.

Then it was back to the kitchen to prepare supper under a tornado of shouted abuse from big Bessie. She bossed a score of under-cooks, dishwashers, and assistants with a stream of curses, slaps, and kicks. Many of the poor creatures quailed in fear of Bessie.

Not Maria.

After the supper dishes had been washed and dried and the kitchen readied for breakfast, Maria shambled back to the room she shared with Anne and Tante Osa.

"You poor dear!" cried Anne as she helped Maria off with her kitchen tunic. "Tarald is furious. He thinks you're shaming the family."

"I am not," Maria said. "Hard work never shamed anybody."

"And Mister Schallert now thinks Tarald is penniless and you are wealthy."

Maria huffed. "I don't know how in the world he got that idea. Did I not come to him begging for work?"

Anne's lips quivered. "I only report what I observe."

"It is not your fault," said Maria. "And just so you know, the three dollars a week I earn will not cover a room for me and Tante. But it is something. One way or another, we will not go with you to Kansas. Try to help your brother understand that."

96

Maria's long workdays left her no time to speak with Tarald. On Wednesday, he knocked on the door of the women's room at night, right after Maria's return.

"May I come in?" Tarald asked.

"As long as you don't stay long," said Maria. "I need to sleep."

Tarald came in. He occupied the lone chair. Maria sat on the bed she shared with Anne and Tante. They stood in the corner and listened.

"I cannot let you stay here in Illinois," Tarald said. "You have come to this wild land as my dependents. I must protect you."

Maria yawned. "I'm sorry, I am tired. Listen, Tarald. Illinois is a settled place, not a frontier like Kansas. Tante and I will find a practical way of life here. Besides, Cousin Gunder Jørgen is nearby to watch over us."

"You are not his responsibility, but mine."

Maria stood up. "Go to bed, Cousin. Think about it more." She swept him out the door.

#

By Sunday, Maria was more tired than she had ever been. Sharp knocks woke her. She stumbled to the door.

The bellhop stood there. "Miss Nybro—a man is at the desk asking for you."

She dressed hurriedly and descended to the lobby, still yawning.

There stood Anders, dressed again in his best suit, beaming. "I borrowed my employer's wagon and team. Come, bring your aunt and cousins. I want you all to meet Kirsten Haraldsdatter's family."

97

"Today? But I am so tired. This is my day off." *Why must he look so charming?*

"Tut-tut, Maria," said Tarald, who suddenly stood behind her. "Though bound for Kansas, we still must honor the social conventions. Anders has invited us to meet his friends." He flashed a wicked grin.

They all joined Anders in the wagon as he drove the big black horses west from Petersburg to Osmundsgarden. He pulled in at a gap in the split-rail fence.

A wizened old woman, wearing a white Norsk headcloth embroidered with bright flowers, came out to greet them. "Anders, my lad! A pleasant surprise. Who are these folks you've brought with you?"

As they climbed down from the wagon, Anders introduced them one by one to the woman he called Kirsten Haraldsdatter, starting with Tante, then introducing Maria, Anne, and Tarald in that order.

Kirsten's children having emerged from the cabin, she introduced them. "This is my eldest, Reier, the shy one. The other boy is Thor, and then there are Karen and Britta."

Reier nodded once, then seemed to shrink into his thin shoulders. Thor—a dark, broad-shouldered young man—stood like a bull, yet showed an open smile. The two girls, for their part, giggled and hid behind upturned hands.

"Now, girls," said Kirsten, "I did not raise you up to be mice in the floor beams. Stand straight and show your faces." She turned to Tante. "They forget the manners I've been at pains to teach them."

"Out berry-picking, maybe," said Tante.

Kirsten Haraldsdatter led them into the square-hewn timber cabin. It bore no resemblance to the fancy Petersburg Hotel, Maria noted. It looked more like a mountain *hytte* in Norway. Just one room for kitchen, pantry, and parlor; a small window beside the door; a fireplace for cooking and heating at one end of the room. The other end of the room had a door to what must have been a separate bedroom. A wooden table and five straight-backed chairs almost filled the dim space of the main living area.

"My late husband, Osmund, built this cabin himself," said Kirsten. "He was a shoemaker, not a carpenter. He made it a tight fit, like a good shoe. There is barely room for me and my children." She brightened. "But you, Miss Osa, shall have the place of honor." She seated Tante at the head of the table. Anders and Tarald took one of the long sides. Anne sat acriss the table from her brother; Maria sat across from Anders.

"Karen, Britta," said Kirsten—"stir up the fire and make some tea."

The girls got busy at the fireplace while their mother rolled an empty lard keg to the foot of the table and sat on it. "What a joy to have someone besides my children to speak Norsk with. So, you all were friends of our dear Anders, back in Norway?"

"Ja," said Anders. "I knew them all from Øiestad and Lindtvedt."

"We have just arrived," said Tarald. "Passing through on our way to Kansas."

"Kansas! Oh, my. I have heard of this place but do not know where it is."

Reier, who stood by the wall with Thor, leaned forward. "It is west of here, Mother."

"Some will go to Kansas," Maria said. "Tante and I will stay here in Menard County."

Tarald glared across the table. "That I cannot permit."

"I have a job already," Maria said, "working for Herr Schallert at the hotel."

Kirsten snorted. "That spectacled puffin!"

99

"So he may be," Maria said, "but he pays a good wage. Still, not quite enough to rent a room for Tante and me." She made a wry face.

"How unfortunate." Kirsten's mouth was severe. "A shame we have no room here."

"Oh, no," said Maria. "I did not mean to suggest—"

"Use the good teacups, girls—the mussel-painted ones from the royal factory in Copenhagen. And bring some of that special cake."

Nimble Britta placed white saucers and cups with blue flower patterns before Kirsten and her guests, while stolid Karen focused on pouring tea from the pot.

Tante beamed. "That is just how Mamma used to instruct me. She never minded the way I look." The skew-headed old woman winked down the table at Kirsten. "I know I am odd of face and figure. I am one of the huldrefolk. My mother told me so when I was little."

Kirsten laughed, which Tante took as skepticism.

"Well, I saw my face in the lake, so I asked Mamma why I was so different from my brothers. Also, why my toes had webs and theirs didn't. She said, don't worry about those things. It's not something the hidden people are meant to know. And I said, what do you mean, Mamma? So she told how I had been left as a babe, swapped by the hulder at midnight for Mamma's real baby. So, for that reason, she took me under her care."

They all sat mute, perhaps stunned, while Karen and Britta served small squares of dark brown cake with white icing. It looked even darker than the molasses cookies Mamma made back in Øiestad.

"It's called chocolate," said Kirsten. "The Methodist ladies brought me some. So, I have learned to make it myself."

Anne took a bite. She raised her eyebrows, gave a cryptic smile, and turned to Tante. "That is ridiculous.

Had you been one of the huldrefolk, would you not have a long, hairy tail?"

"I did have a tail, a short one, as a babe. When I was a week old, Mamma wrapped me in a christening gown and had me baptized. By the time I grew old enough to walk, my tail had shrunk to nothing."

Kirsten sat with her mouth open, cake forgotten. "I never knew someone of your background before," she said, her eyes a-twinkle. "I'd like to hear more of your story, to help pass the long winter nights."

"That may not be possible," said Maria. "Cousin Tarald has his heart set on Tante's going to Kansas to help break his new farm."

Kirsten impaled Tarald on her gaze. "Is this so? You require her assistance?"

Tarald blanched. "It is not that. Rather, I am concerned for her well-being, and Maria's, were they left here to fend for themselves."

Kirsten burst out in laughter. "Don't you worry about that. We can make room for them here at Osmundsgarden. They'll be snug as bedbugs."

That settled things.

Kirsten would charge Maria and Tante three dollars a week for room and board—just what Maria earned at the hotel, much less than the hotel's room rate. Maria would have a two-mile walk each day to and from her workplace. She did not fear a two-mile walk.

The next week, the cousins left for Kansas, Tarald still miffed at Maria's stubborn resolve to control her own life.

#

When Maria and Tante moved into Kirsten's snug cabin at Osmundsgarden, the family made adjustments. Kirsten

101

welcomed Tante to share her bed on the ground floor, while Maria slept in the loft with Karen and Britta.

Kirsten Haraldsdatter banished Reier and Thor to the barn, they who had until now slept in the loft, separated from their sisters by a curtain. With autumn approaching, the men built separate houses for the pigs and chickens. "We don't mind sharing the barn with the mule and cow," Thor explained to Maria with a shy smile, "but my brother and I shall never sleep with pigs and chickens."

Maria rose before dawn every day to hike into town for work, carrying a few crusts of bread, which she ate on the way. She returned to Osmundsgarden fourteen hours later, consumed a bowl of soup that Kirsten Haraldsdatter set before her, and went to bed. After a week, Maria became inured to this routine.

Bessie, the chef, soon learned that Maria could not be bullied. Maria took pride in meeting Bessie's demands, which came without venom, and even the chambermaid service for Mistress Stephenson made for pleasant breaks in the kitchen wars.

#

Maria's sole respite from toil occurred on the one day each week that the Lord had set aside as a day of rest. On Sundays, the whole household rose late and enjoyed a light breakfast. They read scriptures, prayed long prayers, and sang hymns. After these devotions, Kirsten Haraldsdatter oversaw the cooking of a large Sunday dinner.

Anders often came to join them at dinner, having made the long trek from Sweetwater—sometimes on foot, sometimes on a borrowed horse. Cousin Gunder Jørgen, who worked nearer by, at the farm of Alastair Kinnaird, sometimes came to Sunday dinner as well, since Kirsten had sent word to him that he would be welcome.

Sometimes Gunder Jørgen or Anders brought a bottle of schnapps or American whiskey. Toasts were proposed and drunk to Oskar, King of Sweden and Norway, and to President Franklin Pierce—although Anders disapproved of Pierce's weakness for slavery. Then, after the men moved the large table to the side of the room, the little band of friends would dance to the sound of Reier's fiddle.

The pattern of the dance paired each man with each woman in turn as partners. The bluff Thor held Maria so gently, so awkwardly, that she wondered: How could any man be so shy?

When she danced in Anders' embrace, on the other hand, her pulse quickened. She became so conscious of her sweat that she feared her hand would slip right out of his—and then what would he think of her?

Anders, for his part, danced on unperturbed, with no apparent cares in all this world.

12. Anders

Illinois

October – November 1854

Anders thought, *I should be well enough pleased.*

Arriving in America with nothing, he had taken Benjamin Lake's job offer out of hunger. Despite Anders' first doubts about Lake, the lantern-jawed farmer had shown an admirable character. Anders saved up almost two hundred dollars in a year and a half. He had also been trusted from the start with Lake's big secret—his frequent violation of the federal Fugitive Slave Act.

The job, the savings, and Lake's trust were all reasons to be pleased with himself. Yet, had Anders become a man among the men of Illinois? Did they respect him as a member of the community?

"It is just that my father is the village schoolmaster, back in Norway," he said as he shared in Lake's fine Dutch tobacco in the comfort of Lake's parlor. "I thought when I came here, I would become a teacher as well."

Lake tilted his head. "A schoolteacher? Drilling children in their letters and numbers?" He took a puff on his own pipe.

"Yes, a teacher," Anders said. "Why not?"

"A teacher is lucky to get five dollars a month."

"My father also is ill-paid, but he has the respect of the town."

Lake made a wry face. "Your room and board would be at the mercy of one family, and then the next family in the subscription, and so on. You move from one house to another. You get whatever they're cooking—cabbage, beans, rutabagas."

Anders bridled. "What is wrong with rutabagas?"

"As a steady diet?"

"Besides, as schoolmaster I would have the respect of the community."

Lake choked on a stream of sweet Cavendish smoke. "In Norway, maybe."

#

Anders borrowed a horse from Lake to go see one Abner Tobias in Indian Creek Township about a teaching job. He rode between fields of dry corn. Maples flashed orange leaves, and oak trees brown, touched by last week's frost.

Tobias had an open and well-drained farm, with fields of dense corn already half harvested. The farmhouse itself was the hardscrabble cabin typical of Menard County.

Abner Tobias, a stringy man with an acid expression, came out the cabin door and stared at Anders, measuring him silently, with a critical eye. Smells of cabbage oozed from inside the cabin. Three dirty children burst out the cabin door and ran to the fields.

106

"We just finished dinner," Tobias said, arms folded, making clear that no food would be offered, despite Anders' two-hour midday ride. "You're Gunstensen?"

"Ja. Anders Gunstensen."

"Foreign accent. Where you from?"

"I came from Norway almost two years ago."

"Norwegian, huh?"

"Ja."

The man's mouth crumpled with disappointment. "Well, come on. I'll show you the schoolhouse. You can leave your horse here. 'Tain't far."

They walked a quarter of a mile across a meadow to a tiny log cabin. "This is it," said Tobias. He pushed the front door open.

Anders stepped inside. A high desk stood in the front of the room. Three rows of low benches faced it.

"Dark in here," Anders said. "Is there a lamp?"

Tobias sighed. He gazed at the ceiling. "We'll get you one."

"And a stove?"

"I gotta get the board together. We ain't allowed for a stove yet. 'S more expensive."

Anders spread his arms. "You expect the pupils to learn their lessons when they are freezing?"

"Reckon not. We'll get to it. Session don't start till November."

They walked back.

"You sure you can read and write?" asked Tobias.

"Ja. In English and Norwegian."

"All we need is English. Pay's three dollars a month plus room and board."

Anders halted. "The notice posted in the Sweetwater store said six."

Tobias shot him a look of exasperation. "That's before we knew you was a foreigner."

107

The next Sunday, Anders stumbled down the dirt road toward Osmundsgarden. His gloom dissolved a bit under a fine dinner of roast pork with its own gravy, boiled potatoes, and garden vegetables.

"Maria's tante has proven a great blessing to us as a cook," said Kirsten. "She has her own way with kale and rutabagas."

Aunt Osa, seated at the end of the table—which Thor had expanded to seat up to ten people—nodded her toad-like head and beamed.

"Even I took a hand," Maria said. "The dilled potatoes are mine."

"Everything is delicious," said Anders, pleased with an image of himself as master diplomat. He pulled out his pipe and began to plug it with tobacco.

Maria pushed her chair back. "Come. Let's you and I walk. It's a nice day, and you can smoke your foul old pipe just as well in the open air."

So well-acquainted was he with Maria's blunt talk that Anders chose to accept this suggestion as the open-hearted invitation it was, not the upbraiding it seemed to be.

They strolled down a lane between fields of dry corn. They had not gone a quarter mile when Maria said, "Out with it, lad. What's on your mind?"

"On my mind?"

"Something was breaking you down when you walked in today. Even after a good dinner, you do not seem your usual happy salmon. What is it?"

Anders halted. He puffed his pipe and exhaled a cloud of smoke. "If you must know, I have turned down a headmaster position."

It reassured him to see the look of surprise on Maria's face.

"Oh, they wanted me, all right. They did not want me enough." He resumed strolling through the cornfields.

Maria kept pace with him. "What does that mean, they did not want you enough?"

"Three dollars a month. Nobody can live on such a wage."

"Even as a farmhand, you must make more than that."

"Mister Lake pays me a dollar a day. He is a good man to work for. He gives me room and board as well. And respect."

"I know just what you mean," Maria said. "Bessie the cook is a hard boss, but she is learning to respect me."

Though Anders could not imagine Bessie the cook's respect to be so great a matter as Mister Lake's respect, he kept his mouth shut, again preening his diplomacy.

"Just what is it you want, Anders?"

He puffed out a little cloud. "I already have a good income. I want to be a respected member of the community."

Maria looked sideways at him but said nothing. A dozen crows burst with raucous cries from the brown leaves of an oak and flew toward a tree far across the fields.

"That is why I wanted to be a schoolmaster. For the respect. I did not care so much about the money. However, the pay they offer is so little, it's an insult. Where is the respect?"

"Money and respect together would be good," Maria said.

"Do you know they cut their offer in half because I am what they call a foreigner?"

Maria's jaw dropped. Fire came into her eyes. "Your English is good. What can they be thinking?" She knit her brows. "Does your Mister Lake pay you less than his other hands, because you are a Nordmann?"

"No. I get a full American wage. That is what I mean by respect."

Maria nodded, impressed no doubt by the wisdom of his words.

"Another thing," he said. "Another sign of respect, I suppose it is. Well, I ought not tell you . . . but I shall. Benjamin Lake trusts me with his secrets."

"Secrets?" Maria looked askance. "Lake has secrets?"

Anders puffed his pipe and nodded.

"What kind of secrets?"

"Noble secrets."

13. Anders

Illinois

November 1854

"Hei!" shouted Anders. "Halt what you are doing!" Whatever the two men with the buckboard were up to in the wooded ravine, it was no good.

Seeing Lake's heavy wagon juddering toward them pulled by four horses, with Anders at the reins, the two skurks scrambled to finish their business in a hurry. Anders stopped the wagon so it stood athwart the strangers' rig, blocking its exit from the ravine.

The larger man dumped the limp body of Josh Quimby, Lake's black foreman, into the bed of the buckboard, where his younger partner sat rocking, howling, and clutching his foot.

No, the younger man did not clutch his foot. He held the end of his leg, where his foot should be. The foot itself lay on the ground, encased in the bottom half of a boot. Nearby lay Josh's felling axe, its blade bloodied. Anders stared at the revolting scene, open-mouthed.

"Move yer wagon!" the big man shouted. "You're obstructing the lawful capture of a fugitive slave." He hauled out a large revolver and aimed it at Anders.

Anders frowned. "I think not." He jumped down and strode toward the buckboard.

"Stay back." The man cocked the hammer of his gun.

Anders walked on by him.

The younger man, sitting upright in the buckboard, squeezed his leg hard with both hands. Blood trickled from its severed stump.

Quimby lay still, hatless. The side of his head was big and purple.

"You have injured our foreman badly," Anders said.

"Foreman? A nigger? You can't be serious." The big man shoved the gun into Anders' chest. "Listen here, boy. My name is Bullamore Crawley, licensed contractor for the Commissioner of Fugitive Slaves. We are in the midst of apprehending a runaway. You're gonna be in trouble with the law."

Anders snorted. "This man is Josh Quimby, a free man you have tampered with. And our boss, Mister Benjamin Lake, comes now with two of his sons." He tipped his head toward three riders who approached from behind Crawley. "I believe they have guns."

Crawley glanced back over his shoulder.

Anders felt a thrill of relief.

"Pa, don't let me die," said the accomplice in the wagon, his face white.

Crawley grimaced and stamped his foot.

Anders bent into the buckboard's bed. He lifted Josh by the shoulders. "You ought to help your son," he said to Crawley.

Benjamin, Matthew, and Luke Lake pulled their horses up at the lip of the ravine. Benjamin and Matthew

112

aimed guns at Crawley. Luke rushed to help Anders carry Josh.

Crawley sighed, uncocked his pistol, and holstered it. "See what your nigger did to my boy!" he shouted at Benjamin Lake.

"Mister Quimby is not my nigger," said Lake as Anders and Luke lowered Quimby into the farm wagon. "He is my top hand. He wouldn't have lopped your boy's foot off without cause. You'd better see your son to a doctor, if you don't want to lose him."

Crawley leapt onto the buckboard and snatched up the reins, his son moaning in the wagon bed, while Luke moved the Lake wagon out of the way.

Anders picked up Crawley's son's foot, which still lay on the ground. "This belongs to you." He tossed the foot into the bed of Crawley's buckboard as it left the ravine.

#

Anders drove the wagon, with the unconscious Josh in its bed, back to the foreman's house on Lake's farm. Polly Quimby received her husband with tears of alarm. Anders and Luke laid him in his bed.

Benjamin Lake sent Matthew to fetch the physician from Petersburg.

Anders peered at Josh's misshapen head. "Is not there still some ice in the icehouse?"

"Of course," said Benjamin Lake.

Anders ran to the farm's icehouse. He found an icepick and chipped off a few chunks. Scooping hem up into his hat he ran back to the Quimbys' house. Polly wrapped the ice chunks in a cloth and laid it across Josh's head.

She bit her lip. "You reckon that do any good, Mister Lake?"

113

The big man shrugged. "It might keep the swelling down."

Six hours later, Matthew and the doctor returned. The doctor examined Josh's battered head, took his pulse, listened to his heart.

"That ice was a good idea," the doctor said. "You have any more left?"

"A little," said Luke. "Enough for this, anyhow."

The doctor turned to Polly. "I can't tell you anything. It's a bad injury, but human bodies recover from bad things, Lord willing. Let him rest. Keep ice on his head 'til it stops swelling."

Mistress Lake walked over from the main house with a loaf of bread and a kettle of soup. She also brought knitting, to occupy her hands while she sat with Polly.

The men left.

"The doctor liked your ice therapy, Anders," said Lake as they walked home. "And sending Luke back on foot to raise us was quick thinking. Also brave of you to go on alone and confront them."

"Well, we needed to save Josh. Those two men were about to enslave him."

"Polly has her whole mind on Josh, so let me thank you, on her behalf and his, for keeping him a free man."

"Yes, free," said Anders. "But will he live?"

"It's in God's hands."

"How can they just take a free man like that?"

"We see more slave catchers every year. They get a reward every time they nab a runaway. But if they can grab a free Negro and sell him to a slave dealer, that's pure profit. It's happened before."

Anders pointed at a plume of smoke rising from a chimney on one corner of Lake's horse barn.

"What?" said the lantern-jawed man. "It's just that little stove in the corner of the barn."

"It reminds me how good it is that we stopped those slavers at the ravine. That they did not get this far."

Lake grinned. "You're right. That's a good thing."

Both men, and Lake's two sons, stood admiring the smoke from the little chimney. All four shared its secret: For that stove in the barn would be fired only when needed to draw fresh air for human breathing into the underground room below it—a chamber intentionally hidden from any prying eye.

14. Maria

Illinois

December 1854 – March 1855

Maria's ears pricked up at the word "Scandihoovian." She slowed her steps as she crossed the lobby with bed linens from the laundry.

"This big Swede stopped a bunch of slavers from grabbing Lake's black foreman," a round-hatted man told his friends. "A few days ago this was, after the frost, before the snow." Although they called him a Swede, they must be talking about Anders. Lake had no other "Scandihoovian" hand.

"Faced their shootin' irons and backed 'em down, just like that," the man said. "Chopped off one feller's leg with a big old axe."

Maria's stomach churned as she ascended the stairs with her stack of linen. Of course Anders would ignore guns. He did not believe he could be hurt. But chop off a leg? Anders?

If someone lost a leg, it must have been a deadly affair.

Anders would dance with joy to hear those men in the lobby praise his courage. Respect! Man among men! The wide-eyed idiot.

She stood on the landing, halfway to the second floor. Anders could have been killed by those slavers with guns. The next time she laid eyes on him, she would set him straight.

"Miss Nybro, what is keeping you?" The voice of Mistress Stephenson came down from the top of the stairway. "Don't dawdle, you're not paid to daydream."

#

She awoke earlier than usual for a Sunday. What Norwegian could sleep late on Christmas Eve? It was the main day for celebration.

Karen and Britta rose. Their nightdresses rustled on their straw pallets. The ladder creaked as they crept down from the loft to wake up the fire and hang a kettle of water. By the time Maria came down, the girls were giggled as they place paper versions of helping elves, *nisser*, about the cabin.

While Maria helped Kirsten make breakfast, the cabin door opened. Thor entered in a swirl of snow, carrying the butt end of an evergreen. Reier, just behind him, held its top end.

"After we milked the cow," said Thor, "something came scratching and whining at the barn door. It turned out to be this poor little tree. It wants a good home, out of the weather."

Backward he may be, she thought, *but he hopes to please with his humor.*

Thor and Reier stood the tree on a cross of wood planks while Kristen hunted up the small beeswax candles she had made just for the Yule tree.

118

Tante and Karen toiled at the fireplace. Soon smells of roasting meat, and the baking aromas of seven traditional kinds of cookies, filled the cabin. *Glögg*, a spicy sweet wine fortified with hard liquor, simmered in a pot by the fire.

Maria climbed back to the loft. She donned her best dress from Norway, white with a red bodice and many-colored flowers around the skirt—the outfit she had packed in the very bottom of her trunk. She began to brush her hair.

Tiny Britta scurried up the ladder to join her. She carried a spill in one hand, a burning shred of paper lit from the fireplace. She lit the upstairs lantern and blew out the flaming spill. "Turn around, Maria."

"Yes, my lady." Maria sat still while the girl braided her hair into thin loops. "Such clever fingers you have, so tiny."

"The better to make you irresistible," said Britta.

"Me, of all people? Irresistible to whom?"

"You know, in case any wise man comes from the East just to see you."

Anders would arrive from the east, as Lake's farm lay ten miles east of Osmundsgarden. But he would not find her irresistible when she spoke what occupied her mind. She did not say this to Britta but gave her a swat, as her saucy remarks required.

When Maria's head had been decked with loops of blond hair, she turned and did the same service for Britta. "Your hair is so fine my big fingers can't control it. And fiery red. Any farmhands who stop by will notice you before me, if indeed they are wise men."

Britta made no reply. Her face glowed red like her hair.

They descended from the loft, and there came a barrage of thuds on the door.

119

Maria flung open the door with a big smile. "Welcome! Good Yule!"

Anders stood there. "Maria." Wordless for a change, he stood gazing at her.

She reached out and pulled him over the threshold.

Behind him, Gunder Jørgen stumbled in. "It's a long walk from Kinnaird's place in snow this deep."

Maria helped Anders off with his snowy greatcoat and muffler. She hung them on a peg.

Anders removed his boots and placed them by the fire, beside Gunder Jørgen's. He sniffed the air. "Something smells good. You are baking sand bakkelser, ja? And you look as good as the food smells, jenta mi."

Maria saw that Anders, with only Lake's bunkhouse to live in, was missing the comforts of a real Norwegian home. But now, her sympathy for his plight began to sap her resolve to set him straight. She must speak up, while her indignation still glowed.

She frowned. "It's a wonder you are here among us to see or smell anything. What do you mean, romping about the woods, chopping men's legs off?"

Everybody stared at Maria and Anders.

"I did not chop anything, jenta mi. It was—"

"Do you deny those men held you at gunpoint?" *Let him wiggle out of this.*

Kirsten was horrified. "What men? What guns?"

Anders shook his head. "Nobody was shot, jenta mi. Least of all, me." He narrowed his eyes. "Who has frightened you with such tales?"

"It's the talk of the county. I overheard a harness salesman talking about it at the hotel."

Gunder Jørgen clapped his hands. He raised his arms in the air for silence. "I also have heard of this event," he said. "However, I did not hear it the way Maria heard it." He turned to Anders. "You had better have the truth out and be done with it."

"In that case, I shall sit down." Anders fumbled in his pocket, brought forth his ever-present pipe. He filled it, lit it with a spill from the fire, and sat. "Two slave catchers, Bullamore Crawley and his son, happened upon our foreman Josh Quimby, who is black, cutting firewood in a ravine not far from the Lakes' farmhouse. They decided, since he was all by himself at the moment, to make a slave of him, though he is a free man."

A chorus of sighs and "ohhs" greeted this news.

Anders puffed out a cloud of smoke. "I was driving the wagon back to the ravine to pick up another load of wood, with Luke beside me—he's the youngest son. We saw something was amiss, so I sent Luke running back to the farmhouse for help. Then I drove to the ravine."

Maria shivered with dread for what would come next.

"When I got there, Josh Quimby had already chopped off the foot of Crawley's son—not far above the ankle. Well, you see, to defend himself, his axe was all he had." He looked around at his hearers. Thor listened grimly, Reier seemed withdrawn, Kirsten and the girls showed pure terror.

"Bullamore Crawley had clubbed Josh over the head and thrown him unconscious into their wagon. The son, also in the wagon, was screaming over his severed foot, while the old man calmly went about his business.

"I stopped our wagon in front of theirs to stop them from driving off with Josh. Crawley ranted at me while his boy pleaded for help. I saw that Josh was injured and started to lift him from their wagon. About then, Luke came back on horseback, with his father and brother. They had guns and compelled the slave catcher to put away his."

121

Anders sucked on his pipe. "It was a dreadful mess. Our foreman, Josh, still lies in his bed, unaware what is going on around him."

"What happened to the man who lost his foot?" asked Thor.

"Oh, they drove off. Seeking a doctor, I suppose."

"But they had guns," Maria said, fixed on the main point. "You might have been killed."

Anders looked on her with pity. "You know me better than that, Maria. Besides, what was I to do? Let a man be taken into slavery?"

"You're missing my point," she said.

"If you have a point," he replied, "I fail to see it."

Kirsten nudged Maria with a sharp elbow. "Our Yule feast is ready. Let's all sit down and use our mouths for what Our Lord intended."

#

No more was said that day about the sad event in which Anders had embroiled himself. Maria forbore to mention it further, and no contrition came forth from Anders. He did not even deign to notice the fear for his life that gripped her heart.

"This wicked slave system will be the downfall of this country," he said. "While we enjoy our Yuletide fare, I cannot help wondering what kind of Christmas the slaves can celebrate—like Daniel, that poor devil I could not protect from being recaptured in Memphis."

Of course slavery was evil. That was obvious. But must Anders risk his life to oppose it?

The Christmas delicacies, so welcome in times past, were like ashes in her mouth. Anders, however, seemed to enjoy them. How could he?

She went to bed in tears, gnashing her teeth.

122

#

The Christmas Eve snowstorm brought in a long spell of cold weather.

Maria had thought America to be a land warmer than Norway. In summer it was. The Illinois winter, however, wielded sharper winds than she had ever felt in the coastal village of her birth. She bundled up and fought her way through snowdrifts to Petersburg for her daily drudgery.

"Cold enough for ya, Ioway?" said Bessie every day, with a challenging grin. It seemed that the worse the weather, the cheerier the big woman's spirits.

"I am glad for the cold wind," said Maria. "It makes me walk faster."

Cold and snow could not bar Maria's way nor quench the fire inside her.

One day near the end of February, Mister Schallert met her at the kitchen door after breakfast, as she was on her way to help Mistress Stephenson. "Miss Nybro," Schallert said, "I think it only fair to warn you that the snowfall which begun this morning shows every sign of becoming a dangerous storm."

"It snows?" She recalled there had been an iron smell in the air before dawn. Since then, Maria had been buried in the kitchen.

"Yes, it is snowing now." He led her to a window, and they looked out. "Very tiny flakes, as you can see. You know what that means."

The snow looked like a fine mist over Øiestad harbor. "No, Mister Schallert. I do not know what it means. The snow here does not behave as it should."

The hotel manager suppressed a smile. "That is why I'm warning you. These little flakes will start to blow sideways and pretty soon you'll have a blizzard. You will

123

have to stay in town overnight. Maybe for two or three nights."

What? Impossible. "I have not brought my things. Nobody told me."

"Your things?"

"My sleeping clothes, Mister Schallert. I have not sleeping clothes."

The man looked her up and down.

If he raises his spectacles for a better look, I shall scream.

"Americans," he said at last, "sometimes sleep in their day clothes in emergencies."

"Norwegians do not." A stronger statement than the truth would bear, but why confuse the poor man?

He sighed and gazed at the ceiling. "All right, then. You had better go back and get them, for you'll be here overnight, for sure. Hurry, those tiny snowflakes mount up fast."

The wind cut through her, bundled though she was, as she hiked back up the road to Osmundsgarden. The snowflakes, now visible, became grains of ice flung in her face as she marched along, head bent low to front the wind.

Tante looked up as she plunged into the cabin. "Dear me, has night come already?"

"No, Tante. I have come back for my sleepwear."

"You are moving?"

"Mister Schallert says I must stay at the hotel tonight." She scurried up the ladder, grabbed her nightdress, wrapped her toothbrush and hairbrush in it.

Kirsten met her at the bottom of the ladder. "On your way quickly now. One does not want to be caught in these prairie snowstorms."

Maria tucked the bundle inside her coat.

124

"Here," said Tante. "Drink this before you go." She gave Maria a mug of tea.

"Tante, I have no time."

"You'd better drink it, Maria," said Kirsten. "Otherwise, she'll give us no rest."

Glancing at the fierce look on Tante's face, Maria sat and sipped the hot liquid. She drank it down as fast as she could. It scalded her mouth. She got up to go.

"Hurry," said Kirsten.

Maria flew out the door and on her way. At least the wind would now be at her back. It was a keen wind, and she prayed to Jesus that she might reach the hotel alive.

When she stumbled in, half frozen, Mistress Stephenson met her at the door. "Where have you been?"

"I went to get my sleepwear. Mister Schallert said I am staying the night."

"Hmph. Come along."

Mistress Stephenson showed her a cramped sleeping room in a cellar beneath the lobby, a place where all kinds of linens, utensils, and equipment were stored. "You'll be fine here. Warmest place in the hotel in winter. Now, back to work."

Maria worked round the clock for the next three days. Hotel guests, cooped up by the blizzard, became cranky. The snow crept up over the doorsills. Maria, emptying dustpans and kitchen scraps, had to shovel a path from the back door to the trash bins.

Hotel guests ate more, they ate more often, and they drank more. Some of the men got rowdy. On the third day, a bushy-bearded drummer, who often mentioned his wife and children in pious tones, tried to corner Maria in a dark hallway. The sour smell of beer was on his breath. She brought him to his senses with a sharp slap. The man was merely intoxicated.

125

At last, the snow stopped and Maria went home. Bessie, in a rare act of thoughtfulness, lent her a pair of wool leggings to wear back to Osmundsgarden. "Below zero out there, Ioway. Best to have your limbs wrapped well." Bessie's leggings were so large that Maria had to secure them with butcher's string from the kitchen so they would not flop or drag. But they did keep her warm all the way to Osmundsgarden.

There she told tales of all the things one had to do to please finicky guests, and to keep the rowdy ones in their place, during the blizzard. Now that it was all over, it seemed that it had been grand fun.

But at the end of the week, she received only one dollar instead of the usual three.

"Where is the rest of my pay?" she demanded.

"You took off work several hours the day the blizzard started," said Schallert, "so we docked you half a day's pay. That's twenty-five cents right there."

"I had to go home because you told me I must stay overnight."

"You did no work during that time."

"What about the rest?"

"A single room for two nights at fifty cents—half the usual rate—that's a dollar. And twenty cents each for four meals—suppers and breakfasts—which you do not normally take here. We owed you only ninety-five cents. We rounded it up to a dollar in recognition of your willing service."

Maria stared speechless, for once in her life unable to fight for what was hers.

She turned and went home. All the way to Osmundsgarden, her stomach burned.

#

"How much was it, jenta mi? Half a day's pay?" Anders' brow furrowed.

"I was not gone half a day even," Maria said. "No more than three and a half hours."

"Besides, you were absent so you could prepare to serve Schallert's customers, was it not?" He spread his hands.

Thor grimaced and slapped the table. Reier, Kirsten, Karen, and Britta all nodded in agreement, their faces fierce in support of Maria. Tante frowned.

"True," she said. "I was called to serve the guests. And then there was—"

"The money he charged you for room and board. A room which you would not have needed, and food you would not have eaten, except you were called upon by the hotel to stay at your post—all through the terrible blizzard—and keep the customers satisfied. Ja?" Anders raised his eyebrows.

"Ja," said Maria. "Still, I don't see what good it does to tell you this."

"Why did you not tell me before? The storm happened three weeks ago."

"Anders," said Kirsten, "you have not come to dinner the last three Sundays."

Anders struck himself in the head. "Three weeks. Can it be so long?"

"Yes, it can."

"Please forgive my absentmindedness."

"That Schallert," said Thor. "He is asking for something." He leaned forward, about to rise from his chair and go deliver what Schallert asked for.

Anders laid a hand on Thor's shoulder. "Patience, old friend," he said. "I'm sure it will all work out." He added a wink.

The next day, when Maria came down to the kitchen after helping Mistress Stephenson through the afternoon, Mister Schallert called her to the desk.

"I'm afraid I made a terrible mistake." He handed her a gold quarter-eagle, worth two and a half dollars. "I should not have withheld two dollars from your pay for the blizzard week. Please accept an extra fifty cents as a bonus for the delay in payment."

Maria, mouth open, stared at her employer.

He fidgeted. "You have friends, my dear."

"I do?"

"Mister Gunstensen stopped by this morning. And he brought with him Brother Claymore." Schallert coughed. "My pastor."

"He did?"

"The two of them explained how fortunate we are to have a woman of your dedication and principle working here. Also, how unfair—even, unbiblical—it would be to charge you money for serving our customers."

Maria grinned. She enjoyed seeing the spectacled puffin squirm.

"And I quite agree with them, by the way. I am grateful they pointed it out. Good day, Miss Nybro. Back to the kitchen now, quick."

15. Maria

Illinois

April 1855

Maria hiked into Petersburg as usual the Saturday after Easter. On this fine day, however, she had arranged in advance to have the day off work. She had insisted and Schallert had given in. So now she walked past the hotel and kept going.

She wore her best dress, the one that had so impressed Anders at Christmas. She had sprinkled it with a bit of bergamot and lemon oil. Her bag of coins and paper currency hung from her waist.

The night before she left Norway, Pappa had roused her after midnight. He led her to the kitchen chimney and, to her surprise, pried out a loose stone—a stone Maria had passed a thousand times on household errands.

From behind the stone, he pulled a box filled with money.

Pappa took out one hundred speciedaler in Bank of Norway notes, plus twenty-five silver speciedaler. "For your journey," he said.

He kissed her forehead. Tears flowed down his cheeks.

Then his fingers dipped again into the box and took from it a silver ring topped by a gleaming gem. He turned the ring this way and that under the candle, showing the stone's facets. "It is a diamond. I don't know what it's worth. A seafaring man, a bit of a skurk, left it with me as bond for a boat he never came back to claim. I sold the boat at a loss. I kept the diamond ring."

"It is beautiful, Pappa."

"Maybe it is worth enough to get you out of trouble sometime, across the sea where I can't protect you." He lowered his brows. "Do not ever wear this or flash it around. There are people in this wide world, Daughter, who would cut your hand off to get a ring like that. A jeweler in Christiania told me the stone itself weighs a full carat."

"It must be worth a fortune."

"I don't know. Just keep it safe. If you have to sell it, make sure you sell dear."

She had placed the ring in a small red pouch and placed the pouch in a button-flap pocket she had made high up inside her skirt, where no man should ever lay a hand. It dwelt there at this moment—a year later—separate from the money in the bag hung from her waist.

Red-winged blackbirds scolded her, and meadowlarks burbled pure joy up from their lemony throats as they teetered on stems of tall prairie grass. The fields smelled black and fecund. Warmth was in the offing.

Gaining the Athens-Springfield road, she slowed her pace, walking south toward Springfield just fast enough not to appear to be dawdling.

The first driver to overtake her, a farmer with a load of fresh manure, waved as he passed. The second, a drayman driving a loaded freight wagon, reined in his team and asked if she would not prefer riding to walking. She smiled. "No, thank you." He tipped his hat, flicked his reins, and rattled on down the road.

The third driver was Anders. He wore his good American suit and drove Mister Lake's fine buggy. "Maria!" He reined the big chestnut to a halt. "What are you doing here?"

"Anders. I wondered when you would come along."

"You expected me?"

"Of course I expected you. Why else would I be walking along this road?"

He scratched his head. "Come, jenta mi, I have no time for riddles. I am on my way—"

"To Springfield to start your citizenship papers."

"Why, yes." Anders sat a bit taller.

"And since all your other friends are absorbed in their little chores and preoccupations, I thought, Anders ought to have company, someone to share his time of glory."

He gazed at her, speechless.

"Will you not invite me to join you?"

Anders leapt out of his seat, helped her into the buggy, then got back in and sat beside her. He clucked the horse into motion. "I didn't know anyone would pay attention to my little errand today."

"Maybe to Kirsten Haraldsdatter and Cousin Gunder Jørgen and the rest of them it seems a small matter. But to you, it is a great thing, is it not?"

"Of course."

"So, it is important to me also."

He stared at her. A tear formed in his eye.

"Come, do not cry. It's a joyous occasion." Maria touched the money bag at her waist, as if checking to make sure it was there.

131

Anders chuckled. "Yes, it's a joyous occasion. What's in the bag?"

"Just something of my own. A little piece of business maybe I can take care of in Springfield. If we have time."

"We shall make time for your little business, jenta mi." Anders glowed with goodwill.

"So, what is your next step?"

"Next step?"

"After applying to become a citizen."

"Well, jenta mi, that by itself is a good start."

Maria tipped her head to acknowledge his point. "But not a finish, ja?"

"People here have no respect for teachers. So I am content to make a good living in Mister Lake's employ."

"Truly, Anders?"

"I like the Lakes. We do important work. We are not just farmers. We support good causes, like freedom. Mister Lake is an important man."

"Ja. People talk about him." Maria leaned closer. She touched his arm. "What if you had your own place? Would not this noble man respect you even more?"

Anders said nothing.

"Oh, Anders—have you given up on yourself?"

He scowled.

"Listen." Maria rattled the bag at her waist. "You hear that clinking?" She took the bag from her waist, opened the drawstrings, and spilled money into her hand. "Twenty-five silver speciedaler and another one hundred in Bank of Norway notes. My father gave me these, to help me in any kind of misfortune, or if a great opportunity should come along. In Springfield we shall find out how much American money I can buy. I expect it will be more in American dollars than in Norsk money. Maybe one hundred fifty dollars."

Anders raised his eyebrows. "And you show me this because?"

"How much have you saved thus far from your earnings at Mister Lake's farm?"

"First I had to pay back fifteen dollars I owed him—"

"You owed Mister Lake money?"

"He helped me out of some trouble. It had to do with a slave named Daniel. I will tell you about that sometime, if you want. The main thing is, after paying back the fifteen, I still have almost two hundred dollars in savings."

"Anders!" Maria squealed. "That's wonderful. Don't you see? With my money and your money together—"

"We could buy a farm." Anders' face glowed.

"You would be a landowner, a man among men here in Illinois."

His eyes narrowed. "Maybe not, jenta mi. It may not be enough. Still ..."

"Of course it will be enough. We'll make it be enough."

"Enough to buy the land, maybe. We'll also need livestock, seeds, equipment. However, I know a man—"

"Yes?"

"Mister Eliot. Rance Eliot, the storekeeper. He is quiet and soft-spoken, for an American. And dresses very well. The important thing is, he has money. I've heard he is willing to lend it to people he trusts. If we needed, we could borrow—"

"No need to decide that now. Wait and see if we have enough without borrowing."

"Yes, of course. That's sensible." A cloud came over Anders' face. "I hate to give up my work with Mister Lake. The freedom work, I mean."

"When you become his fellow farmer—a land-owner in your own right—then you can be a better partner to

Mister Lake in his freedom work. More valuable as a partner than as a hired hand. Ja?"

Anders smiled. "Ja."

By the time they reached Springfield, they had settled the matter.

Maria stood beside Anders in the county clerk's office as he swore an oath declaring his intent to become a citizen of the United States of America.

She stood again with Anders one hour later, when she and he were joined in marriage by Hiram G. Tolliver, presiding judge of the Sangamon County Court.

To celebrate their wedding, Anders drove her from the County Courthouse to the Statehouse. They sat in the buggy, on Sixth Street, before the large building with its high dome.

"It is the house of the people," Anders said, "where the people's business is done. We could go in there right now to see the legislators as they hand down the laws."

Maria shuddered. "We dare not, Husband." Anders was too forward.

He seemed disappointed.

"What do you see up and down the street?" Maria asked. "Nothing but stores and shops. Places where people spend money. Look, there is even a jewelry store—Chatterton's. They have gold and diamonds, fine watches, and all manner of things. Next to them stands a clothing store for women and another next to that for men. And so on down the line—with yet another jewelry store at the end of the block."

Anders looked befuddled. "What are you saying?"

"I am saying that we have come to a wealthy land. Springfield, not even the chief city of the nation, yet has all these wonders."

"Do you think, Wife, perhaps that I should buy you a diamond ring from Mister Chatterton's store?"

"Now you are being ridiculous. Such things are not for us. We have a farm to buy."

There was no need to tell Anders that she already possessed a diamond ring.

16. Anders

Illinois

April 1855

Anders found Rance Eliot in the doorway of his store, listening to the chatter of half a dozen men who stood on the porch, ranting at one another over slavery.

"Mister Eliot!" Anders shouted. "May I speak to you in private?"

Eliot, after a moment, refocused his gaze and smiled. "Mister Gunstensen. Don't you wish to join the donnybrook?"

"Donnybrook?"

"A fight." Eliot tipped his head toward the debaters.

"If I join, it will be on the side of freedom. I am here for something else, however."

Eliot bowed his head. "By all means." He led the way into the store. There were no customers, only two clerks busy counting the inventory. "What is on your mind, my friend?"

"I need farm equipment and supplies, seeds, and livestock."

Eliot raised his eyebrows. "Going into farming on your own?"

"Ja, I hope so."

"You're getting to be an old hand at Lake's. He must be sorry to lose you."

"He and I shall continue friends. My farm is not far south of his."

"The Haraszthy place?"

"That is it."

Eliot glanced about, hunched his shoulders, motioned Anders closer. "Mind if I ask what you paid for the land?"

"Five dollars an acre."

"He had my standing offer of four. You outbid me." Eliot pursed his lips.

"The storekeeper wants to become a farmer now?"

Eliot chuckled. "Not exactly, no. I'm always interested in land. There are many ways to acquire it, and many ways to turn it to profit. If I had to lose the parcel, I'm glad it was you that got it." He beamed as if he had scored a coup. "To your question. I can sell you whatever you need, except livestock."

"That is no problem, I can get livestock." Anders shuffled his feet. "The problem is . . ."

Eliot waited calmly.

"I have heard," Anders said, "that is—I need to borrow money."

"Ahh. So, you cannot pay for equipment, supplies, seed, and livestock. Yes?"

"Ja, that's it." Anders squirmed. "We can afford most of it, not—"

"We? There is more than one of you?"

"I have married. Miss Maria Nybro, who arrived last summer from my old country."

"Well, I say. Congratulations are in order." Eliot opened a drawer and drew out a long cigar. He gave it to Anders with ceremony. "My little gift to the bridegroom."

"Thank you." Anders took the gift cigar in his hands.

"Allow me." Eliot struck a match and held it under the cheroot's end.

Anders puffed. Smoke billowed forth.

Eliot smiled as he waved the match out. "Now. How much do you need?"

"One hundred dollars?"

Eliot squinted. He scrutinized Anders. "How long have we known each other?"

Anders had trouble framing a reply. "I . . . I came here more than two years ago." He lowered the cigar and gulped fresh air while his head swam in circles.

"That long, already?" The storekeeper smoothed his long locks. "My, how time flies. Well, I must say, I have heard nothing bad about you—and if there had been anything bad, I would have heard. You strike me as the kind of man who pays his debts."

"You can ask Mister Lake. I paid fifteen dollars I owed him."

"You don't say. And now you're asking for, what?"

"One hundred—"

"Right. A hundred dollars." Eliot closed his eyes, then opened them. "I'll go it."

Anders felt a wave of relief.

"Of course, we'll need a legal agreement."

"Ja, sure. Of course."

Eliot reached under his counter, brought out a steel pen and a bottle of ink. "Why don't you go amuse yourself at the Debating Society, while I draw up the paper? Go on, I'll come get you when it's ready."

#

139

Anders returned to the porch and listened to the noisy argument. He stood beside a roof pillar and dropped his smoldering cigar into a brass spittoon.

The chief debaters were the old Whig Charlie Simmons and the two Blodgetts, York and Merv, Democrats who always took the pro-slavery side. Bystanders included Will Cargill, a likeable chap whose views Anders had not yet figured out, and two other men, Slim and David.

Anders knew Slim and David, like Charlie, were Whigs. They all faced the same problem. Their party crumbling around them, they had to choose a new one.

"Your midget, Douglas, done kicked over the hornets' nest," said Charlie to the Blodgetts, "and now the whole federal Union gets to pay the price."

York Blodgett's eyes blazed. "Stephen A. Douglas is God's and Illinois' gift to the Republic. That's why they call him the Little Giant. He knew folks from the South, movin' into new territories, would want to bring their niggers with them."

Slim, standing at Charlie's elbow, raised a finger. "If that's so, Mister Know-it-all, how come the Kansas-Nebraska Bill gives voters the choice to keep slavery out?"

"Shit," said York Blodgett.

Meaning he has no answer, Anders thought.

"Well," said Merv Blodgett, "popular sovereignty."

"Aha!" cried Charlie. "Don't it occur to you two that your popular sovereignty is the opposite of your special pleading for slaveholders?"

"Now, that just ain't so!" York shouted.

"Excuse me," Anders said. "What about the wishes of the black man to be free? Are they not to be considered?"

York and Merv rounded on him. "Niggers' wishes don't fall in the same category as white folks' wishes," Merv said. "They are a whole different kind of beast."

"Ja, you call them beasts, but they are men, like you or I."

York Blodgett's eyes narrowed. "Where you from again?"

"Norway, as I've told you before."

"You got any niggers in Norway?"

"No. None."

"Then you don't know what you're talking about. Shut your damned foreign mouth and leave these arguments to the Americans."

"In less than three years I will be an American. Will you listen then?"

Blodgett waved his hand in dismissal.

Anders felt a tap on his shoulder.

Eliot the storekeeper stood beside him, smiling. "Your papers are ready."

#

In the cool darkness inside the store, Anders considered the paper Eliot held before him. It was a printed form, on which Anders' name, the amount of one hundred dollars, and the figure "10" had been inserted by hand.

"What means the ten?" Anders asked.

"That's your interest. Ten percent a year. The fee you pay me, in addition to repayment of the principal, for the use of my money."

"Of course. Interest. I did not know it would be so much."

"Ten percent is pretty standard these days."

"I see," Anders said. "What is this word, mortgage?"

"That refers to the security."

141

"Security?"

The storekeeper, smiling, smoothed his side locks. "It specifies the arrangements in case you don't pay."

"I told you I pay. Ask Mister Lake."

"Yes, yes. However, sometimes things come up. Things that make it impossible to pay, like death or other disasters. You know that. In such a case, how would I get my money back?"

"What does that have to do with mortgage?"

"A mortgage simply pledges your land against the loan in the event of non-payment."

Anders drew in a breath. "So, if I can't pay, you take my farm."

Eliot smiled. "That's it. You've got it."

17. Daniel

Louisiana

June - December 1855

Daniel beamed as little Jubilee tumbled in the dirt with a couple of older children. The light brown boy, now more than a year old, played just as lively as his all-black playmates.

Daniel cared for Jubilee though he sprung from Mas' Petitbon's loins. The black half of the boy came from Betsey, who now lived under Daniel's protection. She considered the child her great treasure, so she called him Jubilee.

Daniel had built them a hut at the edge of the new village, which Luc had christened Camp Espère Pas. They were shunned by the maroons because Daniel and Betsey had triggered the planters' raid that killed Sammy. When Betsey brought forth Jubilee, the babe magically embodied the taint that Daniel had brought on the colony.

Although Jubilee's washed-out skin and blue eyes were just as unappealing to Daniel as to the maroons, he did not think the boy or his mother should be shunned because a white man had forced himself upon her.

Luc's first inclination had been to shoot both Daniel and Betsey, or else banish them to the swamp. But Luc's sway did not hold absolute sway. Bijou, in her own grief for her son Sammy, forbade Luc's summary vengeance. Still, most of the maroons reflected Luc's views—so Daniel's little family of three lived a dodgy existence.

Instead of sharing in the common produce, Betsey had scrounged a few seeds and started a garden of her own, an hour's walk outside the colony. Daniel trapped and hunted on his own, farther and farther from the maroons' hunting grounds. He spent many nights away, sleeping in his pirogue or in the limbs of a tree. He always came back with a little game for Betsey. She, in turn, stayed healthy enough to suckle the baby.

Banishment hung over their heads. Luc talked about sending them away once the child was weaned. Without the slight advantage of living with the maroons, they would soon be dead. Such little things as salt, vinegar, and molasses were crucial to survival.

Those items had been provided by Sammy's raids on the plantations. With Sammy dead, Luc himself made the appropriation runs. It had always been dangerous work. It was more dangerous with the colony farther removed than before from the plantations. And Luc, though a master of stealth and woodcraft, had grown older.

For all the maroons' hostility, they did not deny Jubilee access to his playmates. Not yet, anyhow. That time might come, however, if the family became more isolated.

Daniel had begun to have an idea what to do in that case.

#

As autumn set in, things got worse.

144

Luc's steady outlook and common sense had vanished since Sammy's death. As the colony's supply runner, he now appropriated more corn whiskey and less of the other necessities from plantations. The extra whiskey, Luc himself consumed. The scarcity of vinegar, salt, and other staples caused grumbling among the maroons, none of whom dared challenge Luc to his face.

Instead, they cut off Daniel, Betsey, and Jubilee. For supplies that used to be shared by all colony members, Daniel now had to pay a price—two dead rabbits for a small jug of molasses, for example. It strained his household economy. The success of each hunting trip became a grim necessity.

However, because he ranged farther than any other member of the community, he made a startling discovery. He found another group of maroons, living in an upland forest to the northeast, near the Arkansas line. The first hint had been snares set for wild game—snares like his own, but not set by him nor by any of the maroons of Camp Espère Pas.

On his next trip he walked into the upland maroons' camp, carrying a small bottle of vinegar as a peace offering. From then on, he brought them something every trip.

#

In December, he returned from a hunt and found Betsey running about, crying and tearing her hair.

"What's goin' on, woman?" he called.

"Jubilee! Jubilee! My baby!"

"Jubilee, what?"

"Wandered off. I was fixin' up some greens, I turn around, and he's gone."

145

The boy must have gone into the swamp. Daniel ran to his canoe. He poled furiously.

Ahead of him, screams.

A 'gator had the boy in its mouth.

Daniel leapt into the water and plunged his big knife into the beast. In death it opened its jaws. The boy floated free—and so did his bloody right arm, no longer attached to Jubilee.

Daniel grabbed Jubilee and flung him into the pirogue, then climbed back in himself. The boy's face was pale. Daniel squeezed the upper arm stump to stop the bleeding. Having lost his pole, he paddled back to camp with one arm while holding the boy with the other.

Betsey waded in to meet the canoe. She screamed when she saw her baby.

"Get a rag or somethin'!" Daniel shouted. "We need to tie off his arm."

The other maroons forgot their boycott and rushed to lend aid. They brought cloth for bandages, tubs of maroon balm—no help at all for Jubilee's injury—and concoctions of herbs meant to ease pain.

The child lingered near death.

They cleaned the stump of his arm. In a few days it turned black and smelly anyway. The rot crept to his shoulder, then to his little chest, his breaths grew labored, and after a week Jubilee died.

Betsey plunged into grief, awash in tears, talking out of her head. One thing she said made sense. "From jubilation to tribulation. I come out here to save my baby. Now the swamp done took him."

Daniel smoldered. "This no place to live. They is no freedom here."

He strapped on his big knife and strode to Luc's hut.

146

The big man raised his head when Daniel entered. A mug of whiskey stood before him, but he did not seem drunk, for a change.

"I'll have my gun now," said Daniel.

Luc turned his head. "Bijou, honey, go get them pouches."

Bijou rose without a word and left the hut.

Luc reached under his bed. He pulled out the musket. "Damned thing never did me no good." He tossed it to Daniel. "Take it and go."

"How it works?"

Luc frowned. "We gotta learn you everything."

Bijou re-entered with the ammunition pouches.

Luc showed Daniel how to load the powder, wadding, and ball, how to ram them down with the ramrod, and how to place the percussion cap. "Then you pull the trigger. We not gone do that here. You have to take my word for it."

#

After they buried Jubilee's small remains, Daniel and Betsey set out in the pirogue, heading for the camp of the upland maroons.

That would be just a way station. The words at the top of Daniel's mind were: "Benjamin Lake, Sweetwater, Menard County, Illinois."

Daniel had a sense he was leaving his old life behind when he poled the pirogue away from Camp Espère Pas. That night, halfway to the upland maroons' camp, he dozed against the trunk of a live oak while Betsey slept in the beached pirogue.

He awoke trembling. He had seen Mammy. He had been back in her old cabin at Hurricane Plantation. She had been frying something, smelled like catfish. It was all

147

so real. Mammy set the dish before him, saying, "What a fine boy, runnin' off and leavin' your friends behind." The catfish on the plate became a giant cottonmouth, stretching its fangs up to bite him—and he woke up.

He looked up into the tree and down at the ground all round him. No movement. No sign of a snake. He shook himself. Why would Mammy serve him a snake?

He turned his body and tried to go back to sleep.

18. Anders

Illinois

January – March 1856

Anders strapped on the skis he had fashioned from two oak branches. He went out to harvest more corn. His horses could not pull the wagon through the snowdrifts, and Anders had no sleigh. Therefore, he had made runners of willow and attached them with pegs to a wooden box. This he dragged behind him on a rope harness, to fill with corn, when he skied out to the field.

Never in Norway had he met such a winter. Gray-haired Americans said the prairie itself had never seen such a winter. The first blizzard came at the end of October. After that a blizzard came every week or two, with lesser storms between. He had bought long ropes and strung them from house to barn and from house to outhouse. Sometimes on his way back to the house after tending the stock, halfway along the rope in sideways-blowing snow, he could see neither house nor barn. Men had frozen to death outdoors on their own farms in such storms.

When the snow relented long enough to do outdoor work, the temperature plunged, which prompted Anders to don every item of clothing he could wear while still retaining the ability to move about. Thus far he had taken fewer than two-thirds of his corn ears into the crib. He had cut but few of the stalks, which could be chopped and mixed with hay and oats to extend the animals' feed.

The early cold had given Anders no chance to plant winter wheat. He had tried to keep the seeds dry for future use. Water leaking into the corner of the barn had spoiled them.

One special seed had grown well, however; it would bear fruit in the spring. As he skied to where the tan cornstalks stood half-buried in snowdrifts, he imagined holding in his hands the robust new son Maria would soon deliver.

So lost did he become in this reverie that he almost failed to see a movement across the field. When he did see it, he stopped in his tracks. Two bucks ambled at the far edge of his cornfield, placidly munching his crop.

What a stroke of luck, for he had his rifle with him.

He had bought a used Hawken rifle with a double-set trigger from a man in Sweetwater. He took it with him to the fields in case he might bag a deer, as Thor had done the winter before at Osmundsgarden. Deer tracks in the snow showed that the beasts ate his corn. He understood their winter hunger, but no law of man or God required him to feed them. Killing a deer would protect his crop while also getting meat for the table.

He unslung the loaded rifle from his shoulder and sank to his knees. He slipped the wool mitten off his right hand, placed a percussion cap on the gun's nipple, then waited.

150

The deer meandered about a hundred yards away, half-hidden by dry cornstalks. The shot would be too difficult.

He waited. They had not sensed him. There was a chill breeze; luckily, it came his way.

When the larger of the two bucks parted the cornstalks, making himself seen, Anders pulled back the icy rear trigger—which armed the front trigger with a *click*. The buck froze and swiveled its head straight toward him.

He touched the front trigger. The gun leapt in his hands, with a loud bang. The buck dropped. The other bounded away, the white flag of his tail marking his path across the fields.

Anders skied over snowdrifts, between corn rows, to the buck—its eyes glazed in death, its body warm. A ragged gasp: Did the deer yet breathe? No, it was his own panting he heard.

He stood up. He took three long breaths. His heartbeat slowed.

Why this sudden excitement? He had killed chickens aplenty, slaughtered pigs on Uncle's farm in Norway. *This is different, Anders. This marks your first kill as a hunter. Your first time to kill with a gun.*

A wild thrill shook him. The next moment came a wave of remorse for the life he had taken. Something told him to pray. "Thank you, O Lord, for this fine buck you have given me. Forgive my hand in his death. May I use him wisely to provide for us, your children here at Søtstrøm. Amen."

Anders dragged the buck to the farmyard, hung it up, gutted it.

When the meat cooled, he cut it into steaks, roasts, loins, and stew meat. He scraped all flesh off the inside of the deerskin and stretched it flat in the barn. He spread

151

salt on it to draw the moisture out. Later, he would tan the hide with the deer's brains and rub the skin till it became supple.

He cut the meat into small packages, wrapped them in cotton sacking, and stowed them in the cold woodshed.

The next day he led Webster and Clay, two fine horses that Benjamin Lake had sold him at half their value, up the Sweetwater Road. Presenting six venison steaks to Lake, he asked to borrow a sleigh for the day. Lake lent him a bobsled with wide front and back runners that would ride well through almost any drift. Anders hitched his team to the sleigh and drove it back to Søtstrøm. He loaded half the remaining deer meat in it and set out for Petersburg.

At the Kinnaird farm he found Gunder Jørgen Nybro by a pot-bellied stove in the bunkhouse with the other hands. He gave half the venison to Gunder Jørgen for his own use and to share with his bunkmates.

Gunder Jørgen poured coffee for Anders. "Sit down, Mighty Hunter. We also have warm rolls from the bunkhouse oven for you. How is the great hunter's wife, and her aunt?"

To be called a mighty hunter, though spoken in jest, pleased Anders. It pleased him also to extend his boast. "Maria is well," he said. "Nothing wrong with her that a bit of childbirth won't cure."

"Childbirth! You mean she—that is, you two—are expecting a baby?"

Anders smiled.

"And when will this happy event come about?"

"Late March, I should think."

Gunder Jørgen raised his eyebrows. "Not too long, then."

"No. Not too long."

Gunder Jørgen sent Anders on his way filled with rolls, coffee, and good cheer.

He drove to Osmundsgarden. Kirsten Haraldsdatter received him, and his gift of frozen meat, with gladness.

When he told her about the expected child, Kirsten rose from the table and hugged him. "And who will help Maria with the birthing?"

Anders was stunned. He had never considered this question until now.

"Anders! Have you never seen a midwife go to the house of a woman in labor?"

"Well, in Norway—"

"Should America be different? Even in a land of freedom, babies are not free to deliver themselves." Kirsten had fire in her eyes.

"You're right," said Anders. "Would you—"

"Dear Anders." Kirsten took both his hands in hers. "I would be delighted to help your Maria. Only it's such a great distance. It will take you half a day to come fetch me, and another half day for us to get back to Maria. That child really would need to deliver itself."

Anders frowned. "What about Maria's Aunt Osa?"

Kirsten bit her lip. "Old Tante does many things well. Cooking, storytelling, and such like things. But does she know much about the birth of babies? What experience did she have in the old country?"

Anders had never asked about this. He looked down at his boot tips.

"Anders, midwifery demands experience but also takes good judgment. Is there not someone near your farm who could help Maria's old aunt with her delivery?"

\#

Anders, remembering it to be Good Friday, said a prayer as he squeezed the last milk out of the cow Rødsidet's udder.

Rank bedding straw mingled its scent with those of hay and manure, filling the barn with a warm, earthy smell. In the solemnity of Lent, a hope of new life filled Anders: Any day now, his son would be born.

He stepped out into sunlight. Meltwater dripped off the icicles that hung from house and barn. Winter's back had finally been broken.

He entered the cabin and placed the oaken bucket on the table. There sat Aunt Osa, sipping coffee through a lump of sugar held in her mouth, like a lady of leisure.

Maria dashed about the cabin, dusted and swept in every corner.

Anders frowned. "I've brought fresh milk. Come, sit. Rest, like Tante."

Maria, on her knees, scrubbed at a spot on the puncheon floor.

Aunt Osa made a sound, half croak and half cluck. "No king, home from the hunt, finds cleaner quarters than a new babe in a crofter's hut."

"Oh!" Maria dropped her scrub brush. Suddenly pale, she tried to rise.

The old woman hurried to her side. As she helped Maria to her feet, Aunt Osa spoke to Anders. "What did I tell you, boy? Go get the woman from up the road."

#

He hitched his two horses, Webster and Clay, to his farm wagon. He drove to the Lake farm on a road of new mud and icy ruts. He leapt from the wagon seat, ran to the front door, and pounded. Mistress Lake opened the door.

Smiling at his news, she gathered up medicine jars and bundles of herbs. He placed them all in his wagon bed, hemmed in with burlap sacks, then helped her up to the wagon's seat.

They got back to Søtstrøm at noon. Maria now wore a tentlike linen nightdress. She lay on the main-floor bed Anders had built for her when she could no longer climb to the loft. Aunt Osa sat by the bed, croaking odd tunes—songs of the huldrefolk, for all he knew.

Mistress Lake waddled in the door at his heels. Anders helped her out of her coat.

Aunt Osa said, "A well-fatted sow! She'll know all about dropping a litter."

Anders cringed, then realized Mistress Lake had not understood Aunt Osa's words, spoken in Norwegian. He frowned at Maria's tante. Had she meant criticism, rustic humor, or a heart-felt compliment? Who could tell?

Mistress Lake smiled down to her third chin. She glided to the side of the bed and beamed at Maria. "How do you feel, my dear?" she asked.

Maria groaned, rolled to her side. "Ready to get it over with." She rubbed her belly.

Mistress Lake said, "Hadn't you better see to the horses, Mister Gunstensen?"

How could he leave his wife at her time of need?

Maria nodded agreement with the old woman's stern decree, so out Anders went. The horses did need attention.

When he came back in, the three women seemed united in an unfathomable mystery. Aunt Osa and Mistress Lake drank tea, their eyes a-glitter. Maria lay on her side, staring straight ahead as she breathed in and out.

He wanted to do something. Anything. "Now that Mistress Lake is here—"

155

"Make sure we have enough firewood, then leave us," Maria said. "Go tend the farm."

He brought in two armloads of wood, then stood by the bed in uncertainty.

"You may go now," whispered Maria.

"But—"

"Go!"

Anders stepped back from the bed. He picked up his hat to leave. At the door, he turned back. "One of you will come to tell me, when the child comes?"

"I expect you'll hear its arrival," said Mistress Lake.

#

Anders busied himself in the barn, tidying up the hay in the haymow, mending harness, grooming Webster and Clay, then grooming the cows—Rødsidet and her heifer, Lillerød.

Hours had gone by with no word on the birthing. He sat downhearted in the cow's stall. Why did women keep everything such an infernal secret?

#

Screams woke Anders. He jumped up, ran from the barn, then halted at the cabin door. The shrieks curdled his blood. He quailed at whatever waited inside the cabin.

He stood, foolish and irrelevant.

The screams stopped. Through the door came the voices of Mistress Lake and Aunt Osa—voices, not distinct words. He braced himself, rapped on the door, entered.

The two old women stood by the bed where Maria lay, a white bundle between her shoulder and breast. Mistress Lake gave him a sober stare, then a brief smile. She stood aside so he could see his child.

156

"Why, he's blue! So small."

"Not so small," said Mistress Lake, "and many babes come into the world without much color. By the way, your child is a girl, not a boy."

"A girl?" *A girl.* He had never considered that possibility. What help would a girl be?

It all changed in an instant. His mind cleared and he thanked God for this delightful little woman. Delightful and small. Tiny.

She lay in the crook of Maria's arm—skin pale, eyes closed, body quiet.

"What will you name her?" asked Mistress Lake.

"Gunhild," said Anders.

"Ja," Maria said. A first-born daughter always took the name of her father's mother.

"I am told you are Lutherans. Is there a minister of your faith nearby?"

"No," said Anders. "I do not think so."

"This child should be baptized. Any Christian believer may perform the rite. May I baptize her for you?"

Anders' mind groped for a tactful response. "We—ah, we usually do it about a week after the child is born."

"In this case, it would be better not to wait." Mistress Lake stared at Anders.

Tears rolled down Maria's cheeks.

What can all this mean?

Trembling, teeth clenched, Maria raised the infant into the arms of Mistress Lake.

The old woman stepped to the table, where stood a bucket of water. She bowed her head. She dipped a hand in the water, touched it to the baby's head. "Gunhild Gunstensen, child of the Covenant, I baptize thee in the name of Jesus Christ the Lord. Amen."

Anders' jaw dropped open. How strange to have a layman christen a baby . . . in fact, a laywoman . . . and

157

with words that made no mention of God the Father or the Holy Ghost.

Strangest of all, the surname: "Gunstensen."

Maria met his gaze, her eyes wide, as they shared a thought: *Does this woman not know the child's name is Gunhild Andersdatter?*

The answer leapt into his brain: *Of course not.* As Mistress Lake returned the child to Maria's arms, Anders thought: *We are not in Norway anymore.*

They were Americans now—all of them. Americans took their father's surname and that was that. He was Gunstensen; all of his children, male or female, would now be Gunstensen—no Andersens, no Andersdatters.

The old Norsk ways had no force at all.

He whispered, "God knows her true name. It will always be her name in Heaven."

Maria's eyes declared something fierce, implacable, and terrible. She stared at him until he wept salty tears.

Then she cast her eyes downward, at the still child in her arms, who, in the few moments given her, had already slipped away from the strange American name and flown to her Heavenly home, where she would be Gunhild Andersdatter for all eternity.

19. Anders

Illinois

March 1856

Anders sat on a stump and held a horseshoe nail in cold fingers, scoring letters into a flat of sandstone. He had finished "GUNHILD" and prepared to start on "GUNSTENSEN." He raised his arm for a stretch, seeking not comfort but only to resume work on the stone.

Yesterday he had made a small coffin. That work, done in the barn, surrounded by horses and cows, had occupied his hands and eased his mind. This present task, inscribing an unnatural name on a bit of stone, had a different feel. A work of separation.

Maria had lain in bed several days, visited by would-be consolers. Kirsten Haraldsdatter had come first, with Karen, Britta, and Thor. "We left Reier to tend the farm," said Kirsten. Having arrived to celebrate a birth, they stayed on to mourn a death. Kirsten made Maria eat the sweet cream porridge she had brought. "Even a bereaved mother needs fløtegrøt, to regain strength for living."

Gunder Jørgen arrived from Mister Kinnaird's farm. He glowered down at Maria, tugged away the small cool bundle she held so tight in her arms. He and Anders took it out the cabin door. The earth being frozen solid, they packed little Gunhild in snow and put her away in the lean-to.

A few days later, with everyone gone and Maria still in bed, Anders used a froe and potato fork to make a hole in the half-thawed earth. He made Maria get up. She and Tante came out of the cabin. They stood in mud while Anders prayed aloud for the soul of their daughter.

Maria stared at the small wooden box as Anders lowered it into the grave. "Do not ask me to shovel earth upon her," she said, then went back inside.

#

The rumble of a wagon heralded Matthew Lake. He drove in through the gate and halted his team. Anders set down his nail and stone.

Matthew, seeing what work Anders had in hand, shook his head. "A terrible thing, Anders. A terrible thing."

Had Matthew not said the same words, a few days ago? Had he not visited after the baby's death? Anders could not remember.

"I hate to ask at a time like this," Matthew said. "We need your help."

How can Benjamin Lake's son, who has everything to make life worth living, come to someone like me for help?

"Ja, Matthew. How can I help you?"

Matthew peered both ways along the Sweetwater road. He dropped his reins, stepped into the wagon bed, and shifted two of the large white bags piled there. A narrow tunnel appeared under the other bags.

Matthew reached in and poked. "Come out."

A dark form emerged from between the bags, then jumped to the ground.

The young black man, dressed in a new set of work clothes, stood thicker than Anders remembered from three years ago. More muscular. The mouth a bit puckered, no doubt from loss of teeth. But the face was the same.

What had those Memphis jailers called him?

"Daniel?"

The man smiled. "Thass right, sah. Daniel."

Anders turned to Matthew. "This Daniel is the slave taken from our steamboat at Memphis, when I first came to America—the time when your father got me out of jail."

"We had a message from a friend in Springfield," Matthew said. "This gentleman asked after us by name."

Daniel grinned. "Mister Benjamin Lake, Sweetwater, Menard County, Illinois."

"So, I went down and picked him up," Matthew said, "along with our seed corn. Only it wasn't just him."

Daniel leaned into the wagon bed and reached between the bags, just where he had emerged. He drew out a slender dark wrist, followed by a calico-clad arm and then a whole person—a slim woman in a long, loose dress and white cap, her face etched with sorrow.

"This be Betsey." Daniel helped her down from the wagon.

"I can't get them to our farm," said Matthew. "We're under watch. Slave hunters just up the road, checking every wagon goes by. Daniel and Betsey need a place to stay. Out of sight."

161

A picture came into Anders' brain—himself huddling overnight in the boathouse of Maria's father, back in Øiestad.

"Come," he said. He led them into the barn. He extended his arm toward the hayloft.

"Thank you," said Daniel. He allowed Betsey to go before him.

With her foot on the first rung of the ladder, she gazed up at Anders. "Thank you, sah," she whispered.

#

Matthew Lake rumbled off, his wagon bed now innocent of any commerce except bags of seed corn.

Anders entered the cabin and took down the Hawken rifle, which hung above the door. He poured powder down the gun's barrel and followed that with a lead ball and a bit of cloth, jammed it all down with the ramrod, replaced the ramrod under the barrel, and re-hung the gun on its pegs above the door.

Aunt Osa's eyes bulged. "The soldier rests on his arms."

From her sickbed, Maria murmured, "Will you go hunting?"

"Not now. We have guests for supper."

"Guests?" She swept her gaze over the cabin.

"Ja. I will take their supper to them in the barn."

"Black folk, a man and a woman," said Aunt Osa. "I saw them out the window."

Maria blinked. "Are they slaves, then?"

"No, jenta mi. They are guests."

#

162

Aunt Osa cooked a bit of the pork Anders had butchered last week from his October piglets, with potatoes, onions, and rutabagas. Anders filled two plates and took them to the barn.

Daniel and Betsey came down the ladder. They sat on the edge of the water trough and ate by lantern light.

Anders asked about Daniel's new escape. "Did you ride the steamboat again?"

"No, sah. Thass how they caught me before. This time, we walked."

"All that way, from Mississippi?"

"No. Loosiana." Daniel munched a potato, wrinkled his brow. "See, when Mister Davis got me back, he sold me downriver. Sold me to a man owns a cane plantation in the bayous."

"And he sold you because . . . why?"

"How he could trust me not run off again? Only cure for that's a whuppin'. Well, Mister Joseph Davis too fine a gentleman. He would never whup one of his people. Mister Davis be upright, like that top hat he wear. So he sold me to a man that does believe in whuppin', Mas' Petitbon, and he took care of it."

"This man beat you?"

"Just the once. Look you here." Daniel raised his shirt. He turned and showed Anders his back.

Anders brought the lantern near and saw scars. A map of brutality. How could one person do this to another?

"They's all healed up now," Daniel said. "But you can still see 'em."

Anders wept for Daniel.

Daniel lowered his shirt. "When we started, I reckoned if we get to Illinois, we be free. Man in Quincy say Illinois full of slave catchers. Got to go all the way to Canada, now."

163

"Ja, it is true." Anders sighed. "At this moment you cannot go to Mister Lake's farm. Instead, you stay here, and we get you past the slave catchers and on to freedom."

Somehow, he thought. *Somehow*.

#

After dark, Matthew Lake returned, his wagon still piled high with seed corn.

Anders, holding a lantern, led him into the barn, to the foot of the hayloft. "Daniel!" he called, his cold breath swirling in the lantern light. "It is safe now. Matthew has come to take you away."

Daniel and Betsey peered over the edge of the hayloft, their faces lit by the glow from Anders' lantern. They came down the ladder. Betsey, shivering, huddled in the warmth of Daniel's embrace.

Matthew stepped forward. "We have the chance to get away now. We'll take you by back roads to a man we know in Tazewell County."

"It be a trial to get on, from there to Canada?"

Matthew Lake smiled. "Easier than from here, that's for sure."

Daniel released Betsey. He stepped away. "Go where the man tell you. Folks protect you, it be all right."

Betsey's eyes opened wide. Open-mouthed, she shook her head. "No! Why you say that? You got to come, too."

"Don't make a fuss. You be safe, all the way to Canada."

"What?" Terror crossed Betsey's face. "Why you leave me now?"

Daniel touched her face. She slapped his hand away. Tears rolled down her cheeks.

"I join you in Canada by and by."

She closed her arms across her chest. Her shoulders quaked.

Anders could not believe his eyes and ears. "You abandon your wife?"

"She not my wife, Mister Gunson. We friends, thass all. I 'scaped her from the plantation. We been through a lot together."

Matthew knit his brows. "But this is your chance to go to Canada."

"I can't."

"What else can you do? This county swarms with slave catchers."

"Reckon I head back south."

"South!"

Daniel spread his hands. "They's others down there need to get free, too. Now I know the way, I can help my friends."

Anders scratched his head. "This was your plan all along?"

Daniel, eyes hooded, said nothing.

Betsey wept.

"You walk into danger," said Anders.

"My mammy told me I got to help my friends. And these men in Loosiana, Quintus and Micah, they is my friends. I told them, when I found the way I would come back for them. And I found there is a way, goin' slow, puttin' one foot in front the other. So I gotta show them."

What could Anders say to that?

"Don't worry, Mister Gunson. I have a gun. Left it with a man in Quincy. I go get it back before I cross the river." Daniel turned to Betsey. "You go now. This your chance."

Mournfully, she climbed into Lake's wagon. He carefully piled grain bags close around her, then drove off.

Anders and Daniel stood watching the wagon until it disappeared from view, then a few minutes longer, until no more sound of it reached their ears.

#

"Time I be goin'," said Daniel.

"Not yet. There is more to be said." Anders put his hands on Daniel's shoulders. "It is cold out here. Come, let us go in with the beasts, where it is warmer."

Anders picked up his lantern and led the way into the barn. He entered the stalls of the cows and horses and moved among them, running his hands over their flanks, inspecting them with his eyes. Daniel followed him.

"Three years ago, Daniel, when I came to this country, I tried to help you in Memphis. I failed and you suffered, being returned to a cruel owner—"

"Thass not your fault. Besides, Mister Davis not cruel."

"Because he would not whip you himself?" Anders leaned an elbow against the chest-high stall wall of Rødsidet, the cow. "Then what do you call a man who would sell you to another, knowing you would be ill-treated?"

Daniel opened his mouth to speak, then fell silent.

"You have made it to Illinois. This time I have succeeded in helping you. Only, you will not accept my help. For Betsey, yes. Not for yourself."

"I told you, I got friends to think about."

"Ja. I admire a man who thinks of his friends. Our Lord says, Greater love hath no man than that he lay down his life for his friends."

"Doubt it'll come to that, Mister Gunson."

"It might."

Daniel remained silent.

166

"Since I came to America," said Anders, "many things amaze me. One of them is slavery. I try to make sense of it, but it makes no sense." He moved on to the horse stalls, gave a carrot each to Webster and Clay. "Maybe, before you go south, you could tell me about yourself. Who you are, who your friends are, and how you live under slavery."

Daniel bit his lip.

"I really would like to know."

Daniel stretched and blew out a long breath. He rubbed the top of his head. "I had me a mammy and a pappy. Don't hardly 'member my pappy, on accounta he died. Mammy say he's a fine man. He died stoppin' runaway horses that run away with Miss Davis carriage. Miss Caroline, that was, the youngest."

Anders came out of the horse stalls. Daniel followed him to a bale of hay on the barn floor. They sat side by side.

"I also had a brother and a sister—older brother, younger sister. They both die when the cholera come round, a few years back. That left me and Mammy, just ourselves in our little cabin. Mammy was a house servant, did washin' and laundry and whatnot. When Mister Davis calc'late I's twelve, they put me out in the fields with a big, long bag, learn to pick cotton. This was just after my brother die, so I's like a replacement."

"How much do they pay you to pick a bag of cotton?"

Daniel roared with laughter. He rolled on the ground. When the tears of his mirth subsided, he said, "Now you tell me, Mister Gunson—whose cotton is it?"

"Well, I suppose it is Mister Davis' cotton."

"Thass right. And whose nigger is I?"

Anders frowned. "Mister Davis'."

"Now you got it," said Daniel, wiping a tear. "So why they pay me anything at all to pick that cotton?"

167

"You have needs. Your mamma has needs."

"They give us a little food, which Mammy cooks up after she done at the big house, and after I come in from the fields. And they give us a new set of clothes, almost ever' year."

Anders considered Daniel. He described the most degraded conditions of life, yet he did not seem depressed.

Daniel seemed to read his mind. "You got to remember, Mister Davis figger he's the best owner in the whole South. We kin learn to read and write. Not many of us does, but we can, 'f we got the time and innerest. We got our own courts, if somebody does a wrong thing. One nigger, Ben Montgomery, so smart he almost run the whole plantation for Mister Davis. No better place to be a slave than Hurricane Plantation."

"If life was so good for you there, why did you run away?" It sounded sharper than Anders intended. "I really want to know."

"Mammy died."

"Oh. I am sorry. I did not know."

Daniel pressed his lips together. "She was the best thing in my life. So when she went, I had nothing left. Only more work. Thought I might as well see the world."

"So, you climbed on board the steamboat."

"And you know the rest of the story."

"No," Anders said. "Not all of it. What happened after you were captured?"

"They put me in leg irons and took me back to Mister Davis. He axed me did I want to be a good nigger and stay on the plantation. I said no, not specially. So he sold me to Mas' Petitbon. Now they's a world of difference from a cotton place in the Delta to a sugar plantation in Loosiana."

"How so?"

168

"Hotter. More bugs. More snakes. And the work is unbearable. Most unbearable after harvest, when they squeeze the juice out'n the cane. Thass miserable work in the cane press. Least, so they tell me. My friends, Micah and Quintus, they done plenty work there." Daniel flashed a mischievous smile. "I din't stick around long enough to find out for myself."

"How did you get away?"

"Stole the master's pirogue—thass a kind of a boat. Went off deep in the swamp and found a bunch of maroons to live with."

"Maroons?"

"Black folks what live back among the bayous. They was slaves once and run off like me, and now they is nobody's nigger. But it's a hard life."

"So, you ran away from the maroons, too."

"Not 'zactly. First, I stole Betsey from Mas' Petitbon. Then they was a lot of commotion about that. Then Betsey and I lived with the maroons, and she had her baby."

"A baby? Yours?"

"Naw. Mas' Petitbon's."

Anders was shocked.

"Betsey din't want to share the child with his father," Daniel said. "So she named him Jubilee, and we all lived out in the swamp, among the maroons. Till the alligator got him."

The alligator got him. Unbelievable.

"The baby? An alligator ate the baby?"

"Told you it was a hard life. Then me and Betsey picked up and come north." Daniel stared into Anders' eyes. "Now you know the whole thing."

Anders took a deep breath. "Thank you. I . . . wanted to know." He stood, stretched his limbs. "Listen, it is too late for you to start out, and you cannot travel by day. Stay

169

with us tonight and tomorrow, rest and eat. Then after dark you can be on your way."

"Thanks, I'll do that, Mister Gunson."

Anders started to leave, then turned back to Daniel. "One more thing."

"Whazzat?"

"My name. It is not Gunson. It is Gunstensen."

"Ain't that what I said? Gunson?"

"No. Listen. Gun-sten-sen. Gunsten, sen. My father's name is Gunsten. Say it."

"Gunsten."

"That is right."

"You Mister Gunsten."

Anders sighed. "No. My father is Gunsten. I am Gunsten's son. That is, Gunstensen."

"Gunsten's son."

"Gunstensen. If I am Gunson, as you say, then my father is a gun. And he is not."

Daniel's mouth hung open. His eyes swam. "Your pappy not a gun?"

"No, not a gun. He is a schoolteacher."

"Oh."

Anders swung the barn door open. "I am glad we had this talk."

"Yeah, Mister Gun—sumpin'-sumpin'."

#

Anders went back to the cabin. Maria sat at the table.

She looked up when he came in. "Well?"

"Betsey has gone off for Canada. Daniel will stay one more day, then leave at dusk."

"Then we shall be in danger one more day."

"I had a long talk with him just now, jenta mi. You cannot believe what things he has been through."

170

"I cannot believe what things we will go through, Husband, before it is over."

20. Anders

Illinois

March 1856

Anders rose before dawn.

He took a plate of pork scraps and boiled oats to Daniel in the cold barn.

"Thank you again, Mister Gunson."

"Call me Anders."

"Yes, sah." Daniel bit his lip. "I be a danger, long as I'm here. I be gone at sundown."

"Ja, that is for the best," Anders said. "Meanwhile, stay out of sight."

#

Anders hiked into Sweetwater. He carried a package of butter and cheese to Mister Eliot at the store. Every bit of cash income helped.

While there, he kept his ears open. His real purpose was to listen to the town gossip. He heard no mention of a wagon intercepted on the road to Tazewell County, no suspicion of the Lakes or of himself, no mention of slave catchers, of Betsey, or of Daniel.

He walked back home at noon, relieved.

Maria confronted him. "Husband, explain why he is still here."

Anders smiled. "I see you are out of bed and moving around the house now." He hung his hat on a peg, stepped around Maria, and sat.

"My daughter sleeps in the ground. I myself am not well. How can I rest with danger on my doorsill?"

"Daniel will go south again to help his friends. Tonight, after dark. Is it a problem that we help him?"

"When you helped slaves before, that was at Mister Lake's farm. Now the Underground Railroad makes a stop here at Søtstrøm."

Aunt Osa set a dinner plate before Anders. "Many's the time I've caught sight of trolls or drauger, yet I never saw the like of these creatures for darkness."

"Daniel is neither a troll nor an undead soul," said Anders. "He is a man like us, with a darker skin. He can speak. He can eat potatoes and pork and beets, just as other people do."

"And when he brings these friends of his out," Maria said, "then he will bring them here again, ja? Will put us in further peril."

"When has he endangered us?"

She came and stood over him. "When have we not been in danger, since he arrived?"

"The threat is from slave catchers, if anyone. It is not Daniel who is the danger." His brow furrowed. "Why must I explain this? Is it not clear as a bell?"

"Idiot!" Maria cried, dashing her hands against his shoulder.

"Hei!" Anders stood, knocking his chair over backwards. He grasped her shoulders in his large hands.

174

"Calm down. He will go on his way tonight. Let us not worry about dangers that do not exist."

Hoofbeats and wagon sounds came from outside.

Anders stepped to the window. Slave catchers stood in the barnyard—the same ones who had tried to take Josh Quimby—their horses' breath steaming.

He crossed the room in two strides and took down the loaded Hawken from its pegs. He pulled a percussion cap from the pouch and placed it on the priming nipple.

"Stay here, bolt the door behind me." He stepped outside. The door slammed shut behind him. The bolt thunked into place.

Anders raised his rifle. Too late.

The old slaver sat a tall horse, had a gun already aimed at Anders. "Seems we have a stand-off, farm boy." His mouth turned up at the corners. "I'm Bullamore Crawley. I believe we've met before."

Anders nodded. "You go away now."

"We'll be happy to leave you to your shack, Oley. But we've got a sworn duty. Runaway slaves all through these parts. Some white folk harbor them."

"We have no slaves here."

"Don't matter. The law requires you to assist our searches." The man beckoned his son, who sat on the spring seat of their buckboard.

The son climbed down laboriously from the wagon. Once balanced on the hard ground, he limped toward Anders' barn.

My God, he has replaced his lost foot with a wooden one.

"Hei!" Anders swung his rifle toward Crawley's son.

The old man cocked his gun with a *click*. "Don't pay no mind to Teddy, he won't touch your stock or your feed. If you ain't hidin' slaves, you got nothin' to worry about."

Anders could swing the gun and shoot the old man now. The shot would draw Teddy away from the barn. By that time, Anders would need to have another round loaded.

But his powder, balls, and caps were inside, behind a bolted door.

What if he shot the old man at the very moment his son emerged from the barn with Daniel? Perhaps then he and Daniel together could overpower the son.

Teddy limped out of the barn, tottering over frozen wagon ruts. "He ain't in there, Pa."

"Not in the haymow?"

"Not in the haymow, not in the stalls with the horses, not nowhere."

"Take a gander out back. See if he's holed up behind the barn."

Teddy limped off. After a long while he returned, grinning. "Nothin' there but a big, steamy manure pile and an old wagon. Your Oley is fixin' to spread pig shit all over the land."

Bullamore Crawley swung his gaze back to Anders.

"We've got to search your shack, boy."

Anders' heart beat faster. "You may not search my home. I know American law. You need a paper from a judge."

Crawley pulled a paper from under his coat. "You mean this?"

"Hand it to me. I can read English."

"How do I know you won't rip it up, or maybe set fire to it?" The big man stuffed the paper back inside his coat. "Come on, Teddy. It ain't worth the battle here. We'll get the sheriff to enforce our writ."

They drove off.

After making sure they had gone, Anders ran to the barn. There was no sign of Daniel. Even the hay in the loft did not appear to have been disturbed.

He stepped to the open hay-loading door. On the ground below stood the farm wagon, full of manure he had loaded yesterday for spreading today. As he looked upon it, the manure in the wagon stared back at him.

It spoke. "They gone?"

"Daniel!"

The former slave stood. Clumps of dung fell away from his body. That which still clung made Daniel non-human. It also stank. He scraped manure off his body and dropped it back into the wagon bed.

"Best not leave a trail of this shit all over," he said. "If they come back, they figure out where I hid."

Anders came out of the barn, drew a bucket of water, carried it across the yard, and dumped it over Daniel. He did so again and again. Daniel, shivering, rubbed the manure off with his hands.

Anders brought him a cake of lye soap. "Go in the barn, take off your clothes, take a bucket and wash yourself all over. I will bring you some dry clothes."

He turned toward the cabin. Maria's tense face watched him from the window.

She threw the bolt and swung the door in to admit him. He climbed to the loft. He picked up a long shirt, trousers, and a pair of socks, and brought them back down.

"You would give away your spare set of clothes!"

"What else should I do? The man is freezing and has nothing fit to wear."

Maria shuddered. She crossed her arms, paced back and forth. "How could he abide hiding in cow dung?"

"I don't know," said Anders.

Back in the barn, he posed Maria's question while Daniel washed and dried himself.

"No choice," Daniel said. "If you was ever a slave on a sugar farm, then you knowed, an hour in hog shit not so bad. Worth it for the freedom."

"I was a slave myself," said Anders. "Back in Norway."

Daniel scoffed. "Yeh? A slave?"

"I was indentured to my uncle on his farm. He treated me very ill."

Daniel stepped into the clean trousers Anders had brought. "Not the same as bein' a black man in Loosiana."

"No. Still, it gives me some idea."

Daniel laughed.

"What is funny?"

Daniel laughed again. "Yes, sah, Mister Gunson! You make one mighty fine slave." He marched around the barn, imitating Anders' bouncy, free-as-a bird gait, with comic effect.

Anders picked up Daniel's manure-stained clothes. He draped them over a low beam. "Later, I will soak them with kerosene and burn them up."

He took the Hawken rifle back inside. He hung it back in its place over the door. He turned around to find both women staring at him.

"What now, Husband?" asked Maria.

Anders thought a moment. "Daniel shall rest in the barn, out of sight, until after dark, when he will be on his way. I shall work near the house and barn for the rest of the day, in case those slavers come back. You may start preparing a fine supper to see our guest off."

#

178

Anders mended harnesses that did not need mending. He took a scythe, sharpened it, and mowed the dry grass near the gate down to the snow line, so that Søtstrøm would present a neat appearance when viewed from the road. He even applied a bit of bacon fat to the creaky hinges of the barn door.

When the sun neared the horizon, he called Daniel in from the barn and placed him at the table with himself, Maria, and Aunt Osa. Aunt Osa had roasted the last bit of venison from the deer Anders had slain. Thank God, the wild meat's strong aroma overwhelmed any whiff of barnyard that might still hover about Daniel.

Aunt Osa brought the venison, along with potatoes and rutabagas. She ogled the black guest all the while she served the food.

Anders asked the Lord's blessing, in Norwegian as usual. All present, including Daniel, said, "Amen."

Aunt Osa kept staring at Daniel, while Maria stole sidelong glances. To make Daniel more of a human in Maria's and Aunt Osa's eyes, Anders tried to engage him in conversation about his life as a slave and his escape to freedom. Daniel, so talkative in the barn, seemed shy in the cabin, giving only the briefest of replies.

Maria stood. With rare ceremony, she offered Daniel more potatoes.

Daniel shook his head. "It's time I be going."

Maria put bread and the last of the venison in a sack. She handed the sack to Anders, tipping her head toward Daniel. Anders gave him the sack and offered a jug of water.

"No, thank you, sah. That heavy to tote. I reckon I'll find cricks to drink from."

He strode off through the sere cornfield south of the cabin and disappeared in the dusk. Søtstrøm lay quiet in the evening chill, as if neither Daniel nor Betsey had ever visited.

"Thank God he is gone," Maria said.

"What is so bad about him?" Anders asked. "The fact that he is black?"

"No, Husband. He cannot help being black. But while here, he was a danger to us—to our safety, our farm, our future." She shivered.

"Well, you can relax now," Anders said. "Things are back to normal."

21. Maria

Illinois

March 1856

Maria helped Tante clean up after supper, while Anders went to the barn to tend the stock.

She had just hung a kettle of water to boil when rough shouts came from outside.

She ran to the window. In front of the barn, two men kicked something on the ground.

Anders.

Her body quaked.

Lord, help me now.

She stood on tiptoe and bumped the rifle down from above the door. It toppled into her arms. Anders had loaded the gun, but she needed something else—a yellow, shiny bit.

The powder horn and pouch sat near. Her fingers scrabbled in the pouch, found hard metal things—"caps," Anders called them. She placed a cap with trembling fingers. She leaned the rifle on the wall, swung the door open, and picked up the rifle in both hands.

"Bolt the door, Tante."

She dashed across the yard.

"Skurker!" she screamed. "Uslinger! Stop!"

One man stomped Anders' limp form, the other one, larger, turned toward Maria and raised a threatening hand.

She stopped ten feet away. "Go!" She waved the rifle.

The big man shouted, "Let's go, Teddy! We've given him enough to think about."

The kicker kept on kicking—stumbling, almost falling over, yet kicking with vigor.

Maria pulled the trigger. Nothing happened. The trigger did not budge.

The man kicked at Anders, over and over.

Her fingers found a second trigger, behind the first. She pulled it. No shot erupted. Instead, the forward trigger made a click. She touched it again.

Flame and smoke blasted from the muzzle. The gunstock bashed her shoulder.

The big man staggered back and howled.

"Skurk! Kjeltring!" Maria screamed.

"Pa!" cried the younger man. He limped over to the big man, extended an arm.

Why does he limp? It's the other one I shot.

A sound made her glance backwards. Tante tottered out from the open cabin door.

Maria whirled the gun in a great arc. She aimed it at both men, who huddled together. "I shoot!" she screamed. *Maybe they don't know I fired my only shot.*

"Let's go," said the old man. He groaned. They lurched off toward Sweetwater Road, leaning on each other, both limping.

Their wagon stood beyond the barn, nearer the road. Maria watched them hobble to the wagon, get into it, and depart.

She turned, full of dread for Anders.

A stiff form stood behind her—Tante, casting an evil eye down the road where the men had vanished.

22. Maria

Illinois
March – April 1856

Maria leaned over the bed in which she and Tante had laid Anders. Two lanterns, one on each side, showed his face a muddled mask, its nose misshapen, eyes closed.

She had watched hours. She touched his forehead. *Why do I seek for fever? Those men brought mayhem, not malaria.*

At last, Anders woke. He gazed out through slits in purpling flesh, confusion in his eyes.

She placed a finger on his lips. "Shh. I told you that slave endangered us."

"But—" He writhed, as if to get up, perhaps to make an argument.

"*Altfor djerv blir ofte dengd,*" Tante said. "Too bold, oft brings a thrashing."

Anders writhed again, contentious.

"Shh," Maria said. "Tante has a proverb for everything. You lie back. We can talk later."

He lay still.

At least he follows my advice when he is hurt.

Maria watched until he went back to sleep, a flame of anger rising inside her.

She whispered, "If he wakes again, give him broth."

Then she slipped out the door and stomped up the Sweetwater Road.

#

By the light of the setting moon, Maria banged on the Lakes' door.

Dogs, hens, and rooster erupted as one. Moos and whinnies sounded from the barn.

Then she realized the day had not yet dawned. No matter. Time for these people to wake up. She pounded again on the door. Her shoulder throbbed where the gunstock had bashed it.

Behind the frost-etched glass a lantern glowed. A fat form moved with it.

Mistress Lake threw open the door, drawing a robe over rounded shoulders. "Maria. What's wrong, child? No coat, you'll catch your death." She pulled Maria inside. "What brings you out, so soon after your ... confinement?"

My child's death, you mean.

"Now you have nearly made my Anders get killed!"

"Killed? Mister Gunstensen?" The old woman's eyes widened.

"Not killed. No." Maria's rage robbed her of breath. "*Near* killed! Ja! All because of your son ... and his black friend."

"You mean Daniel."

"My Anders lies bed-struck in our house. His face is like, is like, a pile of boiled beets."

186

"Come." The old woman led Maria through the kitchen to the parlor. She set the lantern on the dark wood table.

Benjamin Lake appeared, disheveled, rubbing his head, his clothing askew. His wife scuttled back to the kitchen.

Lake extended an arm inviting Maria to sit on a red-upholstered armchair. Maria ignored the chair and stood, pouring out the events of the past twelve hours.

She ran out of words. She stood panting.

Lake brooded for a time.

"It's almost time to plant," he said at last. "How long do you think he'll be laid up?"

Exasperated, Maria threw her hands in the air. How could she answer that?

"Excuse me." Lake left the room.

Mistress Lake came. She brought tea, poured a cup for Maria, invited her to sit.

Maria remained standing. "What kind of country is this, where people own each other? Where they erupt a man's home and half beat him to death!"

Mistress Lake held Maria's hand and shed tears with her.

Mister Lake came back through the parlor, with Matthew and Mark. All wore work clothes and heavy jackets. "We'll get things organized," Lake said, and they left.

Maria turned on Mistress Lake. "How thinks he to fix things now? It is his fault, to begin with! He teaches Anders to cavort with black slaves and white skurker!"

"Consort, I think you mean, dear," said Mistress Lake. She poured herself a cup of tea, sat down, and took a sip. "What could those men have been thinking?"

"They thought to kill my Anders. And they would have done it, too."

187

"Yes. But I mean, what business is it of theirs whom you and your husband have as guests? It's your land."

"They did not seem to think so."

"Of course not," said Mistress Lake. Her eyes flashed. "Such men think themselves everybody else's master. They were thwarted in hunting slaves, and they took it out on your husband. Chances are they chose him on account of his foreign accent."

A Scandihoovian, Maria thought. *Yes. It is just so. They tried to cheat him when he applied to be a schoolmaster.* She used a napkin to dry her tears.

"There's only one thing to do with such men, and it's to stand up to them."

"That . . . that is what I tried to do."

"You did just fine. Now we must get your Anders well, so he can get back to farming."

#

Maria sat down, drank tea, and received a good deal more of Mistress Lake's sympathetic yet hardheaded advice. Then the two of them walked to Søtstrøm together through the dawn-pinked landscape. Mistress Lake brought along a bag of herbs, medicines, and cures.

Anders stirred, eager to get up and start plowing.

Mistress Lake pushed him back down. "Let us tend to your injuries, Mister Gunstensen. My husband and sons will begin your field work."

The old woman examined Anders gently. Besides the damage to his face, she said, he probably had cracked ribs. His swollen left foot made it seem one or more bones had been broken there as well. "He won't be walking much for a few weeks."

Lake and sons began plowing, manuring, and harrowing the fields. They worked all day while Mistress

Lake cared for Anders and talked with Maria about the wickedness of slavery. Near sundown, she went home with her menfolk, promising to come back often to check on Anders' progress.

Maria remained, with Anders and Tante. Anders slept. Tante offered Maria bread and a bowl of soup. Bone tired, Maria sank into the chair and took her supper.

Tante sat down on the other side of the table and tilted her square head toward Maria. "In dizzy times, the butter still spoils."

In the silence that followed, Tante's words buzzed around in Maria's head, contending with her need for sleep. *Dizzy . . . butter . . .* Butter!

Now she remembered. It was not just one of Tante's sayings. Butter sat in the pantry, churned yesterday before the slave catchers came. Butter and some cheese as well. Had not Anders been beaten last night, he would have made one of his trips to town today. He would have taken the surplus butter and cheese with him and sold them to Mister Eliot for resale in his store. The small payments from Eliot for butter and cheese were an important source of cash. Butter would not go rancid in a day or two; still, it had to be fresh. Maria had almost forgotten.

Anders had always handled business in town. Maria had never set foot in the Sweetwater General Merchandise Company store. But tomorrow, she, not Anders, would take the butter and cheese to Mister Eliot.

#

The man who faced Maria across the counter was groomed with uncommon care. Unlike most American men, clean-shaven Rance Eliot dressed with cool elegance and kept his long hair brushed. The air near him tingled with a spicy fragrance.

I wonder if his money smells as good as he does.

"I was shocked to hear what befell your husband, dear lady." The voice, soft and cultured, matched the face, a portrait of sympathy.

Maria grimaced. "Ja. We shall get over it." She tipped her head toward the counter, on which lay her butter and cheese.

"Oh, yes." He lifted them and placed them in his hanging scale. He jotted numbers on a scrap of paper. "Thirty-five ... forty," he mumbled. He looked up and, seeing her, smiled. "Oh ... let's make it fifty cents."

Maria held out her hand.

Eliot placed two coins on her palm and rolled up her fingers over them. "Please convey my best wishes to your good husband." He gave her hand an extra squeeze.

Maria turned and left. She wondered whether the extra ten cents represented the value Eliot placed on a fleeting squeeze of her hand.

#

Kirsten Haraldsdatter arrived with her children on the third day. Reier and Thor took over the plowing from the Lake men, while Kirsten and the girls helped Maria and Tante with nursing and housekeeping.

Toward sundown, while her sons were still in the fields, Kirsten helped Maria set the table for supper.

"We heard it was slave catchers who beat Anders," Kirsten said.

"What of it?"

"Why would they do that to Anders?"

"They did not catch their slave, and they got angry at Anders about it."

190

Kirsten frowned. "Has he been harboring runaways?"

Maria set down her cutlery, faced Kirsten, and took her by the shoulders. "Suppose he has. It is our farm. Whose business is it?"

Kirsten squirmed. "That's true. You should do as you wish. Only—"

"Only what?"

Kirsten shook off Maria's grasp. "If you play with fire, you will get burned. Too bold, oft brings a thrashing."

Maria snorted. "Tante loves that old saying, too. But I learned an American saying I like better." She continued to set cutlery on the table.

"Yes? What saying?"

"There's only one thing to do with such men. It is to stand up to them."

23. Anders

Illinois

April – June 1856

Anders stumbled across the field with the best gait he could manage while holding a heavy bag of seeds. He turned a hand crank, and a rotating disc at the bottom of the bag flung seeds out over the field. It was an easy way to plant wheat.

He must march straight ahead. Walking a straight line would be easy, except for the pain that jabbed his ribs and squeezed his injured foot with each step. He tried not to grimace. Maria, if she cast her eyes this way, ought to see a contented man doing pleasant work in his field.

His face had mostly resumed its normal color and proportions. And, praise Jesus, the fog in his head had mostly cleared.

He had a good start on planting, thanks to the help of his friends. By mid-May, he would plant all fourteen cultivated acres—half to wheat, half to corn. Then he would start to pull tares from the wheat fields.

#

When mid-May arrived, Anders' plan remained on schedule. Maria came out when she could to help him with the weeds—more than a one-man job, even if he had been healthy. He stood for a moment to ease his back.

"Tomorrow," he said, "I will go down the road to rent a yoke of oxen for a few days."

"It is good to break new land," Maria said, "but what about all this?" She pointed to patches of cutleaf teasel already shooting up among the corn seedlings.

"I will break only a few acres of sod. Then we'll weed some more."

He took comfort in talking of such matters with Maria. They were straightforward, unlike that other thing they could not talk about: the infant whom God had entrusted to their care, then snatched away from them.

The child lay under a crude stone on which he had scratched GUNHILD GUNSTENSEN. What purpose did all this serve? Why did God give you a child and then take her away? What gain did God get from dashing a couple's hopes for posterity? Did Gunhild now rest safe in the bosom of the Lord, or did her unquiet spirit hover near the grave? Now that she was gone, how soon would it be safe to entertain another young soul? How could Anders and Maria talk about that? When would they begin?

#

Anders rented a yoke of oxen and a long-beamed breaking plow from a farmer named O'Bannion. He broke four new acres in as many days. He took the oxen and plow back to O'Bannion and came to work again with Maria. Side by side they attacked the teasel and lambsquarters.

194

Working with Maria in the field, Anders said: "I don't believe God meant us to be childless. He will surely give us a new son in the near future."

Maria made no reply.

A few days later, he brought up the subject again. This time she answered, "What if our daughter's death is a sign from God?"

"How could that be, jenta mi?"

Tears burst from her eyes. Her slight frame trembled with sobs. "Husband, I left Norway to escape the despair that gripped my family. Too many babies lost, too much sadness. Now that sadness has followed me here."

Anders gathered her in and held her in his arms. "My dear, that does not mean our loving God abandons you. He has sailed you across the sea to place you on a new course, in spite of any setback."

#

One day in early July, Anders came in from the blazing fields to the cool shade of the cabin. He found his wife in a state of excitement.

With shaking hands, Maria gave him a folded paper. "It's a letter. The first we've received here."

"Hallelujah!" said Anders.

"Amen," said Aunt Osa.

Maria folded her hands under her chin. "I almost killed the postman. Mister Smithson. He is a giant, hairy man who rides a mule. I took down the gun when I saw him approach. I thought he might be another . . . you know."

"Another slaver, come to thrash us again? Put that out of your mind, jenta mi. At least you did not shoot him, ja?"

195

"Ja. When he approached holding the letter, I put the gun down and let him draw a bucket of water for his mule."

Anders broke the wax seal and unfolded the single paper. "I recognize the hand. It is from my brother Gunder. That prissy schoolmaster writing of his. Everything spelled just so."

"Yes, yes. What does he say?"

Anders skimmed the letter. "Hm. First of all, Father does not feel so well." He frowned. "It must be serious. Gunder thinks the Ministry of Education will soon appoint a new headmaster for the village. Also, he says Mother and Father were much relieved to get my letter which explained about Uncle Torgus' death. And he scolds me for not writing sooner." He lowered the letter and sighed.

"You have that off your conscience now, Husband."

"Ja." He took up the letter again. "Oh, here's news. John decided to emigrate. He will come here."

Maria opened her eyes wide. "Your younger brother? When? When is he coming?"

Anders searched Gunder's neat handwriting. "He says John has already left for America. Let's see. The letter is dated the Third of May, almost two months ago. That means—"

"We can expect him any time."

24. Maria

Illinois

July 1856

Maria carried the butter and cheese to Sweetwater once again. She would rather Anders dealt with Eliot. But since his brother John had arrived, Anders kept busy in the fields, the two men planning together the empire they would build on thirty-four acres of Sugar Grove Township.

Yet the butter and cheese payments could not be neglected, so Maria trudged two miles over hill and dale to the Sweetwater General Mercantile Company.

When she entered, Eliot greeted her with a smile. "Missus Gunstensen! I declare you're pretty as a picture. How nice to see you again."

Maria placed the dairy goods on the counter. She fixed her gaze on them, hoping they would speak for her.

The corners of Eliot's mouth twitched upward. "Not that I don't also enjoy Mister Gunstensen's visits. He's been missed here."

"You will see him soon. Right now, he is busy with his brother from Norway. They work together on the farm."

"His brother. How wonderful." He weighed the butter and cheese. "I'll get your payment for you in a moment. First, let me show you something."

Maria did not like the gleam in Eliot's eye. She did not want to offend the storekeeper, with whom Anders remained on good terms. But what did he want to show her?

"Your husband has already seen it. Follow me." Eliot scooped up her butter and cheese. He marched out the back door. Maria hurried after him.

Behind the store a high mound rose from the earth, a door set into its near face.

"It's a cellar. Come." He took a candle in a holder from a shelf near the door and lit it with a Lucifer match. Holding the light in one hand and the dairy goods in the other, he disappeared down a wooden stairway.

Eliot had Maria's dairy goods, not yet paid for. For that reason alone, she followed him into the loam-scented dark, making sure to leave the door open behind them.

"This will assure you of the care we take with your cheese and butter." Setting the dairy goods on a shelf, he turned to her and placed a hand on her shoulder. "Notice how cool it is?"

What she noticed was his hand. She jumped back, breaking contact.

"There you see it," said Eliot. He thrust the flickering candle into the darkness ahead. "My pride and joy."

The candle lit blocks of ice, stacked with layers of straw between them.

Eliot's eyes glittered. "There is no spring on the property. No cold water bubbling up from the ground. Therefore, no way to keep your goods cool." He hovered

198

over Maria while lecturing. "So, I dug this cellar when I came here fifteen years ago and I paid for tons of ice to be hauled in from Brady's Pond, five miles away. Just to keep your butter and eggs cool for my customers to buy." He leaned closer and giggled. "This way, I also have ice for the occasional mint julep."

Maria stepped backwards again. "What is mint julep?"

"It's a southern drink. Best with ice. A small comfort after my long day's work." He leaned forward. "O, my dear, do not think me a drunkard. I assure you, I am a temperate man."

Maria could think of nothing to say.

"Did you know I came here from Mississippi?"

"No. Anders never said."

"Perhaps I've never told him. But I am strangely drawn to divulge things to you. I was, you see, a young man of substance and property, until the so-called Panic of Thirty-Seven."

"Panic?"

"That's what they called it. As if the fearfulness of a few men could stampede the markets and ruin the Yeoman Farmer. They conjured it up on purpose, don't you see? Yankee traders and bankers. I call it the *Betrayal* of Thirty-Seven, that's what I call it. You must agree."

There was fire in his eyes.

Maria gulped. "Ja."

"My pappy had a thousand acres and a hundred slaves. Poof! Gone in a moment. I was ruined. Mortified." He grasped her arm with his free hand.

She wrenched it free.

He shook himself. "But forgive me, dear lady. This old history is nothing to you. In brief, I came here and started over, that's all." His smile hung heavy with

199

shyness. "Something about you—your sincerity, I suppose—compels me to confide."

He pulled a coin from his pocket and handed it to Maria. "Perhaps we should go back before I forget myself further."

Maria fled up the stairs into the sunshine.

"Good-bye, Mister Eliot," she called back over her shoulder. "Thank you."

Before he could reply, she scurried homeward, clutching the half dollar he had paid.

From now on, Anders must handle all business with Rance Eliot.

25. Daniel

Arkansas

August 1856

Daniel skipped sideways as a red hen darted out with the abruptness of God's providence. It would be blasphemy not to accept the gift.

She saw him and sped up. She meandered, bobbing her head, crisscrossing the road, kicking up puffs of yellow dust. Daniel stayed behind her. After a time, she relaxed a moment. Daniel stooped and scooped. The hen squawked.

Down the road, a drab cabin huddled by the woods. A man poked his head out the cabin door. "Hey!"

Daniel wrung the chicken's neck and ran—back the way he came, around a curve, off the road into the woods on the left. With the noise the farmer raised, it took all Daniel's will to slow down and move as Sammy had taught him. Silently.

He peered from behind a bush as the man stopped and gawked at the woods on both sides of the road. The man raised a shotgun to his shoulder, chose the same side Daniel had chosen, and plunged into the forest.

Daniel's hand rested on the cold metal of his own gun. He breathed slow and deep. The worst thing now would be to fire a shot.

The man with the shotgun turned this way and that. He squinted as if half blind. *Maybe it's so. Lord, let him be short of sight.*

When the man stalked further into the thicket, Daniel slipped back to the road. He trotted in his former direction. Nearing the cabin, he took to the woods on the other side of the road, to avoid the farmer's kin. He skirted the cabin and kept on through the woods. When he had put a mile behind him, he stopped to rest.

The limp hen was still in his hands. Sitting on a downed log, he placed the bird in a moisture-proof bag inside his knapsack. *God bless you, Mister Van Doorn.*

#

When Daniel had sent Betsey on to Canada, he had left Gunson's place and retraced his steps, headed for Quincy. He followed the railroad, traveling by night and hiding by day. Even on the smooth railroad bed with gravel ballast between the ties, the journey took ten days. The meat and bread that Gunson had given him lasted two days. He began taking terrible risks to steal food from small towns along the way. His stomach felt like a useless thing under his ribs by the time he slipped through the pre-dawn streets of Quincy, on the banks of the Mississippi.

He waited until John Van Doorn arrived to open up his sawmill for the day. Daniel stepped out from between two stacks of finished boards and hissed. The red-bearded lumber baron, a large man in his forties, staggered back half a step, his face tense. He held out his hands in a fighting posture, then relaxed.

"Why, bless my soul, it's Daniel." Van Doorn beamed. "We prayed you would come back but didn't know faw shoo-ah that you would." Daniel guessed he meant "for sure."

Van Doorn opened the door of the sawmill, led Daniel inside, and took him up to his office on the second floor. "You look thin. Have you breakfasted?"

"Naw suh. Not that I recollect."

"Sit ye down. Let's have a talk."

Daniel sat.

Van Doorn strode from the room. His voice boomed through the open doorway as he greeted his factory hands and gave them orders for the day. The mill's giant circular saw whirled to life, whining through fresh logs.

The mill owner came back into the room and shut the door, blocking half the sound. "Noisy, ain't it?"

"It is, Mister Van Doorn."

"That's paht of the price we pay for the privilege of sawing timber." Van Doorn sat down in a wooden swivel chair by his big pigeonhole desk. "I must say I'm at least hahf surprised to see you here." *Half, he means.*

"I told you I would come back."

"You must have been tempted to go on to Canada."

"Betsey's on her way there now. I got to go south. Just come back to pick up the gun I left with you."

Van Doorn frowned. "You still plan to go all the way to Louisiana? There are plenty of slaves just ovah the rivah in Missouri whom you could liberate."

"These ones in Loosiana is my special friends."

"So be it." The big man gave him a look of frank appraisal. "Now, what if I told you that I already threw away that old musket of yours?"

Daniel's heart sank. *I thought you was my friend.* He glared at Van Doorn's open, curious face. "You had no right to do that, suh. Thass my gun."

"Very old." Van Doorn knotted his forehead. "A museum piece."

"What that mean, a museum piece?"

"It means the next time you fire it, or the time ahftah, it could blow up in your face. Maim you if not kill you."

"Worked just fine for me." *Once, anyways.* Daniel had shot a deer on his way north with Betsey. The risk of the shot being heard was terrible, but they had been on the verge of starving.

Van Doorn shook his head. "It might explode, or fall apaht, at any time. Besides, it's infernal heavy."

"Guns be heavy. Can't help it."

The big man raised his russet eyebrows as if to argue, but just then the door opened.

Charles Sidener, the owner's black assistant, came in with a package in white paper. He set it on a table by Daniel's chair. "Open it."

"Hello, Mister Sidener. Glad to see you again."

"Fill your belly, Daniel. We can talk later."

Steam rose when Daniel opened the package. "Hot biscuits!"

"From the bakery up the street. There's little jar of honey in there, too." Sidener grinned as Daniel bit into a honey-smeared biscuit.

Van Doorn bent down without leaving his swivel chair, opened a drawer, and brought out an object wrapped in brown leather. "Hee-yah. It's a Colt Navy."

"Colt Navy?"

"Thutty-six calibah."

The leather wrapper was a holster. A brown strap looped over the wooden grip of a handgun. Van Doorn pulled the strap from its slot and withdrew the gun. "It's a repeating pistol." He handed it to Daniel.

Daniel wiped crumbs from his fingers before taking the gun. "Fits right in my hand," he said. "Ain't much heavy, neither."

"It's you-ahs, Daniel. Along with the holster and belt." Van Doorn glanced up at Sidener. "You know that othah thing we talked about?"

"Oh, yes." Sidener went out the office door.

"You won't have to occupy your hands carrying this thing," said Van Doorn. "It will just hang at your side till you need it. And it fires six shots without reloading. Cap and ball."

"Cap and ball?"

"We'll teach you how to use it."

Sidener came back in with something else. "Look at this, Daniel. It's a knapsack." He held out a pinewood box covered by leather on its front, back, and sides. "Those two straps are for your shoulders, so you can wear it on your back. Open it up."

Metal snaps on the front flap came open when Daniel tugged. Inside the box was a bag with a drawstring, almost as large as the box itself.

"That bag's oilcloth," Sidener said. "Waterproof. You could use it for fresh-killed game or other wet items, so your other goods stay dry."

Those other goods included balls, powder, wads, and caps for the pistol, a Bowie knife, a tight tin container with fifty lucifer matches, a flint and steel to help conserve the matches, a tin cup for water, a dozen fishhooks with fifty feet of strong fishing line, and a length of unbleached cloth. "That's in case you get hurt and need to bandage yourself."

"You call this, knapsack?"

"Yes. Simeon and Monroe Clark built it at Mister Van Doorn's suggestion."

"Our troops carried them in the war with Mexico," said Van Doorn. "Thought you might find it useful."

"But you din' think I was comin' back."

Van Doorn laughed. "I said I did not know faw shoo-ah. But it's best to be prepayahd for anything."

Daniel hefted the revolver again. He slipped it into its holster and pushed the cover flap through its slot.

"Anything else you need? Maybe Chahlie can get it for you."

"More of that strong fishing line," Daniel said.

Sidener raised his eyebrows.

"For snares. Catch wild creatures without using my gun."

"I'll get you some, right away."

"And a hat? Lost my old one when I had to ride under a bunch of corn bags."

#

At dusk, having put more miles between himself and the cabin where he had stolen the chicken, Daniel built a small fire in a thicket far off the road and roasted his prize. He reckoned the gloaming to be the safest time to make a fire. The smoke would blend with the dusk. As to the flame, it would not burn so bright in a gray woods as in a black one.

He had learned many such lessons in his trek northward with Betsey. It had been a long spell of unrelieved danger until, in Quincy, Illinois, they were spotted by Charlie Sidener, who had led them to his boss, Van Doorn. Now back in slave country, Daniel put his lessons to use again. This time he had a lightweight gun, a large knife, and that wonderful knapsack filled with useful items like fishing line.

Van Doorn and Sidener had rowed him downriver at night in a skiff, dropping him on a wooded bank below Hannibal, Missouri. The hills and woods of Missouri and Arkansas offered safer haven than the east bank, where Kentucky, Tennessee, Mississippi, and southern Illinois crawled with slavers.

Missouri and Arkansas were slave country also, but the farms were fewer and smaller. Once you got away from the river, you could follow any country road south and even by day you could generally avoid white folks. In these parts, black folk commonly walked the roads, hired out by their owners to work other men's acres. If seen, you might be taken for a local. This day's adventure had been an unexpected close call—all because of the hen's squawk.

As his teeth teased the chicken meat from bone and tendon, it seemed worth the risk he had taken to get it. Nevertheless, Daniel considered going back to night-only travel. It would slow him down, but Louisiana was closer every day.

26. Daniel

Louisiana

October – December 1856

Daniel found Camp Espère Pas just where he had left it. He had used seventeen matches, fifty feet of fishing line— and no caps and balls.

After leaving the upland maroons, with whom he had rested some days, Daniel had spent two weeks on the banks of the big bayou, using his Bowie knife to hew and shape a small dugout canoe or pirogue. Better a boat than by foot, getting around the swamps.

He beached his pirogue near Camp Espère Pas and slipped through the trees into the middle of the camp. He carried his Bowie knife at the ready, remembering how tense things could be in Luc's domain.

"Well, well, well—looky who the Lord brought back to us." Bijou, Luc's large-framed wife, stood up from the pot she tended over the central fire. She mothered Daniel in a fierce hug, heedless of the big knife in his hand.

"It's nice to see you, too," Daniel said when his breath came back to him. "Where's Luc?" Only women and children stood about the campsite, and a couple of old men.

"Luc took the men off huntin' wild pigs."

"Pigs?"

"More hogs in the woods now than when you lived here, honey. They gets away from plantations, runs loose, gets theyselves families. Pretty soon they is wild game, like any other."

"Is that a fact."

"But plenty more dangerous. Big hog can kill a man, he don't watch out. They hunts 'em with lances—is what they call 'em." She snorted. "Really they's just sharp sticks."

#

Late that day the men came back with a dead hog slung under a bowed timber. Six men carried it, three on each end of the pole. The men were in high spirits after a hunt that would give the whole colony meat for a month plus sinews, guts, bones, hooves, and coarse bristles.

Luc led the parade, his chest bare and smeared with pig blood like some savage chieftain. When Luc saw Daniel, he stopped in his tracks. With a cold eye, he raked Daniel from head to toe. "You back again? Thought we was rid of you for good."

Daniel stepped forward, stopping just short of Luc. "Did you know, Mister Luc, they's a whole world out there? And people don't have to live this way no more. They's freedom up north. Thass why I left here."

"Then why you come back?"

"I got friends need to get free. Friends on Petitbon Plantation."

"What that got to do with us?"

"Maybe you could help."

210

Luc stared at him. "Don't you go settin' off that thing."

"What thing?"

"That thing a-hangin' on your trousers. Guns cause us nothin' but trouble."

Daniel smiled. "Got it from a friend up north. White feller give it to me, matter of fact. I not be shootin' it off around here, though."

"You don't get none of this pig. You din't catch it like we did."

"I can catch my own game."

"Not with no gun."

"Tell you what, Luc," Daniel said. "I'll sneak up on 'em and hit 'em over the haid with the butt end of my pistol, how about that?"

Some of the maroons sniggered.

Luc frowned and pointed beyond the row of huts. "If you wants to build you a place over that end of camp, I won't stop you." He turned away to oversee the division of the hog.

#

Daniel built the smallest shelter he could make do with. When Jerry, Amos and other maroons came around to make fun of his tiny hut, he explained that he did not plan to stay long.

One week passed into another. Luc avoided Daniel's company. Daniel snared and cooked his own game. No problem with that. But he needed Luc's help. Having come all the way from Menard County, Illinois, Daniel had no idea how to get back to Petitbon's place.

Unless Luc helped him, how could Daniel ever find his way back to Quintus and Micah, to prove to them by

211

his presence that their fears of escape were groundless? Mammy would not want him to fail in this mission.

O Lord, O Mammy, O Somebody—please unharden the heart of Mister Luc.

#

Daniel gave Luc two weeks. Then he went and stepped in the big man's path when he came back to his hut after a call of nature.

"Get out my way," said Luc.

"Talk to me," said Daniel.

Luc swung a backhand.

Daniel ducked and bobbed back up again, grinning. "Talk to me."

Luc's arm flashed again, this time with a blade at the end of it.

Daniel did not move. The point of the knife touched his throat. "We done this before. Don't you get tired of doing the same thing alla time?"

Luc flung the knife, embedding it in a tree. He glared at Daniel.

"Thass better," Daniel said. "I need somebody show me the way to Petitbon's."

"Haw!" Luc bent double with mirth. "You come here from Petitbon to start with, but you can't find your way back?"

"Don't you recollect? I's lost and bewildered when you and Sammy found me."

Luc glowered at the mention of Sammy. "You went back there with my boy one time. A time I'd like as soon forget."

Daniel sighed. "I could prob'ly find it from the old camp. But thass miles from here."

Luc looked at Daniel squinty-eyed.

212

Daniel tapped him on the chest. "You come over my place round suppertime. I got a big catfish. Give you some." He turned and walked away.

#

Luc approached in the evening, as Daniel roasted his fish on a grill of woven willow twigs over a low fire.

Daniel looked up at him. "Din't you bring no plate? How you gonna carry some fish home to Bijou?"

"Keep your catfish, eat it yourself. We got plenty."

"Happy to," Daniel said. "Then what'd you come for?"

Luc squatted opposite Daniel. His face softened, its planes shifted in the firelight. "If you get your friends outta there, then you leave here for good?"

"Yeh. I take 'em up North."

"You know Henry?"

"Old man, stumbles around, keeps company with Marcellus?"

Luc nodded. "Thass the one."

"He's new to me. Weren't here before, when I was."

"He come into our camp last fall along with his daughter, Dorie. They was slaves at the Avery place. She had her belly full of it and lit out, takin' him along, and they found us. But Dorie took fever and died in the spring. Ever since then, we stuck with him."

"Why, he that much bother?"

"Well, Marcellus, you know, he old like Henry, but at least he can do somethin'. He weaves baskets out of willow wands. He can make pots from clay, too, in the fire. Right handy."

"Yes, he is."

"Old Henry can't do nothing. Just eats. Waiting to die. Can't take him huntin'. He just be in the way."

213

Daniel sniffed the aroma of the baking fish. He turned it over. "Hmm."

"I been thinkin', maybe Henry better off up North."

"He got people up there?"

"He would have, if you took him. You and your friends from Petitbon."

Daniel frowned. He took the fish off the fire and examined it. "That be your price for helpin' me?"

"It is. Then I be done with all of you at once."

"All right. I'll take Henry."

Luc stared into the fire a moment. "Okay, then. I guide you to Petitbon."

#

Daniel spoke with old Henry the next day. Wobbly, palsied, with a glassy film over one eye, it seemed he could do nothing but tell strange stories to the colony's children.

"How old are you, Henry?"

The old man sat on a mat, whittling on a stick. "Mercy me, young Daniel, I don't know. Nobody ever done told me. Reckon I's old enough to be your grandpappy."

"When I get back here with Quintus and Micah, we gonna light out for the North. You comin' along with us. You'd best practice your walkin', so's you can keep up."

"Oh, I keep up, Son, don't you worry. Luc don't want me here, I go with you. Thass all right then."

Daniel wished he could tell how much the old man understood of the trip they would take together. He sighed.

#

Luc and Jerry led the way, poling Luc's pirogue, while Daniel followed in his own one-man craft.

214

"Remember every twist and turn," Luc had said. "We gonna get you there, and we'll pick up some appropriations, but then we leave again quick. No waitin' around for you. Gotta find your own way back."

They left mid-morning and poled most of the day, resting at places Daniel took care to memorize. They reached Petitbon's plantation at nightfall. As before, they stopped short of the plantation landing and beached their canoes under the hidden trail that led to the slave quarters.

"I go first," said Luc. "You stay here with Jerry till I get back. Then we leave, and you on your own." He faded into the bushes, carrying a Marcellus-made basket filled with maroon swamp goods.

"How long he gonna be, you think?" Daniel asked.

Jerry shrugged. "However long he be, thass how long we waits."

Daniel prayed to his mammy for patience. Now on the cusp of fulfilling his vow to rescue Quintus and Micah, he wanted to get on with it.

Luc stayed away a long time. Daniel and Jerry made small talk.

"You really been all the way up North?"

"Yup."

"What it's like?"

Daniel stretched his limbs. "It gets real cold in winter and spring. Snow and all that."

"Man, I like to see that."

"Not so bad, you got enough clothes."

Jerry nodded. "Got mighty cold here, too, 'bout a year ago. In the fall. Hard frost come early. Then everything got colder. Like near froze to death."

"How come you din't?"

"Things got warmer again. You been to Canada?"

215

"No. Not that far. Sent Betsey, though. Hope she's all right."

Rustling came from the bushes. Luc's head appeared, then the rest of him. His basket now held plantation goods. Something clinked as he lugged the basket to the pirogue.

Luc turned to Daniel as he climbed into the pirogue with Jerry. "I spoke with Hattie. She say your friends Quintus and Micah still live in the same old cabin. She gone keep her mouth shut." He turned to Jerry. "Let's go," he said. They shoved off, leaving Daniel alone.

His moment had come. *Look out for me, Mammy.*

He crept through the bushes and up the slave trail, his Colt Navy dragging his belt down, the knapsack with all his possessions on his back.

#

He stood at the cabin door. Low voices inside. Quintus and Micah, nobody else.

He rapped lightly. The voices stopped. He rapped again.

The door opened a crack. Daniel stood in moonlight, but the crack in the door showed only darkness. Micah's voice came from inside. "Who that?"

"It's me. Daniel."

"Daniel! Come in, boy." The door opened wide. "Get some light, Quintus."

A match flared, a lantern lit up. By its soft glow, Daniel entered.

"Daniel, boy," Quintus said. "Good to see you."

The cabin stood just as on the day Daniel left, except his pallet of straw was gone. Quintus and Daniel had pallets, one on each side of the cabin. At the back stood the little potbelly stove they cooked all their meals on. The two slaves' brogans and work outfits lay on the dirt floor by their pallets. They themselves were barefoot and wore their nightshirts.

"Lookit you, boy," said Micah. "Got yourself some nice boots, a pistol, nice little kit on your back. You musta been somewhere since we see you last. Come, sit on my bed, tell us about it." He spread his arm in invitation, and Daniel sat down.

"Here." Daniel took off his knapsack, opened it, and pulled out a couple of items. "I brung you some bacon from a wild hog—traded it off a maroon name of Luc—and a small fish I caught this mornin' in the bayou."

Quintus eyed the offerings with glee. "Thankee kindly, Brother. We eat good tomorrow night. You gonna stay around long enough to dine with us?"

The vision of a satisfying meal shared with his best friends was almost more than Daniel could bear. "I can't," he said. "Got a pirogue down on the stream bank. Somebody finds it by day, we's all in trouble. I got to be gone before sunlight."

"Oh," said Quintus. "Thass a shame."

"Listen. I come to take you two back with me. I think my canoe hold three of us. If not, I take you one at a time."

The two slaves' mouths hung open.

Micah's expression turned to one of joy. "Thass a marvel, Daniel. Ain't it, Quintus?"

Quintus sat mute.

"You take us to freedom," said Micah. "Right, Daniel?"

"Thass it, boys." He felt a warm glow, giving them the news.

"Where we go?" asked Quintus.

"First, we go to Camp Espère Pas. Thass where the maroons live. Then we head north."

"North?"

217

"Land of the Drinking Gourd," said Micah. "The Big Dipper. Ain't you heard tell of it?"

Quintus put his hand to his mouth. "Reckon so, yeah. You been there, Daniel?"

"Sure have. There and back."

"Is it good there?"

Daniel laughed. "Good? Why—"

"If it's good, why you come back?"

"To bring you there, 'cause you my friends."

"Uh huh." Quintus nodded, but his face looked glum. "Pretty fur piece, ain't it?"

"Long walk," Daniel said. "We make it just fine, though."

"Uh huh."

"Whassa matter?" Micah said. He stood and started to pull on his trousers. "Let's get up and go now."

"Hmm. Reckon I got to sleep on it."

#

"They ain't comin'?" Luc boggled.

Daniel, steaming, paced back and forth in Luc's hut. "Micah was all set to go, but Quintus. Well, Quintus got to think on it first." He struck his palm with his fist.

"You still takin' Henry."

"I ain't takin' nobody till Quintus and Micah come."

Bijou laid her hand on Daniel's shoulder. "How you gonna fix that, honey?"

"I told 'em I come back by the full moon, and they better be ready to go."

"Full moon!" Luke bellowed. "Thass weeks away yet."

Daniel shrugged. "Quintus, he mighty fearful. It's just the way he is. He don't like to rush into things."

Daniel left Luc's hut at dawn. Time to go check his snares.

218

Three weeks later—weeks of impatient waiting and dark looks from Luc—Daniel returned to the Petitbon plantation.

Shivering, he slipped out of the woods by the light of the full moon and crept down the row of cabins, seeking shade where he could find it. Moon on frosty ground seemed like day. He felt naked. What if Mas' Petitbon or the overseer, McCutcheon, came along?

He rapped on the cabin door. This time it swung open without words exchanged.

The lantern already glowed in the cabin. Quintus regarded him with a long face. Micah simmered with excitement.

And they had a boy in the cabin.

"Who this?"

"Name's Josiah."

"What he's doin' here?"

Quintus cleared his throat. "Daniel. You goin' without me. But you gotta take Josiah."

"What?"

"We been talkin' about this," said Micah. "They's things goin' on here you don't know about, Daniel."

"Things like what?" Daniel sat down on Micah's pallet to listen.

Micah tipped his head toward Quintus.

"They was a hard frost round here las' year," Quintus said. "Done kilt all Mas' Petitbon's seed cane."

"Yeh?"

"Yeh. So, this year, whole lot less to harvest. We done finished harvest already, squeezed all the juice, sent it off. Maybe half what we usually do."

"So? Why you tell me all this?"

219

"Petitbon and McCutcheon been in a foul mood. Massa don't know whether to buy all new seed cane or change over to cotton. They takin' out their fury on the slaves. Any little thing, they bring out the whip."

"Seems like thass all the more reason to go."

Quintus' long face cracked itself into the saddest smile Daniel had ever seen. "I can't leave all my friends to suffer this without me."

Silence filled the cabin as Daniel took this in.

"Maybe I can help calm things down," Quintus said.

"And I say he's a damn fool," Micah said. "So I'm goin', but he ain't." He got to his feet. "Let's go now."

"But you gotta take Josiah," said Quintus. "Take him in my place."

Daniel shook his head. "I can't take no babies along."

Josiah waved a finger in his face. "I ain't no baby."

"How old you, Son?"

"He almost twelve," Micah said.

Daniel scoffed. "Boy so small?"

"I's bigger'n I look," Josiah said.

"Josiah's all alone," said Quintus. "His pappy died last year, then his mammy. Think how you'd feel if you was a young boy and both your pappy and mammy dead."

Daniel had never told Quintus and Micah of his life before Petitbon Plantation.

"Tonight be Christmas," noted Micah.

Daniel sighed. "All right. Let's go."

They slid down the trail on the frosty ground and got into Daniel's pirogue. He had brought an extra pole so Micah could help. However, the small craft rode so low with the three of them that Daniel told Micah to hunker down, not rock the boat, and throw away the pole. Barely afloat, they made their way back to Camp Espère Pas.

27. Anders

Illinois

January – June 1857

Pounding on the cabin door startled Anders.

He looked out the window. "It is that mail fellow, I think. His mule stands in the yard behind him."

John looked up from strips of harness he was trying to re-join. "Mail?"

"Fiddlesticks!" Aunt Osa scolded her knitting. "An unbelled horse in winter!"

Anders frowned. "Why comes he here in a snowstorm?"

Maria put the kettle on. "Open the door, Husband, and find out."

Anders opened the door. The tall postman, bundled in furs, held a white envelope. "Your second letter from Norway in six months. Thought it might be important."

Anders took the letter. "Thank you."

"Come in, Mister Smithson!" Maria called from the fireplace. "Do not stand with the door open."

Smithson stepped inside. Snow fell off his shoulders. "Thank you kindly, Miz Gunstensen, only—"

"Only what?"

"Well, Katie." Smithson pulled a long face. "Hate to leave her standin' in the cold."

"You can put Katie in the warm barn for a while. Our horses will like that. Anders will help you. Then come back and have coffee."

Anders left the letter on the table and went with the postman to stable his mule.

When they came back, the scraps of broken harness had been swept from the table. Aunt Osa poured black coffee into Maria's good teacups while Maria placed squares of sponge cake on small plates around the table.

"Thank you, Ma'am," said Smithson. "Right neighborly. I thought you said coffee."

"Well," Anders said, "there is coffee, ja. But when we say coffee, we never mean coffee only. There is always something else to go with it."

"And you came all this way to bring the letter," said Maria. "We can't let you rush off."

John picked up the letter and gave it to Anders. "It is addressed to you, Brother."

Anders knew the writer's hand. "It's from Father."

"His writing looks a bit shaky," John noted.

"Hm." Father's cursive script was definite and angular, as always, but John was right. The strong strokes were broken by little waves, as from a palsied hand.

"Well, Husband, will you open it?"

Anders did so. He scanned the page, then read aloud, "Dear Son and Daughter-in-Law, I send you greetings from our good King Oskar and from all your friends and neighbors here in his Norwegian provinces—Father can never start a speech without some sort of ceremony in it.

"I must inform you that my health has declined, so that now your brother Gunder has become schoolmaster for our village—This is what Gunder himself predicted when he wrote us last summer, jenta mi.—Now the education ministry must hire someone else to be assistant teacher. If you had been here, dear Anders, it could have been you."

Anders gritted his teeth. But Maria gazed at him with untroubled brow. He read on.

"Nevertheless, he says, 'I understand your position. I always said you would have to fend for yourself. It grieves me that you felt constrained to do so in America. But that is the way of things. Young men here have not the opportunities afforded across the sea.

'Since you and I may not meet again on this earth, I take pen in hand to say that I am proud of you, my independent son. That is why I am content that your brother John follows in your footsteps. Only, I ask this: That in all things you both continue to comport yourselves with honor and do what is right, not giving any regard to profit or loss.'"

Tears flowed down Anders' cheeks. A lump was in his throat.

"Thus you may know yourselves to be men of consequence and respect in the society where our Lord has placed you.

"Your mother also sends her love. I am humbly and sincerely yours, Gunsten Gunderson, Schoolmaster Emeritus, Village of Øiestad."

#

As the winter wore on, Anders mulled over this missive from his father.

223

The old man clearly meant that he was not long for this world. Anders had always looked to him as an example of the right way to live. From now on, Anders would have to look to himself, to be his own exemplar. And John, as younger brother, had the right to expect that Anders would show him the way of honor and probity.

Sometimes his choices in life, such as aiding the slaves who were so monstrously wronged, placed him at odds with Maria. Not because she approved of slavery, but because her practical mind fastened itself upon dangers— some imaginary and some, alas, real. Still, in examining his conscience could find no decision that gave him shame.

On a sunny day in late January, Anders, hiked into Sweetwater with Maria's butter and cheese. Several locals, including Charlie Simmons and the Blodgett brothers, sat around Eliot's pot-bellied woodstove, debating matters of national and local importance. Simmons, a former Whig, buttressed his arguments with news from the *Illinois State Journal*, a Republican paper.

After Eliot gave him a dollar for his unusually large delivery of butter and cheese, Anders said, "I would like to buy a newspaper."

"You want a newspaper? It would give me pleasure to let you read my copy."

"No, no," said Anders. "I mean, to have the newspaper come to my farm, every week."

Eliot smiled. "You want a subscription." He reached under his counter and brought out a receipt book.

"Ja. A subscription."

"Five dollars for a year. Six issues a week."

Anders inhaled sharply.

Eliot raised his eyebrows. "Of course, you could get just one issue a week for two dollars a year, but then you'd miss so much. These days, a farmer needs a paper, it's just that simple."

"A farmer needs it?"

"They print farm prices. You'll know what hogs or cattle fetch, day by day, in Springfield and Saint Louis. Then you can reckon up what price you need to get here in Menard."

"I see. Still, five dollars ..."

"If the cost is worrying you, Anders, may I suggest you try a three-month subscription? Only one dollar and a quarter. If you don't see the value after three months, you can quit."

"Ja. That will be good. Three months."

Anders gave back the dollar Eliot had paid him and added a silver quarter to it.

"You won't regret it. It'll be a big help on prices. A word to the wise, though: Disregard all that political palaver on the back pages. It's biased."

#

Silas Smithson and his mule became regular visitors. Though letters were a rarity, the newspaper came six days a week. On long winter nights, Anders and John pored over its dense columns by lamplight, trying to decipher the news.

Prices for crops and livestock were shown in dollars. But dollars per what? Anders already knew that "lbs." for some reason meant pounds. He begged his friend Benjamin Lake to tell him the meaning of "cwt." It turned out to be a hundredweight, one hundred pounds.

He and John would soon have a surplus of pigs to sell. The paper would tell him the price at Springfield. If buyers at Petersburg offered far below Springfield prices, they would take their pigs to Springfield. The paper was already starting to prove its worth.

Although Mister Eliot had warned against reading the political news, Anders and John found it engrossing. "Naturally Eliot does not agree," said John. "The paper is clearly Republican. And Eliot, though he tries to conceal it, is sympathetic to the Slave Power."

"What is this Slave Power, Brother? Where did you get those words?"

"They are right here in the paper, Anders."

"What can they mean?"

John grinned. "I think Slave Power means all the men in Congress who make decisions for the nation in light of their own preference to keep slaves."

"Southerners, you mean. The notion of a Slave Power seems like a separate government."

"Let us pray it does not come to that."

But on Monday, March 9, Anders was dismayed to read an article headed, "Buchanan Dances to Taney's Tune."

The editor of the *State Journal* had written: "Democrats who might have supposed James Buchanan to be a smoother pitchman for slavery than his predecessor Franklin Pierce must be unnerved by their new man's clownish posturing on the matter of Dred Scott."

"Dred Scott?" John asked, reading over Anders' shoulder. "What is Dred Scott?"

"I don't know, Brother." Anders moved the paper directly under the lantern and squinted to discern the news unfolded there.

The brothers figured out that Dred Scott was a slave who had sued for his freedom in court. Scott's attorney argued that when his master took him from Missouri into the free states of Illinois and Wisconsin, he had automatically become a free man. The case had been decided by the Supreme Court in Washington. Chief

Justice Taney had declared that a black man could not be a citizen of the United States. If that black man was a slave, he must be considered property only. And the Court ruled the Missouri Compromise of 1820 unconstitutional—casting doubt on whether any state could outlaw slavery, even within its own borders.

This news by itself had Anders and John steaming, but there was more. Buchanan, the new president, had said in his March 4 inaugural address that slavery was "a judicial question, which legitimately belongs to the Supreme Court of the United States, before whom it is now pending, and will, it is understood, be speedily and finally settled. To their decision, in common with all good citizens, I shall cheerfully submit." These words suggested that Buchanan did not care which way the matter was settled. He would "cheerfully submit" to the decision, either way. But the Court's decision was announced only two days after the inauguration. Who could believe that the new president, a pro-slavery Democrat with connections on the Court, did not know the outcome in advance?

"Buchanan's sly semaphore of impartiality must be engraved in the annals of history as the most brazen chicanery ever inflicted upon our long-suffering public," harumphed the editor. Anders and John agreed.

"You asked about the Slave Power," said John. "Maybe I should have said the Slave Power is our own government."

After three months, Anders renewed his subscription to the *Illinois State Journal*. By that time, however, he and John were busy preparing and planting the fields. The leisurely winter gave way to the busy spring. Anders was so tired at night that he fell asleep before he finished perusing the farm prices.

But while he spread manure, plowed and harrowed, planted his corn and spring wheat, and then began the weeding and cultivation necessary to ensure good crops, the question of slavery came back to his mind. How could a whole race of people be relegated to the status of livestock? "Chattel slavery" meant that people were regarded as mere chattels, the personal property of other people, who could do with them as they wished. This could not be right.

Despite his previous work in Benjamin Lake's Underground Railroad operation, Anders had little direct experience with slaves, other than Daniel and his friend Betsey. Daniel had gone south again to free more of his friends. Anders had heard nothing further. He wondered what had become of Daniel.

28. Daniel

Illinois

June 1857

Daniel stepped from the bushes into the nighttime street. He peered both ways. Nobody in sight. Good.

A rustling came from the thicket behind him. "Shh!" he commanded. The sound ceased. *Josiah thinks now we in Illinois we safe.* The boy's lapses were rare and brief. Since leaving Camp Espère Pas six months ago, Daniel had trained his three traveling mates to be on the lookout always, to move with stealth, to leave no trace at all. *Be a shame to get caught now we so near to Canada.*

Daniel loped across an intersection and down a block of small houses. He counted one, two, three . . . the fourth house on the north side of the street. Sure enough: one and a half stories, white house, best on the block, like he'd been told.

Light beckoned, yellow in the window. Daniel tiptoed up the porch steps. He knocked on the door. Nothing happened. He checked both directions again.

The door swung open. A tall, bearded black man stood there.

The man pulled Daniel inside. "Yes, Brother? Something on your mind?"

"This be Springfield?"

"That's right."

"Mister Donnegan?"

The man smiled. "William K. Donnegan. At your service."

"I'm Daniel. I come with three friends. They in the bushes." He jerked his head back toward the vacant lot. "Followin' the Dipper. Need to see Mister Lake in Menard County."

Donnegan's gaze raked Daniel from top to toe, lingered at his boots, scarred from slogging hundreds of miles. A double winding of shellacked muslin, almost worn through, bound the sole of the right boot to its upper. Frizzy threads stuck out at angles.

"Mm-mm. We'll do something about those boots. I'll make you a new pair."

Daniel frowned. "You do know Mister Benjamin Lake? Sweetwater, Menard County?"

Donnegan pursed his lips. "Never met the man. Heard of him, though. Pretty sure I know where he lives."

Daniel had hoped for a more solid connection. Could this man be trusted?

Donnegan turned his face to a young woman standing in the parlor. "Honey, rustle up some bacon and beans for Daniel and his friends."

The woman went out through a door in the back of the room.

"You hungry?" Donnegan asked.

"Some, I reckon."

"Were you followed?"

"No. I made sure."

"Run back quick and bring them on," Donnegan said. No time for further doubts.

Daniel went and brought back his traveling mates—Micah, young Josiah, and Henry. On the long trek from Louisiana, Josiah had failed to become the burden that Daniel had feared. Instead, he had boundless energy, endless cheerfulness, and the ability to learn many new skills. He excelled at trapping, fishing, and woodcraft but had also mastered the light-fingered and swift-footed appropriation of food from farms and town lots they passed.

Henry, despite his assurances to the contrary, was the one who could not keep up. His aged joints slowed their progress. On three separate occasions the little band had holed up for a week or more while the old man recovered from fits of ague. Nevertheless, Henry, like Micah and Josiah, made no complaints.

When Daniel had gotten his traveling mates into Donnegan's house, the big man, a cobbler by trade, measured Daniel's feet and went out to his shop. His young wife fed Daniel and his mates, then led them up a narrow stairs to a garret under the sloped roof. She left them. The four lay down to sleep.

In the middle of the night, rough hands shook Daniel awake.

"Here, try these on."

A match flared, a candle gleamed. Donnegan gave Daniel a pair of brown leather boots. The nicest boots he had ever seen. He slipped his feet into them. They were perfect.

"A hasty job," said Donnegan. "But they'll do."

"Thank you," Daniel said. "I got no money."

"We'll put the boots on account."

"On account? What account?"

Donnegan cackled. "*On account* you need somethin' to wear on your feet."

Daniel and Donnegan roused the others and herded them downstairs. Outside, in the dark alley, all four of them climbed into the false bottom of a large manure wagon driven by an old white farmer.

To lie long in one position would tax their patience. Especially under a load of manure. *Why must I always hide under pig shit?*

With great difficulty, Daniel turned his head. Josiah's anxious face came into one corner of his vision. "From now till we get out," Daniel whispered, "not a word. Not a sneeze, not a hiccup. Not no sound, hear?" The boy's head nodded. Good. Daniel could not see Micah nor Henry, but he did not worry about them.

The farmer clacked his tongue, the horses leaned into their collars. The wagon rumbled down the street.

After some miles, morning light seeped through cracks in their hiding place. The wagon halted, then lurched as the farmer jumped down from his seat. White men's voices came and went. They sounded like customers at a country store, speaking the harsh accents of the North.

Daniel worked a hand up his body to scratch his nose. Fumes settled from the manure above them, but there was no leakage. Things could be worse.

The wagon rocked again as the farmer climbed back up to the driver's seat. He clucked and flicked the reins. The wagon rolled again. When well out of earshot from the store, the farmer spoke. "My friend at the store said the county's aswarm with slave hunters. They'll have the Lake farm under watch."

"I know where we can go," Daniel said. "On the road south of Lake's farm. Gunson be the farmer's name."

232

When the old farmer pulled boards from the wagon's bottom, Daniel fell to the ground. He rolled out from under the wagon, stood, and brushed himself off.

Farmer Gunson, hands on hips, stared at him as if he were a ghost.

"Daniel! You always drop in unannounced."

"Wish I knew you was double—I'd a brung a extra me along." Daniel tipped his head toward the second Gunson, who stood beside the first.

The first Gunson laughed. "May I introduce my brother John? He came here from Norway last year, after you visited."

Brother John grinned and stuck out his hand. Daniel shook it.

Tears coursed down Anders Gunson's cheeks. "It's good to see you. I have been in fear for your life."

Micah and Josiah came out of the wagon now. They helped Henry roll out from underneath and stand up.

"This my friend Micah," Daniel said. "The old man be Henry, and the boy is Josiah."

"Come," Gunson said. "Let us get out of sight. You never know when the slavers might be watching."

The Norwegian farmer looked older, blunter than before, his nose crooked, a scar across his brow. He limped a bit as he walked. The younger Gunson seemed a mockery of the older brother. John now looked more like Anders than the present Anders did.

The rail-thin wife watched from the cabin door, arms crossed in front of her.

Anders Gunson opened the barn door and ushered them in. "You all must be very careful. Stay out of sight. If slave catchers come before we can move you onward, I do

233

not know where we shall hide you." He and his brother left the barn.

Daniel spied through a crack in the door as the two men approached Missus Gunson. They had an intense talk. The strange old bug-eyed woman he had met last time also came out and joined in.

"Not sure his womenfolk like havin' four run-off niggers in they barn."

Micah cast a worried glance at him. "They gonna turn us over, you think?"

"Naw. I don't think so."

After a long while, the farmer and his brother came into the barn again. They carried plates of pork and potatoes for the four guests.

"Eat up," said Gunson. "That is all you get." He smiled. "My wife made raspberry jam—not for you. She has taken it all up the road. She will walk past the slave hunters and take her jam to Mistress Lake. While there, she will mention to them that we need a wagon for *four sacks of potatoes*."

"We was thinkin' maybe she don't want us here," Daniel said.

"Yeh," said Micah. "Wouldn't be surprisin'."

Gunson took a deep breath and exhaled. "When you were here before, Daniel, there was trouble, after you left. That makes her cautious. She does not want more trouble."

"There it is. Thass why you look beat up."

The farmer grimaced.

"How bad was it?"

Gunson stared back at Daniel. "Not so bad," he said. His brother frowned.

"Now," said Gunson, "you must tell me about your adventures since we last met."

234

As they ate their dinner, Daniel told the Gunson brothers of his quest to free his friends—the help he had received in Quincy, the long journey south, the disappointment of Quintus' decision to remain in bondage, and the longer journey back north.

Gunson's brother, John, broke in. "This work you do, bringing your friends out of slavery, one by one or three at one time—"

"Yeh? What about it?"

"Well, nobody pays you to do this. I think it must be something God calls you to do." He pierced Daniel with a blue-eyed stare. His older brother nodded agreement.

"I think my mammy would want me to do it," Daniel said. "But if God be callin' me to it, then it look like God be callin' you, too—cause here you is helpin' us."

John received this comment with a look of fierce pride.

Gunson lit his pipe and looked around at the group of four black faces plus his fierce, blue-eyed brother. "Maybe there is something to what John says. The hand of the Lord must be in this work. That is why it feels so right."

Two of Lake's sons came that night with a big freight wagon. Daniel, Micah, Henry, and Josiah climbed up to crawl into tunnels under two tons of potatoes.

The two Norwegian brothers watched as they took their places. "After you get these men where you are taking them," the older Gunson asked, "will you go south again to save more?"

"Reckon I will."

"How much longer will you take this risk?"

"Long as it takes."

Both brothers reached up to shake Daniel's hand. "God go with you," each said.

29. Anders

Illinois

July 1857 – September 1858

Anders tied ribbons of red, white, and blue on the horses at the withers, where the hames rose above their collars. Pleased with the adornment, he mounted the spring seat beside John, flicked the reins, and drove out the gate. Maria and Aunt Osa sat in the wagon bed, surrounded by baskets of picnic food.

Fields of green on both sides of the road made Anders nudge his brother and point at the corn. "Knee-high by the Fourth of July."

"You made a rhyme," said John.

"It's an old saying. The top leaves should reach a man's knees by this date."

"What if the corn does not grow knee-high by the Fourth of July?"

"Praise God, this is not the year we will have to find out."

Things were going very well. America indeed was the promised land. Anders had made the fateful decision to marry Maria and become a farmer instead of a teacher. After two years of hard work, the future looked bright. A bumper crop burgeoned before his eyes.

Two times Søtstrøm had harbored fugitive slaves and moved them onward.

Anders' five-year legal wait for American citizenship would soon be over. And on this fine day he would take his family to celebrate the nation's birth, just like all his neighbors. He was becoming a man among men in Menard County.

As they neared Petersburg, the road became clogged with neighbors on their way to the festival of Independence. Anders waved at Benjamin and Dorcas Lake in their fine buggy, stuck in traffic a few wagons behind. Up ahead he caught sight of Gunder Jørgen Nybro, Maria's cousin, riding with his employer, Alastair Kinnaird.

The road came out into a meadow by the Sangamon River, where farmers parked their wagons. Anders did the same. While Maria and Aunt Osa carried baskets of food to the picnic grounds, Anders and John unhitched the team and led them to the river. Dozens of others were watering their horses on a long curve of shallow mud bank.

Anders shouted hello to Will Cargill, whom he sometimes saw at the Sweetwater store. The older man with Will, tending the team of fine bays, must be his father. The family had a farm between Sweetwater and Greenview. Will said something to the old man, perhaps telling him who Anders was, for the elder Cargill tipped his hat to Anders.

Turning to his right, Anders saw York and Merv Blodgett, pro-slavery blowhards who often tried to browbeat other debaters at the general store. He had stated his own views clearly enough in their presence, yet

Merv surprised him with a curt nod in his direction. His brother did the same.

"Those two," he said to John, "the Blodgetts. What a pair."

"Ja. Any time I see them they are always sticking up for slavery. What do you suppose they are doing here?"

"I suppose celebrating Independence, like us."

"You called this a feast day in the American public religion of Freedom. What do you suppose men like that think of freedom?"

Anders chuckled. "It's a good question, Brother. Maybe one day I shall ask them."

As little as he cared for the Blodgetts, Anders noted with satisfaction that at least they gave him a bit of respect as part of this community.

Anders and John walked the horses back to the wagon, removed their harnesses, and staked them in an area with plenty of grass to munch. Then they went to the picnic grounds, where Maria and Aunt Osa had spread a blanket. For the next hour they enjoyed a relaxed lunch of dilled potatoes, boiled eggs, pickled cucumbers, and wild raspberries.

They took the blanket and baskets back to the wagon. Then they started walking, along with everyone else, to a large open space in the middle of the fairgrounds.

"Watch this," Anders said to John. "You won't believe it."

A rope had been strung in a great circle to keep spectators back. Anders and John shoved their way through the crowd. They got up near the rope. At the center of the rope circle stood two anvils. One lay upside down on the ground. The other stood right side up, its foot resting on the upturned foot of the first. Two men hovered about the anvils.

"What are those men up to?" asked John.

"They are going to shoot the top anvil into the air," said Anders. "The bottoms of the anvils' feet are concave. It makes a hollow space between them. They stuff the space with black powder and touch it off."

"What silliness. A bit of black powder could not make an anvil fly very far."

"You're right, Brother. No more than two hundred feet, straight up."

"No." John looked askance, gauging Anders' seriousness.

"Yes. You'll see."

John rubbed his chin. "I would not want to be the one standing underneath when it comes down."

A small puff of gray smoke rose. "They have lit the punk they will use to touch—"

At that moment a known figure appeared behind the rope on the far side of the circle. *How dare he show his face here?*

The men in the center of the circle sprinted away from the anvils.

A BOOM shattered the air.

"Look!" Anders pointed to the sky. "Up there."

"I see it! My God!"

A tiny speck in mid-air, the anvil fell into the woods a quarter mile away.

"Now you have seen your first anvil firing."

"I hope nobody was in those woods."

"Mm." Anders thought how convenient it would be if Bullamore Crawley had been under the falling anvil, rather than safe behind the rope.

#

240

Anders did not cross paths with the old slave catcher after the anvil firing. *Just as well*, he told himself. *I might try to kill him for threatening Maria.*

The four of them—Anders, Maria, Aunt Osa, and John—returned to Søtstrøm. They resumed farm life. The crops did come in very well, as Anders had predicted. He sold part of his corn and wheat, and a few pigs he had raised, for cash money.

In the fall, at the third annual Menard County Fair, he enjoyed talking of good crops and prosperity with other farmers. They listened to his observations just as he did to theirs. He was gaining the respect of the community.

After the harvest, he paid Mister Eliot fifty dollars against his mortgage. This also gave him satisfaction.

The temperature dropped, the snow came, the winds blew. By this time Anders felt himself an old hand on the prairie. He pointed out to his younger brother that this winter had none of the severity of that first winter at Søtstrøm, when he had strung ropes across the barnyard to keep from getting lost in the snow.

Christmas was celebrated at Osmundsgarden, as usual, with Kirsten Haraldsdatter and her children. This Christmas, John's second in America, was special because Gunder Jørgen had announced his engagement to Miss Torbjørg Aleson of Springfield. They would be married in the spring, after Gunder Jørgen had purchased a farm he had his eye on not far from Søtstrøm. They would raise the finest hogs, and sons, in Menard County. "We look forward to having you as neighbors," said Anders.

#

April 14, 1858, marked a special day—the third anniversary of Anders' marriage to Maria and also of his declaration of intent to become a citizen.

241

His example in the latter regard had inspired Reier, Thor, and John. So he drove the three of them to the courthouse in Springfield and guided them to the clerk's office. There they signed papers that declared their own intentions to become citizens in three years' time.

Anders then took his momentous step. He held his right hand aloft and repeated, phrase by phrase, the judge's words.

"I hereby declare, on oath, that I absolutely and entirely renounce and abjure all allegiance and fidelity to any foreign prince, potentate, state, or sovereignty whatever, and particularly do renounce and abjure forever all allegiance and fidelity to the crown of Sweden and Norway, whereof I was heretofore a subject."

The judge said the promise should be made "without any mental reservations."

Yet Anders, who had no sentimental ties with King Oskar, knew that as a United States citizen he would never obey the Fugitive Slave Act. Inwardly, he regarded that law as being still under debate in the high councils of the land. Meanwhile, he wondered when Daniel would arrive unannounced, as he had ten months ago, guiding others to freedom. On the other hand, maybe Daniel had been killed or captured. Nevertheless, the Lakes might still need Anders' help with some other "express package requiring special handling."

The meadowlarks trilled their pleasure in the warmth of spring as Anders drove his two friends and his brother home to Menard County, more prepared than ever to assume his place as a respected citizen in his adopted homeland.

The rest of the spring went well, all the planting ahead of last year's schedule. Anders looked forward to another good crop. As the two brothers worked side by side in the fields, he began to wonder what he would do if

John decided one day to strike out on his own. One must consider that possibility. When a man came to this land of opportunity, it would hardly be a surprise if he started making ambitious plans for his future.

#

So Anders returned to the courthouse six months later. He entered with John at his side and strode down the hall to the Menard County Clerk's office.

"I want to give my brother half my land," he said.

John stood up straight, like someone worthy to receive such a gift.

The white-haired clerk gazed at them over wire-rimmed spectacles. "You'll want a lawyer to help you with that."

"And how much costs a lawyer?"

"I believe a lawyer would charge five dollars for that service."

Anders scowled. "One dollar for every three acres I give my brother."

The old clerk rubbed his head, then leaned forward as if sharing a secret. "Listen, you can write the paper yourself. We would charge you fifty cents to register the deed—to make it official, you understand."

"Ja. Okay."

"You must take care, however, to make it say what you want it to. Once it's recorded, it's the lawful ownership."

"You have paper and a pen?"

On the paper given him, he wrote: "I, Anders Gunstensen, wish to give my brother, John Gunstensen, half of my thirty-four acres of corn." He signed his name and slid the paper across the counter.

The old clerk read it. He raised his eyes. "Wishing is not the same as doing. This paper says you wish to make a gift. Do you want this document to actually make that gift?"

"Ja. Of course."

The clerk dipped a pen in ink and struck out a phrase. He frowned. "It also says you're giving him corn. Are you just giving him half the corn, or do you also want to give him half of the land the corn stands on?"

"Well ... both, I suppose."

Another stroke of the clerk's pen, and he handed the paper back across the counter. It now read: "I, Anders Gunstensen, ~~wish to~~ give my brother, John Gunstensen, half of my thirty-four acres ~~of corn~~."

Anders read it and nodded.

"What is the parcel of land in question?"

Anders wrote the legal description of the property on the bottom of the paper.

"Wait here," said the clerk. He entered a forest of shelves at the back of the room and came out with a large book, which he laid on the counter. He turned to a page halfway through the book, then ran his finger down the page and clucked.

"Ja? What is it?"

"There's a lien on your property."

"Lien?"

"Mister Eliot of Sweetwater recorded a mortgage on your farm, for two hundred dollars, dated June of 1856. You need to get the lien released before we can record your deed."

Ah, so that's how it is.

"What's going on, Anders?" asked John.

"Come on," Anders said. He scooped up the paper, folded it, and put it in his pocket.

In the wagon on the way to Sweetwater, Anders said, "When I started farming, I borrowed one hundred dollars from Mister Eliot."

"Ja," John said. "I imagine you needed the money."

"I did. So he made me sign a mortgage, pledging my farm in case I could not pay."

John frowned. "You do not own your land?"

"No, I own it. But Mister Eliot gets his money first."

"The man in the courthouse said two hundred."

"After the slave catchers beat me up, I borrowed more for seeds and expenses, to get going again. So, two hundred. That is the mortgage Mister Eliot recorded at the courthouse. Only now, it should be one hundred fifty, because I have paid fifty back."

"This is very confusing."

"Mister Eliot will straighten it out for us."

They lapsed into silence as the horses pulled them toward Eliot's store.

Anders wanted to make sure John got his due in spite of any and all annoying legalities. His younger brother—impulsive, always considered at home to be flighty and unreliable—had buckled down here in Illinois and made a good job of farming alongside Anders.

Since John's arrival the summer before last, all the acres had at last been brought under cultivation. This year Anders and John had planted all corn, and they expected a bumper crop. They could retire the remaining debt in the near future.

John had become a member of the little family. Anders had helped him build a cabin to live in, with room enough for Aunt Osa to move in and keep him company. Anders thanked God that he could now share his living quarters with his wife alone. The awkwardness that had come between them since the loss of Baby Gunhild now seemed to be melting, praise God.

John might as well have half the farm, since he did half the work. The neighbors already referred to Søtstrøm as "the Gunsten brothers' farm." John often went with Anders into town. Both brothers frequently observed, and sometimes took part in, the chatter of the Sweetwater Debating Club.

Everyone in the neighborhood enjoyed the debates at one time or another. Simon Borchers, the old drunkard Anders had seen sleeping outside the saloon on his first entrance to Sweetwater, often lounged in the shade and listened to the arguments.

Anders stopped the rig outside Eliot's store. He and his brother went in, heedless of the verbal barbs and arrows flying on the front porch.

Eliot greeted them cordially. When Anders explained the problem at the county clerk's office, the storekeeper promised to fix it. "I can prepare the documents in a short time. Why don't you boys enjoy the hospitality of the house while you wait?"

They went back to the porch and listened.

The large, hairy York Blodgett stood beside a barrel of pickles and brayed, "Your man Lincoln done put both gigantic feet in his mouth. I hope they weigh him down to Perdition."

"Pray tell, Brother Blodgett, of what speakest thou?" Charlie Simmons, former Whig, always enjoyed goading the slavery advocate.

"You know damn well what I'm talkin' about, you miserable old mud puppy. A house divided against itself cannot stand. That's what."

Beside Anders, John stirred. "Ja, what is wrong with that? We have it in our Bible, too—*Hver Stad eller huus, som bliver splidagtigt med sig selv, vil itte blive bestandigt.*"

There followed a thundering silence.

Blodgett stared at John. "Say that again?"

"*Hver Stad eller huus, som bliver splidagtigt med sig selv, vil itte blive bestandigt.*"

"That's what I thought you said." Blodgett circled a finger near his ear, an American sign to mark a lunatic.

Laughter erupted all around, breaking the tension of a moment before.

"The young man's right," said Charlie. "And so is Lincoln. A house divided can't stand. I believe I'm a Republican now."

"This country has always been half slave and half free. It's what the Founders intended. Now this nigger-loving shyster from Springfield says it's got to be all one or all the other. He's worse than that Seward from New York. No doubt which way they want things to go."

Matthew Lake stepped forth. "What you got against freedom, Mister Blodgett?"

"Oh, well, spoken, young Lake. You and your pappy are great champions of freedom, while you sell horses to Mississippi planters who make their living off nigger slaves."

Matthew stood nose-to-nose with Blodgett, his hands curled into fists.

"Gentlemen, there shall be no violence on the premises." Rance Eliot smiled. "Mind your manners or take your fight to the tavern."

"Tavern? Yessir," said Simon Borchers. "Let's take it to the tavern."

Eliot motioned Anders and John inside.

In the calm of the store, Eliot placed a document before them. "This releases the current lien on your property and pledges you both, jointly and severally, to a new mortgage at the current amount, one hundred and fifty. As you can see, I've already signed."

Anders scratched his head. "Jointly and severally?"

247

Eliot smiled. He spread his hands in a show of openness. "As co-owners, you will each be responsible to make sure the loan is paid. Sign at the bottom and bring this paper to the clerk. He will register your deed."

Anders signed and handed the pen to John.

John hesitated.

"It's all right, John," said Anders.

John signed.

30. Anders

Illinois

October 1858 – July 1859

Anders and John rode to Alton on a special train October 15, along with Mister and Mistress Lake and their three sons, to hear Abraham Lincoln challenge Senator Steven A. Douglas in debate. Douglas was the proud author of the Kansas-Nebraska Act, which allowed slavery in territories where it had formerly been forbidden. Lincoln in June had won the endorsement of the new Republican Party for Douglas' seat when he declared, "A house divided against itself cannot stand. I believe this government cannot endure, permanently half slave and half free."

This final 1858 debate between the two candidates for U.S. Senate took place on an outdoor platform in the center of Alton. Thousands of farmers and townsmen attended. A group of Negroes stood listening to arguments in which they figured mostly as bogeymen, while mustachioed slave brokers from downriver raised boisterous cheers for Douglas.

Lincoln, long-limbed and relaxed, showed himself master of the situation while the pudgy Douglas flogged the air with harsh manifestoes. Lincoln secured Anders' vote when he spoke of the eternal struggle between "the common right of humanity and ... the divine right of kings. ... No matter in what shape it comes, whether from the mouth of a king who seeks to bestride the people of his own nation and live by the fruit of their labor, or from one race of men as an apology for enslaving another race, it is the same tyrannical principle."

Anders' excitement for his candidate was briefly eclipsed by a glimpse of two men making their way around the far edge of the crowd. Their gaits told their identities: Bullamore Crawley, walking with an odd hitch imparted no doubt by Maria's gunshot, and his son Teddy, limping along on his wooden foot.

Raucous shouts broke forth as Lincoln finished and bowed. When Anders looked again, the Crawleys were nowhere to be seen. Neither did he meet them on the walk back to the station, a fact for which he gave thanks. Still: How strange that these skurks, whom he wished never to see again, seemed to pop up everywhere, while Daniel, whom he did wish to see, had dropped out of sight completely. Of course, Anders reflected, Daniel had chosen a calling in which one tried not to be seen.

On the train home, Benjamin Lake explained the Senatorial voting system to Anders and John. Lincoln and Douglas would not appear on the ballot. To send Lincoln to Washington in place of Douglas, they must elect Republican James W. Judy to the Illinois General Assembly. Whichever party won the legislature would control the Senate seat.

#

Shouts reached Anders and John from a mile away as they strode toward Sweetwater in the brisk November air. Men's voices rose in chants and ragged songs, louder and clearer as they neared town.

Anders' heartbeat sped up. He, not John, would act in today's drama. John had come along to see Anders cast the first vote of his life.

The brothers reached Sweetwater and found two gangs of men crowding the path to the polling place. They shouted. They danced. They strutted. They passed jugs around and swigged liquor from them. They gathered and staggered under opposed signs: Menard County Democrats on one side, Republicans for Lincoln on the other.

The two groups jostled with sharp elbows to block the path. Men wearing rosettes and stern faces pressed ballots, pre-printed with their party's nominees, into voters' hands.

Anders sought a Republican ballot. A man in top hat and mutton-chop whiskers jammed in and pushed paper at him. "Here's the one you want, Citizen! Vote for Engle, Democrat for General Assembly."

"No, thank you. I shall vote for Yames Yoody, the Republican."

"Yoody, *who-dy*? Why, you don't know who's up for election. We got no Yoodies."

A gaunt man in a straw hat wedged between Anders and the whiskered Democrat.

"James W. Judy, Republican—this one right here." He glared at his opponent. "Man comes all the way from Sweden to vote, it don't give you license to deceive him."

"Norway, not Sweden," Anders said. "But I know Lincoln stands for freedom."

251

Before the two canvassers came to blows, Anders marched on down the path, Republican ballot in hand and brother John at his side.

Men waited in line outside the polling place, located in Eliot's store.

Ahead of Anders, young Will Cargill bantered with Charlie the Whig-turned-Republican. Charlie waved a ballot in Will's face. "Young Man, you may as well go home, 'cause I'm gonna cancel out your vote."

Will smiled. "How do you know that, old timer? Looky here." He showed his ballot.

The old man's jaw dropped. "I had you wrong, young man. I take it all back."

Inside the store, barrels and boxes had been moved aside. A deputy sheriff and a clerk sat behind a table on which rested a large book.

Grim party minions stood near, making notes in little books.

Anders and John reached the front of the line. Anders stepped forward. He handed his ballot to the clerk. The man put a pen in his hand. "Sign at the bottom, if you please."

Anders dipped the nib in an inkwell. He wrote his name on the ballot. The clerk rocked a hand-blotter over his signature. The deputy then picked up the ballot and examined it.

"Andrew Gun-steen-son," said the deputy. "Where do you live?"

"At Søtstrøm."

The lawman's brows knit in confusion.

"South of Sweetwater," Anders said.

The clerk made a notation in the big book. "Andrew Gunsteenson, Sweetwater. One for Judy," he announced to the party men keeping score. He folded the signed ballot and slipped it down a slot in a blue-painted box.

Anders watched his precious ballot disappear.

"That's all, Mister Gunsteenson," said the deputy. "You have voted."

"But, do you not count my vote?"

The deputy chuckled, as did everyone standing within earshot. "Countin' comes later, after everyone has voted. We open the box and then count the votes."

The Americans stood around Anders, grinning.

"Thank you," Anders squeaked.

As he pushed his way out between inbound voters, his eyes overflowed. "After a lifetime of bowing to the king's servants, I have voted in a free election."

John placed a hand on his shoulder.

#

For three days, Anders and John waited for the results. Anders found himself vexed by Maria, by Aunt Osa, by the horses Webster and Clay, even by the rowdy cornstalks.

On Saturday, Silas Smithson arrived on his mule, Katie. Anders ran to greet him.

The postman gave Anders his copy of the *Illinois State Journal*. "'Fraid your man lost. No James Judy in the legislature, no Abraham Lincoln in the Senate."

When Anders scowled and snatched the paper from his hands, Smithson shrugged with impartial federal sympathy.

Anders rolled the paper in his fist and marched up the road to Lake's farm.

#

"Sit down, Anders. Calm yourself," Lake said. "All of us are disappointed. Lincoln was beaten by unequal districts, and by John J. Crittenden."

253

Anders sat down. "Crittenden. Who is this Crittenden, then?"

"He's a moth-eaten old Whig from Kentucky. Holds himself out as heir to the great Henry Clay. This Crittenden wrote to a man named Dickey in Ottawa, favoring Douglas over Lincoln. Dickey held the letter for weeks. Then, he gave it to the press in October—only a week before the election."

"A letter from one man to another changed the election?"

"That's politics, Anders. The Whig Party no longer exists. Every Whig leans either Democrat or Republican. They do respect Crittenden—Lord knows why, the old scoundrel. But there's no doubt his letter swung many Whig voters to Douglas."

Mistress Lake glided into the room. "Here, you two— Herr Gloom and Mister Doom. Be not afraid. Father Abraham will triumph in the end."

Both men stared at her. She smiled.

"These debates will make Mister Lincoln president two years from now."

Benjamin Lake laughed.

"Mark you my words, Mister Lake."

Her husband composed himself. "Of course, Dear."

#

Anders dragged himself home along the Sweetwater Road. He could not fathom Mistress Lake's optimism. On her say-so, could he assure his brother John that Lincoln would soon emerge as president?

Maria stood at the table, slicing bread. "Why so glum?"

"Mister Lincoln lost the election."

She stood silent, making perfect, thin slices of bread.

254

Aunt Osa led him to the table, sat him down, and placed porridge before him. "It's a rare goat that makes its own cheese."

Anders scratched his head.

"She means," said Maria, "that we must pay attention to our own tasks."

"Of course. Why bother to say it?" He sat bemused by Aunt Osa's words. "She herself makes the cheese, and we don't even have any goats."

"Goats or no goats, each of us has responsibilities." Maria held a plate of bread slices before him.

"Yes, of course." He took three slices.

"Our corn goes unpicked while you visit the Lakes to discuss Mister Lincoln's future. What about our own future?"

Anders snorted. "You need not worry about Lincoln anymore, jenta mi. He has lost."

She took a slice of bread, spread it with butter. "Good riddance to him."

She has no sense of politics.

"Lincoln is beaten, yet remains undefeated."

Maria smiled. "Just like our cornstalks, standing straight and unbowed, row by row."

"But one acre remains to be picked. I shall get it all in before the snow flies."

"The thermometer already goes to zero some mornings."

"Quite so. I'll get to it now the election is over." He took a deep breath, plunged ahead. "Speaking of our duties—"

"Yes, Anders?"

"Well, jenta mi, what about children, to carry on our line?"

Maria thought a moment, then raised a finger. "How can we feed another mouth, with the crops untended?"

255

"The crops are not untended. I will have all the corn cribbed in a few days."

"Yes? Truly?"

"I have said it."

"All right then." Maria smiled. "Perhaps we can sow another child."

#

With the election behind him, Anders got all the corn picked as promised.

He, Maria, Aunt Osa, and John traveled to Osmundsgarden and gathered with their friends to celebrate the rich harvest all had enjoyed. Maria shared the contents of a new letter from Kansas, which showed that Anne and Tarald were making their way in spite of civil disturbances in their vicinity.

The rest of the autumn, winter, and spring passed quietly as they all hewed to their appointed tasks.

#

On the Fourth of July, all gathered again in Petersburg to celebrate Independence Day. The day-long festival of fun, food, and speeches took place without the usual launch of an anvil into the air. The anvil firing gave way to an unprecedented event, which had to wait until dark.

A thin orange line shot skyward for four seconds, then vanished.

"Mmph," said Anders. "That's what all the fuss is about."

Where the orange streak had vanished, a chrysanthemum bloomed white against the dark sky, to the awed moan of a thousand voices.

"No, Husband, *that* is what all the fuss is about."

256

The white flower was succeeded by an orange one, then a green one, then a blue one. After a few moments, three flowers sprouted from different corners of the sky.

Each new floral design drew a new "Ohhhhh!" from the crowd. Few had ever seen fireworks. None of the Norwegians had.

Kirsten Haraldsdatter's children hovered about, reviving her from a deep swoon.

Gunder Jørgen Nybro nudged Anders. "They say your friend Lake, and my former boss Kinnaird, were big donors to the pot of money for hiring a pyrotechnician."

"I was a doubter," said Anders, "but these sky-sparkles are so beautiful I am carried away. Can they burn so much gunpowder as this in future years as well?"

"Husband," Maria said, "this is 1859. It is a new age."

On the way home, while Aunt Osa and John dozed in the wagon bed, Maria came forward to sit with Anders. "It was good to see Gunder Jørgen and Torbjørg again, after their sorrow." Her cousin had married Miss Torbjørg Aleson of Springfield. He had left the employ of Alastair Kinnaird and bought a farm south of Søtstrøm on the Sweetwater Road. The newlyweds had begun a family with high hopes, but their first child had been stillborn.

"Gunder Jørgen is back to his old self," Anders said. "He bent my ear for an hour on the future of hogs in Menard County. Torbjørg seemed in good spirits as well."

"Yes. Because she is expecting again."

"Another baby, so soon? Perhaps this one will live."

"Don't spout it off to the world at large. She does not want people to know. The reason she told me is because … I know what it's like. I mean—"

"Yes, yes. At any rate, it's good she's with child again."

"It is." Maria leaned into Anders' encircling arm. "And she is not the only one."

257

"Why, who else?"

She said nothing. Anders fastened his eyes on Maria. Her oval face gazed back at him with glittering eyes.

He smiled. "Oh. I see." He gave her shoulders a squeeze, dropped the reins, and wrapped both arms around her, leaving Webster and Clay to find Søtstrøm on their own.

31. Maria

Illinois

October 1859 – October 1860

Maria had no doubt her baby would be born alive and healthy. The child battered her insides, eager for any fray. Neither Maria's appetite for food nor her drive for work waned in the least.

With Tante she washed clothes, aired linens against the winter. She took cheer from the autumn sun, with the comfort of its appointed tasks.

Even the prospect of being arrested by the sheriff for shooting Crawley—something she had feared for months after the incident—was no longer among her concerns. If the man were still alive, he would lodge no complaint that might draw attention to his own lawless behavior.

Furthermore, Anders' pet refugee, Daniel, had not shown his face at Søtstrøm in more than two years. Perhaps he would not come back. She did not dislike Daniel. She found his simple and direct manner appealing. But whenever Daniel or other escapees showed up, it meant danger. Perhaps Anders could now turn his mind away from politics and conflict.

"Harpers Ferry," he said without preface, raising his head from the newspaper.

"What is that you say, Husband?"

"Harpers Ferry. It's a place. John Brown, the man who killed those people in Kansas, has been arrested for treason."

"Now Anne and Tarald won't be troubled by him," she said with a smile.

Anders frowned. "Well, no. Not by him."

He buried his nose in the paper and became dead to the world again.

Her husband's persistent interest in politics, foolish though it might be, had no effect at all on Maria's cheerful mood.

Torbjørg was another matter. Since Torbjørg had married the ablest Nybro cousin, she and Maria had become friends and confidants. Thus, Maria knew something only Torbjørg and Gunder Jørgen knew. Torbjørg had told her over coffee one day, when Maria had hiked to their pig farm to deliver a gift of Tante's brown cheese.

"Our little boy who died last year," Torbjørg said, "was not the first."

"No!"

A tear rolled down Torbjørg's cheek. "We lost another. I miscarried early on, almost a year before the other. That is why this new baby is so important to us. He is our third try."

#

260

In mid-December, Gunder Jørgen came rattling into the yard at Søtstrøm, jumped from his wagon, and pounded on the cabin door.

"I have left Torbjørg all alone," he said, eyes round and wild. "Please go help her. I must fetch Mistress Lake. The baby's coming."

He jumped back onto the wagon and drove up the Sweetwater Road before Maria could ask questions. She jutted her chin out, ready to play at midwife until the old American arrived.

"It's just two miles," Anders said, "but it will be better to ride than to walk, both for you and for the child you are carrying."

While Maria bundled up, Anders hitched the horses to the wagon.

Pig-stench smacked Maria in the face as they drove onto the Nybro farm.

"How can Torbjørg give birth in such an odor? It's all I can do to drink my coffee down when I visit her."

Anders reined in at the cabin door. "One gets used to the smell of one's livelihood."

Maria bustled into the cabin, praying for the arrival of Mistress Lake. While Anders waited outside, Maria got Torbjørg into her birthing gown, laid her down on the bed, and readied her for the trial to come.

"Take comfort now, dear," Maria said. "Your baby will soon be here."

Torbjørg yielded to strong shivers.

There came a noise. The door opened. Mistress Lake swept into the room with serene confidence. Gunder Jørgen and Anders entered right behind her.

"Thank God you have come," Maria said.

Mistress Lake calmed Torbjørg's shivers by holding her hand. She smiled at Gunder Jørgen and pointed at the door.

261

With a calm hand on Gunder Jørgen's shoulder, Anders ushered him out.

They will go to the barn to discuss swine. Anything, as long as they stay out of our way.

After four hours of Torbjørg's brave whimpers, a baby boy came forth.

A tiny and weak child, yet he breathed on his own. He sought the warmth of his mother's breast, nuzzled his way toward the nipple and its treasure.

Maria went out to fetch the men. She swung the big door open. In the dim barn, Anders sat on a hay barrow, his long arm around the shoulders of Gunder Jørgen, who shook with sobs.

Maria walked to the front of the hay barrow, stood before the two men, and kicked over a bottle of whiskey that stood on the floor between them.

"No!" shouted Gunder Jørgen.

Anders furrowed his brows. "That were, was, the only thing to console him, and you have shloshed it out, jenta mi."

She picked up the bottle, turned it upside down to empty the last few drops, and shook it.

"Come and see your fine son, Gunder Jørgen."

"He lives?" Gunder Jørgen sat upright. He bolted from the barrow, strode toward the barn door—then stopped, mid-stride. A queer look came over his face, and his body shook.

"It is the alcohol," Maria said. "Stay here until you can present yourselves decently. Both of you."

An hour later, when the contrite men knocked and gained admission to the house, Gunder Jørgen gave thanks to God for this live-born son.

"His name will be Henrik Lars," he said. "How strong he is already!"

262

With the birth of her own child near, Maria stayed at Søtstrøm for Christmas instead of traveling as usual to Osmundsgarden.

Anders brought in a pretty evergreen. They trimmed it with candles, as Martin Luther himself had done. Tante loaded the table with roasted pork ribs, rice pudding, and dark *pepperkake* cookies while Maria hoarded strength for her time of trial.

After the Yule fest, wind-driven snow and frigid temperatures kept Maria indoors.

Even Anders went no farther than the barn. Except when tending the animals, he stayed indoors, mended harness, and pored over the *Illinois State Journal*. John spent long afternoons in the cabin with Anders, discussing the politics of slavery.

Maria ran out of things to do. Taking a cue from her mother's perennial mission, she sewed a christening dress for the new infant. It seemed a mad project, for she had no home church where such a rite could be held. Worse yet: A mother-to-be teased the gods if she made advance provisions for her unborn child. Every baptismal garment Mamma stitched in her chair by the hearth at Øiestad was made for a niece, a nephew, a cousin, or a friend's baby. Never for her own—perish the thought! Even with this precaution, only Maria and little Michaelline, of all Mamma's children, had survived.

I'll not be bound by Mamma's dead superstitions.

Maria had to do something, so she stitched.

The child came on January 30.

The breaking of water and the onset of contractions went as before. Maria sent Anders to the Lake farm. Then she changed into a clean gown—a new gown, a gown unstained by sorrow for the lost Gunhild.

263

Maria knew, as Tante helped her into bed, that this birth would be different. The contractions did not slow, nor did they weaken. They continued strong as they started. Each one came sooner than the last.

When Anders burst through the door with Mistress Lake, they were the last to arrive.

Anders blanched at the sight of Tante over the bed, holding a squirming ball of newborn flesh between Maria's naked legs. His face went from white to green.

"Mister Gunstensen," said Mistress Lake, "go to the well for water. Knock on the door before you come back in."

Two full buckets of water already stood nearby, which Anders himself had drawn before he left. Maria smiled as he wobbled to the door, sent away on a fool's errand.

"Now, what about this new child?" The cheerful old woman tied and cut the cord, washed the babe, swaddled him, and oversaw Tante as she cleaned and covered the new mother.

Maria felt elation as Tante placed the warm little boy in her arms, where he burrowed for the comfort of her breast.

"What will you name him?" asked Mistress Lake.

Gunsten, of course, for Anders' father.

But doubts assailed her. In Norway, the boy would be named Gunsten Andersen—son of Anders, grandson of Gunsten, a logical progression. In Illinois, American naming customs would make him Gunsten Gunstensen. How could that be right?

A knock came at the door. Mistress Lake opened it to Anders. John stood beside him, curious about his new nephew, yet reluctant to intrude.

"Here is your bucket of water," Anders said.

264

The old woman smiled with three chins. "Place it on the table. Go see your son."

Anders and John entered.

"Husband," said Maria, "what shall his name be?"

Anders' smile warmed her. He reached out, capped the child's head with the lightest of touches. He gazed into Maria's eyes with love. Even, she thought, with a new kind of respect.

"George," he said.

"George?"

"He is the first natural American in our family. The father of our grandchildren and of their children after them. We shall call him George Washington Gunstensen."

John nodded his approval.

Tante, who made out the name well enough though she spoke no English, stood with her mouth open.

Maria said, "You may call him George Washington Gunstensen, if you please, Husband. I shall call him Georgi. It rolls easier off my Norsk tongue."

Anders rolled his eyes.

Mistress Lake reached down to take the baby. "Shall I—"

Anders stopped her with a wave of his hand. "No need to hurry the baptism this time. We shall have a proper church christening by and by."

#

Maria's life at Søtstrøm was transformed by the presence of a living child.

She regained strength, consuming Kirsten Haraldsdatter's gift of fløtegrøt with joy instead of sorrow. After two days, she resumed all the tasks she had done before. She exulted to realize that not only she, Anders,

265

Tante, and John benefited from her work—so also did this rosy-cheeked, blue-eyed gift from God.

Anders seemed just as smitten with little Georgi. He spent hours holding the baby, cajoling him in earnest tones, or crooning into his ear songs recalled from childhood in Norway.

#

In accordance with custom, they had George Washington Gunsten baptized on the eighth day. With no Lutheran church nearby, Anders asked Brother Claymore to officiate. The rite took place in the Methodists' white frame meetinghouse in Petersburg as part of the regular Sunday service.

Maria thought it an odd kind of worship. The most familiar thing about this baptism was the little white christening garment she had made with her own hands. Her tears flowed. She had never felt so close to Mamma.

Besides Anders, Maria, John, and Tante, other guests present included Mister and Mistress Lake, Kirsten Haraldsdatter, and all four of her children.

Among Anders and Maria's close friends, Torbjørg and Gunder Jørgen did not attend. Gunder Jørgen had hiked up to Søtstrøm to convey regrets. "Torbjørg is not fit to travel yet, and of course little Henrik Lars will not think of going anywhere without his mother."

Maria had smiled at his little joke, thinking it a clever way to put a shoe deliberately on the wrong foot. For it was not Torbjørg who failed to thrive, but Henrik Lars the newborn. His parents would not budge from the farm until their child grew strong enough to be taken about.

Gunder Jørgen and Torbjørg were to have been little Georgi's godparents, but since they could not attend the christening, a panic ensued. Anders had wished to recruit

266

his brother John, but Tante said it would be bad luck for an uncle to stand as his own nephew's godfather. And that still left the question of a godmother. The uncertainty, practical and theological, persisted all the way to the door of the church.

When Maria told Kirsten and her family of the crisis, Thor stepped forth and said, "I would be honored to serve as godfather to your first American-born child"—a pronouncement altogether unexpected. Likewise, his sister Karen volunteered to be Georgi's godmother. Nobody present could think of any impediment, Methodist or Lutheran, to a brother and sister serving as a child's godparents. Thus, it was done.

That Thor, thought Maria. *So shy and quiet, but always there just when he is needed.*

"I have decided to join this church," said Kirsten to Maria after the service. "They do things in a different way, but they worship the same Lord we do. It is no good for us to continue with makeshift services at home when there is a church we could attend."

#

In spring Anders and John took to the fields to spread manure, plow, and harrow. They toiled from the rising of the sun till the last of her rays died in the west. After supper, the brothers discussed politics. Both grasped at every indication that Mister Lincoln would stand for election as president of the United States.

This enthusiasm, Maria thought, might be wise or foolish; it would not be feckless. It would result in something concrete, something that affected her own life. Maybe, something to be dreaded.

When Anders tried to explain the national political system, it seemed senseless to her.

267

Lincoln opposed Douglas, the same man who had beaten him in the election for Senate two years ago. Had the question between the two of them not been settled then?

"Why re-run the last election?" asked Maria. "Since Lincoln and Douglas have already settled their quarrel, why do they not leave it for others to contest this one? Is that not a better way for grown men to behave?"

Anders laughed. "You will never understand American politics."

"And you, Husband, do you understand American politics? Why is it, then, that every time you read an item in the paper, you run up the road for Mister Lake's explanation?"

Anders rolled his eyes.

As Election Day 1860 neared, Maria remained in a sunny frame of mind. Georgi crawled around the floor of the cabin; soon he would learn to totter on two feet. He would need his own set of burnished sheeps' knuckles for playthings. Their little family had plenty of food for the winter. Anders, with John at work beside him, had never been so happy and productive.

And no word had ever come of the slave catcher she had shot four years ago. On that long-dormant subject she contented herself, inquiring no further. As Tante would say, "Best not poke the troll."

32. Maria

Illinois

April – August 1861

Maria scrubbed in the corner by the stove while Tante corralled Georgi. Now that he had gained his legs, the tyke toppled whatever he encountered, screeching in delight over each victory. He had to be watched every minute.

Horses clomped in the yard. Maria rose from hands and knees to peek out the window. Anders and John led the horses back from the field. At this hour of the morning?

"You manage the little child, Tante, and I'll see to the big one." Drying her hands on a towel, she went outside.

"Maria!" Anders called. "We must drive to town immediately!"

"What is the rush, Husband? Sweetwater will be there tomorrow as well."

"Not Sweetwater," said John, leading Webster to the wagon. "Petersburg."

"Petersburg! What about the plowing?"

Anders led Clay to the wagon, and the brothers began to hitch up the two horses.

"Plowing can wait, jenta mi. Big things are afoot."

"Oh, yes?"

"A man came down the road riding a big bay and shouted that the Southrons have fired on Fort Sumter."

"Fired. You mean guns?"

"Ja. Cannon. It is an act of war."

Maria placed herself between Anders and the doubletree. "If it is war, should not the fields be plowed? Where is this shooting fort, anyway?"

"South Carolina. Please step out of the way."

"What has a war in South Carolina to do with us?"

Anders placed his hands on Maria's shoulders and moved her aside. "That is what we must go to Petersburg to find out."

The brothers rattled off at breakneck speed, heedless of Maria's qualms.

#

They came back long after dark.

After they unhitched and cared for the horses, Anders entered the cabin.

"How goes the war, Husband?" Maria whispered, mindful of Georgi's infant snores.

Anders frowned. "Nobody knows anything."

"It took all that time in Petersburg to find this out?"

Anders sat down. "The man at the newspaper office says it's war. Others say President Lincoln will do like Buchanan and let the South go its own way. All agree that if he tries to send food and supplies, the war will be on. Everything is rumors and fantastic prophecies, but men are starting to raise a militia company."

"Do not the southern states always talk about going their own way?"

"Well, now it seems they are ready to do it. They challenge the federal authority. They mean to test Mister Lincoln's resolve."

"If there is a war, will you and John have to go?"

Anders sighed. "There is no telling, jenta mi. Nobody can guess what will happen."

"If there is a war, or no war, we still need to eat, ja?"

Anders smiled. "Do not worry, Wife. We shall put Webster and Clay back on the plow tomorrow. They had their holiday in town today."

#

After the first excitement over the firing on Fort Sumter and President Lincoln's call for troops, nothing happened. Anders and John worked the fields as usual by day. At night they read the *Illinois State Journal*, impatient for any scrap of news about the war. State officials organized a regiment of infantry, the Seventh Illinois, to serve for a period of three months, and sent them off to Missouri, where they languished.

On the night of July 24, the brothers hunched over the newspaper, reading by lamplight.

"A slight retreat," said John. "For tactical reasons."

Anders scowled. "This is the *Illinois State Journal*. If it so much as whispers the word retreat, you may be sure it is a great disaster." He raised his face from the paper. "Jenta mi, the first big battle has happened, at a place called Bull Run—and we have lost."

"Does that mean the South gets to keep their slaves?"

"No. It only means victory will be harder. Lincoln will need more soldiers."

Maria frowned at her stitchery.

271

"Right now," Anders said, "they are about to re-organize the Seventh Infantry for a three-year enlistment."

"And what does that mean?"

He stared into his lap. "Our government is in danger. One man, at least, from our family should go."

She did not breathe.

"And it must be me."

"It must be you. Why?"

"Well, jenta mi—I am the citizen, after all. And, as you know"—he chuckled—"it has long been thought that flames and steel cannot hurt me."

"Anders!" She flung down her needlework. "Now is no time to fall back on a silly superstition. This is serious. You could be killed."

"And is it better John should be killed?"

She stood nose-to-nose with him. "Why must it be either of you?" Where was his logic?

John grasped Anders' shoulder and turned him around. "You are not thinking straight, Brother. I shall go."

"What!"

"You have a farm to run. You have a wife and son. I have no such obligations."

"You are half owner of the farm."

"If I don't come back, my half will be yours again."

#

The argument between the two brothers raged for two days and two nights.

On the third morning, John had gone.

"Tante," said Maria, "did you hear him leave?"

272

The old woman kindled the fire and stood up. "A nightmare visited me. It rode my chest all through the night. That must have been the horse that took him away."

"I'll go find him and bring him back," said Anders.

"Husband, he did this to spare me and Georgi and Tante from a life without you. He will see to it that you never catch him."

"Still, I must try." He snatched his hat off its peg in the cabin wall.

"Even if you could bring him back and tie him to the plow," Maria said, "it would only free you to go to war yourself." She bit her lip. "And it happens there are more than just the three of us who need you here. I would have told you soon, anyway. We shall have another little one in the winter."

#

Anders moped about the cabin and the barn for a time. Then, resigning himself to John's departure for the Army, he plunged back into field work. "Only it is hard, jenta mi, to do all this work myself. I have become accustomed to having my brother's help."

One day he walked into Sweetwater and came back with a bedraggled old man.

"This is Simon Borchers. From now on he will help me with the field work."

Maria smiled, as is only polite. But, such a specimen! Slovenly, loose in his joints, and foul-smelling. In Norsk, she asked, "Will he live among us?"

Anders replied in English. "He shall take his dinner with us and will sleep in the barn."

"Thank ye kindly," said the old man. He dipped his head humbly and touched the greasy brim of his hat.

Anders led Borchers off to show him his sleeping quarters.

Maria waved a towel behind them to clear away the old man's stench.

#

When the day's work was done, when supper had been cooked and eaten; when the new farmhand tottered off to the barn for his night's sleep, Maria quizzed Anders about his choice.

"He has nowhere else to go, jenta mi. And we need the labor."

Maria clucked. "What has brought him to such a low state?"

"He drinks."

"And you have brought home this drukkebolt to our farm?"

"Good workers are hard to find these days. And Simon knows how to work. We keep no spirits here, nor beer or wine. So it will be all right."

33. Daniel

Missouri

December 1861 – January 1862

Daniel huddled in the alley outside a riverfront saloon. Wind-driven needles of rain pierced him. Maybe it would turn to sleet. His clothes were all wrong for Christmas in St. Louis. Yet here he was.

Men came to the saloon for supper as well as drink. Some left the premises reeling. Daniel eyed those. He might relieve a drunken stranger of his wallet. But these men did not look prosperous enough to rob.

The war had put an end to Daniel's profession as Underground Railroad conductor. With no recompense, he had survived six years in the sketchy occupation, always on the run, relying on his wits, his stamina, and a few fortunate connections—like those with Van Doorn, Lake, and Gunson. It had been a calling to be proud of, something that made him think Mammy would be proud of him.

Now that the battle had been joined for real, slaves would walk off the plantation and give themselves over to the Union Army. The need for an Underground Railroad had boiled away in the heat of events.

Daniel's final mission had been to slip through Louisiana to bring the news of liberation to the maroons. Luc had laughed in his face. "Freedom? Look around you, boy. We as free as black folk can get in this world."

"If you foller me out the swamp, they's going to be good jobs with the northern troops, totin' and fetchin' for real money. You wouldn't have to live in the woods no more."

Bijou's eyes opened wide. She looked over at Luc.

The big man curled his lips back like a fox on the hunt. "Tell me, Brother Daniel. You ever see any of this northern army money with your own eyes?"

"Not yet—but it's comin' sure as night follows day."

Luc turned away, cutting off a conversation Daniel had trekked hundreds of miles to have. The other maroons shuffled their feet. Some gazed at Daniel with longing. He tried to wake them to the new opportunity, despite Luc's scorn. However, when he left camp the next day, none followed.

They could not imagine real freedom could be at hand.

So Daniel had walked out of the swamp and headed north, using the routes he had learned by taking others to freedom. Here and there, in the confused economy of the Trans-Mississippi, he got an odd job for pay. At other times he took what he needed, always trying to appropriate it from whites, not steal it from blacks. But most whites were poor farmers, not rich planters. To take from them felt more like theft than appropriation.

He had drifted to St. Louis, the largest city on the river north of New Orleans. Though slavery existed here, many free blacks worked in the city, finding jobs on and near the Mississippi River. Here, Daniel knew he could make his way.

At this moment, however, he was starving. The rain had not turned to sleet. Rather, it seeped as cold water through the cracks that now riddled the boots made for Daniel long ago by Mister William Donnegan of Springfield.

Two men came near, black men.

Only he had never seen a black man swagger that way.

He stepped out of the alley. "Say, there, Brothers— what kind clothes you all wearin'?"

The pair—one thin, one thick—stopped short. They wore identical blue outfits and flat-topped caps with ribbon tails.

The thin one smirked. "Whatta matter, farm boy? You never see a sailor before?"

"A sailor?"

"Thass right. Sailors," said the thick one. He smiled. "We's assigned to the *Essex*, finest gunboat in the Union Army."

The thin sailor scowled. "Who the hell want to know?"

"My name Daniel. Just come up from the bayous. You all got me goin' now. You *sailors* in the *Army*?"

The thick one chuckled. "We sailors in the Navy. Our ship is in the Army."

Daniel scratched his head.

The thin one rolled his eyes. "No use. He can't fathom it."

His sturdy friend winked. "Brother Farmer, look like you could use a meal."

"Couldn't I, though?"

"Come on in here with us. We'll explain it to ya."

So Daniel followed the sailors into the tavern. Cigar smoke filled the room, mingled with the smells of strong drink and fried meat. White men and black men rubbed elbows, though each kept company only with members of his own race. Black bartenders sweated behind the bar, serving customers.

The sailors chased a couple of loafers away from a table. They ordered three steaks and three beers.

"Thass right nice of you," Daniel said. "I'll do the same for you sometime."

"Yeh," said the skinny one. He regarded Daniel with hooded eyes. "How you gone do that, dummy? Lookit yourself."

Daniel's gorge rose. These boys had no idea what he'd been through for freedom. He gave his skinny critic a wry face of his own. "I'll tell you in a minute. Meantime, you ain't told me who you are and how come you in the Army."

The stout one replied. "We's stokers," he said. "We's Navy men on a Army ship. I'm Albert and he's Rufus."

"Glad to meet you both. What that like, being a stoker? They keep you in chains?" The memory of shackled stokers on a steamboat flashed across Daniel's mind.

Rufus glared at Daniel. "Chains? No, sah. We's free men, good as any sailor on board."

Albert waved at a waiter bringing plates of meat and mugs of beer on a tray.

"The work's damn hard," said Albert, his eyes alight at the steak set before him. "But you do get three square meals a day."

"Plus"—Rufus held up his hand like a preacher— "fourteen dollars a month."

"And a dollar-and-a-half extra for grog," Albert said.

"Food, and money too." Daniel rubbed his chin. "Where can I get one of them upside-down hats?"

#

The sailors took Daniel to their ship, the *U.S.S. Essex*, moored beside the quay downriver from the saloon. They stood on the high levee and admired the ship from above.

Brightness dazzled Daniel's eyes. He held a hand before his face.

Rufus hooted. "It's just limelight, bonehead. They use them in theaters and such. Somebody got the idee to put one down here so they could work on the ship all night. Your eyes better get used to it."

"I never saw a boat like that." Daniel had to shout to be heard above the clangs and bangs coming from the ship. "Puts me in mind of a box turtle."

"Box turtle!" Albert laughed. "Yup, reckon so. Them is iron plates they's puttin' on her for armor."

Rufus showed crafty eyes. "The rebs shoots a ball at her, it glance right off, see?"

"We's livin' in tents on shore while they do the work," said Albert.

The two seamen led Daniel down to a tent city on the quay. They threaded their way through canyons of canvas. Finally, they stopped at a large tent and went inside. A table at its center overflowed with books, maps, and papers.

A hatchet-faced white sailor glared at them.

Rufus and Albert stood up straight and tall. "Bosun McGurk," said Rufus, "we brung you a landsman, name of Daniel."

The bosun reminded Daniel of McCutcheon, the dour overseer on Petitbon's plantation, only rougher. "Ever sail on a warship?" he asked.

"I was a stoker on a steamboat," Daniel lied.

The bosun snorted. He squeezed Daniel's upper arm and spat. "Keep your nose clean, stay out of trouble. You'd best resign yourself to injury or sudden death, or I'll not have you."

"I'll take my chances, sah. Fight for freedom."

"Mm. You read and write?"

"No, sah." Behind him, Rufus snickered.

The bosun spread a large book out on the table. "What's your name?"

"Daniel."

"Daniel what?"

He glanced over at Albert and Rufus. They shrugged.

"Daniel . . . Freeman. I guess."

"You guess? Don't you know?"

"Thass it. Daniel Freeman."

The bosun wrote in the book and handed Daniel the pen. "Make your mark right there, Daniel Freeman."

Daniel drew a large X where the man's bony finger pointed.

"Raise your right hand."

Daniel did so.

"Do you, Daniel Freeman, solemnly swear or affirm that you will support the constitution of the United States?"

"Yes, sah."

"And do you solemnly swear or affirm to bear true allegiance to the United States of America, and to serve it honestly and faithfully, against all its enemies or opposers whatsoever, and to observe and obey the orders of the President of the United States of America, and the orders of the officers appointed over you?"

Daniel took a deep breath. "Yes, sah," he said. "I do."

The bosun shook his hand. "Welcome to the United States Navy. May God have mercy on you, because I sure as hell won't." He turned to Albert and Rufus. "You men, show him to the quartermaster."

#

The days blurred as Daniel learned to be a sailor. It was complicated. He studied how to wear his blue uniform, how to tilt the hat, how to tie the neckerchief; how and when to salute an officer, how to stand at attention, how to speak with "aye-aye" and "sir" in every sentence; how to call things by naval words—decks, bulkheads, hatches, fore and aft, starboard and larboard, abaft and abeam; how to give proper respect to every officer and petty officer; how to tell time in bells and speed in knots.

With the ship off limits while being fitted with armor plate, the bosun and others used a large diagram to show Daniel its parts. He memorized the name of every place on the ship. "If an officer send you to Number Three Coal Bunker," said Albert, "thass where you got to go, not the powder magazine."

As a landsman, Daniel would receive twelve dollars a month. After two years' service he would become an ordinary seaman and make fourteen, like Albert and Rufus. He would start at the most unskilled position, as a coal heaver.

He found it hard to learn so many things at once, but these were important things, more important than anything a white man had entrusted to him before.

He still did not know how he, with his black skin, could serve in the uniform of the United States. "Everybody knows they don't allow niggers in the Army," he said to Albert.

"Thass true, old boy. Howsomever, we's in the Navy."

"How can we be in the Navy, when the *Essex* is in the Army?"

281

Albert laughed. "You tell him, Rufus."

Rufus leaned back, looked down his long, bony nose, and held up a finger. "It's very simple, numbskull, if you had any brains. General Grant own these boats. But he an Army man. He don't know nothing about boats. So, he let Admiral Foote run the boats. Thass how the Navy can be in the Army."

"So, when do we sail on this boat?"

"Any day now, Daniel," said Albert. Daniel felt measured by his gaze. "You sure in a big rush to get yourself kilt."

34. Daniel

Missouri, Illinois, Kentucky, Tennessee
January – February 1862

Daniel's ship, the ironclad *Essex*, steamed out of St. Louis and headed downriver to Cairo on January 10, 1862. The next morning, she slipped further downstream, escorting troopships.

"General Grant got a coupla thousand men he want to pay a morning call on Johnny Reb," said Rufus. "And he want us to get 'em there in one piece."

Ta-rum-pum-pump! Drumbeats interrupted Rufus' lecture. *Ta-rum-pum-pump*!

"They beatin' to quarters," said Albert. "Time we go to work."

Ta-rum-pum-pump! Sailors black and white ran every direction, bound for duty stations. Rufus and Albert grabbed Daniel and shoved him down a stairway into the belly of the ship.

"Stay out the way!" shouted Albert.

"Don't get run over!" shouted Rufus. He pushed Daniel toward the coal bunkers.

Coal heaving was the dirtiest job on the ship. Daniel ran large scuttles of coal from the bunkers to the boiler room, where Albert and Rufus, with many others, fired the boilers.

A dull THUD shook the deck below his feet, made him drop half his load of coal. As he bent to gather it back into the scuttle, Albert shoved him out of the way, scooping up the spilled coal in a shovel, which he ran back to the boiler door.

Rufus, also feeding the boiler, glanced back over his shoulder. "Thass a 'leven-inch Dahlgren, Farm Boy! Don't you fall down every time it shoots!"

Two more THUDs rocked the boat as Daniel ran back to the bunkers. The ship lurched, and he staggered.

Heat sapped Daniel's will. Sweat soaked his wool jumper. The stokers, stationed in the hottest part of the ship, worked bare-chested. Back at the bunkers, Daniel stripped off his jumper before refilling the scuttle.

"Get to work, sailor!" bawled a petty officer. Daniel speeded up.

Thuds and booms continued, and the wooden deck tilted right and left.

CLANG! Daniel's ears rang.

"Reb cannonball hit our casemate!" Rufus yelled. "Don't pay it no nevermind!"

Daniel worked in a frenzy, running to and from the boilers with scuttles of coal, which he dumped on a big pile the stokers took from. He learned to run zigzag as the ship thumped and writhed in the agony of combat.

Then it all ceased.

The clamor of battle gave way to the steady roar of engines and paddle wheels.

Shouts and whoops drifted down the companionway from the gun deck. A head and shoulders, upside down, thrust into the boiler room from above—a gunner, a white man turned black as night from cannon smoke. "We done it, boys! Run the rebels off. They're skedaddlin' back to Columbus!"

The engine room erupted in shouts and cheers. The black men who served the boilers shared in joy with the blackened white gunners just above and the unblackened white officers who plied charts and binoculars up on the hurricane deck.

The chief engineer released all but a skeleton crew of stokers and heavers. Daniel mounted the companionway stairs to fresh air, jostling among his fellow stokers. The gunners were lavish in praise. "You boys down there fired them boilers just right." Except for his friends in the Underground Railroad, it marked the first time in his life that white men had ever praised Daniel for anything. He felt like a man.

Weary, sweaty, blackened sailors poured through the forward hatches and climbed the sloping casemate to the hurricane deck, where cool breezes wafted. What a relief, after the heat of the bunkers and boiler room.

A sailor pointed to three dark smudges rising from the water far across the river. "Them's the rebs. Cottonclads."

"Cottonclads?"

"They've got cotton bales for armor, where we've got iron plates. That's why we won the battle."

"I'm s'prised," said Daniel. "I thought sure a battle would take more'n five minutes."

The sailor snorted. "We was fightin' near an hour. You musta been busy, not to notice."

Daniel nudged Albert, who stood beside him. "We done good, din't we?"

Albert smiled.

Rufus was sour. "We got through this time, Simple Simon. Don't expect it to last."

#

The *Essex* chugged back to Cairo for coal, ammunition, and supplies. Captain Porter gave orders to put the vessel shipshape. The ordinary seamen and landsmen were put to work scrubbing everything, shining the brass fittings, and holystoning the wooden decks.

Two days later, they shoved off from Cairo, turned up the Ohio River, and steamed toward Paducah, Kentucky, a major staging point for Union troops. For the next three weeks, the *Essex* made forays from Paducah up and down the Tennessee and Cumberland Rivers—cautious probes into rebel territory. Sometimes they drew musket fire from the shore. Twice they drew ineffectual fire from Confederate cannon. In all this, they fought no real battle.

The sailors worked in watches, four hours on and four hours off. They slept in hammocks slung in the forward hold. But no one could sleep twelve hours a day.

Daniel watched Rufus work a steel pen across a paper laid on an ammunition crate. He gazed at the smooth flow of curves and loops the pen laid down from Rufus' hand. He had seen white men write on paper. Now here, a black man did it.

Rufus raised his head and frowned. "What you starin' at, landsman?"

Daniel swallowed. He pointed to the sheet of paper. "That's—"

"Writin', Farm Boy. Handwritin', to be exact. I don't need you snoopin' around when I write a letter to my mama in Cincinnati."

"No," said Daniel. "Course not. Only ..."

"What?" Rufus' glared icily. "Spit it out."

"Well, them's words you're writin'. They mean somethin'."

"Yeh, they mean somethin'. Thass why I'm writin' them."

"I could learn. You could learn me."

Rufus shook his head. "You'd never get it."

"I want to try."

Rufus sighed. He stood up and led Daniel to where he kept his sea chest. He opened it and pulled out a pencil, a sheet of paper, and an oblong piece of something. "That there's a rubber. That's so you can rub out your letters."

"Why would I rub them out?"

"For practice, Farm Boy. You don't need to use up my letter paper to practice writin'. You can rub out your words and write over top of them." Rufus made a mark with the pencil and rubbed it out. "See? You can do that four, five, six times 'fore the paper comes apart."

"Oh." Daniel received the paper, pencil, and rubber into his hands. He smiled with gratitude. "Well, uh, how do I do it?"

"Do what, landsman?"

"Write."

Rufus stared at him. "Oh, that. Well, for starters. The first thing you got to learn is how to make an A. They's two kinds. A little one and a big one." He took the pencil and drew an example of each on the paper. "There. Now you do it." He handed the pencil back to Daniel.

Daniel put the pencil point on the paper and started to draw an A. The lead broke and gouged a hole in the paper.

"Jesus, Farmer! Not so hard. You got to learn how to hold the pencil."

Rufus spent the next fifteen minutes demonstrating how to grip a pencil, using just the tips of the thumb and first two fingers. "Then you pull it across the paper gentle, this way—not like you done. I said you couldn't do it, and I was right."

Daniel grabbed the pencil from Rufus' hand. He wrapped his fingers around it and copied Rufus' A. Something did not seem right.

Rufus frowned. "No, no, that ain't it a-tall." He knit his brow. "Brother Daniel, which handed is you?"

"Huh?"

"Which handed? Right or left?"

"I never thought on it before." Daniel changed the pencil to his other hand. He held it lightly and moved it carefully on the page. This time it made an A, something like Rufus' A.

"Thass it! Farm Boy, you is right-handed. Now, always write with your right hand. You need to practice a lot. Make your A smaller and straighter. More controlled."

"Yes, yes," Daniel said. "What else?"

"Well, sooner or later, you gonna need B."

#

Daniel spent all his free time practicing his letters. At the end of two weeks, he presented Rufus with copies of all twenty-six letters, large and small.

Rufus raised his eyebrows. "Thass good, Farm Boy. Now, can you say them all?"

"A, bee, cee, dee, ee ..." Daniel spoke his way through the alphabet.

"Very good."

"Now, how they make words?"

Rufus sighed. "That's a long trick, landsman. First, you got to understand, each letter make a sound by itself."

Rufus began teaching Daniel what sounds each letter could make, then how to combine them into simple words like "dog" and "cat."

By the second day, Daniel could write "My name is Daniel Freeman. I am a free man." Rufus smiled, the first time Daniel had ever seen him do so, when Daniel showed him the two brief statements. A sense of power and joy coursed through him.

Then Rufus frowned. "You got a long way to go, landsman. You gonna learn things ain't always spelt the way you would spell them."

#

Daniel's literary life got preempted by war.

The *Essex* left Paducah the morning of February 4 with full loads of coal and ammunition, guarding steamers filled with two divisions of General Grant's troops. They were to attack Fort Henry, a Confederate border stronghold on the Tennessee River.

All day Tuesday and Wednesday, as Grant's soldiers landed just north of the fort, the *Essex* and six other gunboats cruised the river near the landing zone, ready to answer any rebel challenges. All sailors of this "Western Gunboat Flotilla" stood double watches, pausing only for a quick meal and a short sleep.

On Thursday morning, February 6, the drummer beat to quarters. All hands manned battle stations as the flotilla chugged upstream to bombard Fort Henry with their forward guns.

Daniel ran between the bunkers and the boiler room, carrying coal which the stokers, including Rufus and Albert, fed to the boilers. Stripped to the waist, slippery with sweat, he dodged his fellow coal heavers as they ran a loop in the ship's tight quarters.

The Dahlgren cannon shook the timbers, and rounds of artillery fired from Fort Henry clanged off the heavy iron casemate that protected them all. Daniel no longer quaked with fear but accepted these noises as the routine sounds of battle.

He filled his scuttle and turned away from the bunker. Something struck his ears with hammer force. He fell back against the scuttle. His legs launched him forward. A wall of steam pushed him out the forward hatch. He sprawled on the foredeck. Screams rang in his ears. A steam-scalded stoker, skin already sloughing from his upper body, staggered from the hatch and fell into the water.

All around him scalded men lay on the foredeck, moaning or screaming.

He had to get out of there. Best way would be over the side. The mouths of the cannon just above his head would soon belch flame and smoke, maybe toasting him alive.

He got back on his feet and realized the guns were silent. The *Essex* had turned sideways. It drifted downriver, away from the fort. The shore slipped sideways past the bow of the ship.

Nobody's driving the boat.

The *Essex* turned a complete circle as the current carried her downstream. Daniel recognized the timberclad gunboat *Lexington* as the *Essex* slid past her. Booms, thuds, and smoke on all sides testified that the other six gunboats of the flotilla continued the fight.

Only the *Essex* had met with disaster.

#

She limped back down the Tennessee to Paducah. She got up enough steam to return to Cairo the next day with the ironclads *Cincinnati* and *St Louis*. The three gunboats blew their whistles and flew Fort Henry's captured flags upside-down.

The battle, though a victory, had taken a heavy toll on *Essex*. Daniel learned that a thirty-two-pound rebel

290

shot had pierced the armor plating and blown up the middle boiler. More than thirty crewmen, most of them stokers and coal heavers, had been killed or wounded.

Daniel had escaped with a slight scalding, but Albert and Rufus had been at the point of impact. Albert was dead. Daniel felt like a motherless child again. Albert, more than the tart-tongued Rufus, had been his champion in the Navy, the one who watched out for him and showed him the ropes.

Rufus, burned and looking like a corpse, left the ship on a stretcher. He mumbled, "I'll write you a letter, Farm Boy. You'll have to puzzle out the words for yourself."

35. Anders

Illinois

April – August 1862

Anders grasped the crowbar in numbed fingers and chafed the lid of the wet wooden crate. Rain drummed on the platform roof and dripped off into cold puddles beside the tracks. This year's mid-April rains had turned uncommonly cold.

Brother Claymore of the Petersburg Methodist Church held a lantern. His breath steamed in its feeble light.

The station agent squinted at a paper crimped in his stubby fingers.

The crate's lid gave way, scraping Anders' knuckles. He dropped the bar and pried the lid off with his bare hands. Light from Claymore's lantern spilled into the long crate.

It could not be. "This cannot be my brother."

The agent rattled his paper. "Bill of lading says John Gunstensen, corporal in the Seventh Illinois."

"That cannot be right!" Anders cried. Darkness closed in, blocking his vision, and he felt dizzy. Warm arms, Maria's, encircled his waist.

His head cleared.

Maria gazed up at him, fear in her eyes. When had he ever seen that?

Claymore coughed. "Sometimes, when they give up the ghost, it changes their face beyond recognition."

"These here remains were in transit more than a week from Tennessee . . . as maybe you can tell. They may have been short on ice when they shipped him." The agent wrinkled his nose. "Certainly none in there now."

The thing in the bottom of the crate wore a blue coat. A cap pinned to its chest showed brass letters on its crown—Co. I / 7th Ill. No marks on hands or face, no bloodstains on the blue coat. Perhaps the wound lay under the cap.

Anders tried to compare the sunken face to his brother's. O shame!—his memory would not summon John's face.

The man in the box seemed familiar, yet with some features raised, others diminished.

Maybe the ball struck John's face but instead of destroying just distorted its lines, as that cartoon sketch artist did last summer at the county fair. No, that cannot be right. Still, it looks something like him.

"It is John," he blurted.

Maria held him tight.

"Your brother is with the Lord now," said Claymore.

Anders held back tears. "He fought to protect us, all of us, to shelter us from the war. But the war has struck us anyway."

Brother Claymore made all the arrangements and preached a sermon in the Indian Point Cemetery the following Saturday. He called John "a brave fighter in the

294

cause of freedom," and all the Norwegian and American friends present nodded solemnly. A freshening wind chased off the rain of previous days.

Anders dumped earth on John's coffin. He thought, with dread, of the burden of writing this news home to Father and Mother. *To learn such a thing at their age! How shall I tell them? What will Gunder say? And John himself—he will not live to see the final victory of the Union, for which he has given his life. What can I say to his ghost? What account can I give of myself?*

Thor nudged Anders. "You have shoveled enough. Give over, before you fill the grave and leave nothing for us to do." Thor took the shovel from his hands.

Anders drove Maria and Aunt Osa home to Søtstrøm. The farm was all his own again. The knowledge weighed him down like a granite tombstone.

#

Anders walked behind Simon Borchers—a poor substitute for John, yet one he must accept. As Borchers swung the hoe, Anders dropped two kernels into each hole, using his foot to cover them with soil. It made him think of John, tucked into a hole at Indian Point Cemetery and covered with soil. And Gunhild, covered up with soil in a hole right here at Søtstrøm.

George Washington Gunstensen, ambassador of all things brash and alive, rolled in the grass under an oak tree. He stood up and pointed. "Pappa, look!"

A tall man rode toward them—Smithson, the postman, on his black mule.

"Letter for you, Mister G." Smithson, face full of woe, reached an envelope down to Anders. It was franked with "Col., 7th Ill. Vols." and addressed to "Mr. Gunstenson, Sweetwater, Ills."

Standing in the field, under the eyes of Smithson, Borchers, and little George, Anders opened it with trembling hands. One sheet of paper had another sheet folded inside.

Anders walked away.

#

In the barn, by daylight from the open door, Anders read:

> *Dear Mr. Gunstenson,*
> *It pains me to inform you of the death of your*
> *brother John in the Cause of Freedom. You will*
> *find his last letter to you enclosed.*

Borchers, ignoring his need for privacy, entered the barn.

Anders slipped John's final letter into his pocket. Even the official notification, still in his hands, he would have preferred to keep from Borchers' eyes. The old drunk had no business soiling his memory of John.

Borchers spoke softly. "From his commander, is it?"

"It ... yes. Signed by Richard Rowett, Lieut. Col., Commanding. "

Borchers gazed past Anders. He said nothing.

Something dissolved in Anders. Words poured forth. "They fought at a place called Shiloh. This Rowett says John died from a shell that exploded near him. Listen to what he says: We searched for wounds on his body and, finding none, concluded that the mere concussion killed him."

"Tch," said Borchers. "There's a mercy, anyway."

"It was an impossible situation. He says the soldiers called it a hornet's nest."

296

"Know just what he means, Sonny. We said the same thing when we was pinned down at Molino del Rey. In Mexico, you know."

"Simon," said Anders. "I did not know you were a soldier."

"Yep. Private Borchers, that's me."

Borchers shuffled out of the barn. Anders watched him go and shook his head.

Anders folded the letter and slipped it back into the envelope. Then he pulled out the private letter from John.

Dear Brother,

If you see this I have given all. Do not be dismayed, we all must travel the same road.

I give you back half of your farm. I will not need it.

I have learned that things are not so simple as "Free the slaves and that's all"! Lots of men want to save the Union, or punish traitors, yet have no care for the slaves. I hope our struggles will end slavery but no longer count upon it.

What I do insist is, we must fight until the Secession surrenders. They must be defeated, not bargained with. The Union must be on our terms, not theirs. I have lost too many friends to accept less.

I know how Maria and little George depend on you—He never knew about John Oliver!—and how satisfying your labors must be. However, I cannot help wishing for your strong arm in battle, while our Cause may yet be saved.

Your loving brother,
John
Company I, Seventh Illinois Volunteer Infantry
On campaign in Tennessee, April 5, 1862

297

#

The month of June brought heat and lush growth to Menard County. Anders' corn sprouted fast. It promised a big harvest in the fall, if weather or locusts did not destroy it. The winter wheat waxed full in the ear.

As he worked with Borchers cradling the wheat, Anders brooded on John's letter. Suppose he yielded to his brother's last wish, that he join the fight. How could the farm be sustained? Borchers was capable enough but was a drunken old sot, unfit for large responsibility.

Anders thought of Maria's father, Christian Conradsen Nybro, boat builder of Øiestad, Norway. Maria had confided in Anders that her Pappa was paralyzed by strong drink every winter. Yet every spring he turned back with zeal to the business of building boats and making money. The prospect of profit turned him sober and responsible.

"Simon," Anders said, "what if you were paid a half-interest in the crops, instead of a daily wage?"

Borchers frowned and set down his cradle scythe. "Come again, Sonny?"

"Instead of fifty cents a day, I would pay you half of the harvest. You could sell your half at the mill. You would make more money that way."

Borchers cracked a lopsided smile. He removed his hat, scratched his head.

"Naw, you see, Sonny, I can't work like that. Need my cash money, a little at a time, if you know what I mean."

"You old drukkenbolt!" Anders threw down his cradle in disgust. "You drink up all your wages as soon as you get them. You make no provision for yourself, yet we must give you cash every Saturday, on the dot! Arrgh!"

He stomped off. Borchers, though himself a war veteran, would never be the means by which Anders could be freed to serve his country.

He needed to walk in the corn, lest he push the old reprobate too far and be left with no help at all.

#

Anders and Maria stayed home on the Fourth of July 1862. There was farm work to be done and two young boys to care for. Besides, the dazzle of a few pounds of skyrockets shrank to nothing, in Anders' estimation, against the tons of powder used on battlefields to kill young men like John.

On the Fifth of July, a Saturday, Anders took fifty bushels of threshed wheat to the flour mill in Petersburg. Farmers passed the time in conversation as they waited for their grain to be ground. Some of these men Anders knew from the debates at the Sweetwater store.

Charlie Simmons—once a disgruntled Whig, now a dissatisfied Republican—pulled several recent issues of the *Illinois State Journal* from under the seat of his buckboard.

"Maybe you boys can help me understand this," he said. "On Tuesday they said McClellan was knocking on Jeff Davis' door. Here it is, listen: A successful strategic movement which must result in the fall of Richmond at an early day. That sounds pretty good, don't it?"

One or two farmers rumbled their assent.

"But now, listen to this. On Wednesday: The result claimed for the two or three days fighting is that *he now occupies better ground* in supporting distance of the gunboats, with *a more compacted and less extended line* immediately in front of Richmond. Now, that don't sound like he captured it, does it?"

299

"Maybe it means he's just getting ready to capture it," said Will Cargill, who had just arrived with wheat from his father's acres.

Charlie smiled. "I'm glad you said that, Son. 'Cause it *does* sound like that must be it, don't it?"

"Why, sure."

"*Howsome-ever*," Charlie said, "here's what yesterday's paper says about it: Though compelled to bear the *repeated* and *violent* attacks of superior numbers, our troops seem never to have been betrayed into *anything like a rout*. Ya hear that, boys? Nothin' like a rout. No, nothin' a-tall like a nasty old *rout*."

Anders, knowing Charlie's love of long debates, just wanted to get to the point.

"If it was not a rout, then, Mister Simmons, what was it?"

Charlie gave him a professorial glance. "That's a very good question, young man. Let's see, now . . ." He buried his nose again in the paper. "Oh, here it is. Listen: *Retiring* deliberately and in order, to the position *proposed to be occupied*, they received each tremendous shock of the foe with a firmness which was *their own best protection*."

He fixed Anders with an owlish gaze. "Well, there you have it, sir. General McClellan, you know, they call him Little Napoleon. On accounta he's so short, you see. Retiring—that means retreatin'—*Retiring* deliberately and in order . . . *for their own best protection*. Anything about that sound Na-po-leonic to you?"

"Not too much, no," said Anders.

The miller's boy came out and told Anders his wheat had become flour. Anders drove his wagon to the mill's loading port. He received almost a ton and a half of white flour and bran, in gunnysacks.

With the Union Army's costly missteps weighing heavy on his heart, he drove from the mill to Osmundsgarden, to see Kirsten Haraldsdatter.

#

"Anders! What a pleasant surprise."

Kirsten led him into the cabin, sat him down, poured coffee. "What brings you here, all by yourself?"

Anders sipped his coffee, hesitated. "Things are tight all over, Kirsten. Since last summer, I have had no help but old Borchers—"

"I wanted to assist you, Anders, only—"

"I know." He smiled. "We got through the winter somehow. This spring already I have made a good harvest of wheat, with Borchers' help."

"Praise God, Anders! So even without our help, you managed."

"Now I'm concerned about the corn."

Kirsten flapped her hand. "That doesn't come till autumn."

"Just so."

Kirsten stared at him for a moment. She wrinkled her brow.

"What are you getting at, Anders? Say it straight out, I am a simple old woman."

"Maria may need to harvest the corn by herself."

Kirsten's mouth fell open. "Anders—"

"Our armies grind away at the rebels. My help will soon be needed to put down the curse of slavery."

Kirsten's face crumpled. Tears welled in her eyes. "Oh, Anders, how can Maria spare you? This war is a problem for the Americans to solve."

301

"We are the Americans, Kirsten Haraldsdatter, whether you like it or not. I shall not have my brother's death go for nothing."

"How will Maria get along?"

"She would have Borchers."

"Borchers." Kirsten frowned. "I have heard of him. Not the best of men, is he?"

"Nor the worst, either, I suppose. In time of war, we must use what God sends us."

She sighed and cast her eyes down.

"I came here to ask you right now, Kirsten, whether you can spare one of your sons to help Maria and Borchers with the corn harvest."

Having said what he came to say, he lapsed into silence.

Kirsten stared down at the table, her mouth pressed into her fist, for a long time. Then she lifted her face. "It will be so. You shall have Thor, he's stronger than Reier."

Anders smiled. "Thank you, Kirsten Haraldsdatter. I shall pay a dollar a day."

"You shall pay nothing!" she barked.

Anders recoiled at her outburst.

She glared at him. "Since you mean to desert your family, then we must help them from our own substance."

Anders drove home in darkness.

All this so I may follow my brother into the flames, which may consume me, caul or no caul. Leaving Maria and the boys alone so my friend Daniel may attain his goal of freedom and I my goal of being a man among men—a true American.

And to achieve all this, he brooded, *I must accept Kirsten Haraldsdatter's charity.*

#

The *State Journal* reported a series of battles in Virginia, all fought within one week.

Anders ignored the stalwart optimism of the paper's accounts. These battles had dashed McClellan's plan to march up the peninsula and capture Richmond. Now the cautious leader would regroup his forces, resupply them, restore their morale, and plan his next meticulous campaign. Prospects for a swift victory appeared dim.

Then, on July 20, Lincoln moved General Halleck from Corinth, Mississippi, to Washington, D.C., to be general-in-chief of all Union armies. Whether this would revive the Eastern campaign, Anders did not know. But Halleck's departure left Grant in charge of the West, giving hope of progress in the Mississippi Valley.

Grant, if anyone, would get Union forces back on the offensive.

And more soldiers would be needed.

#

The August sun brought forth sweat, which ran down Anders' arms, making the logs slippery as he and Borchers unloaded them from the wagon.

"The world has been turned upside down," said Maria from the cabin door. She held five-month-old John Oliver in her arms while George chased the rooster around the yard.

"What do you mean, Wife? That sounds like something your Tante would say."

"Since when do you gather firewood in July?"

Anders straightened up, took a few deep breaths. "The wheat is in, and most of the potatoes. It will be another six weeks before the corn is ready. We may as well keep busy making firewood."

Her eyes measured him.

303

"Firewood is essential in wintertime, jenta mi. Without it, you, the boys, and Aunt Osa might freeze."

Maria parked the baby on her hip and stared at Anders. "You would not freeze with us?"

"I … am not so worried about myself."

"Hmpf." She turned and went inside.

#

At dinner, after Anders asked the blessing, Maria said, "Of course, it makes sense to get the firewood done now, if you will not be here later."

Anders, helping himself to sliced beets, stopped with the serving spoon in mid-air.

"That is what this is all about, isn't it?" she said. "You mean to join the Army."

Maria looked straight into his eyes. Aunt Osa, bringing baked potatoes from the fire, stopped to stare at Anders with her mouth open. Georgie played with his spoon while little John Oliver nuzzled at Maria's breast.

"I don't know when I have smelled food this good," Anders said. He smiled at each of them in turn. To the silence which greeted him he added, "Our country needs more soldiers."

Maria took Georgie's spoon from him, dipped it in his porridge, and guided it to his mouth. "Your family needs you more than the Army does."

"My brother gave his life—" He could not say more.

Maria scooped porridge up into Georgie's mouth and over his lip. She laid the spoon down and turned her eyes to Anders. "Your brother's life means more to you than your own."

Anders took a deep breath. "They will enlist Menard County soldiers for Company K, 106th Illinois Volunteers, at Athens next Thursday."

304

Maria, John Oliver at her breast, picked up the spoon again. She made quite a production of feeding Georgie his second bite. Not a glance in Anders' direction. "Eat your food, "she said. "It will get cold."

Aunt Osa, having laid a baked potato on each adult's plate, looked up at Anders. "Soon or late, what's warm goes cold," she said.

36. Anders

Illinois
September 1862

Anders stood straight, like a soldier, before his tent on the baking street of K Company, his uniform dusty from daily drills. He had cleaned it as best he could, had brushed his limp brogans and smeared them with lampblack. He had honed his razor and shaved off thirty days' growth of sandy whiskers.

The beard would grow back, for it would not always be convenient to shave in camp or on the march. But today Maria would see him for the first time since his enlistment. He wanted her to see the man she knew, not the hairy savage he had become in a month's time.

Today the 106th Illinois Volunteer Infantry Regiment would be mustered into federal service at its training camp in Lincoln, the new railroad town established nine years ago and named for the Springfield lawyer who had assisted in its founding. Mothers, fathers, sisters, brothers, and wives of soldiers had come to

Lincoln from miles around for the mustering ceremony. Maria had traveled more than twenty miles.

His breath caught in his throat as she came in view wearing her best Norwegian dress, her golden hair braided and looped as she had worn it at Yuletide before their marriage. John Oliver wriggled in her arms. Georgie, made shy by a tent city bustling with soldiers and starched civilians, clung to Maria's dress. She, though encumbered by the two boys, glowed like a ray of sunshine in promenade with Aunt Osa and the Lakes.

The drab civilians who crowded her path—the women more than the men—turned to stare as she passed. Anders knew she had not dressed to please him, much less to show approval of his decision. Rather, she flaunted her stiff-necked way of holding her head high in the face of adversity. He had never been prouder.

Maria and Aunt Osa detached themselves from the Lakes. The old woman took Georgie's hand and parted him from his mother's skirt.

"You are beautiful, jenta mi. I am sorry to leave you. And my two big boys."

She frowned and placed John Oliver in Anders' hands. He held the warm bundle of his youngest boy, who smelled like the newness of the earth in springtime. The baby's deep blue eyes mirrored his soul. Anders kissed his forehead and handed him back.

He reached for George with both hands and tossed him in the air. The boy screamed with delight. He quieted for Aunt Osa once his feet rested on the ground again.

Maria placed a hand on Anders' chest.

Why must I leave this loveliest of women?

Something wanted to burn a hole in his pocket. He dug deep, brought out a small booklet, and placed it in her hand. "Coupons. Worth ten dollars cash each month, from the government. I have signed an allotment to send you most of my pay. You must bring this coupon book to the local pay officer at the courthouse."

Maria sighed. "Ja. Good. I shall."

"I spoke with Simon Borchers before I left. He pledged to stay on until I get back. He is a good worker. He promised me that he would try not to drink too much."

Maria cast her gaze downward. "I hope he will not *too often* drink too much. If he can be sometimes sober, I shall be grateful."

"And Kirsten Haraldsdatter will lend us Thor for harvest. That is worth a great deal."

"I know it, Husband."

A bugle blasted nearby, startling Maria.

"That is assembly, jenta mi. We must go line up to be mustered into service."

He filled his eyes with Maria and the boys. "One more thing, Wife. The mortgage to Mister Eliot." *Did Maria just shudder?* "It is down to seventy-five dollars now. It is recorded at the courthouse. When harvest comes, try to pay it off. I would prefer not to be in Eliot's debt."

All around them, soldiers hurried from their tents to the parade ground.

Maria stood stiff, her lips pursed. Tears sprang from her eyes. "Oh, Anders! You will come back to us in a box."

"Nonsense."

She wrapped her arms around his neck and pressed her lips to his in a kiss plainly meant to last through eternity.

#

Anders stood in formation on the dusty field as the regiment was mustered into service.

309

At the head of the formation stood the new sergeant major, said to be a blooded soldier, one who had seen battle. He had been transferred into the new regiment to help Colonel Latham lead the untested 106th to war.

The sergeant major was a tiny figure, far up the field from where Anders stood in Company K. Yet when this important person shouted—"Regiment ... form by companies!"—Anders knew the voice.

He doubted his ears.

The voice shouted again: "Companies ... report!"

Anders strained, stood on tiptoe to see over the ranks ahead. He saw the sergeant major trooping the line behind the colonel.

The voice ... the size. That gait, altered by Maria's musket blast. The old slave catcher, Bullamore Crawley.

When dismissed, Anders ran to regimental headquarters, breathless with urgency.

A guard barred his way. "Who goes there?"

"Anders Gunstensen, private, Company K."

"State your business."

"Crawley. I must warn the commander."

The guard frowned. "Crawley's the sergeant major."

"Yes, but he should not be!" Anders heard his voice rise; he could not help it. "I know him before the war. He were ... was, a slave catcher."

The guard frowned. The tent flap parted and Colonel Latham came out. Anders snapped to attention.

"At ease, soldier," said the colonel. "Who are you?"

"Private Gunstensen, sir. Company K. I come to tell you about the slave catcher Crawley. He is not qualified for Army, he is a—"

"That's enough, Private." The colonel's mouth clenched. "When something bothers you, talk to your platoon sergeant. Not me."

"But, this Crawley—"

310

"Dismissed, Private." The colonel stepped back into his tent.

#

Back in his company, Anders found Sergeant McCann, a neighbor from Sweetwater.

"Jayzus, Andrew, you bought all of us a peck of trouble. You ain't supposed to go to the commander with every little thing."

"This man is a slaver. Does that mean nothing?"

"Yer talkin' about the man's occupation before the war. What he done for a livin' was legal. He's as welcome as any man to serve his country. And don't you forget it."

"How can—"

"Button up your lip, Private. Now back to your platoon. We've a big day of drill tomorrow."

#

Anders sat under an oak tree a few minutes later, cleaning his musket beyond perfection. It galled him to be rebuffed by both his commander and his platoon sergeant, when the facts were so plain.

Crawley suddenly stood before him. The sergeant major grabbed his lapels, yanked him to his feet, rammed him up against the oak tree. His musket fell in the dirt.

"Listen to me, Oley," said Crawley, his hot breath in Anders' face. "I do remember you from Menard. And your wife, with her musket. It's your hard luck she weren't a good shot."

"Skurk!" Anders shouted. "Kjeltring!"

His comrades in Company K stood gawking, unsure what to do.

311

Crawley glanced at the crowd of soldiers who had gathered as spectators. He backed away from the oak and stood Anders on his feet. He moved in closer.

"I'm back in your life now, Oley, and I forget nothing ... ever." His voice threatened by its softness.

"How can you be in the Union Army? You are a slaver. You and your son."

"Don't bother about Teddy. Your nigger friend with the axe took care of him. He can't fight with a wooden foot. If he could, the damned fool would fight for the rebs."

"Why do you not fight for them?"

Crawley took a deep breath and sighed. He stared daggers at the soldiers who hung around, curious about their now low-toned conversation. The soldiers moved away.

"Don't take much of a brain to see the North's gonna win. Your so-called Confederacy will be swept away, and slavery with it. I don't know what I'll do for a livin' after the war, Oley. I do aim to be on the winning side."

"You fight only for your advantage. I fight for freedom."

"Bravo, Oley. Bully for you. Army Regulations say I must care for you as one of my own little ducklings. All I say is, you better watch every move you make. I can break you any time I want." Crawley spat at Anders' feet. "And I will."

The sergeant major stalked away.

37. Maria

Illinois
October 1862

Maria pitched cornstalks into the wagon bed.

Borchers flicked the reins, and the horses started back to the barn. Tired and short-tempered, Maria cut a new swath of corn. The work must go on, the corn harvest just beginning, winter wheat still to plant. The warm sun continued from September, of necessity, for she was behind schedule.

Georgi was his usual boisterous self, Janni had begun cutting teeth. She would wean him when convenient, but as long as he would nurse, it was thriftier than feeding him solid food.

Tante minded the boys all day, cooked and cleaned. Maria did Anders' work—the corn harvest, the wheat planting, the care of the animals—with the aid of Simon Borchers.

Borchers drank through Sunday, slept it off Monday, and came to work Tuesday at noon. The most reliable thing about him was his devotion to whiskey. Every

Saturday Maria had to pay his week's wages of three dollars or risk losing his help altogether.

She had gone to the courthouse to receive her ten dollars from Anders' pay. The officer there said he could not pay out until the end of the month. So the day spent en route to and from Petersburg bore no result. Twelve dollars for Borchers this month would have to come from her small cash reserve. Next month would have five Saturdays, so the old goat would need fifteen dollars! If she ever got the ten-dollar stipend from the Army, Borchers' pay would still exceed it by two dollars in most months and by five dollars three times a year. And she would use up a day each month traveling to the county seat. *What an abomination is war,* she thought.

If only she could have her husband back! Then it would not matter how dire the finances were. She and Anders would face things together.

Anders had urged her to pay off the mortgage, but unless she could sell some corn for cash, she would have to go to Mister Eliot and beg for an extension of the loan.

She dared not think about the precious stone in its little red bag. It remained hidden on her person eight years after Pappa had given it to her. Neither Anders nor Tante knew it existed. That diamond would not be used, except in the direst emergency.

If she could get enough corn into the bin now, the swine would be fat enough to sell in a few weeks. Maybe she could hold off Eliot's demands, if her need for cash were not too great. The butter and cheese payments might just be enough to make up the extra to pay Borchers. So she would continue to take dairy goods into Sweetwater each week, fronting an icy indifference in the face of the storekeeper's noxious demeanor.

The corn harvest and the sowing of wheat were the chief concerns. Kirsten Haraldsdatter had promised

314

Thor's labor at harvest. If she could not have Anders, Thor would be the next best thing. But Kirsten had not said just when to expect him.

When, oh when, would Thor arrive?

\#

On Sunday, October 12, Tante lay abed, eyes open and fixed on the ceiling. When Maria spoke to her, she rolled her eyes and said nothing. Spittle ran down her chin.

"Tante, what is wrong? Let me help you up."

Maria reached below Tante's bony shoulders and lifted her. When she withdrew her arm, the old woman slumped sideways.

"Tante, speak to me."

The old woman gazed into space. Her face, which had been square, had become lopsided. Maria straightened her up again, then lowered her gently back down.

A smell rose. Tante had wet herself.

"Tante! What is wrong?" Maria, despite her Christian upbringing, could only think to slap Tante in the face. So she did, again and again. But it made no difference.

Maria ripped off the bedclothes and stripped the soiled nightdress from the old woman. She got warm water from the stove, bathed and dried her, then put a clean nightgown on her. When she replaced the bed linens under the old woman, she had to roll her to the side. Tante's body was limp.

Maria fed and dressed the boys, Georgi and Janni. Then she went back to see Tante, who lay, eyes open, unresponsive.

"Tante sleep more?" Georgi leaned against the footboard of the bed, quiet and pensive.

"That is right, Georgi. Tante needs more sleep."

315

Maria took both boys outside to play with sticks in the dooryard.

Tears upon her face, she prayed to Jesus, asking that the old woman's burden be lifted.

#

With Tante bedstruck, Maria's workload doubled. Every morning she cared for both boys and tended to her old aunt's insensate needs. She could not get into the field to help Borchers with the harvest until mid-day. She had to quit early, too, since both the boys and Tante needed her supervision again as each day wore on.

The old drunkard's unaided efforts were feeble. By the third week in October, he and Maria together had cribbed half the corn. With the weather turning cool, they would need to plant the winter wheat.

One day she saw a silhouette in the sunset—a barrel-chested, broad-shouldered man, out on the Sweetwater Road. He walked with a rolling gait, like one who had just disembarked from a ship and had not yet got his land legs.

A familiar gait, a saving moment.

"Thor! At last! Praise God!"

He strode into the farmyard, a smile on his face.

"I'm sorry it has taken so long. We had a good deal to do at our place, too."

Maria's prayers were answered. Now, the souls at Søtstrøm might survive the winter.

#

That night, at supper, Maria unloaded her mortgage worries upon Thor. When she spoke of how much she loathed any further indebtedness to Eliot, Thor's brow flexed downward.

316

"This Eliot," he said. "I have heard of him. A lot of farmers borrow money from him. He is quick to foreclose on mortgages and take over the farms of those who cannot pay."

"It does not surprise me," Maria said. "Whenever I see the man, he seems greedy and calculating. He used to be rich. I think he means to be rich again, any way he can."

Thor's mouth set in a firm line. "He already owns several small farms. Their owners have become his tenants. They pay him rent now. They had no choice."

Maria drew in a sharp breath.

Thor looked into her eyes. "Don't worry. I'll take care of him." His muscular hands bunched into fists.

"Oh, no," Maria said. "You must not do anything rash, Thor. It will only cause trouble. Let us concentrate on getting the corn in."

38. Anders

Tennessee

December 1862

Anders, coming back from the field latrine, urged his legs to move faster.

"You there, Gunnison! Get to work, Oley!" The sergeant major's voice banged through the noise of axes, hammers, and men's shouts. Company K, defending a railroad bridge in West Tennessee, had been ordered to prepare for a battle Anders did not believe would come.

Crawley ran lurch-legged to meet Anders as he rejoined his platoon. "You shit when I tell you to, soldier, not before!" He grabbed Anders by the arm and shoved him toward the twelve-pounder field howitzer at the gate of the stockade.

Anders wrenched his arm free. He stood rooted to the spot. "You cannot control nature, Crawley. If you want to regulate my bowels, get us some decent food."

The old slave catcher leaned into Anders' face. "You'll face a court martial for insubordination next week—if you survive Forrest's raid this week."

"Forrest! You think the genius of rebel cavalry will trouble himself about the Forked Deer River bridge?"

"That's why the colonel sent me here from Jackson, Oley. To make sure ole Nathan stubs his toe on Company K." Crawley grabbed Anders again and shoved him toward the howitzer. "Now get busy with that rag and make sure this piece is spotless."

Anders accepted a shine rag a burly soldier named Silas handed him. "What is the use of polishing this cannon when we have no artillerists to fire it?"

Crawley got in his face again. "No more thinking, Oley. Just do what you're told."

He strode away to yell at soldiers digging a trench in front of the wooden palisades that made the stockade wall.

The brawny soldier polishing the gun beside Anders spat in the dirt. "By God, if I was you, I'd a popped him one."

"It's a good thing you are not me, Silas," said Anders. "What would you get from striking the sergeant major?"

"Satisfaction."

"Ja. Plus a firing squad to celebrate your birthday."

Will Cargill, Anders' former neighbor from Sweetwater, chuckled. "Reckon he's right about that, Silas. It'd be your last birthday, too."

Silas scowled. "All I'm saying is, we was doin' fine here. Had us a nice little post guarding a no-count bridge over a piddlin' little stream. Then along comes Sergeant High and Mighty preaching war and calamity. Now we're all worked to the bone fer nothin'. I got half a mind to run—"

The drummer beat the long roll.

"This is it, boys!" shouted Crawley.

320

A moment of awed silence. Soldiers all over camp stopped what they were doing and scanned one another's faces. They saw surprise.

"Go on, get at it!"

Everybody ran at once, grabbing Springfield muskets from stacks of four in front of the tents, then dashing into the stockade to pour fire down upon the rebels.

Anders went to get his musket.

Big hands grabbed him and spun him around. "Not you, Oley." Crawley pushed him back toward the howitzer. "Welcome to the field artillery."

Anders dropped his jaw in disbelief as the sergeant major corralled a dozen men to serve the big gun. "This is crazy! We are infantry, we don't know how—"

"Welcome to artillery *school*, I should have said. Now pick up that trail, six men on each side. Lift it and roll the gun forward."

Crawley cursed and badgered them into wheeling the heavy gun out from the stockade wall. "Keep her movin', Oley. Don't stop now."

They moved the gun to a hillock fifty feet out from the wall, facing the lower timbers of the wooden railroad trestle. "That's what they'll go after," said Crawley. "That's what they're here for."

Anders glanced back at the fortress behind them, where muskets bristled from between the sharpened logs of the parapet.

"Don't worry 'bout your comrades, Oley. They'll be firing over your head. Mostly."

"Steel and fire don't worry me, Sergeant Major."

"Then you're a bigger damned fool than I thought."

Crawley gave each man a task. He called Anders Number Three, to work at the rear end of the cannon barrel. "First, you take this leather thumb stall and cover

321

the vent tight. Keep 'er there till I tell you. If air gets in that tube too early, she'll blow to pieces."

Trembling with the danger and weight of the task, Anders pressed his leather-encased thumb tight over the vent hole.

Crawley taught others the arts of swabbing and ramming the barrel and loading the muzzle with powder, wadding, and shell. "Gimme canister, boys. Canister at point blank'll cut 'em to pieces."

Will Cargill, designated Number Two, shoved a canister shell, filled with small iron balls, down the tube. Another soldier, Number One, rammed it home with the rammer.

The ground rumbled. Anders raised his eyes. Gray riders boiled out of a yellow dust cloud, raised sabers gleaming, hoofbeats thunderous.

Anders had let his thumb off the vent hole. Horrified, he scrambled to cover it up again.

Crawley swatted his hand out of the way. "No time, Oley! Stay on it better next time. Here." He slapped a long piece of metal into Anders' hand. "That's your vent prick. Jam it down there to open the powder bag."

Anders did so.

Crawley grabbed his wrist and yanked it back from the vent hole. "Time's a wastin'! Don't freeze up."

Silas, Number Four, stuck a primer into the vent hole and stepped aside, pulling the attached lanyard tight.

Musket fire blasted from the stockade behind them as the rebel riders neared the bridge.

"Fire!" Crawley bawled.

Silas pulled the lanyard.

BOOM!

The howitzer jumped backward. Anders felt its breeze as it passed.

"Jesus, Oley! Stay out of the way or get crushed."

322

Crawley made them pick up the heavy wooden trail and re-position the gun. "Now, Oley! Plug that hole again."

Anders jumped forward and pressed his thumb on the vent hole. He felt heat through the leather thumb stall, as Number One swabbed the barrel.

Out where the iron pellets had flown, dead and wounded men and horses lay in shallow water under the bridge timbers.

"Quick, boys, they're comin' back!"

Mounted rebels rode forward in place of the fallen.

The howitzer barked again. More riders fell.

As Anders and his mates reloaded the gun for a third shot, Crawley dashed forward. He fell on a soldier in gray who stood beside the timbers, doing something at their base.

"It's a sapper!" shouted Will. "He's got bags of powder to blow the bridge!"

The gun reloaded, Crawley was in the center of its field of fire. Silas stood uncertain, the lanyard taut in his hand.

Crawley pummeled the sapper with his pistol, then shot him. A rebel horseman rode down on Crawley and slashed him with a saber. Crawley fell into the water.

"Fire!" shouted Anders.

Silas stared at him, his mouth open.

"Fire, damn you! Crawley's down."

Silas yanked the cord. The gun jumped. A score of rebels went down.

Anders tossed his thumb stall to Silas and sprinted into the maelstrom of blood, water, and screaming horses. He raised Crawley half out of the water. Blood poured from a gash in the old slave catcher's neck.

"I'm dying, Oley." Crawley's eyes were white with terror. "Go back. Leave me."

323

"I cannot." Anders struggled to lift Crawley on his shoulders.

Will Cargill came to help. Will and Anders got Crawley to his feet and staggered back toward the howitzer, dragging the sergeant major between them.

The gun blew to pieces before their eyes, metal shards and body parts flying past them. A BOOM struck their backs.

"Rebel horse artillery, damn their eyes," said Crawley.

They staggered into the stockade, past the ruined gun. Silas' torn body lay across it.

39. Daniel

Mississippi

April – May 1863

Daniel stood on the hurricane deck of *U.S.S. Pittsburgh*, enjoying the breeze, when the drummer beat to quarters.

Ta-rum-pum-pump!

Here we go again.

Daniel had answered the drum often since transferring to *Pittsburgh*. The week after *Essex* met disaster at Fort Henry, he had been in *Pittsburgh's* crew when Grant attacked Fort Donelson on the Cumberland River. Though damaged by rebel fire, *Pittsburgh* played an honorable part in the Union's first great victory.

Two months later, she trained her guns on Island Number Ten in the Mississippi. Later she destroyed batteries below New Madrid, Missouri, clearing the way for Grant's army to cross the river. Other operations followed, all aimed at restoring federal control of the Mississippi.

The great obstacle was Vicksburg. The city stood on bluffs high above the river. Its guns prevented the passage of Union boats. To take the town, Grant had to get his army downriver below Vicksburg so he could attack from the east.

Not two weeks ago, *Pittsburgh* had been part of Admiral Porter's grand fleet that brashly steamed past Vicksburg's guns by night to begin the campaign.

Now, as Daniel slid down the casemate to take his station in the boiler room, he saw today's likely objective: a town on the east bank of the river, maybe a place to land Union troops. *Okay, General Grant, the Navy will come to your aid once again.*

Daniel ran to the bunkers and started heaving coal. The booms of the Dahlgrens almost cheered him, mixed with clangs on the casemate as *Pittsburgh* absorbed shots from the shore.

As he scooped into Number Two portside bunker— BAM!

A sheet of flame and blood swept over Daniel. He lay on his back, flung between bunkers and boilers. Coughing amid acrid smoke, he tried to rise.

Something held him down.

It was a leg. No man attached. He shoved the leg aside and rose.

Pain flashed through his chest.

"Lay down, landsman, lemme he'p ya." An unknown voice.

Daniel looked down at himself. His ribs were exposed, a large flap of flesh falling away to the side. As he sank back to the deck, strong hands pushed him up against the coal bunker and pain engulfed him.

"I done shoved the skin back on your chest, and a big wad of cotton over it. Now clamp your arm down to hold the flesh in place. Lay still and keep on breathin'."

Daniel never knew who had helped him. The battle raged for another hour, and he passed out from the pain.

326

He woke on a litter, being carried off the ship.

"What happened?" he asked. "What goin' on?"

"Fight's over," someone said. "You goin' home."

Home? Sounds good. He thought of Mammy, knew she was gone. *Where's home, then?*

They carried him aboard *U.S.S. Red Rover*, a hospital ship. A surgeon examined Daniel's chest, unwrapping the cotton wadding and linen bandages that held it together. Daniel gritted his teeth against a wave of pain.

"Easy, sailor," said the surgeon. "We're going to sew that up."

Someone placed a funnel over Daniel's mouth. "Breathe deep."

A strange smell ...

#

Daniel awoke in a large room, one man among dozens laid side by side. His chest hurt. Sailors all around him moaned.

"Jesus' mercy, you all. Don't you think I feel like moanin', too?"

They kept on moaning. He plugged his right ear with a finger. He worked his left hand up the side where his chest hurt like hellfire and plugged his left ear also. He lay that way, fingers in his ears, for a blank epoch.

He did not know when he slept and when he woke, nor for how long. Sometimes daylight filtered in, other times the light was dim and the air reeked of kerosene.

Plagued by dull pain, he felt hungry. *When did I last eat?*

Dim forms scurried by. He waved his hands, opened his mouth. Nobody came.

327

At last, a man loomed over him—an old white soldier, ragged and hairy, with a black eye patch and below it a grotesque scar. He stared at Daniel.

"Hungry," Daniel whispered.

The man said nothing.

"Hungry," Daniel whispered again, as loud as he could.

The old, wounded soldier shuffled off.

Daniel lay too weak to speak. His chest throbbed and his empty gut howled.

If I starve to death before my chest heals, maybe that's a good thing.

He entered a muddled state. He stood behind white surgeons, gazing down at himself. He could only glimpse himself on the bed when the doctors in front of him shifted left or right.

"He died for freedom," said one doctor. "What was his name?"

"Daniel Freeman."

"Daniel Freeman. Died a free man." He laughed.

The other surgeon joined his laughter until they both roared, clutching their sides, tears streaming down their faces.

I don't see what's so damned funny.

The laughing doctors dissolved, and Daniel lay on his back, eyes open, staring up.

The old soldier with the eye patch loomed over him. "I brung ya some soup. Kin you sit up to take it?"

Daniel tried to sit up. The world went gray, then black. A brawny arm gripped him under his shoulders and raised him partway up, gently. Pain swelled in Daniel's chest. He began to moan.

"Take a sip o' this. It'll help." The man held a spoonful of broth before Daniel's lips.

Daniel slurped.

328

"That's right. Jest a leetle at a time."

He slurped again.

"Don't hasten it," said the ravaged old man. "You got plenty time. I ain't goin' nowhere. I'm casual."

#

The man returned a dozen times a day. Daniel noted that day and night had crept back into his head. He slept as much in the day as at night; he lay in teeth-grinding pain as much at night as by day. But whenever conscious, he knew the difference.

The old soldier fed Daniel three times a day—at first broth from a bowl and spoon, then a hard cracker in addition. "Sumpin' to whet your teeth on, I reckon."

He came at non-meal times, too. Sometimes he relaid Daniel's covers or helped him with the mess and stink of relieving himself in a bedpan, for Daniel could not stand and shuffle to the head on his own. At other times, the old man just stopped by for a chat.

Such conversations revealed the wounded soldier's name to be Jubal. He was one of a small group of treated patients called "casuals"—not well enough to be released but well enough to bear a hand with those more helpless than they.

"How long I been on this here ship, Sonny? I reckon a coupla month now. Lost an eye, you know. Maybe you kin see that."

Daniel smiled. "Reckon I can. Thass why you have a hard time findin' my mouth with that soup spoon."

Jubal brought the spoon to Daniel's lips, then pulled it away, teasing. "Near half my face was shot off by one o' your damned Yankee minnie balls." He spat. "Lucky to be alive a-tall."

"You were shot by Yankees?"

329

The old man nodded. "Right up yonder at Steele's Bayou, in a scrap with Uncle Billy Sherman's boys."

"You a damned rebel!" Daniel lashed out, knocked away the soup bowl and spoon. Jubal jumped back as they crashed on the deck.

The old man shook a stern finger. "Hush now. You disturbin' the other boys."

"I don't care! You an old slave driver, makin' believe you's my friend."

Jubal scowled. "I never druv a slave in my life. Nor owned one, neither."

Daniel glared at him.

"You should be ashamed, smashing that soup bowl like that. Your mammy musta taught you better."

Tears welled in Daniel's eyes. *Mammy*. He could hardly recall her face. How many years since he had seen her? Where would she be now? With Jesus?

He wiped the tears from his eyes, pressed his lips together, and glared at the old rebel.

"And you don't have to call me your friend, neither," Jubal said. "But remember, I'm the casual what's got your soup that you need to live on." He stooped, picked up the spoon and the broken crockery. He shuffled off.

#

Daniel refused to be fed the next time Jubal came around.

Jubal sighed. "Suit yourself." He walked away.

The time after that, Daniel said, "Just leave it there on the nightstand. I can feed myself."

Jubal squinted. With elaborate care, he set the bowl and spoon on the table by Daniel's bed. He stood back, rocked on his heels, folded his arms, and watched.

330

Pain shot through Daniel as he tried to sit up. He lay back and caught his breath. "Well, can you help me sit up?"

"Think you can handle it from there, huh?"

"Just help me sit up."

The old man bent over, put an arm under Daniel, and lifted. Again Daniel felt mothered by the rough old rebel.

Daniel reached out to the table, brought the soup bowl to his lap, then lifted the spoon and took a sip.

"Well done, Sonny."

"Tell me somethin', old man. If you's not a slaver, what you was doin' in their army?"

Jubal's off-kilter smile appeared. "Why, I reckon it's just natural to us Miss'sipians to fight Yankees when they comes a-callin'. Wouldn't you, if you was me?"

"I's not you. I don't want to be you." Daniel sipped more soup. "What you think about playin' nurse to a free black man such as me?"

Jubal's eyes went round. He chewed on his whiskers for a moment. "Mighty surprised. Once I got to where I could walk upright and find my way around the ship, they told me to make myself useful to the patients. I figgered all them patients'd be white Yankees, see. I didn't think the mighty Union Army would be lettin' any niggers into its ranks."

"The Army don't. I'm a Navy man."

Jubal rubbed his chin. "Well, huh. Don't that beat all."

\#

From then on, Jubal just brought Daniel's meals on a tray, helped him past the pain of sitting up, and sometimes stayed for a bit of conversation.

"Listen, Daniel," he said one day. "I'm about as healed as I can get. You know this boat chugs up and down the river. One day soon I reckon they'll put me ashore and into one of them Yankee prisons. So, is they anything special I can do for you before then?"

Daniel frowned. "Special, like what?"

"Some of the white boys likes to send letters home, stuff like that. I can't write so good, but I could find somebody to come and do it for you."

What an idea!

"You just get me a paper and a pencil, Brother Jubal. I'll write it myself."

Jubal brought paper and pencil. As he watched in amazement, Daniel began to write.

> *Dear Miss Betsey,*
> *It has bin many a whil since we met last*
> *at mister Gunson's farm an you took a wagon*
> *to Canada.*

He stopped a moment to collect his thoughts. What should he say?

> *I hope you dont bare me no anger for*
> *sendin you on like I did. It wer for the best then,*
> *befor the war, so I coud help my frends get*
> *free. I hope you dont mind I come callin when*
> *the war is over. I like to see your place and you*
> *all settle down.*
> *Your true frend from old days,*
> *Daniel Freeman, sailor in the U.S. navy*
> *Aboard the U.S.S. Red Rover*

He smiled. "Is they a, whatchacallit?"

"Envelope? Here."

332

To Postman, Winzer, Canada
Letter for Betsey, a Young Black Woman was once a slave on Pettybone Plantation in Loosiana.

He folded the letter, placed it in the envelope, and gave it to Jubal. "I got no postage."

Jubal smiled. "Don't worry. The cap'n got a special pile of stamps just for these letters."

40. Maria

Illinois

June – July 1863

Maria raised her head at the sound. A buggy hitched to a magnificent black horse pulled into Søtstrøm's drive, driven by Mister Ransom Eliot, the storekeeper. He wore his usual swallowtail coat and silk tie. A gaudy, beribboned box sat in the seat beside him.

Dear Lord—what does this creature want from me today?

Maria rose, brushed dust off her skirt, and lifted Janni from between the corn rows, where he had been playing in the soil. "Georgi—you stay here. Help Mister Borchers pull weeds. Mamma will be back soon."

Hefting the dirty sixteen-month-old Janni on her hip, she trudged to the cabin to greet the unlooked-for guest. By the time she got there, Eliot had stopped his buggy and dismounted. He awaited her with a smile on his face.

He held the fancy box in his hands.

"Good day, Mister Eliot," she said. "What business brings you to Søtstrøm?"

His eyes popped wide open in surprise. "Business?" He tossed his head. His long tresses teased his tailored shoulders. "Oh, no, my dear—you misunderstand." He pulled out a handkerchief and dabbed sweat from his brow. "My word, the sun's hot. May we take shelter?"

Maria sighed and led him into the cabin. She motioned him to the best chair.

"Ladies first," Eliot said, sweeping his hand toward the other chair.

"Mister Eliot. I have not time to sit down today. What is it you wish?"

Janni wiggled to escape from her hip. She trapped him with both arms and brought him to the front, between herself and the storekeeper.

"It is just, dear lady, I got to thinking of you, here alone on this farm—"

"I am not alone. There is Georgi and Janni. And Mister Borchers."

"Be that as it may, dear lady"—*how dear can one lady be,* she wondered—Eliot dabbed with his handkerchief again—"be that as it may, you are husbandless for the duration of this war. And you have so many cares. I merely thought to bring you something to lighten your days a bit." He held out the gaudy box to her.

"Ja?"

Janni began wiggling again. *Good boy,* she thought.

Eliot tried to hand her the package. Seeing her hands occupied with Janni, he gave up and set it on the table. "A box of fancy European sweetmeats. Imported. For you."

Maria shook her head. "No, thank you. We cannot afford such things." She pressed her lips together.

"You don't understand. It's free. A gift. From me ... to you."

336

"No. I cannot accept."

Eliot heaved a dramatic sigh. "French bonbons. Even some Swedish truffles." He smiled and wiggled his eyebrows. "I don't want you to misunderstand my intentions."

"No. I understand. Take them with you."

With another sigh, he picked up the box from the table. "By the way, as long as I'm in the neighborhood..."

"What?"

"I beg to remind you that your mortgage falls due in full the first of December. It amounts to seventy—"

"Seventy-five dollars. I know."

"Plus interest, of course."

Maria held Janni tighter. "We are working on it, Mister Eliot. We may have to ask—"

"I'm afraid no further credit can be extended."

What a tasty sweetmeat that is.

"Of course," Eliot added, "it's always possible something can be worked out." He swept his gaze from her head to her feet.

She pulled the door open. "Good day, sir. You shall have your money."

#

On the second Sunday in June, a classic prairie morning, Maria sang her hymn outdoors, in Norsk.

> *I walk in danger all the way.*
> *The thought shall never leave me*
> *That Satan, who has marked his prey,*
> *Is plotting to deceive me. ...*

Two little voices sang with her, accompanied by the trill of a meadowlark. With Tante resting in the Indian

337

Point Cemetery these past five weeks, the boys' singing comforted her, though they could not master the tune or the words.

> *Death doth pursue me all the way,*
> *Nowhere I rest securely;*
> *He comes by night, he comes by day,*
> *He takes his prey most surely. ...*

Over the hill appeared the familiar form of Thor.

He comes by himself. How strange.

He came bounding down the hill with a farmer's gait.

"Hello, Thor!" she called. When he drew near, she asked, "What brings you?"

He bit his lip, seemed ready to say something, but no sound came out.

It must be important. But he's too shy. When will he grow up?

She made small talk. "We planted our corn so late. I don't know if it will be knee high by the Fourth of July, as they say it should."

Thor knit his brows. "Why did you plant late?"

She shrugged. "No Anders to do the work. And Tante was sick, so I had to care for her. And our man Borchers is no help, though he must have his pay each week. So, with one thing and then another—"

"I understand."

"How do things go at Osmundsgarden?"

"Oh, Maria!" he moaned.

His outburst startled her. She took his hands in hers. "Thor. What is the matter? Trouble with your crops, too?"

"No, no. The crops are all right. But, what is Mother to do?"

"What do you mean?"

"Reier and I have been drafted."

338

Drafted. The word they use for conscription.

"Lincoln wants more soldiers," said Thor. "A lottery was held in Springfield. Reier and I must report for duty in ten days."

"Oh, Thor, what will your mother do?"

And what will I do?

"It costs three hundred dollars to be exempted." He frowned. "To raise that kind of money, Mamma would have to sell Osmundsgarden."

"If she could find a buyer. Not many people buy farms these days."

"My father purchased our land with his life. Now Reier and I must do the same."

She squeezed Thor's hand. "Maybe it will not come to that. Please, come in. Sit. Let me give you dinner, at least."

She already had a stew simmering. She sliced and buttered some bread and set it before him, then served him a plate of stew to go with it. When he had finished that, he asked for another. With a grin of good cheer, she served him the last of the stew, which she had planned to eat for supper.

The worry lines disappeared from Thor's face as he filled his stomach. Simplicity, she reflected, can be a good thing in a man.

"Do not worry about the draft," she said. "And tell your mother not to worry. You don't know, but the Lord has already provided for your deliverance."

He stared into her eyes. "You think so, Maria?"

"Yes," she said. "I am sure of it."

#

The next morning, Maria walked into Sweetwater. Georgi walked beside her, but Janni had to be carried most of the way.

Finding Borchers was easy. He lay sprawled on a bench in front of the Sugar Grove Tavern.

"Look the other way, boys." Georgi and Janni were such innocents they did as she asked without hesitation. While they were looking away, she gave Borchers a sharp kick on his shin.

He leapt up, swearing.

"Halt your bad language, Simon. My young boys are here."

He stared at her in disbelief.

"Come. We have work to do."

Reeling, he sat back down on the bench. "What day is it?"

"It is Monday morning, and you smell terrible."

He reached in his pocket and pulled out two silver coins. "I got almost a dollar left. Ain't time to go back to work yet." He stood and turned toward the tavern door.

Maria kicked him again, harder than before.

"Ow!" He doubled over in pain, rubbed his leg where she had kicked.

"Listen to me, Simon Borchers," she said. "For once in your life, you shall stop drinking while you still have silver. Your help will never be as badly needed as it is today. You come back with me to Søtstrøm this instant, or I'll never give you another penny!"

\#

She made the sullen Borchers throw the heavy harnesses over Webster and Clay and hitch them to the wagon. Meanwhile, she put on her best outfit and dressed Georgi and Janni in their best shirts and trousers.

340

"Team's ready, Miz Gunstensen," Borchers growled. "Where we goin'?"

"Take us to the Lake farm, if you please, Simon."

"Lakes? Why, sh—I mean, heck, Ma'am, you coulda walked that."

"Yet I choose to ride. Come."

She swept the boys out the door and put them in the wagon bed.

At the Lake farm, she had Borchers wait with the horses while she took Georgi and Janni inside.

"Maria! And the boys—how nice."

Mistress Lake ushered them into the parlor. She sat them down, insisted Maria take tea. She gave the boys cookies.

"Now, what brings you here?" The old woman's eyes sparkled with the hope of intrigue.

"Mistress Lake, do you know Mister Chatterton?"

"Chatterton?"

"He has a store in Springfield, on Sixth Street. I thought maybe you had met him."

"Oh, yes. That Chatterton. I believe we've met once or twice. Why do you ask?"

"Can he be trusted?"

"Trusted?" Mistress Lake bit her lip. "Yes, I suppose so. As much as any merchant can be trusted, if you take my meaning."

Just what I would have said.

"Why, child? Have you dealings with Chatterton?"

Maria laughed. "Oh, never mind. It is not why I came to see you. Listen." She lowered her voice. "I am going to have Mister Borchers take me clear across the county. It may be quite late when we get back. Can you keep the boys for me? I would not ask, only—it is a sudden thing. An emergency."

341

"An emergency? Oh, dear, I hope everything's all right."

"Everything is fine. I must help some Norwegian friends."

The old Yankee woman squinted at Maria, waited for more details.

Maria kept silent.

At last, Mistress Lake smiled with all of her chins. "Of course. We'll have a lovely time, won't we, boys?"

#

Borchers balked when Maria gave him the directions to Osmundsgarden. "Why, that's near sixteen mile, Ma'am."

"Why do you care? You would be working one way or another."

"I was thinking of the horses."

"They are good, strong horses. They will live."

With a dark look, he clucked and shook the reins.

Somebody awoke on the wrong side of bed today.

#

At Osmundsgarden, Maria again left Borchers outside.

Kirsten Haraldsdatter came to the door. Her eyes were red and puffy.

"I must show you something," Maria said.

Kirsten blinked, wiped her nose, and led the way inside.

"Reier and Thor must wait outside," Maria said.

Kirsten raised her eyebrows, then nodded. The two brothers left the cabin.

In the company of Kirsten and her daughters, Maria raised her skirt. Her fingers found the flap, undid the button, plucked the little drawstring bag from within.

342

Letting her skirt fall, she held the red bag before their eyes.

From it, she drew the ring.

Kirsten's, Karen's, and Britta's eyes went round.

"A diamond," said Karen. She reached out to touch stone. Maria pressed the ring into her hand. Karen held it up for her mother and sister to see.

"Is it real?" asked Britta.

Their mother held out her hand to Karen, who placed the ring in it.

Kirsten brought it up to her eyes to see better. "It is breathtaking. And big."

"Pappa gave it to me the night before I sailed. He said: Maybe it is worth enough to get you out of trouble sometime. Now is that time."

"How so, child?"

"This stone will keep both Reier and Thor out of the Army."

"Six hundred dollars!" Tears sprang from Kirsten's eyes. "Maria—you do that for me?"

"Not for you, Kirsten," Maria said. She patted the old woman's hand. "I will do it for us. I shall sell the diamond and I shall pay to commute both boys' service. In return you must give me Thor, full-time, to farm Søtstrøm until Anders comes home."

Kirsten stared at her.

"You may keep Reier here, to work your farm."

Kirsten kept staring.

"It is not that I dislike fiddle music," Maria said. "But I need someone strong as an ox."

#

Maria had Borchers drive her into Springfield. There she went to see Chatterton, the leading jeweler in the city, as his shop across the street from the Statehouse.

When she showed him the ring, his face told her what she needed to know. He composed himself and examined the stone with a small eyepiece. "Off-white . . . a couple of inclusions . . . though minor. A little over a full carat. It's a nice piece. I can give you five hundred dollars for it, right now." He smiled and rubbed his thin hair. "Cash on the barrelhead."

Maria held out her hand, palm up. "Thank you. I will take it down the street to see what the other man says."

Chatterton's smile grew larger, showed a gold eyetooth. "No need, Madam. I assure you my offer was merely . . . exploratory. How much would you like?"

"One thousand. In gold."

"Gold? Oh, my." His expression showed dismay. "I had thought to give you paper money. And certainly not a thousand."

Maria chuckled.

The jeweler tapped a pencil against his desk.

"Well ... I suppose I could go to seven hundred. Gold."

After two minutes' haggling, the jeweler offered eight hundred fifty dollars in gold.

Maria came out of the shop with almost four pounds of gold coins in a cloth bag, placed inside a larger bag for concealment. "Drive to the bank, Mister Borchers."

At the bank, Maria traded four hundred sixty dollars in gold coins for six hundred dollars in greenbacks. The greenbacks were official U.S. currency, which the government must accept as payment to keep Thor and Reier out of the Army.

And her cloth bag still held three hundred ninety in gold.

"That's a pretty tune you're hummin'," said Borchers on the drive home.

"Was I humming a tune?" She smiled. "It is an old song from Norway." She continued to hum all the way home.

#

Thor came on foot the next day, with just a carpetbag. She took him to the small cabin, which had been vacated, first by Anders' brother John and then by Tante—both of whom now enjoyed the bliss of eternal life in Heaven.

Thor glanced once around the place, set his carpetbag in the corner, and returned with Maria to the main cabin.

She poured him tea.

"We have this old drunk, Borchers," she said. "He gets fifty cents a day, and he does do some work for it. You be the judge. If you still need his help, then keep him. Only make sure he works. Otherwise, I will let him go."

Thor raised his dark eyebrows. "You would fire him on my say-so?"

"Ja. Of course."

Sounds of a carriage came from outside.

Thor rose and went to the window. "Huh. It's that fellow from the store. Eliot." The corners of his mouth turned down.

Maria smiled. "Please let him in. And you stay with us, please."

Thor opened the door.

Eliot stood there, his coat and tie spotless. His dark hair hung lustrous about his face. In his hands, he carried a small, decorated box.

Thor glared at him.

345

Maria, seated at the table, smiled. "Mister Eliot. Do come in."

Eliot sauntered in the door. A whiff of violets entered the cabin with him.

"You smell nice," Maria said.

"Why, uh, thank you." He cast a nervous glance at the truculent Thor. He held out the box to Maria. "I, uh, brought sweets. Bonbons and such. A gift."

She reached up and took the box of candy. "*Tusen takk*. One thousand thanks," she said, setting the box on the table.

Thor stared at Eliot.

"I, uh, received the strangest message," said Eliot, "from, that is, through, Missus Lake, of all people."

Maria fluttered her eyelids. "Ja?"

"Yah—uh, yes. She came into my store, approached me directly, and said: Mistress Gunstensen will entertain you at her farm."

Maria smiled. "Quite so."

Eliot cast a glance at Thor, then turned back to Maria. "I supposed . . . that is—"

"Did you bring paper and a pen with you?"

"Paper and a pen?"

"No matter. I have." From under the table, she brought forth a few coins. Three gold double eagles, one eagle, a half-eagle, three silver dollars, and three quarters. She stacked them one by one on the table. "Seventy-eight dollars and seventy-five cents. Our mortgage plus one half year's interest."

Eliot ogled the pile of coins.

"Please take a seat, Mister Eliot." Maria rose and went to a cupboard. She came back with a sheet of paper, a pen, and a bottle of ink. She set them in front of Eliot. "You will please write a paper to release the lien on our property."

Eliot looked down at the writing materials, then raised his head with a blank gaze.

Thor, standing over Eliot with his hands curled into fists, said, "Do it."

#

A few minutes later, Eliot was out the door and back in his buggy.

Maria leaned out the door. "Good-bye," she said with a smile. "Thank you for the sweets."

She closed the door, went to the table, scooped up the signed lien release paper, and put it in the cupboard with the writing materials. She would take it to the courthouse tomorrow.

She turned back to the table and picked up the decorated box. "I would offer you some, Thor, but they would spoil your appetite for wholesome food."

She cast Eliot's gift of candy into the fire.

41. Anders

Mississippi

June – July 1863

Anders held the rag on Will's head all the way downriver. When they reached the Union lines at Vicksburg, twenty-four hours' worth of Will's blood had seeped through the rag.

The steamer landed. Time to stand up and walk. Anders bound the rag around Will's head. Homer Goodpastor helped him escort the wobbly Will up a long hill to a tent hospital.

In the sweltering shade of the tent, a plain woman in a prairie bonnet probed the wound. "No brains leakin' out. That's good. He seems a bit woozy. Here, Sonny, sit ye down."

Anders and Homer lowered Will to a cot.

"What's your name, Sonny?" The woman wrung fresh water from a clean bandage, used it to swab Will's torn flesh. She peered into his eyes. "Cat got your tongue?"

"His name is Will Cargill," said Homer. "He was wounded about this time yesterday. Rebs opened up on our transport as we was coming down the river."

"Here, Will, just lay ye down." The woman laid Will down gently. She covered him with a blanket. She rose from the cot and bumped into Anders. "You boys still here? Clear out, now. Go get some shut-eye and come back tomorrow. We'll see how he is then." She bustled away to attend to another soldier.

Anders watched her go, crestfallen.

"Come on, Andrew," said Homer. "Let's go find our regiment."

As they walked through the Vicksburg siege camp in search of Company K, Anders gawked at the webwork of trenches, tunnels, forts, redans, and redoubts that sprawled over this land of caked yellow dust. "Homer, see what is around us. It must have taken a thousand men to build these earthworks."

"Yup," said Homer. "And I'll bet she was all designed by engineers, too. We in the big Army now, Andrew."

#

Will Cargill walked into Company K's camp on his own two days later, a large bandage on his head and a smile on his face.

Anders and Homer cheered.

"Reckon that old lady knowed her business after all," said Homer.

"Mother Bickerdyke. All the boys love her," Will said.

An artillery shell screamed overhead. A few moments later came an earth-jarring boom from somewhere in the city of Vicksburg.

"Reckon we've seen the elephant for sure now," said Will. "A chap in the hospital explained it to me. This army

350

is like a city of its own, wrapped all around the city of Vicksburg. General Grant means to starve them out."

"Meanwhile," Anders said, "we still eat salt pork and hardtack, still relieve ourselves in huge foul ditches, and crawl to sleep at night under a piece of canvas. Just like in Tennessee."

Homer chuckled. "All the comforts of home, you might say."

"Excuse me," Anders said. "Now that you talk of it, I must go and answer nature's call."

"You feeling all right, Andrew?" Will knit his brows. "You look a mite peaked."

"I will just be glad when I can go home to Maria's tante's cooking. No Norwegian Army could exist on what they give us to eat."

"Maybe that's true," said Homer. "You ain't in Norway anymore, neither."

Another shell whistled overhead, silencing the conversation.

Anders made a dash for the pit toilets.

#

Every day, Anders and his platoon walked to the most forward trenches to take shifts as riflemen. The works were manned at all hours, lest the rebels try to break out of their entrapment.

Immersed the giant enterprise of Grant's siege, Anders got a truer sense of the scale of Army operations. As a new American, he took pride in the role he played, as small as it was. From other soldiers he learned that he was not the only recent immigrant in the war.

There were whole regiments at Vicksburg composed of immigrants—the Germans of the 37th Ohio and 27th Wisconsin, for example, and the Irish of the 17th

351

Wisconsin. Off to the east, somewhere in Tennessee, there was even a Norwegian regiment, the 15th Wisconsin, commanded by Colonel Hans Christian Heg. Anders, having settled in Central Illinois, away from the main avenues of Scandinavian immigration, did not mind being one of the few foreign-born soldiers in his regiment. Nevertheless he was proud of the many thousands of his fellow immigrants who swelled the cause of the Union.

Every soldier believed Grant's ultimate weapon to be simple starvation. It would be pointless to get oneself shot manning the works. Nevertheless, it did happen. One day Anders saw a private killed by a Confederate Minié ball when he stuck his head up, blood and brains flying backward as the man fell.

Anders had never entirely forgotten the caul under which he had been born and the claim that went with it, that he could not be harmed by fire or steel. Without any firm reason to believe in the old superstition, he had always acted as if it were true. Still, when on the works, he used caution.

#

General Pemberton surrendered the city to Grant on July 4th. Though at Grant's insistence they refrained from outright cheers, the soldiers rejoiced.

Anders had no share in this jubilation, having been confined to bed for a couple of weeks. He had been laid low by a chronic bowel syndrome, which the surgeons called camp dysentery. Mother Bickerdyke used the more graphic phrase "bloody flux." Bad food and squalid conditions had gotten the better of him. The crusty woman's care, however, improved his condition. She believed in cleanliness, fresh air, and a high-quality diet.

Rumors said she had, somewhere nearby, a dairy herd of her own to give fresh milk for her convalescent troops.

Anders felt better when, on July 5, he boarded the hospital steamer *U.S.S. Red Rover* along with many others listed as unfit for duty. Orderlies carried him on a litter and placed him in a real bed, in a room with three other patients.

"We're taking you to an Army hospital in Memphis," said a doctor. "The trip usually takes about twelve hours. You may as well relax until we get there."

Anders closed his eyes and drifted off.

He awoke to see a black face staring down upon him.

"Have I died and gone to Heaven? You resemble an old comrade of mine whom I never thought to see again in this life."

"Daniel Freeman," the man announced with pride. "U.S. Navy."

42. Maria

Illinois

July – September 1863

Maria churned butter by the cabin door on a cool morning in mid-July. With each stroke of the churn's dasher, she visualized the coins she would receive for the butter at the Sweetwater store. Mister Eliot no longer conducted the transactions himself but delegated the chore to his assistant. Maria did not mind his neglect, as long as she received her money.

Silas Smithson the postman arrived on his mule. He reached a letter down to her.

Maria's heart beat faster.

"Ain't nobody's writin' I ever saw." The postman's bushy eyebrows scrunched as she took the letter from his hand. "Postmarked Memphis, Tennessee."

Silas dismounted and led his mule to the well. Georgi and Janni ran along to watch and get in the way.

Maria sat on the threshold. She tried to puzzle out the strange envelope, addressed in a childish hand, the address written in pencil, not ink:

Miz Gunson
Ander Gunson farm
Sweet Water Illinoy

The upper corner had a return address:
Daniel Freeman Landsman
U.S.S. Red Rover
At Memphis

Maria withdrew the letter from the envelope.

Deer Miz Gunson,

I am your frend Daniel you helped exape to FREEDOM.

I met your husband Ander on this boat. It is a hospital boat. He appere verry sick. Pizen from bad army food. Doctors take care a him now. Him an me, we have us a good long talk about them old daze.

You can find him at OVERTON HOSPITAL in Memphis.

Your frend,
Daniel FREEMAN
now sailor in U.S. Navy

"Miz Gunstensen—you all right?" Smithson had returned from watering his mule. "Is everything all right?"

Maria came to herself. She sat on the threshold of her cabin, the letter clutched in her hand, tears running from her eyes.

"It will be all right, Mister Smithson." She sniffled. "At least I know where he is now."

#

When she read the letter to Thor, he wanted to hitch up the team immediately and set out for Memphis.

"No, Thor," she said. "It is not practical."

"Anders is perishing there," said Thor, his face red with concern.

"He is not perishing. He has doctors. Memphis is hundreds of miles. You cannot drive it in a week."

Thor lowered his brow and sulked.

"I shall write," she said.

She wrote immediately and waited without patience for a return letter. The corn grew high and began to tassel, yet she did not hear from Anders. She wrote again. At last she received a letter from an Army doctor:

> *Private Gunstensen received your previous letter, Madam, but was not well enough to write. We do hope to restore him and send him home to you on a medical furlough in the near future.*

This infuriated her. Could not these doctors speak plainly? When would Anders be well enough to write? What could this "furlough" mean?

The tassels had fully emerged on the cornstalks, and the silk had begun to spill out of the ears, when she received the next letter, this one from Anders himself.

> *Dearest Wife Maria,*
>
> *At last I am well enough to write, and all I can tell you is I am on my way home to see you.*
>
> *Look for me at the station in Springfield on 5 September.*
>
> *With all my love,*
> *Anders*

Janni sweetly touched his older brother's face, then yanked on his ear. Georgi squealed and raised a fist to thump Janni's head.

Maria caught the thump in her eagle grip. One hand on each boy, she jerked them upright and set them down, beyond each other's reach, on the wagon bed.

"Boys—"

A whistle piped from the south edge of Springfield, a mile away.

"Listen, here comes the train. Pappa is coming. You must be good."

Georgi leapt from the wagon and ran toward the platform.

"Wait!" Janni cried.

Thor jumped down and ran after Georgi while Maria climbed from the wagon, lifted Janni down, and walked to the platform, clutching his little hand. By the time they caught up with Georgi and Thor, the train came into view, gray smoke streaming from it.

The locomotive overshot the station, but its passenger cars stopped precisely at the platform, as if by a happy accident.

Maria stepped forward, holding both boys' hands.

A porter placed a box under the boarding steps.

Georgi and Janni wiggled and twisted in Maria's grip. In truth, she felt like doing a dance of her own.

After eight weeks in the Memphis hospital, Anders was coming home.

Passengers descended, civilians and soldiers. Maria glanced at Thor. *Where is Anders?* His telegram from St. Louis had said he would be on today's train.

The porter helped a man down, a frail old soldier who tottered on the steps.

An old man like that never should have been sent to war.

The soldier placed one foot down on the platform, then the other. He swayed.

Thor rushed forward to catch him. The man, leaning on Thor's strong arms, gazed at Maria. "Hello, jenta mi."

Her heart broke.

She forced a smile. "Anders! Husband!"

A shy smile wreathed his face. "Home comes your soldier, from the war."

She grasped his shoulders, steadied him, then leaned away to inspect him. "Husband, what has become of you? How could the army let you go, in this condition?"

"I wanted to come. Most desperately." He cast his gaze downward. "Can these big boys be my George and John?"

Janni, not yet two, shrank away. Georgi, old enough to remember Anders, stepped forward yet hesitated.

Anders seemed to wilt. Then he smiled. "No matter. They will get to know me again."

Maria pursed her lips. "Anders, I brought some nice food along—trout, lefse, raspberry jam, cheese—"

Anders uttered a soft groan. "Not now, jenta mi. Perhaps later."

Why had they sent him home to her like this? If he could not eat wholesome food, how would he recover? Maria's own appetite fled as well.

#

Thor lifted Anders in his arms and sat him on the second spring seat, which he had bought for cash in Petersburg and installed before they drove to the Springfield station.

359

Anders carried a brown bottle and a spoon in his pocket. He took a spoonful of medicine from the bottle before they set out for home. "Laudanum," he said. "You would not wish me to ride without it. It would be a shame to make a mess of this nice new seat."

Before a mile had gone by, Anders fell asleep. Maria laid him across the seat. She knelt there to keep him from rolling off. *The medicine they give him does not cure him,* she thought. *It only makes him sleep through his misery.*

When they arrived at Søstrøm, Thor carried Anders into the cabin and helped Maria put him to bed.

#

The next morning, Thor came to the main cabin for breakfast. He sat with Maria at the table, sipping thin porridge.

"How is Anders?"

"He woke after you left and ate a small square of lefse. Then he slept through the night." She could not help the tears rolling down her cheeks.

"Poor Maria." Thor set down his spoon, reached out, and touched her cheek. "Do you think he will get better?"

"I don't know, Thor. He says they sent him home on furlough, whatever that means." Thor's face worked, absorbing her words. "I think they did not know how to cure him, so they sent him home to die."

#

News went round about Anders' return home. By ones and twos and threes his friends came by to see him.

Gunder Jørgen and Torbjørg brought a fat, marbled slab of pork belly, convinced it would set Anders to rights. The smell of it set Anders' stomach on edge. "Take it away,

360

please," he said. He smiled apologetically. "Your ham is well cured, my friend, but for me it seems there is no cure."

Getting up to talk with Gunder Jørgen and Torbjørg seemed to drain Anders of energy. He lay in bed all the next day, too weak to rise.

The Lakes arrived. Benjamin Lake went into the bedroom to exchange a few words with Anders, while his wife sat with Maria and held her hand. They left after a few minutes.

Brother Claymore arrived and inquired after Anders' conditions, both physical and spiritual. "He gains no strength, Mister Claymore," said Maria. "I fear he is not long for this world. As to his soul, he prays to Jesus just as you and I do."

Claymore looked in on the sleeping Anders, uttered a brief prayer, and left.

#

On Sunday, when Anders had been home almost a week, he arose and sat on a bench outside the cabin.

Kirsten Haraldsdatter and her family arrived in their farm wagon, with Reier driving.

Anders waved when they pulled in. He stood to greet them, grasped Reier's hand.

"It is good to see you all," he said. "When I was in the hospital, I thought of you often."

Kirsten held out her red-painted *anbar* to Anders. "You must eat fløtegrøt, for I heard you were weak and in need of recovery."

Maria took the wooden vessel from Kirsten's hands. "Thank you, Kirsten." She carried it inside and set it on the table. Kirsten, Karen, and Britta followed her in.

"How thoughtful of you to bring this," Maria said. "Do not be surprised if he eats little. Most foods are too rich. I have had some success with a plain gruel of oats."

Kirsten knit her brows. "I didn't realize things were that bad with him."

Tears sprang from Maria's eyes and with no forethought she fell into the old woman's arms, racked with great sobs.

Kirsten held her and stroked her hair. "Gather round, Daughters. Do not let the menfolk see her like this."

Maria wept in Kirsten's arm for several minutes.

Outside, the sound of a fiddle began.

Kirsten wiped Maria's face with a cloth. Then the women stepped out to join the men.

Reier played a country dance tune. Thor stepped forward to whirl a few steps with his mother, Karen, Britta, and Maria, each in turn. Maria hesitated, but Anders seemed to enjoy the dance, keeping time with taps of his hand on his knee. And Thor's arms and shoulders gave comfort, just as his mother's had.

When the tune ended, everyone clapped for Reier's performance.

Anders beckoned to Thor and whispered in his ear. Thor ducked into the cabin and came back with Anders' rucksack. Anders reached into it. He pulled out a small, flat bottle.

"Real American whiskey. From Kentucky. Maria, bring glasses for our friends."

"Where did you get this?" asked Reier.

"I bought it from a sutler at Vicksburg. Stuffed it in my rucksack to save for a special occasion." Maria brought tumblers, and Anders poured a dram for each of his friends. "Skål."

They drank to Anders' health. He grimaced as he sipped the harsh spirits.

362

Alarmed, Maria snatched the glass away from him. "That's all for you, Husband."

Anders got up and limped in the door on unsteady feet. He beckoned Thor to follow.

Thor got up, cast a glance at Maria, and followed Anders into the cabin. The two men disappeared into the bedroom.

Maria listened at the bedroom door. She heard only the murmur of low voices.

After a few minutes, Thor came out. "He asked me to send you in, Maria."

"What were the two of you discussing?"

Thor stared at her. His face got red. "Men's affairs," he said.

#

In the middle of the week, Silas Smithson came by on his mule, Katie. "Sorry, Ma'am. I have no mail for you. I was passin' by and thought I might pay a call."

"I fear you will be disappointed, Mister Smithson. He had a sip of whiskey a few days ago and has not risen. He does not eat, either, but only takes the opium the doctor gave him."

Smithson followed her into the house. From the bedroom door, he murmured, "Hello, Mister Gunstensen."

Anders opened his eyes. He gazed vacantly at Smithson. "Hallo, old friend."

Does he even know which old friend he is talking to?

"Have you my copy of the *Journal*?"

"Not today, I'm afraid."

"Just as well. All the news has been ill of late."

#

Maria placed Georgi and Janni on Anders' bed where he could see and touch them. "Do not wiggle for Pappa, boys. He is too tired."

Anders smiled and caressed their unshorn locks. The boys sat quiet and receptive.

"Pappa," said Georgi, "will you get well soon?"

Anders beamed. "I am almost well now, my son. You take your brother out to play."

The boys scrambled down off the bed and out the door while Maria struggled to keep her composure.

#

On Sunday, September 20, Maria and Thor stood at the foot of Anders' bed. They sang an old hymn in duet. In her weakness, Thor braced Maria with an arm about her shoulders. His strong singing breaths, felt through her own thin frame, imparted vitality to her.

Anders lay with eyes closed. He breathed but lightly. When the tune ended, he whispered, "*Det er fint som snus, min venner, fint som snus*. That was fine as snuff, my friends. Fine as snuff."

And he breathed his last.

43. Maria

Illinois

September 1863

Maria stood straight as the spindle of Tante's old coffee grinder, believing that by uprightness she would not disgrace the memory of Anders and their happy union. She wore her best dress, the one from Norway, her hair braided and looped in the old style. Torbjørg, who knew sorrow, had helped her with it.

The oaks surrounding the cemetery had already turned brown, foretelling an early fall. The mist that filled the air was only half water. The other half was smoke from trees felled on nearby farms, and burned in large piles just to get rid of them. A waste.

Brother Claymore stood by the grave and droned on, his black beard tumbling down, pooling into his black suit. At last, he launched into the final prayer.

Good. Only half an hour to go.

Her knees were bumped from behind. "Janni," she hissed.

She reached back to control him. Georgi had already shoved his younger brother back into line. In the small black suit and hat that Kirsten Haraldsdatter had bought from a store in Petersburg, Maria's firstborn son looked like an undertaker.

When at last the prayer ended, Maria stepped forward to shovel earth into the grave. It thumped on the wooden coffin lid.

She helped Georgi and little Janni to do the same. It might mean something to them, later, that they had done this for their father now.

Kirsten came and hugged her. "Dear Maria, what will you do now? How will you work the farm?"

She could only shrug.

Sometimes the troll pokes you.

Anders, born under the caul, who had defeated his Uncle Torgus, who had plucked the fire tongs from her own hands, who had withstood beating by slave hunters, who had passed unscathed through the fire of battle—in the end had succumbed to a foul disease, against which even Mister Lincoln and his mighty army held no power.

He had been blessed with true friends and blessed with Maria's whole love, as fierce and demanding as she knew it to be.

But that was all over now. Her married life with Anders was completed for all eternity. For had not Jesus said, "in the resurrection they neither marry, nor are given in marriage, but are as the angels of God in heaven"?

Maria was left with two small sons and thirty acres of standing grain. True, she now had three hundred gold dollars buried beneath the corncrib. Borchers, at three dollars a week, would drink his way through that before long. And her precious diamond ring was gone forever.

What could she do?

Back at Søtstrøm they gathered. They spoke in low tones, and they ate. Kirsten, Torbjørg, and Mistress Lake had provided plenty of food.

One by one her guests took Maria aside to give words of consolation.

Mistress Lake squeezed Maria's hands in her own chubby ones. " good man, your Anders."

"He was a true fighter for freedom," her husband added.

Kirsten brought tears to match Maria's. "Anders was our first friend in America. Considering how he was, you could say he was our first real American friend."

That made Maria smile. *Anders the American.*

Torbjørg brought no words, only a squeeze and flowing tears.

Reier played a slow lament on his fiddle. When its last strains died out, everyone coughed, shuffled their feet. What else could be said or done?

Then Reier struck up a livelier tune, a country dance familiar to all of them except the Lakes. Nobody danced, but people did tap their toes and smile.

When the song ended, the guests acted restless. They began to mill around, sigh, and turn their eyes homeward.

Kirsten gazed at Maria with pity. "Poor dear," she said, and gave a sympathetic hug.

Maria knew what she meant. Thor's term of labor at Søtstrøm had never been meant to extend past Anders' homecoming. Kirsten could not help it that Anders was dead. Reflected in Kirsten's sad eyes, Maria could see herself, Georgi, and Janni trekking, with only the clothes on their backs, to the county's poor farm near Petersburg.

"Excuse me, Mamma." Thor led his mother a little apart.

Then turned back to face Maria. "I have something to say to you."

All the guests in the midst of leave-taking halted.

Thor's entire earnest self focused on her.

"Ja, Thor?"

"Anders was my friend," he said.

"Ja. He was."

"I mean no disrespect to his memory, but . . ."

"Ja, Thor?"

"Will you have me in his place?"

His eyes made appeal to the guests ranged about them. "Winter is coming. It is not too soon to speak of such things."

Broad-shouldered, oxlike Thor. Sincere and true. She looked at him and her head spun. What had become of the young man she knew, tied to his mother's apron strings? She saw now that he was a grown man, his old mother hovering in the background. When had that happened? How cold Thor expect her to marry? Yet, how could she not?

"Besides," Thor said, "Anders wanted it."

"He did?" She recalled the time, a few days ago, when Anders and Thor had murmured behind the closed bedroom door.

"Ja," Thor said. "I promised him I would marry you. After a decent period, of course."

Maria took a long, deep breath. *Georgi and Janni cannot grow up beholden.* "Thor, you do not have to do this, just because Anders made you promise. I release you from his bond."

Thor's face sagged. Then he composed himself.

"It is not because I promised Anders," he said. "I love you, Maria. In my own way, but no less than Anders did."

She felt dizzy.

"I am only a poor farmer. I work hard, and we shall make a living."

So it was settled.

"It is what Anders wanted," Maria said, "and I want it, too."

Sometimes the troll is driven away.

44. Daniel

Arkansas

December 1863

Daniel, off watch, relaxed and watched the shore go by as *Pittsburgh* patrolled the Mississippi River near the Arkansas confluence.

It's good to be back on the battle-scarred old tub, he thought, *no matter what.* The white sailors scorned him for his skin, yet they tolerated him because they needed somebody for the lowest order of work.

The rebs had tried to kill him and had almost succeeded. But not quite. *Sorry, Johnny Reb. Not dead yet. Try harder next time.*

The bosun's pipe sounded general call. All sailors not manning the engine or the helm gathered on the top deck. Bosun Finley came up the forward stairs, a pile of mail in his hands.

Finley reminded Daniel of Bosun McGurk, who had sworn him into the Navy two years ago—grim, tough, and profane. The Navy seemed to like petty officers of that stripe.

"Drexel!" Finley shouted, passing an envelope to one of the sailors gathered around him. "Rawlings! ... Howell! ... Burnham! ..."

Daniel, who never got mail, stood on the rail, out of the mob of sailors around Bosun Finley. Odd, he thought, that all the sailors stay on deck, those with letters holding them unopened, not going off to read their letters in private.

The bosun sounded his pipe again. "Now hear this!"

Daniel stood to attention, prepared for some new information the bosun wanted to impart. Papers remained in the bosun's hand.

"Landsman Freeman, Daniel, front and center!"

The bosun frowned when Daniel arrived in front of him. He read aloud from a piece of paper. "Landsman Freeman, Daniel, having served honorably in the U.S. Navy for a period of two years, is hereby advanced to the grade of ordinary seaman, pay and privileges to increase accordingly." He folded the paper and handed it to Daniel. "Congratulations, sailor." With a sour look, he extended his right hand to Daniel.

Daniel shook Finley's hand. "Thank you, Bosun."

"Goddam it, Seaman, take care. I don't want you spending your extra two dollars on none of your frivolous nigger hijinks."

"Ha! It's my two dollars, ain't it?"

The sailors around them laughed. Black or white, they laughed, because an ordinary seaman had sassed the bosun and would get away with it.

Finley frowned. "Dismissed!"

Daniel turned away with a smile on his face.

"Wait a minute."

Daniel wiped the smile off his face and turned to face the bosun.

"Here's your mail." He handed Daniel an envelope.

372

"Aye-aye, Bosun. Thank you."

Astonished, Daniel read the envelope, addressed in ink, in a very flowing hand.

Sailor Daniel Freeman
U.S.S. ~~Red Rover~~ Pittsburgh
Mississippi River, U.S.A.

Someone had crossed off "Red Rover" and written "Pittsburgh" in a different hand.

But he was amazed by the return address.

Miss Betsey Pettybone
Buxton, Ontario
Canada

Daniel frowned to see the name Pettybone. Ex-slaves often adopted or kept the names of their former owners. He himself might be Daniel Pettybone if the name Freeman had not popped into his head at the moment of his enlistment in the Navy.

He had written Betsey six months ago. Somehow the letter had found her—all the way up in Ontario, Canada. Now her letter had come back to him on *U.S.S. Pittsburgh.* He wondered if Mammy, from Heaven, had somehow guided both letters on their way.

It seemed an omen of good things to come.

Depending what Johnny Reb had up his sleeve.

THE END

Historical Notes

Anders Gunstensen—the real one—was my great-great-grandfather, second son of Schoolmaster Gunsten Gunderson of Øiestad, Norway. He came to America on the brig *Victoria*, arriving at New Orleans on 29 March 1853. Unlike most Norwegian immigrants, who went farther north, he farmed in Sweetwater, Menard County, Illinois. He married Maria Nybro, eldest child of boat builder Christian Conradsen Nybro, also of Øiestad; fathered two sons; fought in the Civil War; and died at home in Sweetwater September 20, 1863, of dysentery contracted during the Vicksburg campaign. More Civil War soldiers died of diarrhea and dysentery than of any other cause.

The real Maria Nybro—Johanne-Marie Elisabeth Nybro Gunstensen, to be exact—married Anders' friend Thor Reierson (whose name I have changed to Osmundsen in this story) a year after Anders died.

The *characters* Anders and Maria in this book, who share the aforementioned facts with my real ancestors, are in every other way fictitious. I have made everything up, freely fabulizing to suit the story's needs.

Daniel Freeman, the third major character of this book, is not based on any one individual. He is a composite character, invented for the sake of a dramatic plot. I hope in telling Daniel's story I have done no injustice to the memory of those real African Americans who bore frightful oppression and braved daunting challenges to seek freedom—before, during, and after the Civil War.

Besides the basic facts of Anders' and Maria's lives, the following matters mentioned in the book are true:

Maroons, self-liberated former slaves, lived in hidden enclaves in every slave state before, during, and for some time after the Civil War.

Numerous individuals, white and black, operated a so-called Underground Railroad for the purpose of aiding fugitive slaves in their escape to freedom.

Black sailors were rife in the Union Navy during, and long before, the Civil War—far earlier than the more well-publicized enlistment of black soldiers in the Union Army.

Jefferson Davis' older brother, Joseph Davis, operated Hurricane Plantation near Vicksburg on the basis of Robert Owen's social ideals while continuing to keep the black people on his plantation in chattel slavery. His black overseer, Benjamin Montgomery, was a successful businessman and inventor both during his enslavement to Davis and after his emancipation by Messrs. Lincoln and Grant.

Other real people who appear as characters in this book include:

• John Van Doorn, Charles Sidener, Simeon and Monroe Clark, abolitionists and Underground Railroad operatives in Quincy, Illinois.

• William Donnegan, cobbler and Underground Railroad operative in Springfield, Illinois; and later, in

1908, a martyr in the Springfield race riot which gave impetus to the formation of the NAACP.

- "Mother" Mary Ann Ball Bickerdyke, legendary volunteer nurse.

- Charles W. Chatterton, silversmith and jeweler of Springfield, who went west in 1860 to become an Indian agent in Kansas. (I have kept him in the jewelry business an extra three years in order that he might buy Maria's ring.)

- Abraham Lincoln and Steven A. Douglas, noted Illinois politicians.

QUOTES

All scripture quotations, unless otherwise noted, are taken from the King James Bible.

The Lutheran hymn "I Walk in Danger All the Way," by Hans A. Brorson (1694-1764), translated by Ditlef G. Ristad (1863-1938), is quoted from http://www. traditionalmusic. co.uk/ lutheran-hymnal/413-i-walk-in-danger-all-the-way. htm.

All quotations from the *Sangamo Journal/Illinois State Journal* are verbatim from copies in the Illinois Digital Newspaper Collections at https://idnc.library.illinois. edu, except for the headline "Buchanan Dances to Taney's Tune" and two brief passages from that putative article—all inventions of the present author—in Chapter 27.

Acknowledgments

This book would not exist had not my wife, Joelle Caroline Nelson Sommers, an expert family genealogist, brought my Norwegian great-great-grandparents to my attention and asked that I write something about them.

It also might very well not exist had not the fabulous Laurie Scheer encouraged me, before a word of its text was written, to tell the story of my immigrant ancestors.

It would surely have remained a very half-baked first novel if not for continual encouragement and detailed feedback from Christine DeSmet, book coach *extraordinaire*.

I am also much indebted to:

- My late Uncle, Edward Foster Sommers, who in the 1960s dug up significant parts of Anders' story, aided by state archivist Sigrid Skamedal of Kristiansand, Norway.

- The helpful employees of the Menard County Clerk's Office; Ruth Slottag and Mike Kienzler of the Sangamon County Historical Society; Curtis Mann, Sangamon Valley Collection Manager for the City of Springfield Lincoln Library, who provided useful information on the Underground Railway in Menard County; and a nameless but helpful undertaker in Athens, Illinois, who directed me to the Indian Point Cemetery—where, alas, the grave marker of "Pvt. Andrew Gunstensen" was not found.

- Distinguished beta readers who gave time and expertise generously to read and comment on the first draft of the novel: Bill Martinez, literary consultant and a former executive with Bantam Books; Peggy Bendroth, then Executive Director of the Congregational Library in

Boston; Eric Schlehlein, author of the Civil War novels *Black Iron Mercy* and *The Dim White Light*; Jerry Paulsen and Solveig Schavland Quinney of the Norwegian American Genealogical Center and Naeseth Library in Madison, Wisconsin; Paige Brien, Wisconsin-based writer and filmmaker; and Regina Rotar, a friend and fellow writer who happens to be a descendant of slaves. Kira Henschel of HenschelHAUS Publishing, Inc., also read the manuscript and saved me from several embarrassing errors.

• Colleagues in two writers' groups, "OYOS" and "Tuesdays With Story"—especially Rebecca Williams Spindler, Allen Youngwood, Helen Kenyon, Randy Bixby, John McGuigan, Pat Edwards, Tracey Gemmell, Mike Austin, Amber Boudreau, John Sneller, Kashmira Sheth, Amit Trivedi, Cindi Dyke, Bob Kralapp, Paul Wagner, Lisa McDougal, Chris Zoern, Jessica Smith, Huckleberry Rahr, and Jack Freiburger. High kudos accrue to Jerry Peterson, dean of the Tuesday group, whose forthright critiques made me convert many limp wastelands of expository prose to real scenes, in which characters and actions tell the story.

Any defects that remain in this book are the exclusive intellectual property of the author, who also wishes to thank Daniel Willis of DX Varos Publishing, Inc., who not only gave this story a chance, but gave it a second chance when it needed one.

David Kruh
INSEPARABLE

Shawn Mackey
THIS WORLD OF LOVE AND STRIFE

Jeanne Matthews
DEVIL BY THE TAIL

C.K. McDonough
STOKING HOPE

Fidelis O. Mkparu
SOULFUL RETURN *(Nov 2022)*

Phillip Otts
A STORM BEFORE THE WAR
THE SOUL OF A STRANGER
THE PRICE OF BETRAYAL

Erika Rummel
THE INQUISITOR'S NIECE
THE ROAD TO GESUALDO
EVITA AND ME

Vanessa Ryan
THE TROUBLE WITH MURDER

J. M. Stephen
NOD
INTO THE FAIRY FOREST
RISE OF THE HIDDEN PRINCE
SILENCE AND RUPTURED WATERS
THE RISE OF RUNES AND SHIELDS

382

Jessica Stilling
THE WEARY GOD OF ANCIENT TRAVELERS
BETWEEN BEFORE AND AFTER (*Nov 2022*)

Claryn Vaile
GHOST TOUR

Felicia Watson
WHERE THE ALLEGHENY MEETS THE MONONGAHELA
WE HAVE MET THE ENEMY
SPOOKY ACTION AT A DISTANCE
THE RISKS OF DEAD RECKONING

Daniel A. Willis
IMMORTAL BETRAYAL
IMMORTAL DUPLICITY
IMMORTAL REVELATION
PROPHECY OF THE AWAKENING
FARHI AND THE CRYSTAL DOME
VICTORIA II
THE CHILDREN OF VICTORIA II

Joyce Yarrow
SANDSTORM

Printed in the USA
CPSIA information can be obtained
at www.ICGtesting.com
CBHW020749131023
1276CB00012B/3